LOSING NICOLA

A compelling tale of childhood trauma and sinister discoveries

Alice and her brother Orlando lived a quiet life growing up in post WWII Britain; that is until the arrival of the precocious, manipulative and sexually aware Nicola. But on Alice's twelfth birthday, Nicola disappears, only to be found days later, battered, bruised and dead. Twenty years go by until Alice becomes determined to dig up the past and solve the mystery of Nicola's death. But will the truth be too much to handle when she starts to suspect her own quiet and bookish brother Orlando?

LOSING NICOLA

Susan Moody

Severn House Large Print
London & New York

This first large print edition published 2013
in Great Britain and the USA by
SEVERN HOUSE PUBLISHERS LTD of
19 Cedar Road, Sutton, Surrey, England, SM2 5DA.
First world regular print edition published 2011 by
Severn House Publishers Ltd., London and New York.

British Library Cataloguing in Publication Data

Moody, Susan. author.
  Losing Nicola. -- Large print edition.
  1. Murder--England--Kent--Fiction. 2. Brothers and
  sisters--Fiction. 3. Kent (England)--Social conditions--
  20th century--Fiction. 4. Detective and mystery stories.
  5. Large type books.
  I. Title
  823.9'14-dc23

  ISBN-13: 978-0-7278-9620-9

Severn House Publishers support The Forest Stewardship Council
[FSC], the leading international forest certification organisation. All
our titles that are printed on Greenpeace-approved FSC-certified paper
carry the FSC logo.

Printed and bound in Great Britain by the
MPG Books Group, Bodmin, Cornwall.

'Only by acceptance of the past, can you alter it.'
T. S. Eliot

In memory of
Barnaby
All things bright and beautiful

PART ONE

PART ONE

ONE

When I was four, my mother took me to see *Mrs Miniver*, because she couldn't find anyone to leave me with. The programme started with a newsreel of current events. A triumphant white cockerel crowed, then tanks moved along a road, men in tin hats with long guns in their hands leapt in and out of ruined windowless houses, there were explosions and smoke and bewildered faces. Although I was too young to understand what it all meant, the images disturbed me. In the film itself, there were more bombs, more ruins, more loss and fear, bravely faced by Greer Garson in a tweed suit which I recognized as the twin of the one hanging in my mother's wardrobe.

For a long time after that afternoon, I suffered from nightmares of soldiers pursuing me through smoke, of guns firing in my direction, the crump of bombs, people weeping.

At four years old, I didn't have the equipment to deal with something as amorphous as terror; that summer, many years later, when Nicola was murdered, I still did not.

Only desperation could have driven Fiona – my mother – to move to the little town of Shale on the coast of south-east Kent. She detested the seaside in general and this one in particular; the thick grey water, the corrosive salt air, the lumps of tar washed ashore from wrecked ships which we tracked in from the beach to ruin her worn carpets, the gales which prowled beneath the roof tiles and nightmared her sleep with the prospect of unpayable repair bills.

The war was over, and my diasporaed family should have reassembled in Oxford to await my father's return from Germany. But affordable housing in Oxford was non-existent, as students and academics crowded back from their various fields of conflict and in the end, frantic for somewhere to live, my mother persuaded my father's great-aunt into giving us temporary house room while she found somewhere more suitable. Aunt lived alone by the sea in a many-roomed house long since emptied of her naval sons and late husband, the Right Reverend Canon Lowe. According to my mother, Aunt, now an aged, humpbacked crone, had been a spy during the First World War and became a pioneering aviatrix after it, until she settled down with the Canon and took up cabinet-making and occasional journalism.

The two women came to an agreement. Fiona would keep an eye on Aunt, in return for a roof over our heads. And Aunt enjoyed the bargain, too; life in the house again, the sound of young voices on the stairs.

Trains, buses and a Model T Ford brought us to Glenfield House one blustery afternoon. The wind was whipping up the waves, trees groaned

12

in the garden. As we banged at the front door (the knocker had long since vanished), slates fell from the roof. We numbered eight. There was my mother with her indeterminate brood of children, plus Ava Carlton, a runaway wife, and her daughter, Arabella.

I was seven, that first year, Orlando a year older. There were two older brothers – Dougal and Callum – and a younger one, plus Bella. Orlando and I were not twins, though we shared everything except gender, but we might as well have been. Our brains moved along parallel tracks, side by side, anticipating each other's reactions as though they were our own, a single entity. Even when apart, our world consisted of each other. Orlando-and-Alice, Alice-and-Orlando

'We're joined at the hip,' I said once.

He shook his head, touched his chest, grinned his ferocious grin. 'Joined at the heart.'

For Orlando and me, there had only ever been the other. He was everything to me. My God, my companion, my hero. His eyes were the deepest blue and his over-large head was covered with thick black hair except for the area above his left ear, which was a silky silver. His eyebrows were striped black and white, like a road crossing, giving him a piebald and eccentric look. We all knew he was a genius.

Fiona may have hated our new home. We, on the other hand, loved it. In those years following the war it was an extravagant place in which to spend our holidays, a town full of drama. From

13

the windows of our vast house we had extensive views of the sea, bounded at one end by a chalky headland crowned with a cap of bright grass, on the other by a stretch of coastline curved round a bay. Between the two was a pier broken in two halves, the damage done either by a drunken sea captain or from enemy action, depending on who was telling the story. Beyond the pier wallowed a rusting hulk, perhaps the very ship steered by the drunken sailor.

On the horizon, the spars of ships that had been wrecked on the Goodwin Sands jutted upwards, masts flung up to the heavens like the pleading arms of drowning seamen. When the light was right, you could gaze across the Channel to France, see their War Memorial, the twin of the one on the cliffs above Dover, and the sunlight reflecting on their French windscreens. On weekend mornings, white sails dotted the water, white birds soared above. Along the Esplanade, a red-painted land mine, like the shell of a giant chestnut, solicited alms for wounded service-men. Although it was never spoken of, the war was still part of our daily lives.

Even on dull days, sea-light poured brilliantly through the windows. We loved the movement of the sea outside, its constantly changing outlook, now grey, now green, now banded into thrilling lines of turquoise and purple blending into blue. We loved too, the presence of the Royal Marines, who marched past the house on their way to Sunday parade, jingling and jangl-ing, the sun bouncing off their brass instruments, their white pith helmets gleaming. At night, bugles from the barracks played the Last Post; every morning we were woken by Reveille.

In winter, the wind was so strong you could spread your arms and lean back on it. There was a lifeboat, too, and sometimes we would startle from sleep to hear the maroons going off, one, two, three, to call in the volunteer lifeboatmen.

Fiona, raised in the dour house of a college principal in Edinburgh, had grown up being looked after by a string of servants, and had never quite got the grasp of domesticity. Nor of motherhood. Over the years, she had even tried to give one or other of us away, though without much success. Once, a childless couple agreed to adopt Bobby, my youngest brother, then aged two. But by the time Fiona had wheeled him in his pram down an unmade-up road which ended at a cliff-top to their neat seaside villa – 'The Laurels' – and was about to open the gate and abandon him, she realized she couldn't go through with it. Despite the fact that Mrs Childless Couple had already opened the front door and was swooping towards the perambulator with small cries of welcome, Fiona turned and fled back up the road as fast as she could, the heavy black pram, which had been used for us all, bumping and lurching along the road before her.

She told us this story often, her abrupt change of heart apparently emphasizing her maternal instinct, apparently unaware that the original decision to give her youngest child away demonstrated quite the opposite. Nobody had to tell us that Ava Carlton would never have given a child away, never even have *thought* about it. Although we were originally prepared to treat with hostile caution this intruder into our family circle, we soon learned to value and love her for her steadiness, her stability and her warm heart. Instinctively we knew Ava was vital to the continued well-being of our raffish household. She habitually spoke with her head cocked, listening, listening, in case her abandoned, wife-beating husband finally caught up with her and kicked her to death, before taking Arabella back to live with him and his mother. When we first knew her, she kept a bag ready packed by the door of the room she shared with her daughter. It was, she often said, best to be prepared, because You Never Knew.

Later on, perhaps finally feeling safe, she started wearing a ring on the fourth finger of her left hand. It was a beautiful aquamarine, cold and still as the sea, water-pure and square cut, set in white gold, flanked with tiny diamonds. People's eyes were always drawn to it, and Ava had only to hint at the war years, give a rueful little shrug of the shoulders, for them to get entirely the wrong picture. Instead of an Ava on the run from a brute, they saw a woman still mourning the handsome young pilot lost over the Channel, the brave soldier killed at Dunkirk, the fearless sailor who'd been torpedoed or bombed and gone like a hero to a watery grave. She played the part of a grieving widow, faithful even unto death, so sad, and yet so, I don't know, so *marvellous* really, with such aplomb, that no

16

one, not even Orlando, was bold enough to enquire as to where the ring came from and what had happened to the wife beater.

Glenfield House was large and many-roomed, on the corner of a road of similar houses which faced the sea across a stretch of grass. There was a shrubbery to one side of it, a carriage house at the back. The house contained any number of pantries, sculleries, laundry-rooms and stone-shelved larders. Extensive cellars spread below, attics flourished above. A back staircase led up from the big kitchen to what had once been thin-walled rooms where maids slept with the tiniest of fireplaces to keep them warm.

There were outbuildings, a tumbledown green-house, its glass panes long since smashed and its slatted shelves rotting, a stables with wisps of straw still littering the floor of the stalls, hay in the semicircular iron baskets attached to the wall, and mildewed leather harnesses hanging from heavy iron hooks. Neglected grounds thriv-ed beneath war-neglected roses, sagging bowers of overgrown honeysuckles, rioting clematis and Virginia creeper. Shrubs and bushes drooped heavily to the ground, creating green shelters into which we could creep, and behind a clump of bamboos, a pond green as poison sprouted water-lilies and dragonflies. It was our jungle, our rain forest, our chaparral, the secret garden where we played out every sort of adventure, from the Last of the Mohicans to Dickon and Mary.

There was a great deal of large and shabby

furniture, but the house was so big that even with our own pieces added, the place still looked spacious. Aunt's things were different from ours; huge chesterfields, a mirror that was at least twelve feet by twelve in an ornate wooden frame which she had carved herself from fruitwood, and enormous mahogany chests-of-drawers which smelled of mothballs and lavender. There was an elephant's-foot stand in the front hall which held assorted walking sticks, umbrellas, golf clubs, lacrosse and hockey sticks, alpenstocks, even a spear which Aunt and the Canon had brought back after a stint on the Ivory Coast. Hot water in the bathrooms was provided by ancient geysers, both of them corroded with green-stained lime and given to spitting tiny drops of scalding water over anyone within reach. When we moved in, there was still a line painted round the inside of the baths.

'That's all we were allowed, in the Dark Days of The War,' Ava told us dramatically. 'Five inches of hot water and not a drop more.'

'Sounds like the *Merchant of Venice*,' said Orlando.

'Oh no, dear, nothing to do with Italy. It was because of Mr Churchill. Saving water for Our Brave Boys sort of thing.'

'What did Our Brave Boys do with our bathwater?' Orlando quirked his eyebrow, sucked in his dimple.

'Um...'

'What happened if you made a mistake and ran a drop too much?' I asked.

'The police would come.' Ava sounded quite

positive, always a sign of uncertainty.

'What, while you were sitting naked in the bath?'

'I expect so, dear.'

Because the town was a naval base, there had been many local war casualties. Looking back, I imagine that the widowed mothers had nowhere else to go and so they stayed on, tucked inside their private griefs, bringing up their orphaned children, contriving to send them to the kind of schools their officer husbands would have wanted, making do, drawing only a modicum of comfort from each other.

Our accents were middle class, our poverty genteel. We attended boarding schools, and on returning home for the holidays would join up with an amorphous troop of children like ourselves. We knew each other, but not the local children. Orlando and I spent most of our time with Julian and Charlie Tavistock, Jeremy Pearce and David Gardner. Certain things were taken for granted. We all belonged to the snooty lawn tennis club, though our whites were often considerably less than white. Money for dancing lessons was found because our mothers believed that all gentlemen should be able to steer a lady competently round the dance floor and all ladies should know how to follow. Quicksteps, waltzes, rumbas, foxtrot, we learned them all at the Strand Palais, clasped to the bosom of either Mr Sheridan Fox or his colleague Miss Esmée. Both had false teeth and halitosis. We also learned Scottish reels under the guidance of an ancient Brigadier of some Highland regiment, whose moustache bristled and whose blue eyes constantly watered.

The town was full of men like him. Major This, Lieutenant-Colonel That, Captain Somebody-Else. Every morning, winter and summer alike, they emerged from gates set in the high garden walls along The Beach. In dressing-gowns of striped towelling and beach shoes of faded canvas, they crossed the road onto the green, crunched over the shingle, and slid down the steep shelves of the beach. Off with the robes and into the sea they plunged, wearing baggy black woollen bathing suits which had probably belonged to their fathers, or even their grand-fathers. With the war over, perhaps it was the only challenge left to them. Or were they reliv-ing their days at spartan boarding schools, where a cold shower first thing, with Matron barking at their heels, was *de rigueur*? They had red faces and shiny false teeth. They wore flannel trousers and brass-buttoned blazers with elaborate crests on the breast pocket made of gold wire and green or red felt, with flags and crowns woven into them. If they weren't wearing regimental ties, they had cravats thrust into the necks of their shirts.

In all the years we lived there, I never saw any of them with a wife. Once, Major de Grey spoke to me, clattering his teeth and mumbling through his military moustache. He put a hand on my arm. I used to see him sitting above us on the shelving beach, watching as we changed into our bathing costumes. He had a magnolia tree in his front garden, which was the most beautiful thing I'd ever seen.

Occasionally, excursions were arranged for us, and a bus hired. We would sometimes be taken to places of historic interest but much more often to the races. Sometimes the mothers clubbed together and hired the Village Hall for a Hop, paying an older son to act as what we were learning to call a disc jockey.

Every Easter Day, we found a chocolate egg beside our breakfast plates, hollow and patterned like a crazy paving garden path, wrapped in silver foil which could be smoothed out flat and then sculpted into tiny silver fans or goblets. At Christmas, we were taken either to the circus or a pantomime. Orlando and I hated both, especially the clowns with giant lipsticked mouths, eyes surrounded by huge white circles, and baggy checked trousers. We couldn't see why people laughed at them, any more than we understood Widow Twankey or Mother Goose. Pantomimes bewildered us, with their baffling references to vulgarities and catchphrases of which we had no knowledge. I've never understood why they were considered suitable entertainment, since we were not allowed to listen to anything on the radio (we still called it a wireless) except the news, nor read comics, and especially not use what my parents termed 'Americanisms', like *kid* and *okay*.

'They're trying to make us more normal,' explained Orlando once, as we sat unwillingly at the circus. 'They don't want us to grow up as misfits.'

21

'Too late, don't you think?'

'Far, far too late.' Musical Orlando groaned as a clown with tufts of ginger hair sticking out on either side of his chalk-white big-lipped mask did something unfunny with a string of sausages. 'Why can't they take us to the *Messiah*, or the *Christmas Oratorio* or something?'

'Trouble is, we're all too well brought up to tell them how much we hate it,' I said. 'Especially Widow Twankey.'

'Especially the bloody *clowns*.' His hand shook slightly; there was sweat on his forehead. 'There must be a word for hating clowns, some phobia or other. Whatever it is, I've got it.' He grinned his bone-white grin. 'My idea of heaven is never again having to watch Lulubelle and her Flying Ponies shedding sequins like dandruff all over the circus ring.'

Pantomimes and circuses apart, nobody offered us entertainment; we made our own from such pinchbeck as was available. We were always busy. Those long hours of childhood didn't exist for us. We made lists of musicians beginning with B, we read the encyclopaedia, we collected things such as stamps, pressed flowers, sea-glass, stones, quotations, favourite poems. We made constantly revised lists of the books we would take with us to a desert island. Orlando and I were occasionally invited into Aunt's room to have tea with her and listen to her tales of life in Africa, or narrow escapes she had had from naked spear-throwers or rampaging elephants.

In that bleakish seaside town, the one thing

22

there was in abundance was stones. We collected flat stones for skimming, stones with a hole through the middle, stones that looked like amber when they were wet, almost translucent. Green stones, stones with multicoloured seams and striations running through them. There were very few shells on that shingle beach, a few broken winkles, half a mussel, shining like a curve of blue pearl in the shingle, the occasional cuttlefish cast up by the tide and embedded in fierce black clumps of sea-wrack.

Orlando and I were luckier than most. We had a wind-up gramophone, a pre-war instrument that had belonged to my mother. We loved folding back the jointed chrome arm and fitting in the sharp metal needle, which we bought in tiny rattling boxes of painted tin. We owned half a dozen records: *In the Mood*, and *Jealousy*, the drinking song from *The Student Prince*, Max Bygraves singing *Ghost Riders in the Sky*. Henry Hall warbled *The Teddy Bear's Picnic*, with *Goodnight Sweetheart* on the reverse side. We played these songs endlessly, over and over again, until one dramatic afternoon, my mother rushed in like a whirlwind and hurled whatever was on the turntable to the ground, where it smashed into several shiny black shards. To our surprise, we saw that she was crying. 'For God's *sake!*' she shouted.

Our homes were full of hidden tensions.

TWO

Our perpetually anxious mothers were not much involved with us. Although they fed us, saw that we got up in the morning, brushed our teeth regularly, took baths from time to time, they did not talk to us. We were always conscious of things unspoken, of the ordinary textures of our lives constantly on the verge of being brutally and incomprehensibly ripped apart. We knew, without knowing, that our existences were barely held together by the fragile stitches of the not-in-front-of-the-children caution that our mothers exercised. Life was frail, and we were aware of it.

Sex had not sneaked into our consciousness, or if it had, was still unrecognized. There was no television to make us aware before our time, and although we were occasionally permitted to go to the cinema, we groaned when the hero kissed the heroine, or looked away, embarrassed. We weren't allowed to read comics or Enid Blyton. Sweets were still rationed, strawberries were only available in season. Appearances mattered.

We wore shorts and faded Aertex shirts. On our feet were Clark's sandals or white tennis shoes, which we Blancoed vigorously when they grew grubby, setting them out on a window sill overnight to dry to a stiff chalky white. We never wore black plimsolls; black ones were common. Fish and chips were also common, and so was eating in the street. The pleasure and delight of buying three penn'orth of chips and devouring them, hot and vinegary, straight from the newspaper wrapping, was made all the more delicious by the guilty fear that one of our mothers might catch us.

It was always our mothers we worried about. Fathers were rare or non-existent. We never asked about them, partly because in those years following the war, fathers were not a species to which we were used, and partly because we were somehow aware that the answer might be too painful to give or receive. I had a father, though I scarcely knew him and only saw him occasionally. David, Jeremy and the Tavistock brothers, did not. Their fathers had been war heroes, had Gone Down In Flames, according to Ava, or been prisoners-of-war in some German camp and never come home. Mine had spent the war working for intelligence in London, and then, in the immediate post-war years, in Germany, helping, so my mother said, to rebuild it, before returning to his position at an Oxford college. Whenever I thought of him back then, which was seldom, I envisaged my scholarly father in his shirtsleeves, setting bricks into mortar.

Many of the middle-class mothers in the town took in Paying Guests, or PGs. Anything to have a man around the house again, whiskers in the bathroom basin, a smell of tobacco, bass tones instead of trebling pipes or the hoarse croaks of breaking voices. They had not been raised to deal with lodgers, but, finding themselves husbandless, they hoped that the extra income would help to pay for heating their large cold houses, and feeding their families. For such women, life after the war was a series of improvisations as they learned to cope in a new world that was essentially alien. Gardeners, cooks, nursery-maids and housemaids had vanished or else were simply unaffordable.

For the most part, the PGs were misfits thrown up by the chaos of war, men who for reasons of health or age or incapacity, had not fought for King and Country, women whose husbands or fiancés had not returned from the front, or simply people, like Ava, who had quietly seized the opportunity to shuck off their former lives and start again in some quiet place where their pasts could not catch up with them.

During our first years at Glenfield House, PGs passed through in a more or less continuous stream. Most were dull, some were more memorable. Among them was Attila the Nun, a pretty woman who, according to Ava, had Leapt Over the Wall, a mad journalist from Sófia, known to all as the Bulgarian Atrocity, and a tall Army officer called Major John Silver, who came complete with an eye patch and a war wound to the right leg.

Sundry others swam briefly into our horizons and swam away again without making much of a ripple. Fiona found these people in the street, on trains, in queues, occasionally by answering ads requesting accommodation. She had a misleadingly open and sympathetic air so that people, particularly lame ducks, fell naturally into conversation with her, only to find themselves, often without understanding how, not only moving into her house, but also paying rent for the privilege of sharing the discomforts of our daily lives.

Three of them stayed long enough to become fixtures.

Prunella Vane met Fiona on the train, when she came down from London to interview for a job as a domestic science teacher at the grammar school. She was a buxom woman, like all the women in my recollection of childhood, except for someone called Mrs Simpson who, according to Ava, had got her claws into our Rightful King and whose real name was Mud.

Despite her size, Miss Vane was of a nervous disposition and shied like a horse at loud noises and sudden shouts. She occupied a vast freezing attic bedroom on the third floor, from which you could look through dormer windows at the sea and the wrecked pier and glimpse the distant coast of France on summer evenings.

'No need for curtains, as you see,' my mother said briskly, showing her around the first time, while Orlando and I trailed behind, hoping to catch a glimpse of what lay inside Prunella's canvas bag.

'I'm not sure I'd feel quite comfortable...' Miss Vane's hand caressed her throat.

'No Peeping Toms up here, you can be sure of

that,' my mother said.

'What about Peeping Dicks and Harrys?' asked Orlando, at which Miss Vane stepped over to the window and twisted her long neck this way and that, as though to ascertain for herself that no rude man could make his stealthy way across the roof tiles and peer in at her chaste disrobings.

'He'd have to be really determined...' said my mother lightly, glaring at Orlando.

'Unless he was a mountaineer.'

'Don't be silly, dear. Why on earth would a mountaineer want to waste his time spying on Miss Vane?' She looked quickly at her potential new lodger. 'Not that I'm ... Of course I don't mean ... I'm sure that...' The sentence trailed away, leaving behind a possible Miss Vane who wore flimsy undies and posed provocatively in the window, delighting binoculared passers-by on the promenade or even sailors out at sea, provided they had access to a telescope.

Sensing a growing reluctance on the part of Miss Vane to seize this unique opportunity, Fiona smiled at Prunella. 'If you really feel you want to block out the view, then of course we can find curtains for the window, Miss Vane. I'm sure I have something by me.'

'Well, I'm really not certain whether I'll be staying,' Prunella said feebly, but we all knew that it was already too late. Like so many before her, she was caught in my mother's gummed web. Anyway, by this time, she'd been offered, and had accepted, the teaching job she'd come down to the coast for, and perhaps in the end it simply seemed easier to stay than to look for alternative accommodation.

Some time later, Ava *tsked* sardonically. 'Domestic Science teacher? Jam tarts, I would not be surprised if that's all *she's* good for.'

'She does seem to have somewhat exaggerated her cooking abilities,' Fiona said. 'I must say I'd rather hoped she would see her way to mucking in and producing dinner for us occasionally.'

'Why should she?' asked Orlando. 'I bet you lured her here with false promises of home-cooked meals and all mod cons.'

'And that's exactly what she's got.'

'You didn't say she'd have to prepare the home-cooked meals herself. And she *is* paying rent, after all.'

'I suppose I hoped that from natural goodness of heart, she might feel ... Oh well...' Fiona's life was full of these plangent *Oh wells*...

'As for home comforts, she asked me to scrape the ice off her window this morning,' said Orlando.

'Given her circumstances, she should be grateful for a roof over her head, at a rent she can afford,' said Fiona coldly.

'What exactly are her circumstances?'

'That's her business, not ours.'

'Then how do you know she ought to be grateful?'

'Unlucky in love, you mark my words,' sniffed Ava.

Gordon Parker was another long-term lodger, a round-shouldered nervous young man who worked in the public library. He had bad teeth and a high-pitched voice, thinning hair greased back across a lumpy sort of skull and spectacles, which, in Ava's view, did him no favours. He was a member of a local choir, and behind the closed door of his room, we often heard him practising bits of Handel and Haydn in a reedy tenor.

He wore the same clothes every day, winter and summer alike: a V-necked Fair Isle sweater over a checked shirt, a shabby beige corduroy jacket, and chukka boots. There was something nakedly sad about Gordon, which brought out whatever rudimentary maternal instinct Fiona possessed. He was the only lodger she invited in to have a cup of tea with the family; the rest were confined to an electric kettle in their bedrooms. Occasionally she would even send me up to his room with a couple of lumpy iced fairy cakes, the only thing she had ever learned to bake.

My brothers teased him unmercifully, referring to him as Gordon the Barbarian or singing in a high falsetto under his window, until Fiona gave them a lecture on being kind to people who were weaker than they were.

'What exactly did you do in the war, Gordon?' they would ask innocently, blinking the bright blue eyes they had inherited from my father, when it was painfully obvious that the poor man would have registered D4 on any physical scale you cared to use. And Gordon would retort defiantly, flushing a fiery red, that he'd Done His Bit, thank you.

'But what *was* your bit, Gordon? What did you *do*?'

'Not that it's any of your business, but I was employed as a factory worker.'

'Doing *what* exactly?'

'That's for me to know and you to find out.' And he would retire to his room to practise his Handel again.

'He's Not As Other Men,' Ava told Orlando and me once, making sure the door was closed and my mother couldn't hear her.

'What's that mean?'

'You know...' She put a finger to the side of her nose and tapped it.

'No, we don't,' I said.

'You're being very mysterious, Ava.'

'The Love That Dare Not Speak Its Name.' Ava pursed her lips. 'That's as far as I'm prepared to go.'

'Well, it's not very far,' complained Orlando. 'I suppose it's another of the things we'll find out when we're older.'

'Exactly right.'

Our third long-term Paying Guest was Bertram Yelland, art teacher at one of the many boys' preparatory schools in the area. A chronically splenetic man in his early thirties, he was much given to reading pieces aloud from the newspaper and ranting about the state of the country.

'Festival of bloody Britain,' he would say disgustedly in the accents of the minor aristocracy from which he sprang. 'Designed to celebrate what, exactly? The beastly Hun being handed everything on a plate?' He'd spread a slice of toast with Ava's home-made marmalade and attack it fiercely with a set of strong yellow teeth. 'We were supposed to be the bloody winners, weren't we? And look at us now. Christ, you'd hardly know the war was over. Conditions are a bloody sight worse now than they were during the actual conflict.'

He repeated this kind of thing over and over again. Once, Ava challenged him. 'We're struggling to Get Out of the Doldrums,' she said.

'Doldrums is the word,' snorted Bertram. 'The whole bloody country's weighted down by gloom. It's enough to make you join up again. At least you had regular meals in the army, and I don't mean pigswill either. Christ, what was that muck Mrs B served up this evening?'

'A delicious Shepherd's Pie,' said Ava loyally.

'Made from what exactly, Mrs Carlton?'

'Nice minced lamb, of course.'

'Minced shepherd would be nearer the mark.' He groaned. 'The average sheep-herder would run for the hills sooner than eat garbage like that.'

'We all have to make sacrifices, Mr Yelland.'

'Let's face it, the woman's a hopeless cook, even if she has a damned fine intelligence.'

'You do realize that we've recently come through a Punishing War, don't you?' said Ava, who was turning the collar on one of Bella's blouses. 'Cooking for such large numbers isn't easy. And don't forget some things are still on ration.'

'Realize? I should bloody say I do. What do

32

you think I've been doing for the past five years, sitting about on my arse like that poncy little librarian upstairs?'

'That's quite enough of that sort of talk.'

'Making a land fit for heroes, that's what I was doing.' Bertram burped loudly. 'Well, whatever Mrs B's inadequacies – and Christ knows there's a number of them – she's at least what my grandmother would call A Lady. In fact, she'd out-Lady my sainted grandmama any day of the week.'

'I'm sure she'd be delighted to hear you say so.'

Bertram chuckled grimly. 'Woman's got a way with an eyebrow that could shrivel the balls faster than a snowstorm. And when she stares at you with that don't-fuck-with-me look in her eyes, you'd damn well better watch out.'

'I'll thank you to remember there are children in the room, Mr Yelland.'

But Ava, a fearful snob, didn't really mind Bertram's bad language. She knew that his father was a Sir and his mother the second daughter of an Earl.

'Do you enjoy your job, Mr Yelland?' she asked once.

'Hate the bloody place. Hate the little blighters I'm supposed to teach, hate the other so-called teachers. If I wasn't dead broke...'

'Can't your father help?' asked Ava delicately.

'Help? That's a laugh,' said Bertram. 'He never stops sending me letters telling me to forget my highfalutin' notions of being a painter, it's high time I got something behind me, whatever that might mean.' He threw himself around in his chair. 'God, it's like some third-rate cheap romance, kicking me out of the house if I don't toe the line, no son of mine, never darken my door again, cut you off without a shilling, all that hackneyed rubbish that fathers like Sir Chesney throw at sons like me.'

'Really?' Ava was thrilled at these behind-the-scenes glimpses of life in the houses of the nobility.

'But I'll make it one day, Mrs Carlton, I can promise you that. I only need a single break-through, and then it's fame and fortune for Bertram Yelland, and be damned to the pater.'

We children didn't like Mr Yelland, who had a nasty habit of using a wet towel to switch the backs of our bare summer legs if he found us in the passage when he emerged from the bath-room.

'Trying to look through the keyhole, are you?' he'd roar, and with one smooth movement, off would come his black leather belt.

'Why? Is there anything to see?' Orlando asked him, nimbly dodging. 'Are we missing some-thing?'

'None of your damned impudence, boy! I've got your measure, all right. If I catch you hang-ing about here again, you're for the chop.'

'You can't chop us.'

'I most certainly can, you little blighter.'

'But this is our *home*.'

'Doesn't make a ha'porth of difference.' And he retreated to his own room, pulling his loose dressing-gown around him, though not before

I'd caught a disagreeable view of the darkly hairy dangly thing below his stomach.

Whenever we could, Orlando and I spied on these people, gazing enraptured through keyholes at Ava strutting naked around her room, Miss Vane struggling into her ineffectual girdle, the Leaping Nun at her devotions, Gordon clearing his throat with a little flick of his head before letting go of his Handelian appeggios.

But for me, the most fascinating member of the household was undoubtedly Fiona. As well as teaching history at the nearby convent school, she also wrote short stories for women's magazines, making her unlike any of the other mothers we knew. She once told me that she could walk down the street and come back with ideas for ten stories. How she could be so successful on paper, writing about romance, children, domestic trivia, women, when her own femininity was so rudimentary, was another of her mysteries.

I spent a great deal of my childhood trying to break her down into her constituent parts, in an effort to examine wherein her difference to others lay, and also to see how much of her I carried inside myself. What was she like before she had children? What had she dreamed of, hoped for? When I knew she would be out for a while, I would tiptoe into her bedroom, treading lightly as a spider across the carpet, breathing in the ghostly smells of her scent, a precious pre-war bottle of Molyneux No 5, used only for very special occasions, and her face powder, which came in round boxes patterned with art deco black and orange flowers.

One afternoon I found a pile of journals hidden at the back of her wardrobe, each one exquisitely written in Indian ink, with an elegant calligraphic flourish at the end of every paragraph. They described journeys she had undertaken before the war in Germany and Spain and Norway, each page illustrated with witty little drawings of herself in various situations – trying not to fall off a bolting horse whose mane streamed behind it in the wind of its passing; swimming in a striped wool bathing costume with a crab pincered to her toe; rushing through a forest in a sleigh followed by slavering wolves – and with caricatures of people she had met along the way. Each volume was bound with fabric, the sheets of handmade paper sewn together with strong white thread. I was endlessly amused and intrigued by these journals, visualizing a younger, more carefree Fiona, who danced with five o'clock-shadowed men at village *fiestas* under swinging Japanese lanterns, or cycled boldly through the *Schwarzwald* in a pair of long baggy shorts and shoes with big laces. Although I didn't realize it at the time, I can see now how extraordinarily talented she was.

I searched constantly for some point of contact between us. We were the only females in a family of men but I was never able to see what linked us, made us two different and separate from the rest. Nor did I ever find any evidence in her drawers and closets. She was nothing like Ava, who possessed underwear covered in lace, padded sateen bags stuffed with filmy stockings, bottles of face cream, jars of make-up, lipsticks, eyebrows tweezers, powder puffs, orange sticks, nail-polish, cut-glass bottles with rubber balls covered in gold netting which you squeezed to produce a cloud of eau de cologne, a blue silver-topped bottle of *Soir de Paris* by Bourjois. Ava's wardrobe was packed with skirts made of shiny materials, with frilly blouses and little puff-sleeved jumpers, each hung on a hanger of padded white satin. Ava shaved her legs and under her arms.

Fiona possessed none of these feminine articles. A couple of sagging woollen skirts, a few pilled sweaters, a moth-eaten evening dress dating from well before the war. Was it poverty or simply indifference? Much later in my life I would realize that Fiona, a born bluestocking, would have been far better suited to running a women's college in Oxford or Cambridge than trying to run a home.

I loved her, I think, despite the fact that when I was eight, she offered me to a Swedish couple for the summer. They found it odd that after my arrival in their home, they never heard from her again, but after several months, they sent a telegram and dispatched me back to England. Fiona seemed glad to have me home again.

Most mornings, she inexpertly plaited my hair. The tiny tugs of pain as the silky hair was scraped back, braided, secured with rubber bands and ribbons tied over them, were as much part of my daily ritual as getting out of bed or putting on clothes. I loved those moments of intimacy, just the two of us, no noisy interfering boys, no lodgers wanting to know why their laundry hadn't come back or to complain that the geyser had blown their eyebrows off.

I was always eager to know about her childhood. 'Were you like me?' I asked.

'Not nearly as pretty, darling.'

'Did you like being a child?'

'Hated it. I was always cold and Grandfather used to make me and your Aunt Brigid and Uncle William get up at six o'clock every morning, even in winter, to learn Latin irregular verbs and Chaucer and practise the viola. And the cook was absolutely hopeless at cooking, so we always ate horrible meals, and we weren't allowed to talk at meals except in French or Hebrew.'

'How on earth did you learn to speak in Hebrew?'

'Grandfather was a famous Biblical scholar and when we weren't learning the violin or doing Latin, we had to learn Hebrew.'

'What's cornflakes in Hebrew? Or marmalade?'

'We didn't learn that kind of Hebrew.'

'But you could have talked to Moses if you'd ever met him. Or even Jesus!'

'Possibly.'

'Gosh!' To have a mother who might have been able to discuss leper-healing and money-changing with Our Blessed Saviour threw a new light on her.

'But Jesus spoke Aramaic, not Hebrew. Besides, I don't suppose he'd have had time to chat with the likes of me,' said Fiona. 'Too busy walking on water, or making two loaves and five fishes feed five thousand people. I do so know how he must have felt.' She sighed. 'Talking of which ... I wish I had the slightest idea what we were going to have for supper tonight.'

'Did you want to be a mother?' I asked her once, and she answered with her usual hapless honesty, 'Not really.'

'What then?'

'An illustrator,' she said, staring into space, my hair forgotten in her hand. 'I always wanted to draw pictures – not great art, just illustrations. Magazines or books, frontispieces, endpapers, that kind of thing.'

'And why didn't you?'

'My father didn't consider it a proper occupation for a woman.'

'But you like writing stories, don't you?'

'It's an extra source of income, darling, but otherwise...' She seized the hair on the left hand side of my head. 'I swear to you, Alice,' she said fiercely, 'that whatever you want to be later in life, I shall support you in every way I possibly can.'

My favourite story was about Fiona falling in love. 'Tell me how you met Daddy,' I'd say, though I already knew because I'd asked her a hundred times before, so much so that now it was me, not her, who cycled down the Banbury Road from North Oxford to meet the man who'd advertised in the *Cherwell* for someone willing to share the cost of buying a car with him. I was the undergraduate who leaned her heavy green Raleigh against the wall outside the Cadena Cafe in Cornmarket Street, and went into the teashop. It was me who fell instantly and forever in love with the stocky young man who rose, holding a newspaper in one hand, who spoke to me in the most beautiful voice I had ever heard, who asked me to sit down and ordered a cup of tea from the waitress in a black uniform with a little white apron tied around it.

Fiona would insist she couldn't remember what she was wearing, that first fateful time. 'I might have been coming back from lacrosse,' she said doubtfully, biting her lip, my hair lying flat across the blade of her hand. 'Or was it after a lecture? No, I really can't recall.'

So I had to supply the details myself. Sometimes I imagined her dashing in from her college playing field in the Woodstock Road, smelling sweaty (no deodorants back then), in a pleated gymslip and baggy blouse, perhaps still carrying the lacrosse stick, which she hadn't liked to leave outside on the street in case someone stole it, her thin hair wisping around the fine skin of her temples where the blue veins beat. Or she'd be wearing a costume like the one still hanging in her wardrobe, a kind of reddish tweed thing made up for her by her mother's Scottish dress-maker, a felt cloche on her head, her ink-smudged hands hidden inside leather gloves.

In the bottom drawer of the chest in her room, there was a Ramsey & Muspratt portrait of her in an ivory satin evening dress, leaning towards the camera with a cigarette in a long ebony holder, her hair arranged in corrugated waves close to her skull. She looked, for the first and perhaps the only time, beautiful. But even I did not imagine she would have turned up at the Cadena Cafe in a satin evening dress, in order to discuss with a stranger the sharing of a motor car.

I've often wondered what he expected, that young lecturer with the shock of wild black hair, madly in love with a pretty girl called Georgina he had met in Germany while a *lektor* at Heidelberg, a girl whose fair hair stood in massed curls around her face and accented her blue eyes. Georgina was English, the daughter of a rich man in Sussex and, since my father was so poorly paid, she was for him what he called a Quite Impossible She.

So, rising from his seat, newspaper open perhaps at the crossword, perhaps even at the sports page (for he held a half-blue in hockey) did he see the curiously undisciplined inefficient life that marriage to this gawky young woman would provide him with? Did he foresee the wild children, the raffish household, young voices singing round the piano at Christmas time, while turkeys burned and plum puddings boiled dry in their muslin bags? Could he have foretold the unmade beds, the undarned socks, the whole un-wifeliness of Fiona? Did he see cold winds blowing from a grey sea on a winter's evening, and Miss Prunella Vane, flushed and uncertain, Gordon the Barbarian, Attila the Nun, or any of the other assorted curios that Fiona gathered about her?

Did he, above all, have the slightest inkling of Fiona's complete unsuitability for the roles of wife and mother, her total lack of confidence, so much so that she could not even live in Oxford, in case she proved a disappointment to him, which meant that for the whole of his academic life he was forced to live in digs?

What was it about her that made him marry her? The unattainability of Georgina? The intelligence and, yes, a certain pathos that gleamed in Fiona's eyes? Or simply a feeling of pity for this awkward creature coming towards him between the tables, knocking over a cup of tea here, dislodging a piece of iced walnut cake there? Could it, unlikely as it seemed, have been love?

And what had she, the woman who would become my mother, what had she hoped for? Gauche, uncertain, bullied by her scholarly father, ignored by her sister, usurped by her brother, already half in love with a gaunt man from Wycliffe Hall preparing to take Holy Orders, what had she expected from life after she had sat her final exams and graduated? Had she really believed she would become a vicar's wife and live sedately the rest of her life in some country vicarage or inner city rectory, full of solid worth and good works? Had she expected an ordinary life? A cottage in the Cotswolds? A tall cold house in North Oxford, the gentle plod of academia, dry dons and their starchy wives to dinner, herself in a silk dress, her handsome husband in a suit and tie, inviting her husband's awkward undergraduates to sherry once a term, while a docile 'help' passed round crustless sandwiches with the aid of a niece who'd caught the bus in from Cowley? Concerts at the Sheldonian, young academics giving clever parties, playing word-games and charades, discussing frivolously but with just a touch of earnestness whom they would throw off the sledge first to sate the ravening wolves following so closely behind. Had she fancied that there would be picnics and bathing parties, punting up the river with her hands trailing, leaving a tiny drift of artist's ink in the thick green water of the Cherwell? Might she have thought there would be holidays in Scotland or Wales or Cornwall? Is that how she'd seen it, in those days of high expectation before the war? It seemed unlikely.

Maybe she had hoped that, despite my grand-father, she might make it to Paris or to Rome, wear wild hand-painted smocks, meet some Gauloise-smoking artist who would seduce her on a bed of tiger skins and sweep her down to Nice in an open roadster.

Because her father had refused her permission to attend art school, she went to Oxford and read History instead, eventually, when we moved to Shale, becoming a teacher at nearby St Ethel-burga's Convent, forcing the Reformation and the Industrial Revolution into the stolid minds of good Catholic girls who had no other thoughts in their heads except to marry boys of their own sort and perpetuate the race.

At break, she sat in the convent staff room with young women in sensible skirts and blouses, who carried round with them the viscous ghosts of lost fiancés and husbands who'd baled out over Holland or dropped in a ball of flame into some German field, been torpedoed in the cold Atlantic or beaten to death by Japanese guards.

They were mild-eyed, those bereaved and grieving women who occasionally visited our house for sedate cups of tea, Miss Thompson, Miss Jackson, Mrs Ffoliot, Miss Hargreaves, doomed by the war to be spinsters for the rest of their lives, the shades of the men who might have lent them some validity, might have fulfilled their femaleness, still lying like a bruise on their hearts.

THREE

The final summer that we lived at Glenfield, the steady, boring tempo of my life began to alter. At the time, the first change to our routines seemed the least important. It's only with hindsight that I see how the events were set in motion during those long slow weeks that would discolour the rest of our lives.

It was one of those long hot summers that linger on in the memory and stand as the paradigm of all the summers of one's childhood. Day after day the sun blazed from an empty sky, turning our gray Kentish sea to an almost Mediterranean blue. We spent every day on the beach, swimming or sunbathing or endlessly competing against each other to see who could throw a stone the furthest, who could hit a floating piece of driftwood first, who could chuck a pebble into the air and hit it with another.

44

It proved to be the rickety bridge between childhood and adolescence. Julian grew six inches and started to sprout hairs on his upper lip; David's voice began to break. The old freedoms between us suddenly altered. Charles, Julian, even my Orlando, no longer struggled into their bathing suits on the beach, hidden behind an inadequate war-worn towel, but instead wore them beneath their clothes.

And Nicola came.

Nicola Stone had recently moved down from London, along with her mother, Louise, and a brother whom we seldom saw. Among other enticing attributes, she possessed a vocabulary of swear words which even Julian, the oldest of us, hadn't yet dared to use. Although she was tiny – *'I was a premature baby'* – she seemed to be afraid of nothing, especially not the grown-ups. She was two or three years older than I was and she effortlessly took over from Julian as the unacknowledged leader of our pack. She had slanting green eyes and small pointed teeth. Her red hair was cut short, like a boy's, and curled thickly over her head. Freckles covered her nose and in her bathing costume you could see that she had breasts. Apart from Orlando, all of us fell completely under her spell.

Her mother was something to do with fashion, and had bought a smuggler's cottage in the oldest part of the town, long before it became chic. She painted the walls in bright colours, had a wooden upright beam supporting the low ceiling of her sitting-room, drank cocktails from V-shaped glasses of the kind we had only seen in

45

films, smoked cigarettes in a long black holder. Nicola had many more clothes than I did, and boxes of jewellery that had me gaping. Dozens of earrings, long ropes of artificial pearls and blue glass beads, red stones set in gold, chunks of turquoise on silver chains. On top of that, the lobes of her ears were pierced, and she wore tiny gold studs in them. I couldn't imagine having my ears pierced, or even wanting to. Nicola said she'd done it herself with a hot darning needle and a cork. 'Once I'd made the hole, Mum had to get the studs,' she said. 'I could do your ears if you like.'

I could clearly imagine what my mother would say, how vulgar she would consider it, how incredibly unlikely she would be to buy gold studs for me if I let Nicola pierce my ears.

'No,' I said. 'Thanks, but my mother would kill me.' Nonetheless, I was thrilled that Nicola considered me ear-piercing-worthy, that she let me wear her clip-on earrings sometimes, or the feather boa she had hanging on the back of her bedroom door, or try the scent she had in a cut-glass bottle on her dressing-table, though I was only able to do that once as Fiona wrinkled her nose in disgust when she smelled me, and Bertram Yelland made some remark about pox-doctor's clerks.

Something else distinguished Louise Stone from the other mothers.

'Apparently she's a Bit Fast,' whispered Ava, checking that the drawing-room door was firmly shut.

'Do you mean speed-of-light sort of thing?'

asked Orlando.

Ava bent closer. 'She's *divorced*,' she mouthed.

I wasn't a hundred per cent sure what being divorced entailed, but it sounded exotic.

Ava's face twitched as she glanced again at the door. She motioned us towards her and we obediently bent our heads nearer until we could smell her face powder and the scent of *Soir de Paris*. 'What's more, her husband's...' She paused thrillingly.

'What, Ava?'

'Where?'

'...in jail!'

Orlando and I stared at each other and then at Ava. 'Jail? You mean ... in *prison*?'

Ava nodded.

'What *for*?'

'Manslaughter!' The word had an ominous pregnant sound.

'Nicola's father *killed* someone?' Even the urbane Orlando was taken aback.

'Isn't that the same as ... murder?' I asked. My mouth felt dry, as the enormity of the concept of violent death settled inside me. This was way outside our experience. Murder was the stuff of the green Penguin paperbacks that filled my parents' bookshelves, or occasional headlines in newspapers, not something that peoples' fathers committed.

'Yes,' breathed Ava. 'It was a notorious case a couple of years ago, in all the papers for days. I really thought his wife was going to Stand By Her Man, but as soon as he was sentenced, she divorced him and disappeared. And now she's come down here, where nobody will find out who she is.'

'*You* did.'

'Only because I recognized that green costume she was wearing the other day.'

'Maybe you've got it all wrong.' I didn't want Nicola tainted. 'Maybe Mrs Stone just happened to buy her costume at the same shop as this ... manslaughter person's wife.'

'No. She wore it on Day Three of his trial. I remember her in it. I cut it out.' Ava kept voluminous scrapbooks full of newspaper-cuttings about notorious trials.

'Who did Mr Stone kill?' asked Orlando.

Again Ava glanced at the door. Despite their mutual dependency, she was frightened of my mother. 'That's the awful thing,' she whispered. 'It was a little girl. Nicola's best friend. Said he didn't mean to, well, of course, he would say that, wouldn't he? Said he didn't realize what he was doing.'

'Not the old red mist defence, I hope,' said Orlando.

'Is he going to be hanged?'

'They don't hang people for manslaughter.' Ava gave a theatrical shudder. 'I just hope he stays behind bars for the rest of his life. No one's safe with monsters like that around.'

'How can he be a monster if he didn't mean to do it?'

'How did he kill her?' asked Orlando.

'Strangled her with...' there was another of Ava's dramatic pauses '...her very own scarf!'

48

'Does it matter whose scarf it was?' asked Orlando.

'Not as such, I suppose, but somehow it makes it all the more dreadful.' Ava checked the door again, and leaned in once more. 'Pulled it round her neck as tight as he could,' she said graphically, 'until her eyes popped and her tongue stuck out. They found the poor little mite lying on the floor of his daughter's bedroom.'

'Horrible, Ava.'

'How could he not mean to do it?'

Unsure, she moved on to safer ground. 'Not that his name *was* Stone,' she added. 'Louise has obviously gone back to her maiden name or something. He was called Farnham, Geoffrey Farnham.'

'Gosh.' We were speechless, plunged into the reality of the alien, morbidly exciting adult world that rarely intruded into our bookish lives.

Belatedly, Ava realized that perhaps she had been indiscreet. 'Now, don't you go telling anyone what I just told you. It's not fair to visit the sins of the father upon the children. Promise me, now.'

We promised, but the knowledge only added to Nicola's already considerable mystique and my own besottedness.

That was also the summer when I woke one morning to find blood on my nightdress. I looked for scabs on my knees but found none so I went to Ava. 'What's this from?'

'Oh, Alice!' She smiled in a way that made me uneasy and embarrassed.

49

'What's the matter?' I said.

'You've become a Woman!'

'Have I?'

She nodded and winked. 'Better not tell the boys.'

'Why not?'

'Boys can be very silly about things like that,' she said.

Like what? How exactly had I become a woman? What was I this morning, that I hadn't been last night? Adulthood had been something which awaited far off, and which did not affect my current existence at all. Now, I saw that only the thinnest of membranes separated the girl I was from the woman I had apparently become. Somehow, the barrier between my past and my future had been breached. Unusually, Fiona was more helpful than Ava. Matter-of-factly, she explained about menstruating and monthly periods, showed me a sanitary towel, which she helped me to tie on with a piece of string. 'I'll buy you a proper belt when I go shopping later,' she said. 'Of course, you won't be able to go swimming.'

'Why not?' I was appalled at this sudden curb on my freedom.

'Because it's safer and easier for you not to, not while you're bleeding. Don't worry, darling. I'll explain to the boys.'

'Please don't. I'll absolutely die if you do.'

'You're being awfully melodramatic,' she said briskly. 'It's a perfectly normal physical function.' She smiled the same way Ava had. 'People call it The Curse, but it's not really because it means that you'll be able to have children now.'

'But I don't *want* to,' I said. 'Not *now*.'

'You don't have to.' She gave me a short lecture in her embarrassing Wise Woman voice about being careful what I did with boys that left me none the wiser. I was fairly sure I didn't like being a woman. I felt dirty. The string chafed the skin of my stomach, the pad felt awkward. I was sure that everyone could see it bulging inside my shorts. I'd never kept anything from Orlando before, but I felt instinctively that this was something I wouldn't share with him.

Perhaps it was because I was now a woman that Fiona decided I was to take piano lessons. Perhaps she thought I was becoming too much of a tomboy, or perhaps she simply wanted to help the lonely young refugee who was living up the road in Mrs Sheffield's house. Grown-ups didn't explain very much to us in those days but I vaguely understood that Mr Elias had escaped from Germany before the war.

'I don't want to waste the holidays on beastly music lessons.' I kicked at the big Chesterfield sofa in our shabby drawing-room. Orlando had been learning the piano for years, along with several other instruments, but I'd never felt any desire to do so too.

'Some of your friends are already going to him,' Fiona said. 'Mary Stephens. Rosemary Geoffreye. And that strange child from the North End – Nicola Stone.'

'Nicola?' I brightened. If Nicola went to him, it put a different complexion on things. 'She never said anything about it.'

'Well, she began in the Easter holidays, and goes once a week. She'll be taking lessons at school from next term and her mother wants her to get a head start.'

So it was with reasonable grace that I found myself on the stone doorstep of Number Seventeen, five houses down from Glenfield, lifting the green-tarnished brass knocker shaped like a bull's head. When Mrs Sheffield opened the door, she let loose the smell of mould and damp stone and lack of upkeep, which was familiar from my own home.

'Good afternoon, Alice,' she said in her high-pitched, well-bred voice.

'It's for piano lessons,' I said quickly, afraid that she might otherwise think this was a social call.

'Of course. Your mother said you would be coming.' From upstairs, we could hear something sad and beautiful being played on the piano. Mrs Sheffield's face lifted to the sound like a sunflower. She sighed. 'He's such a talented boy. I wish my husband could have heard...'

A boy? I found this strange. None of the boys I knew could have taught someone to play the piano, not even Orlando, and he was already preparing to take Grade 8. 'Should I go up?' I wondered.

'Of course, dear. I'm sure Mr Elias is expecting you. First door on the right. Just knock.'

I climbed the curving staircase while the music swelled. Another brass knocker, polished this time, in the shape of a trumpet-blowing angel, was attached to the middle panel of the door, and I lifted it, let it fall again with a small thud.

The door opened, and Mr Elias stood there, staring gravely at me for a moment.

'You are Miss Alice Beecham?' He had a foreign accent and wore a pullover with holes in the elbows. His teeth were very white.

'Yes.'

'Then please to come in.' He stood aside and motioned me in with a bow.

Immediately I felt lifted out of my usual self. A bow! This was not how I was normally treated. I floated past him and stared around me. The cluttered room smelled of coffee and wool and aniseed; it was an alien smell, and curiously exciting. After the austerities of my own home, it seemed exotic beyond compare. Heavy velvet curtains hung from floor to ceiling on either side of the windows. A grand piano dominated the bay window, through which I could see Orlando kicking a stone along the promenade, occasionally glancing up at the window where he knew I was. The rest of the boys were down on the beach, aimlessly chucking pebbles into the sea. Nicola's hair flamed between them.

A sabre hung above the fireplace with a blue velvet gold-tasseled cap tied to it. On the mantelpiece sat a bowlful of pearls. Records in tattered brown slip-covers lay piled on the floor; a rack of china-bowled pipes stood on the mantelpiece and beside it, a tin where Mr Elia kept tobacco, with a girl painted on it, her long hair rippling over but not hiding her naked body. A red glass decanter stood on the window sill and, instead of lying on the floor, an oriental carpet was fixed to the wall. A record player in a shiny wooden cabinet stood beside the fireplace. On top of it was a primitive radio, with protruding antennae, and a pair of headphones lying beside it. There were faded sepia photographs everywhere. A plump couple beaming, two little girls with long hair held back in a big floppy bow, a group with the couple and the girls with a boy in grey shorts standing in the middle. Were these members of Mr Elias's family? I wanted to ask him but just as we refrained from asking Julian or the other boys about their lost fathers, so I was afraid of stirring up the sadness which I sensed in him.

He was not a complete stranger to me. I had seen him several times walking along the promenade, his head down, his shoulders hunched. And I vividly remembered another time. On a night of storm and gale, Orlando and were I woken by the wailing of the lifeboat maroons. As we lay there in the dark, listening to the wind howling under the roof tiles and rattling the window-frames, Fiona came in to our bedroom.

'Hurry up and get dressed,' she said. 'Plenty of warm clothes.'

'Why?'

'To be there when the lifeboat comes back. You can carry this Thermos of tea, Orlando, and Alice, you take this blanket.'

'What for?'

'There are sailors wrecked on the Goodwin Sands,' she said patiently. 'We must do what we can.'

54

We trudged along the sea front towards the stone-built lifeboat house, battling with the wind and the scream of the storm. People had gathered there, clothes pulled on over their pyjamas, clutching blankets and vacuum flasks, string bags of sandwiches, even ancient sweaters. It was very dramatic. Minutes after we arrived, the lifeboat surged out of the darkness and up onto the shingle bank. A German ship, someone told us, had run aground, its hull holed, men thrown into the waves. They began to unload, first the lifeboat crew in yellow oilskins, then the rescued men, blond, good-looking, bewildered, shivering under wet grey blankets.

Someone behind me began to swear under his breath, on and on in a furious monotone: 'Bastards. Sons of bitches. *Schweinehunder*. *Nazi Schweinehunder*. Filthy bastards. They should have left you there to drown and go to hell.'

I recognized him now. It had been my new piano teacher standing there, cursing the shipwrecked Germans.

Much later I would learn that he was only twelve years older than myself, but at that first meeting, he seemed immeasurably ancient, in his grubby uncollared shirt, and round tortoiseshell spectacles. Orlando had a similar pair. I knew you could prise the tortoiseshell off, like a scab. I wondered if Mr Elias had discovered this, whether I should ask him.

That first afternoon, he sat down at the piano stool and placed me between his knees. 'Now Miss Alice Beecham, we shall start with the scale of C,' he announced, and proceeded to play it, fingers rippling like water on the keys. He put a warm hand over mine and bent my fingers one after the other up the keyboard and down again. 'Up,' he said. 'And down again. Up ... and down.'

'Did you bring that piano with you from Germany?' I asked, when the lesson appeared to be over. I envisaged him bent double, the piano strapped to his back, and wondered what he did with the legs. Perhaps he carried them with him in a bag, or perhaps...

'It is not my own piano.' He smiled at me, and I felt a kind of warmth between my legs, the same inexplicable feeling I sometimes had when I watched Gregory Peck or Audie Murphy when we went to the cinema. 'It belongs to Mrs Sheffield.'

'She's a widow,' I said. 'Her husband was killed in the war.'

And immediately I blushed with mortification. How cross my mother would be if she knew I'd been rude enough to mention the war when this man was from Germany, and might think I was making some kind of dig at him.

'The piano is one of the reasons I came to live here,' Mr Elias said. He spread his beautiful hands and smiled. 'Otherwise I would not be able to become a poor piano teacher.'

He didn't seem poor to me, with his sabres and pearls and velvet caps. 'Were you always?' He smelled of cigarettes, but not the kind my father smoked, of something more exotic, as though some kind of spice had been mixed in with the tobacco.

'I have only done this for a couple of years.'

'What did you do before that?'

'Before that, I lived in London with my cousin and his wife. When his wife became pregnant, they needed the bedroom where I was sleeping.'

'Did you escape from the Nazis?'

'More or less.'

'How?' Orlando was obsessed by the recent war, and had urged me to read the accounts of daring escapes from Colditz and various Stalag Lufts, *The Wooden Horse*, *The Cruel Sea*. We'd seen films starring Jack Hawkins and Richard Attenborough. We knew all about plucky Douglas Bader with his amputated legs, Wing Commander Guy Gibson, *The Naked Island*. 'Did you dig a tunnel, or dress up in disguise?' I wanted to know all the details of fake passports and imitation uniforms, in order to carry the information back to Orlando.

He shook his head. 'Nothing like that,' he said. 'When my family ... when they were...' His face clouded for a moment, '...my aunt Lena brought me to England, along with my cousin, just before the war had started. I was still a boy. I went to school in London, in Richmond, and all the time I studied. Then one day I saw in the paper where there was a job teaching at a school nearby this little town, and I moved down here.'

'Lucky for me, then?'

'Do you really think so?' He said 'sink', instead of 'think'.

'Of course.' We were neglected children, but well-brought up.

'When I came to view the room, Mrs Sheffield

57

told me that this used to be her drawing-room, but that it was too large and too cold for her now. She said she couldn't move the piano, and she didn't want to sell it, because it belonged to her father, so whoever took the room would have to share it with the Steinway.'

'You must have been very pleased.'

'Pleased?' My new teacher lifted his hands in the air. 'I could feel stars in my ears!'

'We say "stars in our *eyes*", not in our ears.'

'Oh, but I felt these stars in my ears,' he said. 'So I asked Mrs Sheffield if I might play the instrument occasionally, and she says...' He clasped his hands together. '"Oh, my dear Mr Elias, it would give me the greatest of pleasure if you would. It might need tuning, of course..."'

'Did it?' I asked. He fascinated me, not simply because of the glamorous strangeness of the space he inhabited but also because of his magical ability to conjure up someone outside himself.

'A little. I did it myself. It took me a long time, but luckily I have perfect pitch, I learned about tuning because back home in Germany, no one would come to the house to tune a piano, so my mother and I had to teach ourselves.'

I frowned. 'Why wouldn't anyone come to your house?'

'They were too afraid of being tainted. Or accused of collaboration.'

'Tainted?' I stared at him in surprise. 'Why?'

'Because we were Jews,' he said.

It was not the first time I had heard that richly sinful, shameful word, though it was never used in my own household. *Jew* ... Although I wasn't sure exactly of the resonances the word encompassed, I was embarrassed and ashamed, both on his behalf and on mine.

'You won't find anything like that here,' I said in the same brisk tones that Fiona might have used, though as yet I knew nothing about anti-Semitism. 'I hope you've found us very welcoming.'

'Of course,' he said. 'Before I came here, I heard very often about the snobbish English, and the way they can smell an alien or an inferior through a wall, but I have never since I got here experienced anything but kindness.'

'Good. That's good.'

'I admire so much these faded, war-weary women here in this little town,' he said. 'So brave, so indomitable, hanging on, keeping their homes going, their children fed and educated and clothed. Just like mothers in Germany, I hope.'

'Did ... do you have a family, Mr Elias?' I asked. Beyond the thick red curtains, I could see the boys on the warm shingle, devising games to pass the time, games I'd joined in dozens of times, over many summers, which belonged to a much simpler world than the one I was hearing about now.

'Pappi, my father, was a surgeon, my mother – Mutti – a Professor at the Conservatoire. She was from Russia, her people were high-class landowners but they had to flee from the Bolsheviks.'

I was storing these words up to ask about when

I got home. *Jew. Bolshevik. Conservatoire.*

'Also,' he went on. 'I had two little sisters, Anna and Magdalena.'

That past tense burned in my chest. *Had.* Beside his mouth, a tiny muscle jumped. I knew that if I reached out and pressed my finger to the flinching skin, I could stop it. I wanted to. I knew how his skin would feel under my touch. Beneath my Aertex shirt, my nipples softly ached.

I watched his face shut down and though I longed to know more about Mutti and Pappi and the two sisters, I kept quiet, sensing something heart-deep and wrenching in him, a loneliness, an unfulfillable yearning to belong.

I needed to change the subject. 'May I look at the books?' I asked.

As well as the piano, Mrs Sheffield's former drawing room possessed a wall of fitted mahogany bookcases, each shelf fringed with gold-tooled leather and filled with the English classics. We had them all at home, but in much worse condition than these beautiful unused volumes of Scott, Dickens, Tolstoy, Kipling, Austen.

He nodded.

Hardly breathing, I took down a copy of *Nicholas Nickleby* and opened it very carefully. It was an India paper edition, with black-and-white etchings that were familiar from the battered copies on our own shelves. I put it back, reached first for *Emma,* and then for my current favorite, *Northanger Abbey.* I felt an almost sensuous pleasure in touching these books, opening the covers and seeing how the pages clung one to another, each one edged with gold that glinted in the light from the big bay window.

'Do you read a lot?' I asked.

'I try,' he said.

'If you want something different from these, there's a public library, here.'

'Where is that?'

For the first time in my life, I knew how it felt to be an adult, in charge, in control. 'I could show you if you like,' I said off handedly, 'one of these days.'

'I would like very much to do that.'

'They even have a few German books,' I said. 'But you've probably read them all.'

'They are still there, on the shelves?' He seemed surprised.

'Of course. Why not?'

He looked away from me, out to sea, his voice musing. 'I suppose I had imagined public burnings of German literature, people in coats and scarves turning up to throw their foreign books upon the pyre, hissing perhaps, hanging effigies of Goethe and Rilke, even the Brothers Grimm, fines for those who try to conceal these heretical books produced by the Enemy.'

I stared at the back of his head, not sure if he was joking. Orlando and I had grown up on Grimms' Fairy Tales. Why would anyone wish to burn them? But we also knew about brave Martin Luther burning the Papal Bull and we had just read *Fahrenheit 451*. 'We don't do that sort of thing here,' I said.

'I think not.' There was a droop to his shoulders that rent me. I picked up a pearl from the decorated bowl which held them. I loved the dull gleam of it lying in my palm, the hint of the life he had abandoned, a life to which he longed – or so I surmised – to return. I put it in my pocket. I started to walk over to stand by him at the window, edging round the piano, when he turned back into the room. Silhouetted against the brightness from the sea, I couldn't clearly see his features. Had he seen me? My face reddened with guilt. He would think I was a thief. What was worse, a thief who stole from someone much worse off than myself. As he bent over an open book of music, I thrust my hand into my pocket, leaned towards the fireplace and quickly pushed the pearl into one of the crevices of the carved marble surround. He looked up again just as I stepped away from the hearth. 'Nor was it customary in Germany until recently.'

He was obviously much more closely connected with the war than I would ever be, a fact confirmed when later that evening, I overheard Ava and my mother discussing him.

'Poor young man...' That was my mother. 'According to the aunt, his entire family wiped out...'

'...Nazis...' Ava's voice was hushed '...God knows what horrors...'

'...I shudder to think...'

'...if it was Bella, I know how I'd...'

'A refugee – what kind of a life can he have?' asked my mother. She paused. 'The *bloody* war.'

Twice a week that summer, I walked out of our

gate and down to Mrs Sheffield's house. Whenever I climbed the stairs to Mr Elias's room, I would hear him playing Schubert's *Trout Quintet* or Beethoven's *Moonlight Sonata* and for me, now, that music is inextricably associated with guilt and with him. Sometimes he would be la-la-ing along to the music and I would stand outside the door, knuckles ready to knock, listening to him, a prey to unfamiliar and exciting emotions to which I was unable at that time to give a name to.

After the lesson we often talked, standing at the window looking out at the stripes of roadway, silver bars, green grass, yellow shingle, blue-grey sea. On those baking afternoons, the sun burned the shingle white. The sea panted with heat, resting like green silk under the milky sky. Between the dusty velvet curtains, I could see the boys waiting for the moment when my hour with Mr Elias was up, ready to scoff, jealous and, at the same time, frightened, realizing that we were all growing up, recognizing that something which had until now been fixed was now in the process of changing. I often saw Orlando, too, the pale parts of his hair bleached white by salt and summer sunshine. Separated from the other boys, he would stare up at the window, frowning, and as I watched, would bend down, pick up a pebble and pulling back his arm, hurl it far out into the sea then stand with his back to the houses, watching as it hit the surface and sent up a spray of white water like an erupting volcano.

'Look down there,' Mr Elias said one time.

'Those are your friends. And the boy with the striped hair, what is his name?'

'Orlando. He's terribly clever.'

'And you, Miss Alice, are you clever?'

'Quite clever,' I said. 'But nothing like Orlando. He's awfully talented, too. He plays all sorts of instruments and he won a scholarship to his choir school. My mother says he's a genius. He had his IQ tested and it was something enormous. My father says he'll either end up as a Nobel prize winner or on the scaffold.'

'This seems a strange assessment of a boy so young. Do you think your father is right?'

'No, I don't think so,' I said. 'At least, not the scaffold part. He'd escape somehow.'

For the sake of the poor refugee and his wiped-out family, I practised my scales over and over again. I could pick out *Twinkle Twinkle Little Star* on the piano in my own house, and *Three Blind Mice*, but now I began to practise more and more assiduously. Scales ... up, up, up, and down again. Arpeggios. Chromatic scales, octaves. I progressed from scales with one hand to scales with both, and then on to arpeggios and the ripple of chromatics. Over and over, until I could have played them in my sleep. I wanted Mr Elias's approval. I wanted to stand between his knees, feel the warmth of his breath on my neck, the beat of his heart against my spine.

As I grew more proficient, I sometimes envisaged myself seated on a stage, swaying across the ivory keys of a Steinway, the silk billows of my gown rustling, my hands flying, while an entire audience scarcely dared breathe for fear of disturbing the beauty of my playing. The Festival Hall, Sir Malcolm Sargent, applause rippling beneath the domed roof like a swelling surging sea, cries of 'Encore!'

One afternoon, he declared that I was to learn a simple tune played with both hands at once. 'We shall start with a song from my own country, which you shall play first with one hand and then, when you have mastered it, with both.'

'What's it called?'

'Muss i 'den, muss i 'den, zum statle hinaus,' he crooned into my ear. He gripped me between his knees as he put his hands over mine.

'I know that song. My father sometimes sings it when he's shaving.'

'Then you will like to play this, I think, Miss Alice Beecham.' His hands were warm and slightly rough. I could feel his breath on my neck, tickling the roots of my plaits. *'Und du, mein schatz, bleibst hier.'*

I twisted round, stared at him. We were no more than two inches apart and his face swayed towards me so that I thought, lips already wrinkling with disgust, for a moment he might kiss me. I knew about kissing: Julian had tried it once, and I had found it fairly nasty. 'Why do you always call me Miss Alice Beecham?'

'What should I call you?'

'Alice, of course. That's what everyone else says.'

He smiled gravely. 'But I am not everyone else.'

I looked at him more closely. Under a mop of

wild black curls, he had light hazel eyes, surrounded by thick dark lashes and in one pupil was embedded, like a jewel, a star-shaped speck of green, the colour of a sunlit meadow, a revealing glimpse of what lay behind his eyes. Looking deep into them, and beyond, right into his head, I saw that indeed he was not like everyone else. Here was someone who was not just a man enclosed in the shell of maleness, but someone, like Orlando, whom I knew and recognized. His hand grazed one of the breasts I was beginning to develop with a shiver that touched something dark and dangerous at the base of my belly.

'Still, I don't like being called by my full name.'

'Very good. Then I shall call you Alice. But then you must call me Sasha.'

'Sasha?' I could feel a blush surging up from my neck. My hands were sweaty. We weren't accustomed to calling grown-ups by their Christian names.

'My real name is Alexander. Sasha is my pet name.' He rubbed his fingers down my arm and moved back from me.

Should I be calling my piano teacher by his pet name? It seemed wrong.

As I was leaving, he put a hand on my shoulder. 'When shall you escort me to the public library, Miss Alice?'

Pulses jumped under my blouse. I felt sick and apprehensive, but at the same time, exhilarated. 'Um ... soon.' I was evasive. 'I have to ask my mother.'

'Very good.'

'I'll tell you next lesson.'

'I shall be waiting.'

When I woke each morning, it was no longer Orlando that I contemplated. All my life he had been my safe harbour, but now my guilty, undefined thoughts fluttered like coloured butterflies, the scarlet of strawberries, the pinky-yellow of honeysuckle, around the lonely shape of Sasha Elias.

FOUR

Orlando's attitude to Nicola was disconcerting. I could see that he not only disliked her, he feared her as well. It was the first time I had seen a breech in his armour of precocious self-confidence; to a certain extent, despite my own infatuation with her, I could understand his unease.

Fiona didn't like her, either.

'I'd rather you didn't spend so much time with her,' she said one morning.

'Why not?'

'She's not a good influence.'

I didn't argue because I was reluctantly beginning to see that she was right, that my idol had feet of clay. Two days ago, Nicola had taken me into Woolworths and, under her tutelage, I had unwillingly shoplifted a lipstick, two biro pens and some sweets. These were hidden in the back of a drawer, weighing on my conscience more heavily than cannon balls. I didn't want them, couldn't possibly have brought myself to use them. I'd felt none of the elation that I could see in Nicola's face when we finally emerged into the High Street without attracting the attention of the store detectives who, Ava had told us many times, lurked in the aisles, masquerading as ordinary people with shopping bags, keeping an eye out for thieves, ready to clap them on the shoulder as they tried to get out of the store and drag them off to the police station. Even more terrifying was the thought of what Fiona would say if she ever found out.

'And since we're on the subject,' she said, 'I don't want to see you behaving the vulgar way she does, in front of your brothers, or anyone else.'

Again I was silent, well aware of what she meant. Nicola had an apparently careless way of standing or sitting which much later I would recognize in the provocative poses of the Balthus nymphets. More than once, I'd seen Bertram Yelland and even Gordon Parker, staring at the shadows visible under her short skirts. When we swam on the beach, she changed into her bathing costume with only the merest hint of modesty. Sometimes her towel fell down to show her top half; sometimes she would bend over to pull on her skirt, apparently without realizing that we could, if we cared to, see her naked buttocks. Julian, in particular, seemed to be transfixed by her lack of shame. Where the rest of us turned away in embarrassment, he stared openly, his hands folded at the top of his thighs, or with his knees drawn up.

None of these perceptions dimmed my admiration. 'Can I have my hair cut like Nicola?' I asked one morning.

'You're still a bit young.'

'I'm almost twelve.'

'Twelve?' Fiona said vaguely. 'Goodness, yes, I suppose you are.'

'And plaits are so babyish.'

'Some of your other friends have plaits.'

'Not Nicola.'

'Hmmm...' she said drily. She didn't seem to see this as a recommendation.

Orlando, who'd been lounging in an armchair, moved in on my behalf. 'If you think about it, though, Alice's plaits are such a bother to do,' he said, smooth as dripping. 'You'd save a lot of time if you don't have to do them every morning.'

'That's very true.'

'So I *can* have them cut off?'

'Let me think about it. I don't want you growing up too fast.'

When a couple of days later, Fiona agreed that I could go to Bette's Salon and have my hair cut short, I was ecstatic, although I felt a brief pang at the loss of my moments alone with my mother. The desire to enter what I perceived as Nicola's far more sophisticated world was too strong. I believed I would end up looking something like Nicola, that I would become a different shape, a different size, a better, prettier, more fascinating person at the snip of a pair of scissors. With my plaits gone, I too would emerge from my dumpy chrysalis and fly like a butterfly in little denim skirts and skimpy tops, charming everyone.

Enchanted as I was by Nicola, I had to admit that there was a more sinister side to her. Once, as we sat on the beach, idly throwing stones into the sea, she asked us what we were most afraid of. 'I'm absolutely terrified of spiders, for instance,' she confided, gazing at us with wide eyes.

'That's called arachnophobia,' said Orlando.

'Oh, you're *so* clever, Orlando. I wish I was clever like you.'

'Do you really?' He stared at her, one eyebrow raised.

'Of course I do. I'd get top marks at school, and I wouldn't be afraid of anything, just like you.'

'Who says I'm not afraid of things?'

'Like what, then?'

'Clowns,' I said, thoughtlessly. 'You hate clowns.'

'Clowns?' Nicola laughed. 'You're afraid of *clowns*?'

'Not afraid. I just think they're stupid.'

'Isn't that the whole point of them?' said Charles.

'What's there to hate about a clown?' Nicola persisted. 'I mean, is it their big feet you don't like? Or those stupid bobbles they wear? Or is it their faces, all painted up, and those big slobbery

70

lips?' There was a curious light in her eyes, a small smile on her face.

'Nothing particular,' Orlando said. 'I just don't like them.'

'It's their faces, isn't it? Those awful white masks. Terrifying, I suppose, if you're frightened of that kind of thing.'

Orlando got up. His upper lip was sweaty as he stood looking down at her. 'There's a money spider on the collar of your blouse,' he remarked.

She screamed, batting at her neck, twisting around in panic as though trying to shake the thing off.

'Here, let me...' Julian bent close, pretending to examine her blouse. 'I can't see anything. He's having you on.'

Orlando grinned brutally. The pebbles shifted under his feet as he turned to climb the shifting slopes of the beach. 'I'm going to the library,' he said. 'You want to come, Alice?'

'Yes, go on, Alice,' said Nicola, her eyes vicious. 'Go and be a little swot like him.'

I was torn. I could see how badly Orlando needed me to be on his side in the unspoken war between the two, but I wanted to stay with Nicola, be part of whatever hidden spell she exerted. 'I'll stay here,' I muttered, not meeting his eye, knowing I was making the wrong decision, that by letting him down, I was letting down myself.

Although the rest of us were away at school, during term-time Nicola took the train every day to the grammar school, the school where Prunella Vane taught domestic science and Bella had recently started.

'That girl's really awful.' Bella told us, half-admiringly, when we came home for the holidays. 'She cheeks the teachers, and skips classes and all sorts of things.'

'What do they say to her?'

'Trouble is, she gets good marks in everything so there's not much they *can* say.'

'Does she have lots of friends?' I asked jealously.

'Sort of friends. There's a group she goes round with. But I don't know if they really like her. *I* don't,' said little Bella. 'I saw her pinching money out of someone's blazer pocket one day. And another time, she was making fun of Sandra Holden in the meanest way, just because she's got sticky-out teeth. Your mother would be furious if she heard I'd done something like that.'

'So would yours.'

'Gosh, yes.'

I saw Nicola in action not long after that. 'Ghastly lumpy old thing, isn't she?' she said to us one afternoon, as we sprawled on the green.

'Who?'

'Her. Look, over there. Old Fatty Vane.'

I looked down the road and there was Prunella, eating an ice cream and staring at the sea. Although I had no particular liking for her, I felt a need to protect her. 'She's not so bad.'

'If I was as fat as that, I'd kill myself,' Nicola said.

'Why?' asked Orlando.

'Because no one would look at her twice.'

'You're looking at her. And you've looked at her before.'

'No *man*, I mean.' said Nicola.

'Do you want men to look at you?'

'Of course I do.'

'Aha ... that explains it.'

The mockery in Orlando's voice seemed to sting her. 'Explains what?'

'Everything.'

Flushing, she turned to me. 'Don't you want men to look at you, Alice?'

'Not really.' I knew from Ava the perils of having men looking at you; that they were only after One Thing, though I was hazy about what that singular Thing might be. 'Not at all, actually.'

'Well, *I* do.'

'As we've noticed.' Orlando's smile was white in his sunburned face. 'We've seen it often enough.'

'Seen what?'

'How you get them to look at you.'

Currents were swirling here which I was suddenly aware might sweep us into waters too deep for us. Down the road, I saw Fiona emerge from our garden gate and wave in our direction. I jumped up, relieved. 'Lunch time,' I said. 'Come on, Orlando.'

A couple of days later, Nicola showed up with something wrapped in newspaper. As we settled ourselves into the shingle, she opened it. 'Look,' she said, giggling.

'What's that?' asked Charles. He and the other boys started sniggering as she held up a vast yellowing undergarment with suspenders dangling from it.

'They're corsets.'

'What're corsets?'

'My grandmother wears them,' said David.

'They're things that really really fat people wear to try and make themselves look thinner,' Nicola said.

'Where on earth did you get them?' I asked.

'Mum took me to a jumble sale and I saw them on a stall.' Nicola looked at us. 'I thought I'd give them to Fatty Vane. Or you could do it, Alice.'

'She's already got some,' I said.

'Maybe she could use another pair. Make her look nice for her girlfriend.'

'*Girl* friend?' said Julian.

'Yeah. Surely you realized she's a lesbian.'

'What's a lesbian?' asked Jeremy.

'Someone who like girls.'

'*I* like girls,' Charles said, leering.

'Another woman, I mean.'

This was territory I didn't want to explore. I flicked a finger at the corsets. 'Anyway, these are much too big,' I said. 'Miss Vane's not *that* fat.'

'It'd only be a joke.'

'Not a very nice joke,' I said. 'If you want to give them to her, do it yourself.' I felt hot and frightened. I wasn't used to challenging authority. Nor, despite the benign negligence with which we were brought up, were we accustomed

74

to spite or nastiness. I could easily imagine Fiona's reaction if she knew what Nicola was proposing and how embarrassed and hurt Miss Vane would be.

'Okey doke,' she said. 'I will.' She glanced at the watch on her wrist. 'Anybody want to come with me?'

Even the boys in her thrall were uneasy about administering such a direct insult to an adult. They kicked at the loose stones of the beach, coughed, stared about them. They were thinking of what their mothers would say if they were caught in such a piece of discourtesy.

'God,' said Nicola, eventually. 'You're all such wankers. I'll do it myself.'

And she did, because I watched her do it, go up to Miss Vane, put her head engagingly on one side, offer her the package. I saw, too, Miss Vane's shy smile of pleasure and wanted to run up, snatch it from her hands, throw the horrible corsets into the sea. But of course I didn't, and was punished later by seeing Miss Vane's face turn pale, her eyes water, the way she dropped the package into a litterbin. At that moment, I hated Nicola.

One afternoon, things took a different turn. After my music lesson, I came out of the gate of Number Seventeen to find them swinging on the bars across the road.

'How's the Groper?' Nicola asked.

'What do you mean?'

'Hands everywhere,' said Nicola. 'Or is it just with me?' She widened her eyes at me. 'Maybe he likes them a bit more mature than you, Alice.'

'How exactly are you defining mature?' asked Orlando, giving the word an ugly sneer. 'Do you mean like *you*, Nicola?'

'He's a pervert,' said Julian, glancing up at Mr Elias's open window. He feinted an elaborate shot with the golf putter he'd taken to carrying around, since he had started golf lessons earlier in the holidays.

'What's perverted about him?' Blushing with embarrassment, I hoped he couldn't hear them. Was that him lurking up there, watching us from behind the dusty folds of crimson velvet?

'He's a beastly Hun.' said Charles

'A bloody Kraut,' Julian said daringly.

I'd never heard either of them use such words or express such sentiments. 'You shouldn't say things like that,' I said. Thunderheads were building up in the distance, and the air danced and crackled with electricity. An equally powerful surge of energy arced dangerously between the seven of us. 'He's a refugee.'

'He can't help being a foreigner,' Orlando said.

'Kraut lovers, kraut lovers...' Jeremy jeered at us.

I stared at him in astonishment. Over the years I'd known him, he had always been the quiet one, the fatherless boy with the straight-cut blond hair and red cheeks, who usually maintained a timid silence.

'There's definitely something funny about him,' said Nicola. I sensed that while they waited for me, she had been playing them off, one against the other, and that now they were jockey-

76

ing for position, each of them trying to outdo the other, each of them fearful that he would be elbowed out of Nicola's charmed circle.

Was I frightened of rejection too? Was I trying to make up some of the ground that had been lost that summer? Or did I feel some deeper alarm? Whichever it was, I suddenly said, 'Maybe he's a spy.' Immediately I knew, Judas-like, that I had sacrificed Mr Elias, made him a burnt offering laid upon the altar of conformity. I passionately wished the words unsaid, but it was too late.

The boys pounced. 'A spy? What do you mean? How can he be? How do you know?'

My credibility was at stake. 'He's got a radio,' I said reluctantly. 'One of those ones that spies use, with bits sticking out of the top. And head-phones.'

'It's true,' said Nicola. 'I've seen it myself.'

'A crystal set,' said Orlando. He was staring at me with astonishment and a hostility that made me hot with shame.

'What kind of headphones?' asked Julian.

I backtracked quickly. 'But of course he can't be. The war's been over for ages.'

'There's still lots of spies about,' announced Charles. 'I heard about it at school. It's because of the Cold War.'

We could see that he didn't know exactly what the Cold War was and politely refrained from asking him.

'Maybe national security's at stake,' Jeremy said importantly, made knowledgeable by the *Rover*, which he borrowed surreptitiously from a friend.

'I think we ought to investigate,' said Julian. 'I mean, if he's a spy and everything.'

'How're you going to do that?' scoffed Nicola.

'We could keep a watch on him.'

'Yeah, follow him and everything. See where he goes.'

'Why would a spy be living here?' I said.

'Precisely,' added Orlando. 'What's there for him to spy on in a place like this?'

'The Marines,' said Charles. 'It's a naval establishment. They might be researching all sorts of stuff here.'

'Like what?'

Charles shrugged, trying to look as though he knew what he was talking about. 'Submarines, or something. Technical breakthroughs in naval warfare.'

'That's what they do in Portsmouth, isn't it?' I said. 'Not here.'

'What does it matter?' Nicola had that dangerous little flame in her eyes that I was coming to recognize. 'He's German, isn't he? That's evidence enough for me.'

The boys nodded doubtfully.

We went home, me hating myself, ashamed, Orlando haranguing me furiously. 'How could you have said something like that?' he demanded. 'You know as well as I do that the poor man's not a spy.'

The incident caused a rift between us all. For years we'd all spent our summers together, never articulating our affection for one another, but nonetheless relying on it, as part of the changeless predictability that was our childhood. Now

Orlando would have nothing to do with the others and I found that I too didn't want to join them as they hung about on the green, swinging on the silver railings outside Mrs Sheffield's house, staring up at Sasha's window. Led by Nicola, they gave the Nazi salute if they saw him, or sang the Horst Wessel song in voices loud enough for him to hear if he listened. They followed him when he walked past the lifeboat into town; they followed him home again. Julian produced a notebook and pencil and kept an ostentatious record of his comings and goings.

Did he notice? Was he hurt, angered, or merely indifferent? I couldn't bring myself to ask.

Darkness came late on those hot August evenings, and our mothers could see no point in keeping to normal bedtime hours, so we were allowed to stay up much longer than usual. Miserably skulking along the back road to avoid them, I could see them lined up along the railings, taunting and catcalling.

Orlando finally told Fiona what they were doing, without divulging my part in it.

'*What*?' She was outraged. 'Tormenting that poor young man? But why?' She stared at me. 'Do you know why, Alice?'

'They...' I swallowed, avoiding Orlando's accusing gaze. 'They think he's a spy.'

'A spy? What, for Germany?'

'Yes.'

'Are they so pigheadedly ignorant that they think a Jewish refugee would spy for Germany?' As she spoke, Fiona was walking towards the front door. 'Have they no sense of compassion?

Or common courtesy?'

She came back half an hour later. 'I've put the fear of God into them. I told Charles and Julian that Colonel Tavistock would have been thoroughly ashamed of them if the poor man were here today, and that I'd have to think twice about allowing them into this house again. As for that Nicola...' She made a disgusted noise. 'I'm a strong believer in independence, as you two know. I prefer to let you children make your own mistakes, which is why I don't often lay down the law. But there are times when it needs to be done.' She looked at me. 'Alice, I'm very close to forbidding you to have anything more to do with that frightful girl.'

I glanced in appeal at Orlando but his face was stony. All my life he'd been my rock. Now he was rejecting me. 'But shouldn't we show compassion to her too?' I said in desperation, foreseeing that I would have to spend the rest of the holidays as a social outcast.

My mother raised a glacial eyebrow. 'What exactly do you mean by that?'

'Isn't her father –' Too late I remembered my promise to Ava. '– isn't he in prison or something?'

'And how do you know that?'

'One of the boys told us,' Orlando lied easily. 'Can't remember if it was Charles or Julian.' Neither of us dared to meet her eyes.

'This is something you should never mention to anyone,' Fiona said. 'And of course, we have to be understanding. On the other hand, whatever her family circumstances, they don't excuse the way she – and the others – are treating poor Sasha Elias.'

She looked at Orlando and her face softened. 'I'd like a quick word with Alice on her own, if you don't mind,' she said.

Alarm and guilt pulsed through me. What had I done?

'I'll be in the garden,' Orlando said, as he opened the door to leave.

As soon as it had closed behind him, she said: 'How're you getting on with your music lessons?'

'All right,' I muttered.

'Why don't you play me something?' she said.

I was embarrassed, unused to so much attention. I launched into *The Fairy's Picnic*. If she was impressed, she didn't say so.

'How do you get on with Mr Elias?' she asked. There was something in her tone that made me uneasy.

'Fine. He's nice.'

'Does he ever...'

'What?'

'...touch you?'

'Of *course* not.' My face burned. He did touch me from time to time, but not in the way that I suspected she meant.

'I've been told that he sometimes uses ... um ... inappropriate behaviour.'

'Who told you that?'

'Louisa Stone mentioned something.'

Nicola must have been saying things, either in order to divert attention from the campaign of terror she'd tried to initiate, or to excuse it.

'What's inappropriate behaviour, anyway?'

'He's never asked you to ... to sit on his lap?' Fiona was almost as embarrassed as I was. 'Or put his hand ... on your knee? Or ... um ... elsewhere?'

'No! If Nicola said that, she's lying. It's disgusting of you to say such things.'

'I'm only repeating something I was told.'

'It's lies!' I shouted. 'He doesn't do *any*thing. Just teaches me the piano.'

'Are you telling me the truth, Alice?'

'*Yes!*'

'Very well. We won't mention it again. But if you ever have the slightest—'

'I *won't*. He's not *like* that, not in the least.'

'Very well. I shall invite the poor man to dinner. Try to make up for the behaviour of your ... *friends*.' She gave me an ice-cold stare. 'In fact, I'll invite them along too. It's time I had Lisa Tavistock round, and Louisa Stone.'

'Good God,' Yelland said later, told of the impending supper-party. 'She's not seriously contemplating having people to dinner, is she?'

'That's quite enough, Mr Yelland,' said Ava.

'More than enough,' Orlanda said.

'What did you say, you rude little sod?' demanded Yelland.

'Now, now.' Ava reached into her mending basket for more grey wool to darn Orlando's school socks, ready for the end of the holidays. 'When she puts her mind to it, Mrs Beecham can be a very good cook. Very inventive.'

'Inventive says it all.'

'She's going to invite Nicola Stone and her

mother.' Orlando twitched an eyebrow. 'That'll be a real treat. Don't you agree, Mr Yelland?'

'Why the hell should I find some minx of a schoolgirl a treat?'

'I just thought you might.'

He was obviously being significant in some way, but I didn't know how, and had no desire to ask him.

Mr Elias came the next Friday. I contrived to sit next to him at the big mahogany table. With the PGs, the mothers, Nicola, Julian and Charles, Jeremy Gardiner, we were crowded, so that I couldn't avoid touching Sasha Elias's arm or thigh every time one or other of us moved. I'd changed out of my usual Aertex shirt and shorts, and put on a summer dress; my newly-short hair was freshly washed, and I was wearing the turquoise-and-silver necklace my father had given me for my last birthday.

Orlando noticed – he noticed everything – but made no comment. Which was much worse than if he had. I felt soft, as though I were moulded out of marshmallow, yet at the same time, I burned with a heat I couldn't define, so much so that my mother wondered aloud whether I'd spent too much time in the sun that afternoon. I shook my head.

Did he think I looked pretty? Was he aware of the curl of hair over my left eye, achieved by sleeping with my hair secured in criss-crossed kirby grips? Had he noticed my necklace? Did he feel the flame coursing through my body when our arms accidentally brushed? Jealousy

83

seared me as he talked with Fiona and Orlando about music. I was the one who knew him best; he wasn't theirs, he was mine, wasn't he?

FIVE

Each holiday had its own ceremonies but the summer offered another ritual which was exclusive to Orlando and me. We were the blackberry pickers, and we took our duties very seriously. We saw our role as that of hunters and gatherers, bringing home provisions that would see the family through the coming winter. The blackberries would be made into jam, or added to the big greasy-skinned cooking apples Fiona managed to obtain from a nearby farmer. She and Ava would spend a day turning them into the blackberry-and-apple which constituted our staple pudding until the following summer, either in pies or as tarts, or eaten with custard or evaporated milk. Without our annual contribution, we feared that the rest of the household might go hungry.

At the start of each summer holidays, we would pump up the tyres of our bikes and cycle down the coast road to inspect our blackberry sites. We knew from experience that the denser the thickets of brambles, the juicier and sweeter were the fruit. We chose only the most inaccessible places, where the heavily-thorned fronds would deter everyone but the most dogged picker; if we saw broken branches or plastic bags, evidence of picnickers, we would pass by.

Through the summer weeks, we kept a close eye on our chosen locations, going out every few days to inspect them and make sure that the ripening process was proceeding to schedule. We loved the salt winds in our hair as we freewheeled along the road which ran below the cliffs, the smell of crushed fennel, the occasional wizened crab-apple trees which had somehow flourished in among the brambles, the flat scented plates of elderflowers which would later become rich with dark bunches of fruit.

The blackberries ripened early that last summer. Orlando and I visited them every few days, watching as the hard green berries began to fill out, to turn hard and red then plumply purple. Now they were definitely black and lustrous, almost ready for the picking. We'd done our reconnaissance carefully, earmarked the places likely to provide the highest yield for the lowest effort, searched out the hidden patches where other, less experienced pickers, might not venture.

We had refined our picking techniques over the years. Our equipment included two of Aunt's walking sticks, one of the golf clubs from the elephant's-foot stand, punnets for picking into, bowls for carrying. We had to choose the right clothes. That year, an old jacket of my father's to protect Orlando's bare summer arms, a sweater of Callum's for me.

As serious blackberry pickers, we seldom

spoke as we reaped our harvest, and almost never ate any of the ripe black fruit. That year, while I learned to play the piano in the close fug of Mr Elias's bed-sitting room, Orlando spent a lot of time cycling up to the cliffs.

One afternoon, I came away from a piano lesson to find him dawdling by the gate of Mrs Sheffield's house, holding both our bikes. 'I've found a new place,' he said. 'Come and look. I don't think anyone's ever been there except me.'

And indeed, when I cycled down the chalky white road after him, and climbed between elder-trees and overgrown fennel to the top of the hill, I could see that he was right. There were none of the broken branches or trodden grass which signified trespassers into what we had come to look on as our own territories.

'Look...' He carefully hooked aside three or four of the thickest creepers. 'There's even a tiny little glade sort of thing in among the bushes.'

'You could hide in there if you wanted to and nobody'd even know you were there. Only problem would be getting in there without tearing yourself to shreds.'

'If you pull this branch here, and duck under that one...' With me cautiously following, he eased himself through the bushes until the two of us were standing on the little patch of grass in the middle.

He took my arm. 'Alice ... don't tell Nicola about this place, okay?'

'Why not?'

'Because.'

'Because what?'

'Because I say so. And I'm older than you.'

Orlando didn't often pull rank. 'What do you think she's going to do,' I said. 'Sneak up here and pick the blackberries before we can?'

He gave his taut white smile, wrinkled one of his striped eyebrows. 'Maybe. Who knows? It's the sort of thing she would do. But promise me, Alice. Promise.'

'Oh, all right.' I bent down to scratch a mosquito bite on my dusty sun-browned leg.

We could hear someone coming across the brow of the hill, slashing at the undergrowth with a stick and singing hoarsely. Instinctively we ducked down.

'It's old Yelland,' whispered Orlando, peeping through the brambles.

'Hope he doesn't see us.'

'He must have come over the top, not up from the road. We can always run back down if he tries coming after us.'

'Bit scratchy,' I objected.

'Better a few scratches than being beaten to death by bloody Yelland.'

To our horror, Yelland strode about a bit, looking out at the line of the horizon which was a misty blue from the heat, then opened the shooting stick he was carrying and sat down. From the bag slung over his shoulder, he produced a sketch-block and some chalks. He glanced impatiently at his watch, shook his head irritably.

'Creative genius at work,' Orlando muttered.

'We could be trapped here for hours.'

'Oh, God.'

In other circumstances, I might have enjoyed

87

lying there on the dry grass. Above our heads the sky was cloudless. Larks sprang up, trilling invisibly against the blue. I could smell dusty leaves, the aromatic scent of crushed spearmint and bruised fennel.

'Do you know what a group of larks is called?' Orlando asked.

'An ecstasy.'

'Nice, isn't it?' He leaned on one elbow and peered between the brambles. He went very still.

'What?' I looked over his shoulder to see Nicola swinging along the cliff path. She was wearing a short denim skirt with brass buttons in a line down the middle and a little pink blouse. We watched as she called out and Yelland swung round.

'Christ!' he exclaimed. 'Can't you ever be on time?'

'Sorry,' she said cheerfully. As she came nearer, she began to undo the buttons of her blouse.

'What's on earth is she doing?' I said.

Orlando shrugged.

Nicola dropped the blouse at Yelland's feet; she had nothing underneath it and I could see very clearly the round swelling of her small breasts, the pink nipples. She wriggled out of her skirt to show a pair of white cotton knickers. I distinctly heard Yelland groan as she put her hand inside her underwear and stuck out a provocative hip.

'God...' There was sweat on Orlando's upper lip. 'She's not going to...'

'Not going to what?' He shook his piebald head but didn't say anything else.

We watched, appalled and excited, as Nicola pulled off her pants and stood naked in front of Yelland, who was cupping a hand over the front of his trousers. 'You filthy little trollop,' he said, his voice sounding thick. 'Get over here.'

She shimmied closer. 'Let's have the money first,' she said.

He reached into the pocket of his shirt and pulled out a note; I couldn't see how much it was. She bent down and tucked it among her clothes, then climbed astride his knees and wriggled right up close. Slowly, she undid the metal buttons of his corduroy trousers and slipped her hand inside. His big fingers squeezed her buttocks, his mouth sucked at her breasts, while she massaged him, back and forth, in the place between his thighs. I could hear him groaning with each movement of her hand, the sound increasing as her movements grew more frantic until finally, with a great heave which nearly dislodged her, he bucked a few times and then subsided.

'Jesus,' he gasped. 'Oh, Jesus.'

She jumped nimbly off his knees. 'Well, that was fun, wasn't it?'

Yelland, breathing hard, didn't answer.

Nicola stood naked in front of him with her hands on her hips. 'By the way, I may have to put up my price,' she said.

His face turned an ugly purple colour. 'You're bleeding me dry as it is, you greedy little tart.'

'It's called supply and demand. Or the cost of living. Or something.' Nicola bent down and neatly inserted herself into her clothes. 'So, what about next time?'

'If you demand more, I'll be able to supply less,' he said. 'I'm not made of money, you know.'

'I only said I *may* have to put up the price.'

And she ran off up the path trodden into the grass, her short skirt flicking from side to side.

'Little bitch,' Yelland muttered.

Hot, slightly breathless, I couldn't have explained the sick fascination of the scene I'd just witnessed, but I knew there was something immeasurably ugly about it. 'What was ... what exactly was going on?' My voice felt estranged from my throat.

'We-ell...' Orlando blew out a breath. On his face was an expression I could not quite fathom. 'It seems our little Nicola is a fairly nasty bit of work. But then we knew that already.'

'*I* didn't. Not *that* nasty.' My idol had more than merely feet of clay; she was clay up to her knees. It wasn't just the transaction between her and Yelland that made me feel nauseous. The loss of something that only a short while ago I had considered beautiful felt like a physical wrench inside my heart. I wanted to go home. I wanted to see Ava and my mother, just breathe in the dependability of their different presences. 'But anybody could have seen them,' I said. Indeed, a man was emerging from the hanger of trees which ran up the hillside to the top. He stared curiously down at Yelland, busy fastening his flies, and at Nicola who was skipping away towards the green lane.

'That's probably part of the fun.'

'Oh, Orlando, let's go,' I whispered urgently.

'We can't. We're stuck until the old sod leaves,' murmured Orlando. 'Can you imagine what he'd do if he knew we'd seen him?'

'Couldn't we get down the slope below here and out onto the road?'

'Not without him hearing us.'

I sighed. 'Good thing it's not raining.'

'Good thing I brought some light refreshments.' Orlando took a bar of chocolate from one pocket and a square-shouldered National Health orange-juice bottle full of water from another.

All around us the blackberry branches drooped, heavy with almost-ripe fruit. Here and there we could see berries which were at their peak of perfection, but we didn't dare pick them, in case Yelland spotted us.

'Rats in a trap,' said Orlando, picking up on my own thoughts.

So we lay there on the scented grass, playing word-games in whispers, neither of us anxious to think about what we had just seen. Nonetheless, it lay there at the back of our minds. My short hair now seemed more like a stigma, glueing me to someone to whom, for all her dash and bravado, I perceived, too late, I had no wish to be connected. Mr Yelland grew increasingly bloated in my imagination, swaying above us like a vast empurpled barrage balloon, swollen with menace and repulsiveness. That furtive opening in his trousers, the fingers tightening on Nicola's skin, her obvious collusion in whatever nastiness was being enacted in front of our

91

disbelieving eyes. I didn't want to think about it ever again. Even then I knew it would haunt me until some greater nastiness occurred and took its place.

We got back to find Glenfield in an uproar. A pink-eyed Ava cowered in the drawing-room, clutching Bella close to her, while my mother stood in the garden, confronting a man who shouted and gesticulated, his accent coarse, his face red and fierce.

Ava was one of the pillars of my life, stalwart, steady, predictable. To find her weeping and diminished weakened the structures of my own existence in a way that frightened me.

'What's going on?' I asked Callum, home on leave from National Service in the Navy, who was lurking near my mother with a hockey stick in his hand, idly pretending to hit a tennis ball, but in reality there to protect Fiona from any violent outburst the red-faced man might produce.

'It's Ava's husband, come back to claim his bride.' My eldest brother was big, with the broad shoulders and thick neck of a rugby-player. Already in his second year of medical school in Edinburgh, he was a distant figure to me, yet one who exuded the same kind of security as Ava. 'And she doesn't want to go with him.'

'I don't blame her.'

'Nor me.'

'I wonder how he tracked her down.' We knew Ava had absconded while her violent soldier-boy was overseas, had snatched up her child and her fancy clothes, her *Soir de Paris* by Bourjois, her peep-toe shoes and flimsy undergarments and fled. Like her, we had assumed that her husband would never find her.

'I'm afraid you'll just have to accept the situation, Mr Edwardes,' Fiona was saying.

'You fuckin' old cow,' Edwardes lunged in my mother's direction but stopped when Callum casually flourished the hockey stick.

'She's had quite enough of your unacceptable behaviour.' My mother had adopted what Orlando called her Empire-building voice, ideally adapted to calling recalcitrant natives to order, and warding off man-eating tigers.

'You can't tell me what to do.'

'In this instance, I believe I can. Your wife and child live beneath my roof and have placed themselves under my protection.' Fiona was magnificent.

'I've got my rights.'

'So has she.'

'The girl is my daughter too, you know.'

'Are you referring to Arabella?' said my mother, at her iciest.

'She's no more an Arabella than I'm a ... a ballet dancer.' Edwardes rose unsteadily on to his toes and lifted his arms above his head. 'Took her down the registry office myself, registered her as Enid after my mum.'

'That probably counts as a crime against a minor,' said Orlando in my ear.

'Enid Gladys,' said Edwardes. 'That's her name. And as for that bitch indoors, Ava's not *her* name neither.'

'I'm well aware of that. Mrs Edwardes explained in graphic detail the reasons for her choosing to change her name. I think you can probably remember some of them.'

'Don't give me that bollocks,' snarled the man, bunching his fists. 'I fought for King and Country, and I got a right to my family around me now.'

'And they have a right to stay here. This isn't the Victorian era, when a wife was her husband's chattel, you know.'

'You what?'

'And if you haven't removed yourself from my property within the next three minutes, I shall call the police and have you arrested for trespass.'

I loved my mother deeply though I did not always esteem her. But at that moment, I admired her more than I could have imagined. Brave, indomitable, generous of heart and spirit; even if she had once tried to give me away to some Swedes, I knew then that she would fight for us wherever and whenever necessary, that she would always do what was right.

'Keep your hair on,' slurred Mr Edwardes. 'I'll go. But don't think you've heard the last of this.' He looked at the French windows and raised his voice so that Ava could hear. 'You too, you bloody slag! I'll be back, don't you worry.'

We stood in a protective half-circle, shielding the hidden Ava from anything further, and after a hesitant moment, he turned and stumbled off down the short gravel drive to the gate.

'Phew...' Callum let out his breath in a windy

94

sigh. 'Now what do we do? He's bound to hang about here, frightening poor Ava into fits.'

'He might even try to kidnap Bella,' Orlando said.

'Unfortunately, you may well be right,' said Fiona. 'How on earth did he find her, I wonder?'

'It's that Nicola,' Ava said. 'I know it is.' The tip of her nose was red, her eyes were watery. She sniffed into a lace-edged handkerchief. 'She was asking me all sort of questions a couple of weeks ago, and like a fool, I told her.'

'And somehow she tracked down your husband?' said Fiona. 'Surely not.'

'Wouldn't be difficult,' said Orlando. 'Not if you were determined. There's all sorts of information down at the library, if you know what to look for.'

'Are you serious?'

'Absolutely.'

'Well, I'm flabbergasted. That anyone would do such a thing in the first place, and secondly that someone so young could be so ... so malicious.' She surveyed her own brood, and shook her head. 'I simply can't imagine any of you doing such a thing.'

'Perhaps Ava needs bodyguards,' Orlando suggested. 'You could use Julian and the others.'

'It sounds a little melodramatic.'

'Obviously they wouldn't be carrying weapons or anything –' I said.

'I should think not!'

'– they'd just be sort of there, to let him know he's being watched.'

'I don't know...' Fiona's forehead creased. 'I

suppose for a few days, something along those lines can't do any harm.' She gave me one of her cool grey stares. 'I'll have a word or two with their mothers.'

It wasn't until I was in bed that night that I had time to consider the scene played out between Nicola and Mr Yelland. Despite my brothers, I was still largely ignorant of the realities of physical sex, but because Fiona encouraged us to read everything we could, I knew a lot about it in theory. Especially the seamier side. Furtive transactions, red lights, men in dirty raincoats, brothels, tightly corseted Madames, prostitutes with hearts of gold. And try as I might to rationalize it, there was no escaping the fact that whatever Nicola was doing, it could only be described as seamy. What I found particularly difficult to encompass was the matter-of-fact way in which she had handled the incident, as though she had done it many times before, and with other men. I passionately wished I had not witnessed the scene.

A flash of Orlando's face came back to me. In the darkness of my bedroom, I was able to examine it more carefully, and come to the conclusion that while its predominant emotion had been one of shock, there'd been a certain amount of satisfaction there too. But what could he have been satisfied about? I wondered if he'd seen Nicola and Yelland up there before. Whether he had persuaded me up to the Secret Glade in order to demonstrate just what kind of a girl she was. To shatter whatever illusions about her I still held intact.

My mother obviously spoke to the mothers of David, Jeremy, Julian and Charles. The boys found themselves more comfortable with a tangible enemy like Edwardes than they'd been with the possibility of a spy lurking on Mrs Sheffield's first floor. For a few days, Bella and Ava were escorted wherever they went, which proved useful for carrying the shopping. The red-faced husband could be seen from time to time, lurching along the front, or balefully eyeing the house, or, if it was after dark, shouting obscenities at us.

I didn't tell anyone, not even Orlando, but I was sure Ava was right. I'd seen Nicola once, from Sasha's window, sitting on a bench, talking to a man I now recognized as Edwardes. She had been pointing at our windows, and it hadn't looked as though she was using some of her own ripe language to tell him to leave us alone. Quite the opposite.

SIX

Fiona smiled at us across the breakfast table. 'Good news, darlings. Or bad, depending on your outlook.'

Most of us looked apprehensive. 'What?'

'You're sending us all to an orphanage and taking the veil,' hazarded Orlando.

'I said *good* news, Orlando.'

'Maybe the little blighter considers an orphanage good news,' muttered Bertram Yelland. He surveyed his porridge. 'Can't say I blame him.'

'Is this likely to affect us all, Mrs Beecham, or just the immediate family?' asked Gordon.

Miss Vane sipped her tea, one finger neatly raised, and said nothing. I saw her reach one plump hand out for a fourth piece of toast and then, flushing, glancing sideways at me, pull it back, while I carefully pretended not to have noticed.

'Well, obviously it will have repercussions for all of us.' Fiona beamed at us. 'My husband and I have finally found a suitable house for us. It's an old mill house, with the original mill-wheel still there, and a millpond and about an acre of ground.'

'It sounds awfully grand,' said Orlando. 'How can we afford it?'

'It's all down to Aunt.' Instinctively we raised our eyes to the ceiling, where the old lady could be heard shuffling about in her room, burning toast, spilling tea, dropping cutlery, enjoying her independence. Looking back, I can see that Fiona's brand of inattention was in fact the kindest sort of care. The fact that Aunt's teacups still needed washing after she'd washed them, that she occasionally left little patches of damp on her armchair cushions, that food sometimes spilled onto her jumpers, was immaterial. She still had an illusion of independence, she made her own meals, she lived autonomously.

'What's Aunt done?'

'She's put Glenfield up for sale, and is giving the proceeds to us, to buy the Mill House. She'll come with us, of course.'

'And Ava, and Bella?'

'Yes. For as long as they want it, their home is with us.'

We looked at each other glumly. 'I don't know,' said Callum. 'Have you really thought about this, Mum?'

'Of course I have.'

'More to the point,' said Orlando. 'Is this definite?'

'More or less...' Fiona's face grew vague. 'Yes, I'm sure it is.'

Across the table, Orlando raised his striped eyebrows at me.

'What exactly do we gain from the move?' Callum asked.

'We gain a lovely home – a home of our very own at last. We gain proximity to one of the most beautiful university cities in the world.'

'You mean Cambridge?' said Bertram, who was a King's College man.

'You know perfectly well, Mr Yelland, that I mean Oxford.' Fiona beamed some more. 'And best of all, it means we shall have Daddy at home, at last.'

'And do I take it,' asked Miss Vane delicately, pressing a table napkin to her mouth, 'that we...' she indicated herself, Gordon and Bertram '...shall be staying here?'

'I'm not going to turf you out into the street,' said Fiona. 'We shan't move until after the children have gone back to school. That should give you plenty of time to find a place to your liking.'

'I may use this chance to chuck up the whole filthy teaching business,' said Yelland. 'See it as a heaven-sent opportunity to do what I should have been doing for years. Move back to London, get serious about painting, and be damned to my father and all his works.' He folded his napkin and tucked it inside the bone ring with his initials in silver relief. 'This is excellent news, Mrs Beecham.'

'I'm so glad you think so.'

Yelland rubbed his hands together. 'I shall give my notice in immediately. Work until next half-term. Then hey ho, it's the bright lights for me.'

'What about you, Miss Vane? I do hope this won't inconvenience you too much.'

'As a matter of fact, it won't. A friend – a colleague at the school – asked me recently if I was interested in rooming together somewhere. I said I wasn't but the offer's still open, because she mentioned it yesterday. And all in all, it might be...' She looked round at us, her face slightly pink.

Fiona's face softened. 'And you, Gordon? Will you be able to find somewhere?'

'I'm sure it won't be difficult, Mrs Beecham. I'll be sorry to leave all of you, of course...' His eyes wandered vaguely across my brothers. '...but we must always be aware of fresh woods and pastures new, mustn't we?'

'Fields,' said Orlando.

'I beg your pardon?'

'It's fields, not woods.'

'Wood or field, what the hell does it matter,

100

you cheeky little bugger,' snapped Yelland. 'Sorry, Mrs B, but that child would try the patience of a saint.'

'Not that you'd know much about sainthood,' said Orlando, so low that only Bertram and I heard him.

'That's quite enough from all of you,' said Fiona. 'Now, this may be the holidays, but I, for one, have work to do.'

'I read your last story while I was in the hairdressers,' said Miss Vane hastily. 'It was really awfully good.'

'Thank you so much. Which one was it?'

'Something to do with a lonely little boy befriending an old lady ... or was it an old man? I'm sorry, I can't remember. But I know it was lovely.'

'Good. Now, everybody, there's one last thing.'

We stopped pushing back our chairs to listen.

'In view of the coming changes, and since it will coincide nicely with Alice's birthday, I thought we might have a party before the end of the holidays. Even a dance. What do you say?'

'Great idea,' said Callum.

'Do you mean here?' asked Ava.

'We can push back the furniture in the drawing room, roll up the carpets. There's plenty of room. Have food set out in here. A barrel of beer, cider, soft drinks.' Her eyes softened. I knew that instead of plastic mugs and glasses from Woolworths, paper plates and picnic forks, she envisioned porcelain and silver, crystal goblets filled with the finest wine, groaning trenchers featuring roast birds, honey-glazed hams studded with cloves, sides of beef, dishes crowded with creamy mashed potatoes, tender vegetables, buttered peas, a swan carved from ice, the elaborately-decorated sort of dishes in the illustrated Mrs Beeton which was kept on the bottom shelf of the drawing-room bookcases.

'Sounds terrific, Mum.'

'Absolutely splendid. Are you talking about black tie?'

'Don't be silly, Mr Yelland. Do we look like black-tie people? Though of course, before the war...' She looked pensive for a moment. 'Oh well...'

'Who's going to come to this party?' asked Callum.

'The rest of the family, for a start. I want you to think of all the people we might want to invite, and we'll write out invitations this evening and you two...' she nodded at Orlando and me '...can deliver the local ones on your bikes.'

How did I feel about the prospect of leaving Glenfield? How did Orlando feel? When I asked him, he raised his zebra eyebrows. 'Hmmm. I don't know, really. Half of me thinks it exciting. I don't like change, and this has been our home for a long time. But it'd be marvellous to be close to Oxford, all that music, and theatre and stuff. And C. S. Lewis lives there too...'

'Daddy actually knows him.'

'...so we might even get to meet him!'

'And Mr Tolkien,' I said. 'Gosh, he said I must come to tea with him next time I was in Oxford.'

'So all in all,' said Orlando, 'I think we're quite pleased, aren't we?' He pulled at his zebra hair. 'If it ever happens, that is.'

'You think it might not?'

'Don't you?'

'Hmm...' So many of Fiona's plans faltered at the last fence. 'If it does, will we be sad to leave the boys, Julian and the rest of them?'

'Not as much as we might have been.'

I didn't even mention Nicola, knowing his views, but in spite of everything, I would be sorry to say goodbye to her. She was bad, even wicked, but she was exciting, vital, a breath of slightly fetid air blowing through our hitherto staid lives. But it would also be a relief to say goodbye to her. I could throw away the shop-lifted stuff, I needn't worry about her being mean to Orlando or—

'Oh!' I said. 'But I wouldn't be able to have lessons with Mr Elias any more.'

'There are other piano teachers.'

'But not any other Mr Eliases.'

Orlando looked at me oddly. 'Who are we going to ask to your party?'

I didn't want Nicola to come, but Fiona had other ideas. 'You can't leave the girl out,' she declared, when I showed her my list. 'It would be unkind not to invite her.'

'I don't really want her to come.'

'Why not?'

'She's...' Dangerous, was what I wanted to say, but if I did, I knew my mother would want to know what I meant. And I wasn't prepared to

103

mention the shoplifting, or Bertram Yelland. Or the way she had tried to damage Sasha Elias.

'...not really my sort,' I muttered.

'Really? I wouldn't have guessed.' Fiona's glance was too shrewd for comfort. 'I like her mother well enough, but I agree the girl is a bit of a menace. Still, since you insisted on being around her so much this holidays, you can't very well leave her out, so you'll just have to put up with it. Obviously we'll invite Louise Stone, and isn't there a brother? Maybe they'll be able to keep some kind of a check on her.'

'Check?'

'This is your party and I'm not prepared to accept any...' My mother wasn't usually at such a sustained loss for words.

'Any what?'

'Anything untoward.'

'What does that mean?'

'Never mind.'

'If she comes, I shan't,' I said sulkily.

'Don't be silly, darling.'

'I mean it!'

But both of us knew that I didn't. Parties were a rare enough event in our lives; a party in our own house was unheard of. We were such a large group that we rarely needed further company. Julian, Nicola and the rest spent time in our house, as we did in theirs, but for the most part, we remained self-sufficient, disconnected from the world beyond our own. Even when my father was home from Oxford, we never had people to dinner. Occasionally one of his undergraduates would show up, taking a detour from cycling round Kent or visiting Canterbury Cathedral. Sometimes my big brothers would bring home a friend from university or medical school, and very occasionally my mother would suggest I might like to invite a girl from school down for part of the holidays. The girl was always Erin Carpenter, an American from Boston. She spelled a kind of freedom – one quite different from Nicola's wildness. I breathed more deeply when I was with Erin, saw the world in brighter colours, sensed wider horizons spreading below the edge of my own sea-encompassed limits.

'Wow!' she would say. 'Great!', 'Ok*aaaa*y!', the second syllable floating endlessly from her wide mouth, giving it quite a different sound from the word we had been forbidden to use. Mediated through Erin, America with its spacious skies, its purple mountains, seemed boundless, munificent, a land of plenty.

But Erin was in California, staying with her divorced father, and wouldn't be able to come. A disappointment, especially since Fiona had promised that, as the party was partly to celebrate my birthday, I could have a new dress.

'Can it be pink?' I said.

'Pink?'

'Oh, *please...*'

'I'll see if I have something by me.' This was a good start: Fiona nearly always had something by her.

And indeed, a few days later, she showed me a length of pink silk brocade. 'What do you think, darling? I saved it from before the war,' she said. 'Isn't it a beautiful colour?'

'Pink,' I breathed.

'Not pink, Old Rose.'

Old Rose. My mother's words transformed the cloth into something magical, straight from the middle of a fairy-tale forest full of white harts and questing beasts, where a sleeping princess lay in a golden castle deep at its crimson heart.

'And Ava's going to make it into a dress for you.'

'It's all very well,' grumbled ever-cheerful Ava. 'Dressmaking indeed, with all I have to do, where I'm going to find the time I really don't know.' But somewhere she must have found it for every evening I could hear the old Singer sewing machine whirring behind the closed door of the room she shared with Bella. I imagined her snatching handfuls of time from a bubbling cauldron of the stuff, spooning seconds from the brew, dipping in a ladle to measure out minutes, dragging hours towards her across the surface and stacking them beside her sewing table like pink clouds. I saw time, slippery as soap, glisten between her fingers.

A fortnight or so later, I was climbing into the pinned folds of a party dress more gorgeous than I could ever have imagined. 'Keep still!' commanded Ava. 'Stop wriggling about, before I stick in a pin into you by mistake.'

And then the dress was over my shoulders and pulled down to my knees and Ava stepped back to admire her handiwork. Looking at myself in Aunt's antique cheval glass, I saw myself transformed into a veritable beauty.

'Very nice,' she pronounced, 'though I do say

so myself.'

'I say so too, Ava. It's beautiful, absolutely lovely,'

On a hanger hooked over the picture rail was a petticoat, white paper nylon with layers and layers of stiff netting round the bottom, each layer bound in a different colour of bias binding. 'My birthday present to you – mine and Bella's,' said Ava, nodding and winking.

'Oh thank you, thank you!' I kissed her, which turned her face red, for we were not a household given to demonstrations of affection.

'Don't thank me, thank your mother,' she said. She picked up a snippet of the Old Rose silk and rubbed it between her fingers. 'Though where she got it from I don't know. I haven't seen quality like this for years.'

The final numbers for the party slid forwards and backwards, now reaching towards forty, now sliding back towards thirty, once as high as forty-eight. Dougal and Callum arrived with friends from medical school and the navy. By the time the evening arrived, the numbers had stabilized at thirty-six.

The carpets had been rolled back, the furniture pushed back against the wall, a long table set up in the dining room, covered in an old sheet, threadbare from many washings. My big brothers had polished the drawing room floor by scattering it with crystals of soda bicarbonate and then dragging Bella and me back and forth in blankets until it had attained the slipperiness of an ice rink.

A barrel of beer arrived and was set up in the dining room on a wooden cradle. There was cider in brown bottles and the kind of neon-coloured fizzy drinks we were not usually allowed. Orlando and Julian had undertaken to make ginger beer, and the tightly-capped bottles stood on a table, looking like bottled dishwater. There were platters of corned beef, Fiona's inexpert sausage rolls, sandwiches of tinned salmon and egg-with-salad-cream-and-cress. Miss Vane had produced dozens of small savoury tarts featuring melted cheese and onions. There were little pink fairy cakes topped with scatters of hundreds-and-thousands, or glacé cherries, and even a birthday cake covered in pink-tinted icing, and twelve candle holders in the shape of roses, each holding a small candle made of twisted pink wax. My name had been iced across the top,

ALICE

set with little silver balls which winked under the lights.

I couldn't stop staring at myself in my new dress, with my shining cap of bobbed hair which had been pinned into kiss curls the night before. The waist was cinched with a black patent-leather belt Erin had sent from America, and which made me look very close to something out of the fashion pages in Ava's magazines. My parents had given me a strand of pearls as a birthday present, and I thought nobody could have been luckier. Perhaps my destiny was not as the successor to Dame Myra Hess but as the new Jane Russell or Rita Hayworth, for no one could possibly look as beautiful as I did. My usually mocking brothers were complimentary, for once. Even Julian, Nicola's faithful acolyte, told me I was looking awfully nice and ran a sweaty finger up my arm. All this, just for me. I'd never been so happy.

As we stood in the hall, waiting for the guests, Fiona put an arm round me and gave me an unaccustomed hug. 'You look lovely, Alice,' she said.

I was still smiling when Nicola arrived, on her own. She wore her everyday garb of a short denim skirt and a white broderie-anglaise blouse with puffed sleeves. She greeted my mother then turned to me.

'Oh,' she said, looking me up and down. 'I didn't realize it was meant to be *that* sort of a party.'

'What sort?' My stomach curdled, my dress turned instantly into Cinderella rags.

'A fancy one.'

'So what sort *did* you think it was meant to be?' Orlando, looking marvellous in a white shirt and a pink silk tie of my father's, had materialized beside me. I could feel his dislike of her in the tremor of his arm against mine and the set of his beautiful mouth.

'I didn't realize it would be...' She eyed my new frock, my pearls, with disdain. '...a dress-up occasion.'

'What a pity you misunderstood the invitation, Nicola.' My mother's voice was cold. 'I do hope you won't feel out of place, dressed so casually.'

Nicola's face reddened, but even she wasn't about to take on Fiona. 'Of course not,' she muttered.

'Orlando, take our guest to the dining room and find her something to drink,' said Fiona. As we walked away, she repeated reassuringly, 'You look *lovely*, darling.'

'Sorry if I didn't dress up,' Nicola said as we moved away, attempting to regain lost ground.

'It's Alice's birthday party. You jolly well should have.' Orlando sounded as chilly as Fiona.

'Well, with *these* kind of people here, it didn't occur to me to put on something fancy.' The sweep of Nicola's arm took in Miss Vane, uncomfortably squeezed into slippery green rayon, Gordon Parker in his desert boots, Sasha Elias in a grey flannel shirt and too-short tie.

'At least they've made an effort.'

'So I can see,' sneered Nicola.

'Sorry if they're not good enough for you.' Orlando kept his voice low. 'We looked hard but we couldn't find any murderers to invite to make you feel at home.'

She went pale. 'You bastard,' she said softly. She turned and looked my dress up and down again, raised her eyebrows, said mockingly, 'You look *lovely*, darling.'

Orlando smiled, wheeled me round and led me towards one of the ivy-wreathed marble fireplaces, where my father stood holding a glass of gin disguised with government issue orange juice. 'How's my pretty little daughter?' he said.

110

He put an arm round me. It was no use. A ring of cold had formed around my heart.

Sasha Elias came up and shook hands with my father, bowing from the waist. *'Guten abend, Herr Doktor Professor,'* he said. His eyes grew mellow when he turned to me. 'How very nice you look, Alice,' he said. 'That colour suits you well.'

'Thank you.' I had never blushed before in my life, but I felt the heat rising to my cheeks. From the corner of my eye I noticed Nicola standing at the top of the wrought-iron steps that led down to the garden, talking to Gordon. Despite my discomfiture, my social conscience was uneasy. Should I go and talk to her again, make up in some small way for Orlando's rudeness? My mother had told me that it was my job to make sure that all my guests were at ease.

'No!' said Orlando.

'No what?'

'Leave her alone.' He touched my shoulder. 'Nothing you can do will change her, Alice.' He turned to Sasha. 'Are you going to play for us later, Mr Elias?'

'Some German lieder,' said my father. He began to sing softly, *'Muss i denn, muss i denn...'*

'I'd love to hear some Bach,' said Orlando.

'Yes, but ... I think this is not the right occasion for Bach?'

'Why not?' asked Orlando, although Callum had just wound up the gramophone and put a Victor Sylvester record on the turntable.

'I think it is more of a dancing party than a concert.'

111

'It's a bit-of-everything-party,' Orlando assured him.

'We shall see,' said Sasha. He smiled at me. 'And if there is to be dancing, I hope I may dance with the birthday child.'

'Girl,' said Orlando. 'She's a girl, not a child.'

Sasha bowed again, one hand on his heart. 'I apologize, Miss Alice. Of course you are not a child, not any more.' To Orlando, he said, 'Your sister tells me that you are a gifted musician. What instruments do you play?'

Orlando shrugged. 'Piano, of course. Violin. Oboe. I'm thinking of taking up the flute next term.'

'If you already play so many, I think this should not be hard for you.'

'I hope not.'

'He can play *any*thing,' I said.

Mr Elias sighed. 'I should like to be as talented as you.' I was amazed that a grown-up would talk as an equal to someone of Orlando's age.

'Thank you,' Orlando said. As the notes of a quickstep began to fill the room, he grabbed my hand. 'Please excuse me – we know this tune. Come on, Alice.' He swept me away.

'Slow, slow, quick, quick, slow,' I whispered, under my breath. Although I was hopelessly arrhythmic with anyone else, I loved to dance with Orlando, who seemed able to bend his body to mine so that instead of being two people, we were one.

Out in the garden, lit by the candlelight streaming across the lawn, I could faintly see Julian and Nicola, dancing together. She stood so close to him there was no space between their two bodies, and while I looked, I saw him bend towards her and she lift her mouth to his.

Kissing! What did that feel like? If Mr Elias kissed me, would it be nicer than the damp sweaty touch of Julian's mouth, earlier that summer? Over Orlando's shoulder I saw my father dancing with my mother, his hand high on her back, his head held in a rigid and formal way which only emphasized the fluency of their movements. Before the war, perhaps Fiona had danced like this, with boyfriends from University, or with my father, foxtrotting through the Schwarzwald, or swaying at a Spanish *fiesta*, fluttering a fan, throwing back her head in laughter.

The record came to an end and Orlando bowed in the way we'd been taught, then slipped away to rewind the gramophone and put on another record. Then Sasha Elias was in front of me, holding out his hand, his green-speckled eyes warm.

'Miss Alice, may I have the pleasure of the next dance?'

'Of course.'

'What a lovely evening we are having' he said. 'It was very kind of your mother to invite me.'

'We're very glad you were able to come,' I said formally,

'We used to dance in my family, too. In the old days. My mother would play the piano and my sisters would clap in time.' He smiled. 'My aunt Lena loved to dance the tango with my father.'

I tried to visualize this German household, the

father with a gold watch stretched across his waistcoat, mother with her hair up and a long tea-gown, the two little girls in low-waisted dresses with big bows holding back their hair, like the illustrations in my copy of *The Secret Garden*, the aunt with a rose between her teeth.

'I've never danced the tango,' I said.

'Then one day I shall teach you,' he said.

Nicola came towards us. Her mouth looked crushed. Against the far wall, I saw Mr Yelland was watching her, his expression hostile.

'Alice has promised to have the next dance with me,' said Sasha, smiling at her. 'Might I have the honour of the one after that with you?'

She looked him up and down. 'I don't think so.' Turning away from him, she said over her shoulder, 'Unless you promise to wear hand-cuffs.'

I hoped he didn't understand what she meant, but he did. He flinched, paled. 'This is a very discourteous girl,' he said quietly. 'Also – I hope you understand – not a truthful one.'

'I know that.' I burned with shame and indignation. How did she dare to be so rude, and in someone else's house, too? At someone else's birthday party. Looking at the lines of distress around his mouth, I knew that I would never willingly speak to her again.

Another record started up. Mr Elias held out his hand and I slipped into his arms. He held me close, pressing me against him, and whirled me around. My heart beat almost painfully against the silk of my frock. When the music ended, he held my hand and gave a stiff little bow. 'Thank

114

you, Alice.'

There was a sudden commotion out in the garden. One of Callum's friends appeared at the French windows. 'There's a chap out here says he wants to speak to a Mrs Enid Edwardes, whoever that is,' he said. 'Seems a bit the worse for wear, actually.' Behind him, we could hear some confused shouting, raised voices, the crash of breaking glass.

'Who's Enid Edwardes?' I said to Orlando as we crowded towards the windows.

'Ava,' he said, and my heart sank. Why did the brutish husband have to return today of all days?

Outside, Nicola was crouched in the corner of the hedge, though I didn't understand what she was doing. Edwardes suddenly turned on her. 'You didn't say there was people here, you little slut,' he shouted, swinging a fist.

My parents pushed between us. 'What the hell has that wretched little whore been up to now?' my father said, his voice low. It was a shocking enough question, especially given that he never used bad language, at least, not in front of us.

Sirens screamed distantly. At the sound of them, Edwardes swung round. 'I'll get even with the lot of you,' he yelled. He lurched towards Nicola. 'And as for you, you'll get what's coming to you.'

'Can't fucking wait,' she said.

I gasped. I'd never heard that word spoken before, though I'd read it, knew what it meant. But to have this girl using it, and in front of my parents ... it crossed my mind that she might be drunk.

'That's more than enough from you, Miss,' my father said angrily. 'You've caused enough trouble already.'

The idea that whatever was going on in the garden was somehow Nicola's fault, was even more startling than my father's swearing. We were not used to children being able to precipitate events, or manipulate the adults around them. On the whole, knowing ourselves to be powerless, we did as we were told.

I could hear Ava sobbing somewhere behind me, and Orlando's voice soothing her. 'Come on, everybody,' my mother called. 'Supper is served. Everything's ready, just go and help yourself.' She stopped me. Pulled me to her side. 'Happy birthday, Alice,' she said. 'I hope ... nobody's spoiling things for you.'

'No,' I said. 'No. Honestly.'

She smiled apologetically. 'I should have listened to you. Not insisted on inviting that frightful girl.'

There was a surge of movement as people crowded towards the dining room, I looked back. Nicola was still standing by the hedge, staring from the darkened garden. For a moment, she looked baffled and lonely. Behind her someone must have called her name because she turned, looked mildly surprised, pasted a smile onto her mouth and nodded.

'Just a minute,' she said.

SEVEN

The morning after the party, the house was peaceful. The rest of the evening had passed so uneventfully – apart from some kind of skirmish at the side door I was too busy to investigate – that by morning I had almost forgotten Nicola. Perhaps it was easier to do so; otherwise I should have been forced to accept that she had deliberately attempted to sabotage my birthday party. Knowing I wouldn't need to see her again, I felt nothing but relief. Very soon we'd be returning to school, and after that, I would never come back to Glenfield House.

Now Orlando leaned across the breakfast table and with a solemn nod, indicated that today was Blackberry Day. Swelled with importance, I nodded back. Gravely we gathered our kit together: Wellington boots, long-sleeved tops, gloves, walking stick, paper bags, punnets, bowls. Only Ava, keeper of preserving pans and Kilner jars, knew that we would be returning later, laden down with fruit and made preparations accordingly: cooking apples to be purchased, two picnic lunches to be prepared and packed into our father's khaki canvas army knapsack, along with a bottle of water, some sandwiches and four digestive biscuits. As formal as though we were about to undergo an initiation ceremony or an ordination, we got onto our bikes and cycled down the drive.

We trawled our sites, desultorily picking only the very biggest and ripest. We had perfected our technique over the past few years. Grasping our walking sticks, we used the curved handle to pull branches into reach. Carefully, we plucked the shiny black fruit and dropped them into our paper bags. Once they were full, we transferred them to our punnets. By midday, we had already filled our bike baskets and cycled back to Glenfield to unload our haul into Ava's waiting pans.

The house was still quiet, which was unusual. My brothers and their guests weren't up yet. The PGs and my parents had gone about their various businesses. We took two more biscuits from the tin in the larder and cycled back again, anticipation sparkling through our veins. The morning's crop had been merely the prelude to the main event. Dumb with expectation, we laid down our bikes on the edge of the road, picked up our equipment and began the easy clamber up to the top of the cliff where the Secret Glade waited for us, a bountiful treasure trove, a dazzling hoard of berried wealth. We started to pick from the outside, saving the inner part with its circle of grass as the crowning achievement of our day's endeavour.

I'd kept faithfully to my promise not to tell Nicola about the Secret Glade, but was nonetheless apprehensive. I'd mentioned it to Charles, and he could have passed the information on to

Julian, who might possibly have told her. The thorns were thick and vicious; the bushes, as far as I could see and to my great relief, were untrampled. We settled into our picking rhythm.

Reach, pull, pick, drop.

Reach. Pull. Pick. Drop.

The world contracted from sea, sky, sun, horizon, to a narrow prospect of thorn, stem, leaf, berry. The boughs were heavy with fruit, but we knew that on the inner side of the circle of bushes lay the real treasure. We could see the untouched strands waiting for us, fleshy with fruit, lushly black, glisteningly ripe. Our bowls were filled and refilled with nature's bounty.

'Looks like a bumper crop this year,' Orlando said.

I nodded in agreement. 'Fiona will be pleased.'

Reach. Pull. Pick. Drop.

I scratched my inner arm on a hidden bramble spray, and stopped to suck out the soft bramble pins. Reach. Pull. Pick. Drop.

Orlando finally decreed that it was time to enter the virgin heart of the Secret Glade. Shoulders hunched against the bramble barbs, oblivious to the scratches and the nettle stings, we pushed our way through into the little patch of dandelioned grass.

Reach, pull, pick, drop.

Reach. Pull. Pick—Oh ... God!

Both of us stopped, mouths open, flushing with fear. Something lay there on the grass. Impossible as it seemed on this normal, ordinary sunny day, we were staring in horror at a body.

God...

119

Simultaneously, our throats acid with bile, we retched, then gave another horror-struck look. Our baskets fell from our fingers, the berries spilling over the ground like tiny nuggets of coke.

'Holy *God*!' whispered Orlando.

My mind erupted in a cacophony of sensations: screams stifled, throat gripped, blows falling onto resistless flesh. And fear, purple-bright and poison-green, black as pain. The air of this secret place was thick with terror. I gave another wincing glance, my stomach heaving, and looked directly at violent death.

As I clutched at the sleeve of Orlando's rough fisherman's sweater, there was no doubt in my mind. I knew about blood, and murder. My parents' bookshelves were filled with green-backed detective novels. Looking at the crumpled heap lying to one side of the grass, I realized how antiseptic words were, how completely inadequate to convey the essence of this heart-stopping reality.

Woodpigeons clattered in a nearby copse of sycamore trees. Gulls shrieked. Further away, I could clearly hear the chewing sound of the sea on the pebble beach. The bitter odour of crushed dandelions filled the air; blood smeared the grass. A faint sweetish odour lingered among the leaves. The scent of death, I thought.

The body lay half on its side, like a piece of garbage thrown carelessly away. Had the killer carried it here, tossed it between the brambles before fleeing? Is that all she had been to him, a piece of garbage to be discarded when done

120

with? Or had she arranged to meet someone here? Someone who was at the party?

I cleared my throat. 'Or- Orlando...'

'What?' His voice was as tentative as mine.

'She's dead, isn't she?'

'I think she must be.'

'Do you think it ... it happened here?'

'I don't know.'

'Somebody must have seen whoever it was. There'd be blood on them. There'd must have been, blood and...'

'Shut *up!*'

The face was battered beyond recognition. Teeth showed through the torn cheek, white bone under the blood. The mouth had been split by blows from a fist. We could see that the body was that of a young girl. The skirt, short, navy-blue, was torn, raised to the waist, revealing thin bruised thighs. There was no underwear. The fleshy triangle at the base of the stomach was flecked with fine brown fuzz, where the pubic hair had begun to grow. The white blouse was ripped; one small breast was visible.

In those years after the war, there was little money about for clothes. One or two outfits for every day, one for Sunday best, one's school uni-form. I knew that the navy-blue skirt had been run up on the sewing machine by the victim's mother, that the blouse was purchased last week from the general clothing store in the little town. I'd seen them both only the night before.

'It's...' I tried to get the word out but couldn't.

'It can't be.' The expression on Orlando's face was hard to read. Horror and disgust, shock, fear.

I forced my fist against my mouth. Nicola. Oh God ... Don't throw up. *Don't.* My lips trembled.

With sudden clarity, I noticed details which, afterwards, I realized I could not possibly have seen. The blue veins leading from Nicola's tiny wrists up towards her arms. The roughened skin near her right-hand thumbnail. A mole at the back of her neck. A pulled thread at the third buttonhole of her blouse.

Was it because I had observed Nicola so minutely over the previous weeks that I could see them now? Or was it simply that shock had sharpened my vision?

'Nicola,' Orlando said loudly, as though hoping she was asleep. 'Nicola...' His voice faded away

And to my surprise, I found that, once given identity, the thing lying on the ground was less potent. Young though we were, death had been a constant in our lives, either through absence or from effect. The dead were never going to come back. The war had left gaps, forever marking those left behind. Standing fearfully on the rough, sun-streaked grass, I understood that those gaps were abstract.

This was real. This was not death, but Death. This was how it might have happened to father, brother, husband, cousin, this tearing of flesh, this pounding, this blood, this hideous non-existence.

'Do you think she could possibly be still alive?' Normally the more dominant of the two of us, Orlando seemed to have shrunk inside himself.

'No.' I bit my lip. 'At least, I don't see how she could be. Not like that...' I gestured at the torn face, the blood.

'We ought to check whether...'

'I can't.'

'We should, we must...'

Cautiously Orlando stepped towards the slight body on the grass, over the soft slime of crushed fruit. Gagging with fear, breathing as shallowly as a reptile, I tiptoed after him, stood with my knees against his back as he knelt beside her.

She lay on her side, almost tucked under the fountain of bramble sprays, invisible unless you entered the thorny barrier they made. It was nearly September and the bushes had already begun to turn autumnal, red-edged. Small long-legged spiders climbed among the leaves. I could see one on her hair, another on her leg.

Orlando reached out a shrinking, juice-stained finger and warily touched her shoulder.

Not warily enough.

The small body fell backwards so that it lay face up. An open, blood-glazed eye glinted between strands of hair. The legs seemed wider open now, spread. I could see more blood on her thighs, marked with purple bruises, and the mortifying display of her private parts, whorled like a rose. This moment settled into my mind like a stain, permanently inked, indelible.

Whatever doubts he might have had before, Orlando couldn't avoid seeing now that she was truly dead. 'She's ... she's cold,' he said huskily.

I reached out a hand but I couldn't touch her. She'd been my friend, my enchantress, my lack

123

of ease. I envisaged my fingers denting her flesh, leaving themselves imprinted on her body. I would never be able to wash away the feel of it. Intimations of mortality enlaced me. Solemnity. Something which once had been so singularly vital, so full, it had seemed, of maleficent energy, was definitively absent and would be so forever.

Suddenly there was movement among the bushes. Twigs cracked, bent tendrils whipped back. Was someone there, was someone watching us, and if so, who? The murderer? The police?

Both of us whirled round but could see nothing. I thought of shoe prints among the crushed blackberries, of tell-tale fibres left at the scene of the crime, a dropped button. I thought of a madman come back to the scene of the crime, ready to murder again.

Panic gripped me. 'We've got to get away!' I screamed. I pulled at Orlando's jersey, his hair, his arm. 'Quick! Come on!'

We raced for the far side of the little green space, shoved ourselves onto the faint track between the bushes, heedless of the biting thorns. It seemed like an infinity of time before we were clear and standing on the low chalky cliff. I took a deep breath of salty air to steady the faintness which threatened me, then scrambled, stumbled, staggered down through the bushes and dead leaves, dropping at last into the green lane and running to the road.

Retrieving our bikes, we cycled away as fast as we could pedal. Without discussing it, we stopped at the nearest bench, dropped our bikes on the green, and sat down. 'The police,' I panted. My head ached abominably. 'We'll have to tell them.'

Orlando said nothing.

I could sense his resistance. 'We have to, Orlando.' I had always assumed the world would stop, if only for a moment, when death occurred. But I could see how we were being forced to keep moving on, towards whatever came next, that time did not exist in the present but was always the past, just as what we had seen was only part of the current bearing us towards the future, that *now* was and always would be, uncapturable, unpossessable.

He leaned forward and rested his head in his hands. 'I'll never, ever, *ever*...' He began to cry, his shoulders heaving. '...never forget ... never, not as long as I live.'

It was the same for me. I knew the image of that slight body, foully done to death, would remain imprinted on my mind's retina, ineradicable. What made the moment especially terrifying were Orlando's tears. I had never seen him weep before, not ever, even when he had the utmost cause to do so.

'The police...' There were tears in my own eyes, and in my throat.

'Who could *possibly* have done something like...'

'We need to tell someone, Orlando.'

'Will they think we did it?'

'Don't be silly.' I put an arm around his shaking shoulders. Usually happy to defer to his seniority, I took charge, feeling a calm confidence.

'Why do we have to tell them anything?' he said. 'They'll find her eventually. We're not the only people who go up there.'

'But if we don't tell, and then they find evidence to show we *were* there, they'll wonder why we didn't report it. And all our blackberry picking stuff is up there. And Ava will wonder why we haven't brought any more berries back with us. We have to explain.'

'There'll be hundreds of people asking questions. Wanting us to go over and over it again and again. I don't think I can stand it.'

'What about an anonymous call?'

'That's stupid.'

'Yes.' I thought for a moment. 'We could tell Ava, I suppose.'

Orlando violently shook his head. 'I can't face it. It'll be like the Gestapo.'

'We can't just ... *leave* her there.'

As it happened, when we got back, we found the house swarming with people. Louisa Stone was sitting with my mother, her eyes dark with dread. My elder brothers were with them, and the girls they'd invited down for the party, looking uneasy and embarrassed. Simon, Nicola's seldom-seen elder brother sat beside his mother, awkwardly patting her shoulder. A slim woman in police uniform arrived as we did. We followed her into the drawing room, where she began asking questions and recording them in a notebook.

'When did you last see your daughter?'

'I don't know,' Mrs Stone repeated. 'I just don't know.' She turned to her son. 'About half-past ten last night, it must have been.'

'Did you and your daughter quarrel?'

'We had a few words, yes. She wanted me to give her permission to go on to the Top Deck, that little dance hall down in the town.'

'There was a do on,' said Simon, looking down at his feet. 'Micky Monckton and his Band.'

'Yes, a dance,' said Louise. 'I said she couldn't go unless I knew who she was going with.'

'I understood that there was a party here last night,' the policewoman said.

'Yes, that's right. She wanted to go on from here.'

'That would have made it quite late, then.'

'Exactly.' Mrs Stone spread her hands, laced the fingers together, pressed them to her mouth. 'That's why I wanted to know who she was going with.'

'And she wouldn't tell you?'

'She ... she said she was quite capable of looking after herself. And anyway, it was perfectly safe, there'd be friends of hers from school going, and she'd be joining up with them.'

'Anybody know any of these friends?' The policeman looked round at us all.

Simon Stone spoke up. 'She muttered something about going out to meet someone and then walking down there. I didn't take much notice, I'm afraid. She's always ... she was always...' His eyes filled with tears, and he looked down again at the space between his feet.

'Always what?' the policewoman said gently.

'Muttering about things. Doing things she shouldn't.'

'A wilful girl,' said Louise. She looked unutterably bleak, as though a mask had suddenly shifted to show an unfamiliar face beneath. 'She's always been like that.'

'She must have sneaked away when no one was looking.' Simon stared at the policewoman. 'She ... she used to do that a lot.'

The policewoman turned to Louisa. 'So you went home without her?'

'I ... yes, I did. I mean, I'd always intended to.'

'She certainly wouldn't have wanted to walk home with Mum,' agreed Simon.

'Exactly. When I was ready to leave, I tried to find her to say I was going, and she wasn't to be home too late, but she wasn't around – not that I looked terribly hard, she could have been anywhere. I went straight to bed when I got home – I've had a hard couple of days – and more or less fell straight asleep. I vaguely thought I heard her come in about midnight.' She clasped her hands against her chest. 'Oh, why didn't I get up and *check*?'

'And you found in the morning that her bed hadn't been slept in?'

'She does that sometimes,' Simon said. He gazed at us forlornly and added, *sotto voce*, 'Just to give us a fright.'

'And when we phoned round to see where she was, nobody had seen her at all. I came round here, on the off-chance she'd stayed the night here, with Alice or something.'

'Which she hadn't,' said Fiona firmly.

'In that case, where is she?' Louise Stone looked distractedly at her watch, her face crumpling. 'It's gone four in the afternoon. I know she can be a bit ... a bit thoughtless, but surely she'd have let us know by now.'

'Could she have run off somewhere?'

'I don't think so – all her things are in her room. Besides, where would she run to? I've rung her grandparents, her aunts, nobody's heard anything. Oh God, where *is* she? For all we know, she could be lying somewhere, dead.'

I caught Orlando's eye. He looked away. I felt it again, violence, tangible as wood, the brutal sounds of death.

Fiona was watching us. She stood up. 'I'll go and make some tea. Alice and Orlando, you can come and help me.'

We followed her into the kitchen, where she filled the kettle and set it to boil. She leaned against the big dresser and folded her arms. 'All right, you two, what's wrong?' she said.

We stayed silent.

'What do you know about Nicola's disappearance?' demanded Fiona. 'There's no point lying to me, I can see that something's up.'

Orlando closed his eyes. His face was white, except for two red patches on his cheekbones, like a clown's mask.

'Come on, both of you. Where is she?'

'Ask Alice,' Orlando said faintly.

'Alice? What do you know?'

'I – we know where she is,' I said.

'Then it's very irresponsible of you not to say. You can see how distraught Mrs Stone is.' She waited a moment. 'So where is she? Who's she with?'

'She's...' I felt sick again. I bowed my head. 'She's ... *dead*,' I blurted.

'What?' My mother's eyes widened with shock. 'Dead? Are you being serious? How do you know?'

'We saw her, Orlando and me. We saw her when we were blackberrying this afternoon. She was – she was...' I couldn't finish the sentence.

'Dead,' Fiona repeated slowly and I could see how the word spread through her head, heavy with repercussions, arrangements, horror.

'It was terrible.' Orlando spoke slowly. 'I shall never see anything so terrible for as long as I live.'

Fiona, about to chide us for not saying something earlier, realized that whatever we'd seen, the two of us were in a state of shock. 'Tea,' she said briskly. 'Orlando, get mugs down and put them on a tray. Alice, we need sugar, milk and teaspoons.' She put her arms around us and drew us close to her. 'Don't worry, darlings. It'll be all right.'

'How can it be? I can't stop seeing her lying there, with her face all bloody and ... teeth showing, and her head kind of split open...' I gulped. 'It was so *horrible*.'

'Orlando,' said Fiona. 'Go to the drawing-room and ask the policewoman if she could come here for a moment.'

A few moments later, she was repeating what Orlando and I had just told her. 'Someone will have tell the girl's poor mother.'

The policewoman grimaced. 'Would you do it?'

Fiona shook her head. 'I couldn't, I'm afraid.' She bit her lip, frowned. 'Poor, poor woman. I can't imagine anything more dreadful than losing one of your children. And there's all that appalling business with her husband. I feel so sorry for her.'

'I'll have to call my colleagues,' said the policewoman. 'And then I suppose I'll have to...' She looked grim. 'A policeman's lot is not a happy one,' she said, after a moment. She turned to Orlando and me. 'We'll need you to show us where ... where you found her.'

Police work was much more fun in books than in real life. By the time we had repeated our story a dozen times, had backtracked, had answered the same questions put in a score of different ways, Orlando and I were exhausted. I wondered if the father in jail would be told that his daughter was dead. Perhaps there was a kind of poetic justice there: having deprived someone else of their daughter, he himself was facing the same loss. At least he couldn't be implicated in this second battering to death of a young girl.

The case remained on the books for years after that summer, revived from time to time by an investigative journalist, by a true-life crime writer with theories to air, or by new-broom Chief Superintendents seeking to clear up cases that had gone cold. Forensic DNA testing was still unheard of. Nicola, we discovered, had not been sexually molested. The blood on her thighs

131

came from the mess that had once been her face. Despite intensive questioning, no motive was ever established, no suspect discovered.

Orlando and I did not tell anyone about Nicola's earlier tryst on the cliffs with Mr Yelland. Neither of us could possibly have spoken of it, even to each other, so it lay between us, ugly and unmentionable. No one appeared to have seen anything untoward. A check of the Top Deck yielded statements from various school acquaintances, all positive that she had not been there that evening. No witnesses came forward to say they'd seen her after leaving my birthday party. We were all fingerprinted, but the evidence the police were able to gather from the body and the place where it was found pointed in no particular direction. The only thing they were able to say with certainty was that she had been killed sometime between midnight and six in the morning of the day we found her.

At first, although we tried not to think about it, Orlando and I found ourselves speculating about who could have murdered her. We examined the possible suspects: Gordon the Librarian, Ava's former husband, Sasha the Piano Teacher, one of the friends Callum and Dougal had invited down, even Julian or Charles, but none of them seemed suitable murderer material. Bertram Yelland was the only obvious candidate, his motive being the fact that Nicola had put her prices up too high, or started to blackmail him, something along those lines. But though we watched him closely, he seemed to carry on just as before, no more or less unpleasant than

132

previously, and showing no signs of any behaviour that might be attributable to a tortured conscience.

It was never mentioned again at home. Nor did we ask, not accustomed to talking to adults. Back at school, I didn't tell anyone what had happened, though a baffling kindliness from my housemistress and from Matron made me realize much later that Fiona must have informed the school. And then came half-term, when, instead of taking the train down to the coast, my father came to fetch me and drove me for the first time to the new house in a Cotswold village. New activities, new friends, finally drove Nicola to the very back of my mind. I joined the Girl Guides, started confirmation classes, learned how to knit, took and passed my piano exams grade by slow grade.

After the move to Oxford, we lost touch with everyone. Often I thought of Sasha Elias, and when I got to university, I tried in a desultory way to find out where he had gone. I telephoned Mrs Sheffield, who told me he had moved to London shortly after we left ourselves, and that she had no idea where he might be.

By the time I had finished school and university, and moved abroad, no one had been accused of the crime. We got on with the forward thrust of our lives, but we had been pushed too rapidly from innocence into experience. It changed us all. The relationship between Orlando and me became looser and more guarded. What we had witnessed among the blackberry fronds grew between us into a malevolent tree, leaves unfurling, branches spreading, until they obscured us from each other's view, and gradually we found ourselves living on a closeness that had once been, rather than in one which actually existed. Nicola had achieved in death what she never could have alive.

As I grew older, if I ever thought of her, I could see that she must have been a deeply troubled girl, for reasons I could only attribute to her father's imprisonment for murder.

It often occurred to me later, when I thought back to that day, that if Orlando and I had not pushed our way through those falls of bramble in our quest for the ultimate in blackberries, she might have lain there undetected for years, and I saw her in dreams, the flesh falling away from the skeleton, the clothes rotting, birds pecking at her, wild animals gnawing, until there was almost nothing left of the Nicola whom I had briefly known. Nothing but a few delicate bones.

PART TWO

PART TWO

ONE

I've never believed in chance, fate, destiny. I don't want to accept that we have no control over the events that affect our lives, that we're no more than the playthings of the gods, tossed hither and yon by the fancy of an uncaring deity. But, sometimes, choices are made for us, and I am willing to concede the possibility that something more than irrational whim has brought me down to Shale this afternoon, a place I haven't been back to since I left it nearly twenty years before.

I woke this morning with plans to check out accommodation in London while I decide what to do with the remains of my life. Instead, some impulse has pulled me into a taxi for Charing Cross and pushed me into line to buy a ticket to the backwater town where I spent perhaps the most significant years of my life. And before I can change my mind, the all-too-conveniently-waiting train is pulling out of the station, gathering speed through grimy back streets, passing crowded suburbs and settling into a steady rhythm through fields where rough grass grows tall and cows graze beside placid streams.

Freshly back in my own country, after the break-up of my marriage and the abandonment of my life in Michigan, I wonder what I am doing. For years I've scarcely given the little east-coast town a thought, though often it comes back to me in dreams when I hear again the howl of strenuous winds, the sound of salt water fretting at shingle, see drowned sailors floating, red spiders weaving webs between the brambles, the cliffs of France sitting unrealistically just offshore, almost close enough to touch. But awake, I have been far too occupied in trying – and failing – to survive my sad and busy life.

The English countryside slides past me, predictable, familiar. Spires, roofs, clumped trees, a kind of pastoral which, after eight years in the wilder, more dramatic landscapes of North America, I have half-forgotten. Travelling by train is a renewed experience; in the vast spaces of America, Allen and I used autos or planes. I'm soothed by the clickety-clack, the rise and fall of telegraph poles outside the carriage window, the dusty smell of the upholstered seats. I think of Allen with regret. And with guilt. I married my tall academic American, met while he was on sabbatical in Paris, less for love than for shelter. It was unfair of me, and his accusations that I have used him for my own purposes rang too true for me to deny them.

I have no luggage with me. I walk purposefully from the station up to the sea front and turn right. Last time I walked along this beach, there was nobody else about. Just me, and the wind and the relentless rain, spilling out of the sky, splashing upwards from the tarmac, hitting the shingle like bullets so that the suck and draw of the waves and the shotgun sound of the downpour blended into one. I had tramped along this same path, bare-headed, heartbroken, not sure where tears ended and rain began. In the distance, obscured by the curtain of water, I had just been able to make out the cap of grass crowning the cliffs five miles away above Beachdown. Beside me, the sea was a dull unforgiving khaki, with small whitecaps driving inland, one after the other, spumes of spray flying as they caught the wind. Back then, I'd been saying goodbye, to my childhood and to love, for I knew then, as one does at twelve, that I could never love again.

Today, the skies are blue, the water turquoise, banded with darker green and a blue that is almost purple. Thin clouds trail high overhead. The sea rocks gently, lapping at the edge of the steeply pebbled beach. And as seagulls scream overhead, and a dog scampers across the pebbles chasing a thrown ball, the memories of that final summer before we all scattered, lost touch, tried to forget, threaten to overwhelm me.

I push them aside. Not now, I think. Wait. Wait...

Already I can see Aunt's house – *our* house – deprived now of the Virginia creeper which once covered it with glossy triangular leaves that turned apple-red in autumn, though the house next door is still painted white with Wedgewood blue trim. The other houses along The Beach look exactly as they always did, almost unchanged since I was last here, though I can see doorbells now, neat piles of them beside the noble front doors, indicating multiple occupancies.

There are estate agents' boards here and there, clapped against the brick front-garden walls. And one of them ... I stare, I for a moment grow still, while fate, destiny, chance, smiles ... one of them is at Number Fifteen, where Mrs Sheffield once lived – and for all I know, lives still.

'Up, up ... and now down, down, down...' The words are clear in my head. I smell his aniseed breath again, feel his warm hands on mine. Sasha Elias. It's so many years since we met. What happened to him, I wonder? Where did he go? What is he doing now? *Why didn't he find me?*

I walk rapidly over the grass, slide between the gap in the municipal railings and cross the road. **FLAT FOR SALE** the board announces. The office of the selling agent is five hundred yards up the road and I almost run to it, push open the door, rush to the desk as though afraid someone will get there before I do, although there is no one else in the place.

'You're selling a flat along The Beach,' I say. 'Number Fifteen.'

'Yes,' says the greasy young man behind the desk. 'First floor.'

Destiny has not faltered. I had been certain it would have.

'Spacious lounge with magnificent sea views,' he recites, rising to find the details in his filing cabinets. 'Two bedrooms, separate kitchen-cum-dining room, bathroom with separate WC, plus convenient bedroom three or study.'

'I'd like to have a look at it.'

He opens a ledger, runs a finger down the pages. 'Our viewing agent's booked up all day today. *And* tomorrow. We could squeeze you in on Friday.'

'I need to see it now,' I say.

He shrugs. 'Sorry. No can do.'

'I've got to go back to London tonight,' I lie. 'I'm looking for exactly that kind of flat.'

He shuts the book. 'There's no one else available to show it. Sorry...'

'It's a minute's walk from here,' I say. 'Couldn't you close the office for ten minutes and show me round yourself?'

He starts to shake his head.

I lean on the desk and push my face towards him. I use the aggressive firmness I've learned over the years in the States.

'Look, I'm a cash buyer,' I say, checking the points off on my fingers. 'I'm familiar with the place – a friend of mine used to live there – so I already know what it's like. My time is extremely limited. Are you going to show me this flat or am I going to write to your parent company and tell them you refused to do so, and missed a sale out of sheer inefficiency?'

Because of some neediness in my expression, or perhaps simply fearing for his job, he finds a piece of paper and scribbles something on it. He stands up, takes a set of keys from the board behind him, and walks to the door. Turning the OPEN sign round so it reads CLOSED, he wedges his sheet of paper behind it. *2:23 pm, it says. Back in 20 minutes.* 'You'll get me shot,' he says.

Two minutes later, we're standing on Mrs Sheffield's former doorstep and he's wrestling with the key in the damp-swollen front door. The salt-tarnished bull's-head knocker is still there. The letter-flap, also tarnished brass, has some leaflets for a local restaurant sticking out of it. The paint is faded and cracked by the sun.

'Who owns the place these days?' I ask.

'Some old lady,' he says carelessly. 'She's moving to Brighton, so she's had the place converted into flats. Actually, I think she's into property development. Lot of money to be made in that. Wish I could get started on that myself.'

'Really?' I try not to sound sceptical. 'So the owner's still in town, is she?'

'Just about. She's renting a place in the centre, at the moment, while she sorts herself out. These days nobody can afford the upkeep on big old places like these.' He manages to get the door open and we step into the front hall.

The paint is bright, the patterned tiles shining, there is a fine oak table in the hall and a couple of watercolours hang from the walls, but the smell is much the same. I breathe in the fusty odour of damp and stone and salt, unchanged since I stood there, that last summer, my leather music case in my hand. I follow the agent up the stairs and wait while he fumbles with the key to the first floor flat.

'Are any of the other flats sold?' I ask.

'The one on the ground floor is. A couple from London. They use it as a weekend place, not a permanent residence.' With a flourish, he stands aside and waves me in. 'And there's been quite a bit of interest in the second and third floors.'

'But no sale?'

'Not as such,' he agrees reluctantly, as though he has in some way been found wanting.

I walk in, and there it is, Sasha's room, the same in almost every particular. The same view, the same smell – is that really a hint of aniseed? – the same copiously-carved marble fireplace, even the same velvet curtains, looped back with faded red ties.

'How much is it?' I don't really care. I'll pay whatever he asks.

The price he names seems unexpectedly cheap. 'I'll take it,' I say. I have no alimony, nor would have expected any, my former husband being in every respect the injured party. But I was able to earn handsomely in Michigan, and Allen, guilty in his own way, has given me an unasked-for settlement in lieu of my share of our house and furniture.

'Don't you want to see the rest of the place?' He leads me towards the back of the flat. 'Nice light kitchen,' he says. 'Big enough to double as a breakfast nook. Reasonable bathroom.' He sees my expression. 'Might want to upgrade one of these days,' he says quickly. 'And of course, a terrific master bedroom, plus one smaller one. Not forgetting the ... uh ... study.'

'I'll take it.'

He looks at me doubtfully. 'Um...' he says. Is it drains or unlooked-for ingress of water that worries him? Is there a right of way through the flat of which he should warn me?

'I'll buy it,' I repeat, more firmly.

'Well,' he says. 'I'll put your offer to the owner.'

'It's not an offer. It's the asking price. I'm prepared to pay it.'

'I ... um ... I have to pass it on to her. I can't just accept it without consultation.'

'It's not Mrs Sheffield, is it?' I ask.

He looks panic-stricken, as though some inviolable rule has been broken. 'We're not supposed to ... How did you know?'

'I used to live down the road,' I say. I have no doubt that my bid will be accepted. 'Tell her I'm Fiona Beecham's daughter.'

'Fiona Beecham,' he repeats, but I've wandered to the bow window and am looking out at the sea. There's the flintstone lifeboat house. There's the sailing club. In the front garden to the right, there's the Baldwins' flagpole; in the one to the left, Major de Grey's magnolia tree, just as they always were. For the first time in years, I am in a place where I feel a possible sense of belonging. I need this flat, I must have it, this is where I want to be, where I have to be if I am to regain possession of myself. To forget. To reunite myself with innocence.

It takes two months for the sale to go through, despite the fact that I have money in the bank and am ready to hand it over to the vendor right then and there, a whole suitcase full of cash, should the need arrive. In the hope of hurrying things along, I travel down from London having made an appointment to see the manager of the Shale branch of my bank.

144

I'm shown into one of those neutral cells that banks favour, furnished with a blond wood desk on four iron legs, two chairs and a cardboard rack stuffed with brochures advertising the financial services the bank offers. There is a window, but it's set too high in the wall to see out of. When the manager appears, he is tall and overweight. His skin has an unhealthy sheen and his fair hair is receding at a rate, which, at his relatively young age, must surely worry him.

He is, to my intense surprise, Julian.

'Do you remember me?' I say, as he sits down across the desk from me. 'Alice Beecham?' I hold out my hand.

'But it says here...' He looks down at my married name then smiles. 'Good Lord, so it is! How extraordinary! How *are* you, Alice? What are you doing here?'

I explain.

'I can't get over this!' he exclaims several times. 'I never expected to see any of you again, especially not after ... not after...' He stops and we stare bleakly at each other.

'Did they ever find out who...?'

He shakes his head. 'Unsolved mysteries of our time.' His face creases. 'If I remember correctly, you and ... erm...'

'Orlando.'

'Ah yes, of course, Orlando ... you actually found her, didn't you?' It's obvious that he remembers perfectly, both who discovered her and what our names are, though I can't see why he should pretend otherwise. I nod. 'I'm amazed that you're still living here.'

'So am I.' He leans towards me across the broad desk and to my surprise, his eyes are welling up. 'Do you know, I think about her just about every day. Not just her, but the ... what happened to her. I suppose that's partly why I haven't moved on. At least, I did move on, obviously, school and so on, and joining the bank, up in London. But when this position came up, I jumped at it.'

'Why?'

'Good question. I don't really know. Unless it was a way of getting back to ... to a time when everything was so much simpler. Or seemed it. Do you remember old Strafford-Jones, the bank manager here when we were kids?'

'Yes. His son, at least.'

Julian shakes his head. 'Never, even in my most down-hearted moments, did I see myself in the same position as him. Yet here I am. It's like being stuck in a time warp. As though she...' He stares at me across the desk, '...she – or what happened to her – stunted me in some way.' His expression is grim. He seems much older than his ... I take a moment to calculate ... his thirty-five years. 'Emotionally, or something.'

'Julian,' I begin. 'Do you...?' I want to ask if he has any idea who might have killed Nicola but the question is too vast for this lifeless little room, with gulls flying across the viewless window and a dusty plastic rubber plant in the corner.

'Is that what's brought you back here?' he asks. He seems uneasy. 'Are you hoping to make sense of it all or...' He laughs unconvincingly,

'...or even find out whodunnit?'

'I'm not a private detective.'

'No, but someone who was there, who knew the people involved, might have a better chance of finding out what happened than the police, don't you think?'

'Possibly.'

'I mean, I've been interviewed at least four times over the years. I'm surprised you haven't.'

'I was once,' I say. 'Over the telephone. I suppose nobody could find out where I was living. But, moving to other matters, you look prosperous enough, Julian. Are you married?'

'Yes. A couple of years ago. No children as yet.' Again he leans forward. 'You know who else is still here?'

I shake my head.

'David. Remember him? He's with Makepeace & Thring, the solicitors in King Street. Married Mary Arbuthnot, would you believe?' Again he laughs. 'There's a couple of others from the old days. Small world, isn't it?'

Small, I wonder, or simply stopped in its tracks by the events of twenty years ago?

'Now...' Julian spreads papers in front of him. 'About the matter you came to discuss...'

While I wait for my flat to go through, I have several further conversations with the agent, whose name, I unwillingly learn, is Gary. He rings me in London to tell me that there's a bit of damp on the chimney-breast; Mrs Sheffield wants me to be aware of this, though I can tell from his voice that he thinks she's mad.

'*Caveat emptor*,' I can hear him telling her, supposing he knows the phrase. 'That's her problem, not yours.' And Mrs Sheffield, not just the product of a more honourable age but a former friend of my mother's, insisting that I be told.

Another time, he rings to say that there is an outhouse at the back of the property, assigned to Flat Two, and Mrs Sheffield is sorry but she hasn't cleared it out yet. If I could deal with it, she'd be happy to take the cost off the purchase price. 'For goodness sake,' I say, 'tell her not to worry. I'm buying the flat as seen. I can manage to clear an outhouse.'

'More of a coal-hole,' says Gary.

'Whatever it is, I'll handle it.'

He telephones again. 'The grand piano,' he says. 'The vendor wonders whether you want to keep it. Otherwise it'll have to be taken to the auction rooms in Canterbury. Not that she's likely to find a buyer – nobody has room for things that size any more.'

'Does that include the piano stool?'

He rustles through some papers. 'As far as I can see, yes.'

'How much does she want for them?'

'Actually...' He sounds disgusted. 'If you want to keep them, they're included in the price.'

Finally the flat is mine. I've already been able to have it painted throughout with faint sea-greens and blues. The bathroom has been retiled and modernized with a high-speed shower as well as a new bathroom suite. The kitchen, too, has been refitted, more in keeping with my acquired American tastes. The faded red-velvet curtains have been changed for floating white voile, the floors sanded and waxed, the knobbly grey carpets replaced with good rugs.

I have had business cards printed, a paper-boy delivers the daily newspaper, the milkman calls each morning. I am anchored down here.

I travel light these days. Nearly all my possessions were disposed of when I left England to live in Paris and then moved on to Michigan. Leaving the States, I was disinclined to bring back anything that might remind me of my pointless marriage, so all I have are books, one or two treasured pictures, a few snapshot memories.

Apart from them, I possess nothing beyond a few items which once belonged to Aunt (three pairs of heavy linen sheets from Harrods, still in their original wrapping; nine silver spoons; a sandalwood-lined cigar box full of beads; a green glass jar; the Canon's woodcut-illustrated translations from the Hebrew of the Old Testament, a Wedgwood dinner service). There are also odd bits and pieces, things that Fiona has lent, given or dumped on me ('Aunt's books, darling, there are some rather fine first editions, the Canon was something of a bibliophile.') as well as other books I'd left with Orlando before I went to France.

I find myself hiring a car and trekking round the stores in the area to buy essential furniture, kitchen equipment, cleaning things. It amazes me how much has to be purchased in order to set up even the most basic household. But eventually I have the promise of sofas, chairs, a dining table, a chest-of-drawers. I even have a bed, the department store happy to sell me a slightly battered floor model, and, for a price, to deliver it immediately. The people in the flat below have lent me a card table until my new possessions arrive. I can use the music-stool as seating until then.

Resting a hand on the polished top of the Steinway, I wonder what made me so eagerly agree to keep it. I play not very much, not very well. Yet sitting at the keyboard, playing songs and hymns to which I accompany myself, or running through the music of my youth, I recognize happiness creeping between the gauzy white drapes – or, if not happiness, then at least contentment – and my hands grow unaccustomedly nimble until notes pour effortlessly from my fingers. Chopin, Schumann, Schubert, Mozart; I am deep into nocturnes, fugues, divertissements which I scarcely remember learning. *I einem bechlein heller*, I sing, looking out at the blazing sea.

The silk oriental rug I bought in a fire sale in Montreal hangs on the wall. Mrs Sheffield's handsome India-paper editions have long ago been removed from what has become my sitting room, but the shelves remain in place, solid mahogany still edged with remnants of scalloped gold-stamped leather. I have been collecting similar copies for years – Jane Austen, Dickens, Hardy – and now at last they stand on shelves worthy of their leather bindings, their gold-tooled covers and gilt-edged pages. There are many second-hand bookshops in the town and it will be a pleasure to browse at leisure, filling in the gaps in my library. And there are still Aunt's 'very interesting' books to go through; I pick up a few and find either racy thrillers from a by-gone era, or gloomy collections of the Canon's sermons, neither of which will be taking pride of place on my shelves. I have spent several hours unpacking my own books, placing my diction-aries, my reference books, paperbacks and poetry, in an orderly fashion in the bookcases.

I half-expected to be lonely but find quite the opposite: that I am full, sated with my new life. For the moment, at last, I need no other company than my own.

My family rallies round to help me move in. Dougal, my eldest brother, now a GP in Shrop-shire, arrives in his sleek Volvo, his wife Krista sending flowers, a home-baked cake, bath-salts, but unable to come herself since she has flown to Vienna to visit her mother. Orlando is there, of course, as he always is, and always will be. Callum is with us, too, a rare treat since he lives now near Adelaide, and has acquired that lean outback appearance that so many Australians have, as though their eyes are fixed on distant horizons while they count innumerable sheep. Bella comes, driving down from London, leav-ing behind her husband and two young sons. Even my youngest brother, Bobby, who has grown rich on laundromats and coffee-bars, and lives with his fourth wife in permanent exile in the Channel Islands, sends down a couple of men in canvas aprons who have shifted my few possessions into the flat and departed before the rest of us have finished greeting each other.

Efficient Bella has brought piles of sandwiches. Callum produces three bottles of cheap champagne. Dougal provides half a dozen bottles of wine for my 'cellar'.

And Orlando has brought me a house-warming present, a painting. It's a view of the rocking sea, the cliffs of France, the wrecked pier and the broken spars out on the horizon where the Goodwin Sands have lurked for centuries, to trap unlucky sailors.

'Darling!' I am overjoyed, for this is not the current prospect from my window but the much-missed view from our childhood home, ten doors down. 'It's wonderful!'

'Where did you get it?' Callum wants to know.

Orlando grins at us, his parti-colored hair and eyebrows giving him the look of a two-legged badger. 'Recognize the signature, anyone?'

'Whose is it?' Dougal is sprawled on my Chesterfield sofa, placed so I can stare at the sea all day long if I wish.

'Bertram Yelland.'

Orlando and I glance at one another and then quickly away. The ghost of Nicola flutters between us. In twenty years, we have never mentioned her name to each other. I wonder if she is branded on his brain cells, as she is on mine.

'I know that name from somewhere,' says Bella.

'He's now a rather successful painter,' says Orlando.

'He always said he would be.' I remember a summer morning, Ava and Bertram talking, his insistence that he would make his name one day.

'I was walking down Bond Street the other day and saw this in the window of a gallery.' Orlando grins. 'I knew it was the perfect present for Alice.'

'Just a minute...' Callum frowns. 'Wasn't he that awful man who lodged in the side bedroom at Glenfield, all those years ago?'

'That's right.'

'Good Lord!' The others open their eyes in surprise.

'An art teacher, wasn't he?' says Bella. 'A bit scary, if I remember right.'

'A right bastard is what he was,' Dougal says.

'He's apparently all the rage, one of those painters who go in for female nudes with varicose veins and sagging bellies in undertaker blue,' says Orlando.

'I remember him constantly erupting from his room.' Callum laughs. 'Red-faced, smelling strongly of drink and poor dentistry, shouting damn it all to buggery, you little sods.'

'I didn't think it was all that funny.' Dougal shifts on the sofa. 'I wonder if Fiona knew how he flicked at our bare calves with a wet knotted towel. God, that used to hurt.'

'Only if he caught you. I usually managed to get away.'

'Much worse,' said Orlando, 'was the way he'd suddenly emerge from a bush or from

153

behind a tree when we were innocently rambling through the countryside, and start charging at us with a stick.'

'Or even,' I add, 'with a length of bramble he'd torn from the hedge, switching at us, while we tried to outrun him.'

'Hares fleeing the hound.'

'It was clear even then that the man was as mad as a hatter,' Dougal says. 'I don't know why Fiona didn't get rid of him.'

'Anyway,' says Bella, looking at my painting, 'there are no naked blue ladies here, thank goodness.'

'That's just how Shale used to be before they tarted the place up,' Dougal says. For the rusting hulk has long since gone, the broken pier has been replaced with an ugly concrete construction, even the tilting masts have been removed.

'Mr Bloody Yelland ... I don't believe it.' Callum slowly shakes his head. 'Talk about coincidences...'

'People say there's no such thing as coincidence,' I say. Not that I believe it. There are too many other coincidences in my life for me to be sceptical.

'I'll tell what's a real coincidence,' says Dougal. 'That after so many years, Alice should just have happened to be down here and just have happened to find this place, just up the road from where we used to live?'

'Don't you think it was *meant*?' Orlando raises a sardonic eyebrow. Like me, he doesn't believe in such things, and normally I would have made some scoffing remark. But today I don't.

'And what's more,' says Bella. 'This is the very place where Alice used to take piano lessons from that German refugee.' She raises interrogative eyebrows at me. 'Whatever happened to him, I wonder?'

I've so often wondered the same thing. Wondered what might have been the result, if I hadn't taken the coward's way out, ten years ago.

'It must be possible to find out,' I say. 'Do you know, I actually met him in Paris, when I was living there.'

'Is that his piano?' asks Callum.

'It was the owner's. It's mine now. It's the very one I took lessons on.'

'That stool's a nice piece.' Dougal fancies he has an eye for furniture, though you don't need one to see that the stool is an exceptional bit of work, made of fine polished mahogany, with a seat whose lid lifts up to hold music, and an elaborately turned wheel for lowering or raising the height. 'Where did you get it?'

'The previous owner threw it in with the piano.' I look round at them all. 'Mrs Sheffield.'

'Strewth,' says Dougal, sitting up. 'Mrs Sheffield ... she had that stunning daughter, remember?' He makes eyebrow-lifting faces at Callum.

'Linda Sheffield. She was a bit of a goer,' responds Callum.

'You two are so crude,' Bella says. She looks faintly worried, as though hoping that her two little boys will turn out differently.

'I wonder why you and Orlando had lessons and the rest of us didn't,' says Callum.

155

'We looked like more promising material,' I say. 'Besides, Fiona didn't have any money for the rest of you.'

'Besides, it was my godmother, Ursula Motherwell who paid for all *my* music lessons,' Orlando says. 'Good old Ursula. Without her, I wouldn't be half the man I am today.'

Dougal remarks, 'Wouldn't have half the trust-fund either, I dare say,'

'That didn't come from her.'

'If you ask me,' says Bella, 'Fiona could see it was far too late to try to civilize the rest of you.' She pulls her big hold-all closer and starts removing sandwiches and fruit. 'Thought we might need something to eat.' I see that she is wearing Ava's beautiful aquamarine ring, which we learned years ago had been given to her by the man who later became her second husband.

'You're a marvel!' I hug her. She is so considerate, so steady, so like her mother. 'Thanks for being so thoughtful.'

'Well ... trying to get this lot fed...' She shrugs. 'By the way, I brought you a couple of things...' Another plunge into her bag. 'You always used to love him so I thought I'd bring him down to keep you company.'

'Rory O'Sullivan! Oh Bella, you couldn't have brought me anything nicer!'

Rory O'Sullivan is a knitted soldier doll in khaki uniform. From the polished Sam Browne belt across his torso and the gold buttons on his knitted shoulders, I deduced as a child that he must be an officer and a gentleman. Not having any other doll, I had envied him from the first moment I set eyes on him; he was Bella's, a gift from her mother. Now, I set him carefully on the window-seat so that he could look out at the view, and the shelving beach from which so many of the other survivors of the officer-class had once plunged into the sea for their matutinal dip.

'Sorely missed,' Orlando says softly, taking my hand. Our beloved Ava died of cancer three years ago. I'd flown over from Michigan for the funeral, knowing that she was leaving a gap in our lives which nothing would ever fill. In many ways, I believe we miss her more than Bella can, for in the face of Fiona's unorthodox parenting, not only was she our substitute mother, she was the rock to which we clung.

'And something else...' Bella produces some thick albums from the depths of her bag. 'Seeing as you'd moved down here, and you were once good friends with that horrible Nicola girl, I thought you might be interested in these.'

'What are they?'

'They were Mum's. She collected all the cuttings she could about the ... the murder, especially since we were all kind of involved. And I also brought the cuttings she'd put together about the Farnham murder, since Nicola was part of that too.'

'What on earth made her keep track of that?' Dougal said.

'She was fascinated by Mrs Stone – Farnham, I suppose she is really – the way she'd show up at her husband's trial day after day, dressed in amazing clothes. Mum loved all that sort of thing.' Bella laughed, a little shakily, thinking of Ava. 'You should see the stuff she got together about the Profumo affair. Mandy Rice-Davies and Christine Keeler. She was completely captivated by those two.'

'A lot of people were,' says Dougal. 'Including Krista.'

'These'll be fascinating, Bella. Thank you.' I touch the files, not sure whether I even want to read them or rehash the events of that summer. It would make much more sense to forget about it, to consign it to the past. Then I think of Julian. Of Sasha Elias. Of Orlando and myself. Perhaps one rainy afternoon, fortified by a glass or two of wine, I would get up the strength to delve once again into those far off and seminal days.

TWO

As if to accentuate how life constantly repeats itself, this is another exceptionally fine summer. The days pass in a fine web of heat. From the big bay window of my new home, I can see how it sits on the surface of the sea, holding the water steady, weighting down the waves like a paperweight. Along the front, children come and go on tricycles and bicycles, carrying beach balls and cricket bats, aimless, sated with sunshine, just as Orlando and I once were.

There are solitary men traipsing along the

sliding pebbles, metal detectors swaying from left to right. There are fishermen carrying more equipment than an Everest expedition. There are the constant dog-walkers. And one of them, I see with surprise, and a certain alarm, seems to be Louise Stone, looking old and bent, though she can't be more than fifty-two. How could she bear to stay on here, after what happened? I wonder if she still lives in the brightly painted little house she used to occupy; one of these evenings, I might walk down to the North End and find out. Or, more likely, I might not.

More days of breathless heat. I am restless, worn out with trying to keep at bay the thoughts I cannot control. Nicola haunts me. The Secret Glade where we found her body: is it still there? Would it exorcise my memories if I were to walk along the sea front and find the place again? The grass on the green is yellow, like straw, parched for moisture, and I, too, am parched, needing something.

One afternoon I walk along the sea to where the low cliffs begin, then climb up through a green lane still hidden, as it was back then, by overhanging greenery and arching trees so that walking along it is like burrowing into the landscape. At the top, the Secret Glade is still there, though houses have crowded nearer on three sides, new brick developments already melding into the landscape with trees and mature gardens. I'm amazed at how close to Glenfield House the area is. As a child, it had seemed a fair distance, but even on foot it can't have been more than ten minutes from the garden gate. How had Nicola and Yelland been so foolhardy as to do what they did out in the open? Or had the possibility of being seen simply added to the excitement?

Several times I have walked past Glenfield, observing the changes that have taken place. The house and grounds have been done up: the woodwork is freshly painted, bricks re-pointed, the lawns mowed into orderliness. The tumble-down greenhouse has gone, the bamboo thickets have been tamed, the lily pond now contains water-lilies and a flash of neon orange indicating goldfish.

The nights are hot and sultry. I sleep badly. Even with the windows open and a breeze blowing in off the sea, the air in my bedroom is thick and close, almost unbreathable. I am flooded by the remembrance of things long past. That summer. Sasha. The body underneath the blackberry bushes. If only I could erase it from my mind. Late at night, I walk along the seafront in the warm dark, listening to the waves rolling in, churning up the shingle, in and out, the sound like a giant crunching stones and spitting them out. I smell pine trees and salt and green leaves, the scent of lilac and cut grass, blackberries on my fingers.

All day the light pours into my room, searingly hot even with the windows open and the white drapes pulled across. The Steinway stands in the bay and eventually, with some difficulty I manouevre it further into the room, not wanting the fine rosewood case to be damaged. I shove the piano-stool into place and finding it unexpectedly heavy, idly lift the lid. It's stuffed full of music: books, songs, an ancient annotated copy of *Messiah*, another of *Judas Maccabeus*. There was a thriving Choral Society in the town back then. I must find out if it still exists; if so, I shall join.

I dig deeper, displacing Bach and Rachmaninoff, Debussy and Chopin. Further down, I find *The First Book of Easy Pieces*. The paper cover is worn and dog-eared. I remember my excitement when I went into the music shop to order it, the feel of it as I later carried it home, my absolute certainty that some not very distant day I would be the cynosure of piano-loving eyes. I recognize the pieces so well, the annotations made by Sasha Elias, the finger numbering, the musical direction. *The Fairy's Picnic* and *By the Lake*; there they still are, waiting to be brought back to musical life. The music books are dog-eared and old-fashioned. Sasha had several pupils as well as me, Nicola and Mary. Were they all as unpromising as I was? I remember Fiona telling me that he was much in demand as an accompanist. From Gordon the Librarian, I knew he worked with the choir at St George's. Ekeing out, I now realize, what must have been a meagre income as music master at the boys' prep school where he taught. Did they tease him for his accent and shabby clothes? Did they torment him for being German?

We never got round to discussing such questions ... I feel the pain in my heart again, that too-familiar sense of loss and regret.

There are also several books of manuscript paper. When I open one, I see thick black notes scattered across the pages, pieces which Sasha Elias himself must have composed. One is entitled *Homeland.* Another is called *Girls* and underneath the title, in spiky black letters: *Claire, Nicola, Mary.* And there's a third: *For Alice.* I can't help it. I flush with a warmth I recognize only too well. Where is he now? How can I find out?

As for Nicola ... I do not want to think about her. For years I've managed to close all thoughts of her up in a box at the very back of my mind and am not about to release them now. Not for the first time since I moved in here, I wonder why I have chosen to throw myself back into the snake pit of memory.

I open another of the manuscript books and inside are sheets of paper; *Mutti,* I read. *My little sisters.* And on another page: *Here, where the land falls into the sea, I am more than alone. I am deserted, abandoned. I'm parched with loneliness, dying of it. I can smell it on myself, like an aura. Lonely beyond bearing, my clothes are stinking of it, as though I have soiled myself.*

Biting my lip – should I be reading what is obviously some kind of diary? – I carefully remove each sheet, place one on top of the next until I have a pile of ten or twelve sheets. Some only have a paragraph or two written on them; others seem to continue for several pages. I straighten them up, fuss with them, and finally, reluctantly, place them tidily on the lamp-table beside the sofa. I will read them, just as I once read Fiona's diaries ... but not just yet.

One evening, as dusk turns the flat sea to the grey of aluminium, I walk towards the town, to the area they call the North End. Small twisty streets run down at right angles to the beach, crammed with tiny picturesque cottages, one jammed up against the next. The front doors open directly into the little sitting rooms, all of which contain a large brick hearth that must once have heated the entire house. The houses sit on top of cellars, earth-floored and sea-damp, where smugglers could stow the contraband unloaded from small boats run directly up onto the nearby shingle beach. The cellars created a network of interlocking tunnels where illicit cargoes could be hidden away or disposed of before the Excise Men had even come knocking at the door.

I turn away from the sea and walk quietly, almost on tiptoe, along Fisher Street, as though fearful that someone might otherwise lean from a window and accuse me of trespassing. Halfway down is what was once Louise Stone's house. The curtains are drawn only partly across the window and I have a clear view into the front room.

She is there. She is watching something on the television, seated on a sofa I recognize, with a small dog – a glossy little dachshund – beside her. She strokes one of the dachshund's ears, spreading it across her thigh as she does so. How does she look, glimpsed between the half-closed curtains? I don't know what I expected, but she seems calm, composed. Yet I wonder how she can be either of those, considering the double tragedy of the hand she has been dealt. Only a certain tension about the shoulders indicates that she is neither, that she waits, just as Ava used to wait, for something violent to hurtle back into her life.

Because I once knew Louise's house as well as my own, I know that the door to the right at the end of the room leads to a kitchen, that behind the length of beige velvet curtaining which covers the far wall is a patch of grass surrounded by flower beds and beyond the grass, an out-building which Louise had converted into an office.

To the right of the television, on a small side-table, is a photograph of a man with a smiling wife and two children. Next to it, another of the same two children, without their parents. I assume this is the family of Louise's son, Nicola's cripplingly self-conscious brother. I struggle to recall his name. Michael? Malcolm? Simon ... Simon who never spoke. I move my head from side to side of the gap in the curtains, but can see no reminder of Nicola: the pain of her loss obviously still runs too deep. I stand at the door with my hand raised to ring the bell, and then draw back. I know that if I am to ease down into the time and place I have chosen to inhabit, then I shall have to speak to Louise. But is this the right occasion? In front of the window again, I see her abruptly look up, out at me, as if – although she cannot possibly see me – she knows I am there. As if she has been expecting me – or someone from the past – for years.

She looks younger than I had expected from seeing her hunched figure along the front. Her hair, once jet-black and cut like a boy's – like Nicola's – is still very short but now a becoming silvery grey. She strokes the dog again, turns her head and speaks to someone else in the room, and a man suddenly moves into my range of vision, white-haired but handsome. He stoops and tenderly kisses Louise's cheek then moves across the room towards the window outside which I stand. I shrink away, my heart racing and continue rapidly down the street, hoping my snooping into someone else's life has not been noticed. Again, a thought strikes me: do the people round here know that Louise Stone is not her real name, or was the investigation into Nicola's murder conducted under the pseudonym she had adopted?

I was afraid I might be lonely, away from the vigour of London, and indeed, occasionally I do find myself possessed of solitude. I am flooded by the remembrance of things long past. That blackberry summer. That grief. A shock so intense that even now, so many years later, it still stabs like a knife edge between my ribs.

But in the general course of things, I am very far from lonely. My work occupies me. The telephone keeps me in contact with friends both here and abroad, And this particular weekend, Erin is here. She is still my closest friend, a Californian, beautiful and wild, who sometimes spent summers with us, while her archaeologist parents worked in Africa. Currently living in London, she is attached to the American Embassy in some capacity I've never quite understood. She has a State-Department-owned flat in Sloane Street, four times the size of mine, furnished in Scandinavian minimalism, with a few startling canvasses on the walls, painted by Erin herself. She eats out nearly every night, and when she's at home, opens tins of baked beans, a taste she acquired years ago after enjoying the subtleties of my mother's post-war cuisine. This is her first visit since I moved in.

She settles into a corner of the big chesterfield I bought from the auction rooms over in Sandwich, and spreads her arms across the back of it. Her sandy hair springs around her head like a lion's mane. On her elegant feet are gold sandals with the thinnest of high heels. Her toenails are painted a rich chocolate colour which precisely matches the short skirt she wears. She is tanned and lithe, far too exotic for this provincial town. She is beautiful, and knows it, but that hasn't spoiled the sweetness of her character. Men follow her with their tongues hanging out, but she is still waiting for Mr Right, who is proving surprisingly elusive.

'You do realize that you'll go nuts here, don't you?' she says.

'How do you figure that?' I say.

'For one thing, sweets, just take a peek out the window.'

'And?'

'There is no one out there. Not one single

person.'

'I can see at least four fishermen. And a woman on a bike. And two people walking dogs.'

'I mean no one you'd want to spend time with,' Erin says. 'What are you going to do down here, for God's sake? Who're you going to talk to?'

'Give me time.'

'I'll give you all the time in the world and you still won't find a kindred spirit down here. Jeez!' She springs to her feet and strides across the room, her calf muscles bunching, to sit beside me on the window-seat I found a local carpenter to build for me.

As so often, she's wrong. The fishing-cottages at the north end of the town have become bijou weekend retreats for jaded Londoners. Although I don't tell Erin this, I've already met a few of them, through the people who own the flat below mine. Most of them are not fishermen, but nor are they people I'd want to spend a lot of time with. One or two are people whose company I enjoyed. And there's Julian and his wife. Already I'm planning a supper party, enjoying the thought of getting out linen and silver, of buffing up furniture, unpacking Aunt's dinner service for the first time, polishing glasses, preparing food.

'Actually,' I say, 'my bank manager turns out to be someone from the old days.'

'Who?' She presses a finger to her cheek. 'No, let me guess ... that Jeremy kid with the pudding-basin haircut, I'll just bet. He was born a bank manager, poor kid.'

'Not Jeremy. Julian.'

'Julian? The tall pimply one?'

'He's still tall, but luckily the pimples have gone.'

'I'd never have put him down as a future bank manager. He was rather dishy in his spotty way. I'd have thought he'd have gone a bit further afield than two yards down the road from where he grew up.'

'Me too. But ... I guess things happen. Anyway, it's peaceful here,' I say mildly. 'And frankly, after the last few years, I can do with quite a lot of peace.'

'Peace is for geriatrics,' she says.

'I can get on with my work,' I say. 'I've got everything I want here. A reasonable library, which will order anything I need. Bookshops. Marks & Spencer. Even two department stores.'

'Selling old ladies' corsets,' she says scornfully. 'And I'll bet they're the same darned corsets they were selling twenty years ago when we were kids.'

Corsets ... a memory shudders inside me of Miss Vane's frozen expression after receiving what she had assumed was a gesture of friendship. 'And there's access to London,' I add quickly.

'Sure, if you don't mind sitting in a filthy train for two and half hours. I could *walk* there quicker. On *crutches*!'

'And apart from all that, I *like* it here,' I say.

'Why? Can you just explain to me why?'

I think about it. I realize that in fact I can't say

168

what it is that attracts me here. A sense of coming home, perhaps. The deep calm bestowed by the sea, easing my turbulent heart. 'The air,' I say. 'The light.'

'Okay. I'll grant you the light. In fact...' She gazes at me with a grin. 'I was even thinking we might look around for a weekend place for yours truly. A studio apartment, if such a thing exists. I'm posted over here for at least four years, so I might as well take advantage. I could bring my gear down, become a genuine Sunday painter.'

'Erin! That would be absolutely wonderful.' I am mostly delighted at the thought that I might see more of her. A tiny alien part of me, which I hardly recognize, wonders if she will interfere too much in the new life I'm trying to forge for myself. I am astonished at my own ingratitude. Erin has always been there when I needed her, has always provided a shoulder for me to cry on.

'God!' She sits down again, this time in the high-backed oak chair, which once belonged to my father, and slumps against its thick wooden slats. 'I can't believe how long it is since we were here. And you know what's bizarre? The entire world has changed but this place has stayed exactly the same. Exactly!'

'Not quite.' I gesture at the pier.

'Oh, Alice. So they made a few cosmetic changes, a sop to the fact that the war's long over. But the mindset's still the same.'

'Just like it would be in any small place in the States.'

'True.' She smiles at me. 'So, now I'm here, what are we going to do with the day?'

169

'What would you like to do?'

We settle for a walk into the town, a trawl round the estate agents to see if we can find a weekend property for Erin, and if not, we'll drive over to Canterbury, which does at least have some decent shops, according to Erin.

As we're about to leave, the telephone rings. It's my former husband.

'Hi,' he says.

'Hi, Allen.' I glance at Erin, who grimaces back.

'How's it going, Alice?'

'Just fine. How about you?'

'Oh, you know...' he says.

'I don't, actually.'

'Germaine's decided we aren't going to work out, so she's moved on.' He speaks in an offhand way, as though it scarcely matters. Knowing him so well, I can tell that it does.

'Where's she moved on to?'

'She's joined an ashram or something.'

'For such a cutting-edge person, isn't that a little passé?'

'I know what you mean.'

'Is she signing up with a friend?' I wonder, rather meanly. 'A like-minded soul whose karma matches hers? Or is it all on a high-minded level of brown rice and beautiful thoughts?'

'God, you can be vicious,' he says cheerfully. Cheerfulness is Allen's defining characteristic. 'And actually I think there *is* someone else, though that's just a suspicion.' His voice brightens. 'Say, I'm coming over to a conference in Manchester next month, and wondered if you'd be interested in meeting up.'

'In Manchester?'

'No, dumbo. Either in London or ... well, I could come down to see you, check out your new apartment, take you out for meal, whatever.'

'What does "whatever" imply?'

'Still got that sharp English tongue, I see.'

'Not really surprising. After all, I *am* English.'

'So...' I can almost see the goofy chipmunk grin on his face which once I thought as cute as he does himself '...can I come visit with you?'

'When are we talking about? I'm frightfully busy just now.'

Although he can tell I am reluctant, he presses me to name a date, and as I always do, I submit.

'Just make sure it's a weekend when I'm not here,' says Erin, after I've hung up.

'Maybe he's your Mr Right.'

'No way, baby.'

'Just as a matter of interest, what kind of man *do* you want?'

'I don't know, but when I meet him, I'll know at once.'

'He's not going to be a garage mechanic, is he?'

'He could be, you English snob.'

'But what on earth would you talk about? I mean after he's fixed up your car and put new tyres on and given you an oil change, what then?'

'You could say the exact same thing about a brain surgeon.'

'Wouldn't you want him to be a bit arty?'

'Not necessarily. Or maybe a bit but in a different field than painting.'

'An actor? A violinist? A sculptor?'

'Any of the above. Or none. It'll be love at first sight, I'm sure. But not necessarily. Maybe it's someone I've already met, but haven't even considered as a potential mate.'

'Like ... like Orlando?'

'Orlando?' She seems genuinely shocked. 'Are you kidding?'

'What could be nicer for me than to have two of my best-loved people united?'

She wrinkles her nose. 'I don't think I'm Orlando's type, for a start. I'm far too independent. And besides, I fairly sure there's already someone in his life.'

'I didn't know that.' The thought is unsettling. Why hasn't he told me?

'Anyway, Orlando's too clever, too self-contained for me,' continues Erin. 'I like emotion, passion, a sort of feverishness about life.'

'So not an Englishmen then.'

'I think not. If I had to choose between the two of them, I'd take Allen every time, even though I don't dig sandy men with freckles.'

'I don't either. Often I look back and wonder how on earth I could have married him.

No. That's not quite true.

I know precisely why.

The grass on the green is yellow, like straw, parched and dry. For once, there is a light spattering of rain against the windowpanes, but it lasts no more than twenty minutes or so, and

172

provides no respite from the heat. The vulnerable moon rises early tonight. Years ago Orlando taught me about the eight distinct phases of the moon, and I recognize that it is in its waning gibbous phase. Bookish children, we had always thought that gibbous meant with long thin clouds drifting across it. Even more surprising was the information that it also means humpbacked, like Aunt.

Across the Channel glimmers the ghost of France, the cliffs at Cap Gris Nez scored by the same stark vertical furrows as those at Dover.

Erin has gone back to London. I pour myself a glass of white wine and settle into my armchair. On the side-table are the pages I found in the music-stool and I pick up the first one.

I must practice my English. I must write every day, even if it is necessary for to use a dictionary for words I do not know. According to my cousin, from now on I should forget the past and become like an Englishman. I do not know if I can do this. How should I cut out the past from my heart?

How can I forget my mother? I see her endlessly, night after night, long dreams in my head. I see her on the floor of our hallway, her legs spread, the white shine of her pearls scattered on the carpet around her head. I see things I do not wish to see, things I shall never, all my life forget. Spread white legs, the dark hair at her thighs, her bared breasts, things no son should know about his mother.

Mutti ... She was such a proud and beautiful

woman. She would not cry out, because of the girls, though she must have been terrified that it would be their turn next. As the filthy soldiers come in turn and take their disgusting pleasure with her, I can see in her eyes, half-turned towards my hiding place, that she is calculating how to save her daughters who stand shrinking away from the men who hold them, faces white with fear. She is wondering whether to kick out at them, to hurt them, launch herself on them, allow herself to be shot, while screaming at the girls to run, or whether, if she submits, she can shame them into leaving without further damage to her violated family. My gentle Mutti.

I sit with the paper resting on my knee. My hand shakes and my heart feels hot. I let myself think of Sasha. Where is he, what is he doing? Does he ever think of me? Why did he never get in touch with me again in Paris?

I know what star I should have followed.

I pick up the page again.

I think of my little sisters, one dark like me, one fair. I loved them, their lithe young bodies in my arms, kissing their soft heads. I loved them. Here, I have nobody to love.

I should leave this place, but would it be any different if I had ended up in London or Manchester or Oxford, the city of dreaming towers, as my father used to say? Ach, that already my memory of him fades. Already I am forgetting him, them, my pale sisters, my beautiful mother.

174

Tears fall from my eyes. The papers lie on the arm of my chair. I bite my lips to stop the tears, the vicarious pain, and pour another glass of wine which I drink rapidly. If I'd known, maybe I could have done something for him. But what? I was only a child. What could I – or anyone – have done for him? You can't, however hard you try, erase memories.

THREE

'Hi, honey.' It's Allen.

I try to suppress my irritation. He should not be using endearments to me. Especially since we're divorced and he has a new partner, even if she's decided that they aren't going to work out. He no longer has any rights where I'm concerned. But of course he has. We shared our lives for a number of years, and that in itself confers certain rights, on both sides. 'Where are you?'

'Just about to leave Charing Cross. We arrive at 12:42.'

'We?'

He sighs. 'Me and the train.'

'I'll meet you.'

'It'll be great to see you again.'

'Mmm,' I say, non-committal.

I'm not sure how great it will be to see Allen again. We were together for eight years, seven of which were uneasy. We were never unhappy, but

175

never really happy, either. We remained the good companions we'd always been, but increasingly I felt as though I was living only half a life.

I met him in Paris, where I was working as a translator for a big international cosmetics industry. Twenty-one years old, in my first job after getting my degree in Modern Languages – French, Spanish and German – earning good money. I had a flat in the fifteenth arrondissement, a single big room with its own bathroom and kitchen attached. The fact that the bathroom was a cupboard into which, by some miracle of engineering, a shower and a toilet had been installed, didn't bother me. Nor did the so-called kitchen, a series of narrow shelves upon which stood a two-burner electric hob and an electric kettle, a fridge big enough to house a half-litre of milk and three slices of ham, plus a sink attached in some mysterious way to the toilet so that I often found coffee grounds or vegetable fragments floating around in the bowl. Luckily, the traffic never went the other way.

I loved the place. It was like living on the set of *La Bohème*. There was a real view, over the roofs of Paris. I could see the Eiffel Tower, and in the far distance, the roundels of the Sacré Coeur. I bought Bernard Buffet prints and put them up on the walls. I wore black tights and ballerina shoes, black polo-neck sweaters. I became more Parisian than the natives. Sometimes I looked like Juliette Greco, smoky-eyed and waif-like. Other times I put my hair up in a French twist, wore demure little white blouses with full skirts. I bought baguettes and paté, I spoke accentless French, I did French things. I passed for French. Parisians are notoriously insular and unwelcoming, but because of my language skills, I found myself totally accepted.

One evening I went to a concert with a couple of girls from work. Nathalie and Marie-Claire were both Parisiennes, and Nathalie, who worked in the press office, had been given free tickets. We bought glasses of white wine at the bar, before the concert started, and drifted about, watching the audience gather.

'That guy's certainly interested in you,' Marie-Claire remarked.

'Which guy?'

'Over there, by the pillar. Quite dishy, don't you think, Nathalie?'

'*Pas mal*. He's been staring at you for at least ten minutes.'

I shrugged. Laughed. 'Either you have it, or you don't.' After a moment or two, I gazed casually in the direction she'd indicated. And gasped. 'Good Lord!'

'What?'

'I ... I know him,' I said. My voice was unsteady. ''Scuse me, girls, but I better go over and speak to him.'

'Tell him I'm free next Saturday,' Nathalie called after me.

He watched me coming towards him. I held out my hand. '*Bonsoir, Monsieur Elias.*'

'*C'est bien, Alice.*' It was a statement, not question. His fingers were warm as they grasped mine. At the sound of his voice, my heart began to beat faster and harder, like a metronome. He was, of course, older than when we'd last met, but he also seemed much sadder. Perhaps I did too. There was grey in his hair, and when he moved his head, I could see a line where his shirt collar cut into his neck.

'*C'est ça.*' I lifted my shoulders and let them drop. 'How *are* you?' My voice sounded artificial, over-bright.

'So...' The green speckle in his eye glowed. I smelled again the scents of aniseed and tobacco. 'You are living here now.'

'Yes. I work for Sonja Eden, the cosmetics people. What about you?'

'I'm here for the moment.'

'How do you like Paris?' I asked.

He smiled. 'It is a place for lovers,' he said. He spread his hands wide and pulled a rueful Gallic face. 'But I have no lovers.'

'Not even one?'

'Most especially not even one.'

I stumbled hastily in another direction. 'So where are you living ... Sasha?'

'At the Cité Universitaire. What about you?'

'I'm renting a flat in the fifteenth.'

'Do you have a lover?'

'I've got a boyfriend,' I said quickly, embarrassed. Girls like me didn't use full-blooded words such as 'lover'. 'Several, actually.'

'But nobody special.'

'Not really.' I jerked my head over my shoulder. 'Look, I can't stay. My friends ... And the concert's about to start.'

'Of course.'

There were so many things I wanted to ask him. So much I wanted to say. 'Can we ... could we meet up sometime?'

With his index finger he touched each of my knuckles in turn. I felt the same warmth between my thighs as I used to when still a child. Then, I hadn't known what it meant. The imperfection in his eye seemed to glow brighter. 'Alice.' He said my name with a kind of certainty. The word brushed across my skin like a kiss.

I pressed my cold glass against my forehead, and then against my face. 'Gosh, it's hot in here!' There was perspiration under my arms and between my breasts. My forehead was damp. He leaned towards me and for a moment I thought he was going to kiss me. Involuntarily, I gasped. I couldn't think of anything to say. His eyes held mine and I wasn't able to look away from him. Where our bodies touched, I felt the heat of him. We stood without speaking, a milli-metre apart. My nerve-endings yearned towards him, like optic fibres, like glow-worms. I didn't want to break the spell, but eventually, as the three-minute bell sounded, I stirred, I sighed. 'I think I'd better go.'

'I'll get in touch,' he said.

'Fine.'

Only after I'd rejoined Nathalie and Marie-Claire and we were back in our seats did I wonder how he would find me, since he had not asked for my address. I touched each of my knuckles. I thought: I've never realized what it meant before, but now I do. *Un coup de foudre.* Love at first sight.

Except it wasn't first sight. I'd been waiting for him for more than ten years.

I met Allen some months later. By then I had given up any hope of hearing from Sasha, though part of me wondered if he searched the faces on the streets – as I did – cursing the fact that he had let me go without finding out how to get hold of me. Yet, I had told him where I worked; he could have found me if he really wanted to. I knew he was out there somewhere. I knew that he thought of me constantly, as I did of him. I had been dropped into love. I was coated in it, as though I were a strawberry delight or a raspberry crème being dipped into chocolate.

As the weeks went by and my feelings kept me awake at night, I grew more obsessed yet at the same time, resigned to his loss. I could think of nothing else; my work suffered. I had no wish to go out with friends or attend the theatre, even to shop for food, in case he called and I missed him.

Eventually, as so many women are, I was frightened by this consuming emotion, this grand passion. I'd let down my guard, for the first time – there'd been men in my life before, but whatever I felt about them, I kept them at a certain emotional distance. It was safer that way. If I allowed it to ignite and burn, I would be reduced to a cinder, the smoking ruins of myself, all that was left of what had once been Alice.

And as so many women do, I opted for safety.

Allen was one of the guests at a party I went to,

given by some ex-pat American whose name I don't remember if I ever knew it. Newly-arrived in the city, he seemed simple, uncomplicated. He had an *apartement* in Neuilly. I knew Sasha Elias was not going to contact me and that it was time I took up my life again. We did ordinary things together. Went to the cinema, walked along the Seine, ate in cheap restaurants, bought tickets to the opera, visited the Louvre, the Rodin Museum, Sacré Coeur, Montmartre, things I'd done several times before but was happy to do again. We shared a passion for Monet, Russian movies, *pommes frites*, walking.

Allen was always good company. He was well-read, cultured, enthusiastic. He introduced me to new experiences and different names. When he was due to return to his Michigan university, he begged me to go with him, and though I was unused to spontaneity, I agreed that as soon as we could find me a job there, I'd join him.

'Not just join,' he said. 'That wouldn't go down too well, in any case. Marry me, Alice. Marry me.' He dropped to one knee and held out his hands.

'All right.'

Aware that passion was missing from our relationship, I was nonetheless ignorant and naïve enough to believe it wouldn't matter. I thought that his love would be enough for both of us. I thought that this way I would not get hurt again, and at the time that seemed important.

It was some time before we both realized what we were missing. I'd spurned the magic in the blood out of cowardice; he'd fancied that in me he would find a normality he'd hitherto lacked. He wanted children, if only to disguise his own ambiguities about gender and sexuality. At the end of the fifth year of our marriage, I lost the ability to cope with the banality of our lives. America in the Sixties was curiously fettered by convention, even in the university town to which Allen took me. Young women looked and dressed like their mothers, and if there one thing I was sure of in those uncertain days, it was that I did not want to look like Fiona. There were conventions and restrictions at which I chafed. There were coffee mornings, tennis afternoons, Tupperware parties, baby showers. People had food fads that astonished me, having grown up in the deprived post-war years, and I gradually realized what little impact the war had made on most of provincial America.

I didn't lose touch with family and home. After his appointment to Boston, Orlando visited us fairly regularly. Callum came twice on his way to or from Australia. Dougal and Krista travelled onwards to see us after attending a medical conference in New York. My parents came once. And Erin we saw often. Nonetheless, I always felt that not only was I not part of the scene, but that I never would be. Even worse, that I didn't want to be.

Children might have disguised our slow dissolution for a while longer, but somehow they never arrived, which made it much easier when the moment came for me to realize that if I was to save myself, then I must leave without delay.

We remained the good companions we'd always been, but as the years went by in a repetitive round of parties and picnics, Christmases spent with our families on either side of the Atlantic, vacations taken in Europe or Mexico, increasingly I felt as though I was living only half a life. And then the nightmares began. Not every night, at least not at first. But increasingly I would wake and lie in the darkness, sweating with terror, while Allen breathed gently beside me. Once again I would see the red spiders on the collar of Nicola's blouse, or the blood on her naked thighs, those thin splayed legs, the feeling that if we had never found the Secret Glade with its treasure house of blackberries, I would never have had to look at her dead body. I took to calling Orlando, waking him in the early hours for the comfort of his voice, the sound of his breathing, the fact that he alone knew what I meant, what I saw in my dreams.

One day, everything simply fell apart. I got up and looking into the bathroom mirror as I brushed my teeth, realized that as with my mother, years before, I had almost no point of contact with the woman who looked back at me. *Alice, where art thou?* Where had I gone? I needed to find out more about who she was. And clear as a bell came the realization that if I was to save myself, then I must leave without delay.

Which I did. Within a week of making the decision to return to Europe, I was gone. 'Why?' Allen asked, over and over again, as I packed my things. 'Why?'

I could only shake my head. I couldn't have

begun to express to him the feeling that I was wasting my life here, that somewhere out *there*, some brighter star waited for me to hitch my wagon to it and follow where it led me.

'We get on so well together,' he insisted. 'We have so many interests in common. We're such ... *friends*.'

'I don't want to spend my life with a friend,' I said.

'If you were more mature, you'd understand how valuable that is.'

'You're probably right. But I want to...' I was too sensitive to his feelings to say that I wanted to be in love with the man I was spending my life with. I knew that high passion can't last, that ecstasy, by its very nature, must fade, especially in the face of everyday dullness. 'I just don't feel that this is all life has to offer.'

'Of course it's not all. But it's the best part.'

'Maybe, maybe not.'

He cried as he saw me through into the Departure Lounge. My own eyes were wet, but it was regret I felt, rather than sorrow.

He is tall, tanned, smiling. We embrace and for a mercifully brief moment I wonder whether we should get back together, before reality imposes itself once again.

'He is not the right man for you,' Orlando said, eight years ago, when Allen and I had come over from Paris to meet my family.

'Who *is*?'

'Me, for instance.'

I laughed.

But he was being serious. 'You're not in love with him, Alice.'

'What is love, Orlando?'

'Don't try to be clever. It's not fair either to you or, more importantly, to him.'

'I know what I'm doing.'

'What you're doing is making a terrible mistake.'

A mistake, yes, I think now, but not necessarily a terrible one.

As we turn out of the station yard and walk towards the sea front, I think to myself that if Allen and I can resurrect from our marriage at least the semblance of affection, then we shall have gained something.

'Is there somewhere I can take you for lunch?' Allen asks, and I steer him towards the big hotel on the front. We order what is basically fish and chips, with the limp piece of lettuce-plus-tomato-slice which passes for a salad in the outposts of England. In London, cuisine has moved on unrecognizably since I was a child, but anywhere else, the art of cooking or serving fresh vegetables still seems to elude us.

'So why are you here?' I ask.

He pretends hurt. 'To see you, of course, hon.'

'And what else?'

He stares out of the window at the wooden rowboats lined up on the shingle above the high-water mark. His sandy hair is touched with white above the ears and I see in him the physical closeness to his father. 'Thing is,' he says softly, 'thing is, I've been sort of wondering if the two of us shouldn't—'

185

'No,' I say. We were married for nearly ten years, yet I feel such repugnance at the thought of sharing any kind of intimacy with him, that I am unnecessarily brusque.

'Come on, Alice. At least hear me out.'

'No!' I shake my head violently. 'I don't want to. There's nothing to discuss.' Emotions curdle inside me: fear, disgust, something unidentifiable which I half-suspect is a deep sexual longing – but not for Allen.

'Boy,' he says. 'You sure are antsy.'

'Allen...' I lay my hand lightly on his. 'Let's keep things the way they are, shall we? We're friends, aren't we? We enjoy each other's company. Let's leave it at that.'

For a moment he stares at me without speaking. I can see his sharp brain moving like a computer behind his eyes, configuring, assessing, weighing up. Whatever hopes he might have had from this visit have been blighted, at least for the moment, but he is wise enough to know that by keeping doors open, he has more chance of getting what he wants than if he slams them shut.

He shrugs. 'Okay, darlin'. Let's do it your way.'

'So tell me about the ashram lady,' I say. 'Charmaine, wasn't it?'

'Ger, not Char.' He sighs, makes his chipmunk face, nods ruefully. 'What a blooper that was! She'd lived in China for some years, and brought back all sort of kooky ideas. Turned the house upside down. All the furniture at crazy angles to make the most of something called feng-shui, which involves living at peace with your environment by harnessing the life force, multiplying by two and subtracting the number you first thought of.'

He ordered another beer from the hovering waitress. 'Honestly, I never knew from day to day what the place would look like when I came home each night.'

'Poor baby,' I said.

'Plus the darned crystals she had hanging from every available space so that every time I moved I risked losing an eye. And nothing in the icebox but tofu and bean-shoots. I had to sneak out for a McDonald's just to keep body and soul together. To be frank, she left for India only seconds before I kicked her out.'

'Why did you take up with her in the first place?' I am laughing, remembering what a good companion he was. Still is. 'You must have known she wasn't the right woman for you.'

'I've made that mistake before.'

I ignore this. 'Is there anyone else in your life at the moment?'

'I've dated this woman from the English Department a couple of times.'

'What's she like?'

'She's okay.' He waves a hand disparagingly in the air. 'That's unfair. She's actually very nice. *Very* nice.'

'Maybe it'll be third time lucky.'

'Actually, I thought it was first time lucky,' he says lugubriously.

In the face of this unsubtle appeal for sympathy, I smile. After a while, his face assumes its customary cheerfulness. 'So ... what should I see in this windy old town?'

We do the tour. The North End with its picturesque knobby-kneed cottages, the fourteenth-century castle built in the shape of a Tudor rose, the other rose-shaped castle which is full of memorabilia of Waterloo and Queen Victoria. We end up walking along the pier to look back at the pastel-coloured houses lining the long Esplanade.

Eventually, we stroll back to my apartment. My home. The wind off the sea is warm; it strokes my hair like a caress. Waves shift restlessly in to shore, seagulls dive and quarrel.

I brew him some coffee and we sit on the window-seat, looking out at the sea. 'It's nice here, but I can't see you staying long term,' Allen says.

'Why not?'

'What's there here for you? Cute, I'll grant you, but not much else. Or is it the desire to get back to your roots?'

'Could be.' For a moment I contemplate telling him about Nicola. But the subject is too overwhelming to be casually dropped into the conversation. 'Actually,' I say, 'I think I'll enjoy it.' I turn the conversation to mutual friends. 'By the way, how are the Staceys getting along?'

'Fine, Tom's got a sabbatical coming up and is thinking of spending it, of all places, in Santiago. And Nancy Landauer specially asked me to say hi...'

For the rest of the afternoon we hash over memories, do-you-remembers?

Later, we walk back to the station. Before he gets onto the train he hugs me and I feel the treacherous tug of comfort and familiarity. 'If you ever stop enjoying, call me,' he says. 'I'll be happy to come pick up the pieces.'

'I'll do that, Allen. I mean it.'

I wave him off, a small lump in my throat. I wonder how long it'll be before we meet again.

FOUR

Allen's visit has triggered memories which have nothing to do with Nicola. For me, this flat is haunted by Sasha Elias. His music is here, his piano, his diary. I want to know more about him. I want to find him again.

From the pile of his papers I have retrieved from the stool, I pick another sheet at random.

Mrs Sheffield came to my door this morning with a visitor. A strong-faced woman from along the road, who wishes me to give her daughter piano-lessons. Mrs Fiona Beecham. She is very un-combed, but obviously of a good class. 'I do feel that all children should at least be exposed to music when they are young,' she says. 'My sisters and I were all taught to play an instrument from an early age. In my case, it was the viola.'

'Ah yes.'

'The trouble is,' she said, 'that my daughter is in danger of turning into a little savage.'

'A savage?'

'A wild thing. She's what we call a tomboy ... there are so many boys around all the time, d'you see?'

'I ... think so,' I said. Perhaps she is making an English joke. I cannot imagine that Mutti would refer to my sisters as little savages.

'Music hath charms to soothe a savage breast,' she said – at least, so I believe that she said. 'So if you can fit Alice – my daughter, that is – into your timetable, it would be a very good thing. I was hoping for lessons at least twice a week until she goes back to school.'

'I'm sure that I can find a place for her.'

'That's very good.' She asked me for my terms and seemed to find them acceptable. 'So when could she start? As soon as possible would be best.'

'Not tomorrow,' I said. 'But the next day. And then again at the end of the week.'

'Excellent.'

She rested the back of her hand against the delicate skin of her temples. It was a strange gesture. It did not seem as though she had a headache, rather (or so I took it to be) it implied an inability to absorb anything more into a brain already overloaded with information. Her eyelids were very red, as though she had been weeping for hours. Mrs Beecham is not a pretty woman, but certainly she is what they call handsome. She gives me the impression always that she should be somewhere else, doing something *different. Teaching in a university lecture hall, perhaps, or playing some instrument such as a harp, in a long green dress, a velvet band across her forehead. Sometimes I see her gaze rest upon her children and a look of confusion passes across her face.* **Where did they all come from?** *she seems always to be saying.* **Why am I here, when I should be altogether elsewhere?**

I rest the pages on my knee. Sasha has caught my mother precisely. I remember so well that baffled expression on her face as she looked round at the breakfast table, the back of the wrist laid against her forehead, her red eyelids.

She said, 'Why don't you come to our house this afternoon, have a cup of tea with us? Then you can meet your new pupil.' When she is gone, I speak in her voice, knowing that this is the way I must talk if I am to be accepted, if I am to be English, as Cousin Dieter wishes me to be.

'My sisters and I were all taught to play music at an early age...' I say it over and over again, 'My sisters and I...' and then I am weeping, thinking of my own two little sisters who died God knows what ugly deaths.

Therefore, this afternoon I have called at the house of Mrs Beecham. It is ten houses away from here and has its name – Glenfield – on the gatepost. I knocked on the door with my knuckle because there was no doorbell or knocker, and Mrs Fiona Beecham, let me in. 'Ah, Mr Elias,' she said in her good English voice. 'Do come in.'

191

She took me into a big room, where steps of cast iron lead down into the small front garden. There were German books on the shelves in this household and my eyes lit up. So the book-burning ceremonies I had imagined taking place across the length and the breadth of England did not happen after all.

Mrs Beecham saw what I was looking at. 'Oh, do borrow them, Mr Elias,' she said in a voice that was kind. 'In fact, please take them all home with you to Mrs Sheffield's. I don't read German and neither do my children, and I'm quite sure my husband wouldn't mind.'

Home ... I must remember that I am English now. Instead of the big comfortable flat on Lindenstrasse, with its long windows overlooking the garden, this cold room with the worn Turkish carpet on the floor is my home. Outside the window there is a cherry tree here, just as we were having in München. Munich, I must call it now.

'My husband was a Lektor in Tübingen before the war,' Mrs Beecham told me, 'He speaks fluent German, he was in Army Intelligence during and after it, because of his facility with the language.'

She opened her eyes wide, willing me not to make the connection between conquered and conqueror – perhaps she doesn't know that I am Jewish.

I would like to tell her about my sisters. About Pappi and Mutti, all surely dead by now.

When darkness had fallen and I finally dared to leave the wardrobe where I'd been hidden, I

*found my mother's pearls scattered on the floor.
I took time to snatch up a handful of them before
walking out into the deserted street.*

*The screams of Anna and Magdalena were in
my ears. Oh my sisters, poor little gentle girls. I
cannot allow myself to think beyond the threshold of our house in Lindenstrasse, although I
imagine all too clearly what happened.*

*The German books of Mrs Beecham are old-
fashioned and worn. There are scrawls over
some of the pages and I imagine my new pupil as
a younger child, taking a yellow wax crayon or
a blue one in her fat little hands and scribbling
over the paper.*

Twenty years have gone by since he wrote them,
and the world has changed, but his words are
still as painful to read, as they must have been
for him to write. I want to know if he ever found
his family again. Above all, I want to know why
he didn't come looking for me in Paris.

A single star gleams above the horizon, which
is streaked with the fiery reds of a summer
sunset. Twenty-one miles away, French cliffs
squat on the edge of the sea. Nearer to hand,
something is caught among the intricate carvings
of the marble fireplace surround, gleaming dully.
It takes me a moment to recognize this as a pearl,
and then to realize that this is *my* pearl, the one I
hid there twenty years ago. It seems extraordinary that it should still be there. I prise it out and
rest it on my palm. It seems to have meaning of
some kind, though I know it cannot have; it is

just part of a random pattern of events which are only loosely related one to the other.

I take up another sheet of Sasha Elias's writing.

When this child, this Alice, comes to me for her first piano lesson, I see my sisters again and for a while I can forget my thoughts. For a while the loneliness goes. Although I do not say so, because I need the money, in truth I would happily give her piano lessons for nothing. She has dirty fingernails and a grubby dress. Sometimes she smells a little unwashed. She looks as though nobody cares for her. I want to bath her, wash her hair, soap her thin shoulders, the way I did with my sisters. Her hands are beautiful, but very small. I doubt if she could ever be a good pianist because she will not be able to play octaves very easily. My other pupil is much more gifted, Mary Arbuthnot. I can see her becoming very good indeed. She also plays the flute very beautifully, as well as the piano, and is competent on the 'cello although she is still too young and small to get the full range out of it.

I would pay to teach Alice, if only to have, for two half hours a week, someone to speak to. To look into her soft brown eyes and see the shy dimple in her round cheeks. To hold her on my knee the way I held my sisters, Anna and Magdalena. I cannot even think of them because if I do, I will fall into an ocean of despair and will never again find the shore. I am tortured by the fact that I am alive and they are dead. If I had stayed with my family, could I have saved them? I know

*that of course I could not. I would be dead too. I
wish I were.*

*Instead I sit in this big room and look out at the
sea, at the masts of wrecked ships rising on the
horizon, where, my landlady tells me, there are
some treacherous sands, and that on New Year's
Day a cricket match is played there. Only the
English, I think, as I smile politely and drink the
tea she has prepared for me in her chilly base-
ment kitchen, would think of playing cricket on a
quicksand in the middle of winter. 'Every year
there are wrecks,' she says. 'Casualties.' She
gestures in the direction of the red, white and
blue lifeboat that sits high up on the shingle to
the left of my window. 'You can hear the
maroons go off to call the lifeboat men together.
Such brave men...'*

*I think of the sailors screaming for their
mothers as the cold water fills their mouths; my
father told me that this is how most men die in
battle, calling for their mothers.*

'Orlando, it's me. Or should I say it is I?'

'Me, I, it doesn't matter. Either way I recognize your voice.' I can hear him smiling.

'You remember Sasha Elias, who taught me
piano that last summer holidays we were here?'

'I know who you're talking about, if that's
what you mean.'

'How would I find him, supposing I wanted
to?'

'I haven't a clue. He taught music at that prep
school in the country, didn't he?'

'Braybrook Park, yes.'

'Perhaps he's still in the area.'

'I don't think so. I ran into him in Paris, years ago,' I say. 'So he must have left here. He said he was studying composition with some famous teacher.'

'Fiona might know.'

'The name doesn't ring any recent bells with you, does it? I mean, you're both musicians.'

'Sasha Elias ... I don't think so. Tell you what, why don't you get in touch with Vi Sheffield.'

'Who's she?'

'You know, Mrs Sheffield, used to own the house you're living in.'

'*Vi*? Since when did you start calling her Vi?'

He considers. 'About twenty-five years ago. I used to play chess with her.'

'Why didn't you tell me?'

'I'm sure I did.'

'I'm sure I would have remembered.' He was always going off to have tea with what at the time I had considered elderly ladies. He had a way of smiling at them which made them smile back, which perhaps helped them to forget their anxieties for a while. And I'm sure they found his wiseacre manner extremely droll.

I put in a call to Braybrook Park, and am received with total incomprehension. The school has changed hands three times in the past twenty years, their records are not complete, nobody who is on the staff now was on the staff back then. After consultation with someone else in the office, I am given the name of a cousin of a current member of staff whose father-in-law might have been teaching games at the time. I write down the flimsy details I am given, though they are clearly nothing more than a dead end.

When I call the cousin, he tells me his father-in-law has Alzheimer's and lives in a home. 'Poor old boy,' he says. 'Used to be such an athlete. Now he can't even lift a cup to his lips without slopping the contents all over the place. Forgotten just about everything he ever knew, that's the problem. Anyway, even if he was still on the ball, I doubt if he'd be much use to you. He left Braybrook a good fifteen years ago.'

'Nonetheless, it might be worth asking, just in case...' I imagine lonely Sasha Elias confiding in an older man, telling him of his hopes and ambitions. But it's pointless, I know. I met Sasha myself only ten years ago. I give the man my details, without any expectation.

'Get back to you if I come up with anything,' he says. 'But don't hold your breath.'

When I telephone her, Mrs Sheffield sounds efficient and businesslike, not at all like the uncertain woman I used to know. 'I can't do Tuesday or Wednesday,' she says. 'Is Thursday all right?'

'Perfect.'

'Right, then. You'd better come to the house, not my office. So ... after working hours, okay?' She gives me instructions on how to reach her. She's living half a mile away from my flat. 'I look forward to seeing you again, Alice. It's been a long time.'

Violet Sheffield, war widow, had seemed old to my twelve year old self, and, despite her brisk telephone manner and the fact that she is speaking from an office, I am expecting to meet someone now ancient, hair pulled back in a neat bun, tissue-paper complexion, with the upright posture instilled by the governess of a gently-bred Victorian miss. An elderly woman, in other words, reduced to mulling over her memories as she faces the ending of her life with dignity and courage.

The woman who opens the door of a Queen Anne house in the town centre is in her late fifties, seems to be clearly engaged with the present and far too busy creating new memories to be wasting time on the old. I realize then when I last saw her, she can't have been much over thirty.

'Alice ... How very nice to see you,' she says, holding out her hand then, after peering at me over her rimless half-glasses, pulling me towards her to brush my cheek with hers.

'And you...' She is wearing a short turquoise dress with a long glittery scarf flung around her neck. Her tanned arms are decorated with a number of thick gold bracelets. Her hair is artificially blonde and cut à la garçonne. 'It's been such a long time. You look fabulous, Mrs Sheffield.'

'Vi, *please*. We've been through the Sixties. Those dreary bourgeois days when people your age addressed people my age as Mrs are far behind us. Thank God.'

Her metamorphosis is quite extraordinary. 'Fine.'

She pours me a stiff gin-and-tonic. 'Forgive

198

me if I sound preoccupied,' she says, 'but I'm in the middle of a very complicated deal which, if it goes through all right, should net me a very nice profit.'

'What do you do?' I dimly remember my parents exclaiming in surprise at learning that like Louise Stone, she had bought a house in the North End, which in my childhood was considered little better than a slum, and was doing it up for resale. My father had referred to the project as a disaster.

'I'm in property development.' The telephone rings and she looks at it, then at me, winks, mouths '...three, four, five,' then picks up the receiver. 'Yes?'

From her end of the subsequent conversation, I gather – I have no choice but to listen – that her deal has gone through successfully, and she will be several hundred thousand pounds better off when the papers are completed. Her house certainly emphasizes that she is doing well, full of rich fabrics, heavy drapery, voluptuous sofas, good paintings. A long long way from the genteel poverty of the house on The Beach.

'Aaah,' she says, sighing happily, running her fingers through her hair, swallowing a large amount from her own glass. She pulls out the quarter of lemon it contains and sucks it. 'Splendid! Now, Alice, you said you wanted to discuss something. How I can help you?'

In the face of such dynamism, I grow vague. She has moved on at a much faster pace than I have, so much so that I feel as though I have been beached upon the shore of a desert island.

'Not discuss, exactly. I don't really ... I just wanted to...'

'You recently bought the first-floor flat in my former house, didn't you?'

'That's right. And I wanted to...'

'Nothing wrong, is there?' She looks at me hard, focuses for the first time. 'How old are you, Alice?'

'Thirty-two.'

'Not that it's any of my business. But you seem rather ... *worn,* for someone your age.'

'I haven't been sleeping well.' I laugh slightly. 'Not that I came to consult you on sleeping pills or anything.'

'Are you married?'

'Divorced.' I shift uneasily, hating the sound of the word, hating being divorced, hating the guy I once went out with, who'd tried to come on to me using the argument that nobody misses a slice off a cut cake. Bastard! I'd poured my drink in his lap and left.

'What happened?' asks Mrs Sheffield. It's impossible to think of her as Vi.

I shrug. 'He was American. We drifted apart, I guess. And then he found someone else. It seemed best to come home to England.'

'How very *insouciante* you sound, Alice. Why did you marry him?'

'For all the wrong reasons,' I say.

'Is there anyone else?'

I hesitate. 'Sort of.'

'Whose sort of, yours or his?'

I consider. 'Maybe a bit of both.'

She leans back, crosses her legs. 'And how is

your mother?'

'She's fine. Living up in Oxford.'

'She always wanted to move back there. I hope she's happier.'

I would like to explore the possibilities implicit in that comparative. Happier than what, or when? Does she mean happier living in a city instead of beside this inhospitable bit of sea? Or simply that things have changed so much for the better?

Before I can ask, Vi is shaking her head. 'God, they were hard times, those years after the war, all of us grieving, short of cash, children to bring up, the whole country trying to come to terms with victory and its implications. I suppose at the time, Shale was as good a place to live as any. All us women, mothers, had to rely on each other in a way that's almost impossible to imagine now.'

'How is Linda?' I ask belatedly.

'Very well indeed. Two children and a third on the way,' She laughs. 'She finds it a bit irritating that I don't do the grandmother bit, babysitting and so on. I've already done that, I tell her, I'm damned if I'm doing it all over again.'

'Do please say hello from me. And from my brothers.' But I've come about something else. 'The thing is,' I say, stumbling ridiculously over the words. 'The thing is ... the apartment – the flat.'

'Yes.'

'You used to have a music teacher living there. I took some piano lessons from him one summer.'

'Yes, indeed. You and a few others, if I remember rightly. God, I'd almost forgotten him.' She pulls at her drink again, offers me her profile as she stares pensively at the portrait of an officer in naval uniform which hangs above the fireplace. 'Poor young man. Poor, poor boy. I felt terribly sorry for him, such a bedraggled sort of creature, so lost and lonely His entire family dying in the concentration camps ... how do you get over such a thing? How can you possibly?'

'I don't suppose you ever do,' I say. 'Do you have any idea where he is now?'

'None whatsoever,' she says decisively. 'Why do you ask?'

'I'd like to try and ... and track him down, if possible.'

'Why on earth ... still that's your business, not mine.'

Some explanation seemed to be called for. 'It's just ... he left some music behind, some letters, a kind of diary. I thought he might want them back.'

'Left them behind?' Mrs Sheffield frowns. 'Left them where, exactly?'

'In the piano stool ... the one that came with the papers. It's the same one as was there when I—'

'I don't know what papers you mean, but the stool was empty, last time I saw it. I emptied it myself.'

'Perhaps you're thinking of a different stool. This was one of those with a seat that lifts up—'

'I know exactly what it looks like. It came from my husband's family, along with the piano.

I hate leaving it behind, but...' She spreads her hands. '...I've been moving around such a lot.' She narrows her eyes at me. 'You look as though you don't believe me.'

'No, of course I do.'

'You can ask young Orlando, if you like. I paid him to help me clear the whole place out. Obviously this was long after your piano teacher had left.'

'But the stool's full of Sasha's stuff,' I blurt out.

'Sasha?'

'Mr Elias. There are manuscripts of pieces he composed, letters from people, this diary...'

'I can assure you that between us, Orlando and I took everything out when the place was converted,' she says. 'I didn't look at it too closely, of course. One wouldn't, after all. But since there was no means of finding him again, I kept them for a while, in case he came looking for them, and then, as I say, it was all thrown out.'

'But they're all still there,' I say. 'In the stool.'

She looks irritated at my persistence. 'They must belong to someone else. The last people to live there, perhaps.' The phone rings again and after another count of five, she picks it up. 'Yes?' Whoever is on the other end is giving her information she doesn't want to hear. 'No,' she says firmly. 'Absolutely not. I already told them the terms on which we'd buy the property and if they don't like it, they'll have to ... No, Justin, I will *not* call them myself. That's what I employ you to do.' She listens some more. 'Then you'll just have to *make* time, won't you?' Again she frowns. 'Look, I've got people here. We can discuss it tomorrow morning. Better come in early, okay?'

Replacing the handset, she turns to me again. 'I'll bet this is some trick of Orlando's! He's always been a bit of a devil, hasn't he? Why don't you ring and ask him?'

'I'll do that.'

As I am leaving, she hesitates at the door of her beautiful drawing room. 'Tell me, Alice, what brought you back here? After the ... after what happened, I should have thought it was the last place you'd want to...' She leans against the door frame, fussing with her silvery scarf.

'I ... I really couldn't tell you.' I shrug. 'Laying old ghosts to rest, I think. Or trying to.'

'Can one ever do that, I wonder?' Her expression is regretful. 'I've hung on here long enough myself. Far too long, probably.'

'Why?'

'Because when it came right down to it, I found that I simply couldn't give up all that remained of Freddie, my husband.' She gestures at the portrait on the wall. 'He was the one and only love of my life, from the very first moment we met, at a Hunt Ball in the Cotswolds, years and years ago. We were both still at school, but we knew immediately that this was it. When they told me he had died, his ship sunk with all hands, I would have killed myself without the slightest hesitation, if it hadn't been for Linda. She was three by then ... I simply couldn't imagine anyone else raising her but me.' Her voice shakes slightly. 'Me and my darling Freddie.'

'Oh, Vi,' I say, catching hold of her hand.

There are tears in her eyes. 'It's all so long ago now, and yet the pain simply never goes away. I miss him every single day of my life. Silly, isn't it?'

'I don't think so.'

She gives herself a little shake. 'Still, one has to move on, doesn't one?'

'Indeed.'

'Come and see me again, Alice, if you have time. I shan't be leaving for at least another four weeks.'

'I'll try.'

She fishes for another slice of lemon from her glass and holds it between manicured fingers. 'I do hope I'm not making a mistake, leaving, after all these years.'

'No. No, I'm sure you're not.' It's a generation ago, and yet the war continues to wrap its tentacles around our hearts.

Walking away from her house, I ponder the obvious familiarity with which she speaks of Orlando. There's a very definite sense that this is an ongoing awareness, rather than a reminiscence of the past. I wonder what he is up to, if anything.

I ponder, too, the nature of love. We're told that it is ephemeral and fleeting, its very essence ensures that it is so. Yet here was a woman, a strong and attractive one who must have faced off any number of suitors, still mourning her husband, content to have had their short time together and wanting nothing more.

205

FIVE

The full moon spills a band of quicksilver light across an anthracite sea. A faint breeze stirs the white gauze of my curtains. It's half-past ten, late enough for the last of the daylight to have gone. I stand there in nothing but a slip, sweat pooling between my breasts and at the base of my neck, wondering whether to gather together a towel and bathing suit and take a late-night swim. Orlando and I had done that occasionally, on just such nights of heat, slipping out of the bedroom we were still young enough to share, running across the green to the beach, sliding down the shingle and into the sea in a wild ecstasy of rebellion and disobedience. We had never been expressly forbidden to get out of bed and go outside late at night, but only because it had never occurred to Fiona that we might want to. I still remember how silky the water had felt along my limbs, and the shadowy swirl of waves around my body.

I remember, too, Fiona's journals, and her description, written in that thick black Indian ink, of skinny-dipping with my father in a reed-fringed pool somewhere up in the Yorkshire Dales. *'Breathless we flung us on the windy hill,'* she wrote, *'laughed in the sun and kissed the lovely grass.*' I'd tried to imagine Fiona casting herself to the earth to kiss grass, but had found it impossible. Once, with Orlando on the cliff-tops, hunting blackberries, I'd thrown myself down and pressed my face to the earth, but felt nothing much.

'What exactly are you doing, Alice?' he said.

'I'm kissing the lovely grass, like Fiona did in the Yorkshire Dales,' I told him. I quoted the line.

'Ah yes,' he said. 'Rupert Brooke. Always to be relied on for a schmaltzy sentiment. Like the potency of cheap music.'

'Why are you so cynical?' I asked.

'You could answer that yourself, especially after seeing how utterly strange it would be for anyone, Brooke, Fiona or anyone, to start kissing grass. Besides, suppose a dog had peed on it; you'd never even know.'

Brushing frantically at my mouth, I'd had to concede that he had a point.

I open the window wider, and lean forward, fanning myself. Should I go down to the edge of the sea or not? There are a few people about, dog-walkers for the most part, but also a few couples, arms around each others' waists. As I stand there, indecisive, a figure appears from the direction of the lifeboat house. A man, dark-haired, wearing a short-sleeved shirt and jeans. Backlit by the moon, he stops directly in front of my flat, separated from me by the silver-painted railings and a stretch of grass. He looks directly up at my window, and, afraid he can see me, I shrink back. In the white light of the moon reflecting off the sea, he looks so much like Sasha Elias that I almost lean from the window and call his name. But I hold back, partly because I am semi-naked, and partly because I cannot be sure. It is, after all, a good ten years since I met him in Paris.

Nonetheless, I am certain enough of his identity to rush into a pair of shorts and a yellow T-shirt, run down the communal stairs into the front garden and step out of the tall gate onto the pavement. Which way can he have gone? Whichever way he'd chosen, he should still be in sight, which he is not. Perhaps he's turned into one of the many pubs, which are still open on this humid Saturday night.

I hurry along the road that runs parallel to the promenade. At the Boatman's Arms, I peer in through the window but can't see him, or anyone remotely resembling him. It's the same at the Drum Major, the Wooden Lugger and the Admiral Nelson. I slow down. Perhaps I was mistaken. It is easily enough done in the imprecise light, especially given the distance from my window to the seafront path. Besides, what would I say if I caught up with him, if it is indeed Sasha, if I did indeed see him and it wasn't just a figment of my imagination?

So I talk myself out of any further search and go home, where I lie on top of my bedcovers and listen to the gnawing sound of the sea against the shingle, and the occasional squawk of a gull.

At two o'clock I wake from sweaty sleep. I get up and pour myself a glass of iced water. The scrap-albums which Bella brought down with her are still on the window seat, waiting for my attention, and I sit down, open the cover of the first one, look down at a photograph of Nicola. A school photograph, head and shoulders, her school tie loose at the neck, her defiance of authority still burning bright, even in newsprint, even after twenty years. I shall have to read the transcripts of the inquest which, a quick flip through the albums informs me, are all there, carefully glued to the thick card pages. But not now. I anticipate that I shall not enjoy reading these cuttings; that I shall need the steadying strength and clear colours of daylight to get through them. I will deal with them tomorrow. Or perhaps even the next day.

Instead, I return to my bed, carrying a couple of Sasha Elias's pages.

Was it Sasha I saw earlier, I ask myself, and if so, how many times has he returned to the town, walked along the front and stopped to gaze up at the windows where he once temporarily lived?

Later, I stretch out in the darkness and think, as I have done so often, about Nicola. Did she lie there among the brambles, bleeding and broken, aware that even if she had the strength or ability left to scream, no one would hear her? Did she know her killer? Did she regret anything, as life seeped out of her, or was she unconscious from the first? Could any of us have done something to save her?

Fiona believed in fresh air. She believed just as strongly in having some time to herself, because,

she said, she would otherwise go mad. So sometimes she pushed Orlando and me out of the
house and told us not to come back for five
hours. And we would set off on our bikes clutching her erratic tomato sandwiches wrapped in
the waxed inner packet of a cornflake box. I
think she hoped that we went for long bracing
bike rides along the promenade and over the
dunes, but in fact we cycled down to the town
and spent our five hours in the upstairs reading
room of the library. The librarians tolerated us
because we behaved ourselves. We didn't leave
apple cores on the shelves, or tear pages out of
the books. We didn't spill drinks on the floor.
Food was forbidden, in any case, but they might
have suspected that we were trying to sneak in a
sandwich or a packet of Smith's crisps. When we
did, we left no crumbs.

There were two librarians back then, a woman
in a lacy sort of jumper that smelled of sweat,
and Gordon Parker. Looking back, I can see that
they might from time to time have slipped
upstairs and listened outside the door of the
reading room, or even poked their heads round
the door, in order to check on us. In cold weather, they put the gas fire on for us, which popped
and burped as we read our way through the
books on the shelves which housed English
Literature, Humour, History and Travel, or
brought books up from the Children's Library.

We weren't at first allowed to take adult books
out of the library, but after a while we had
exhausted the stock of Noel Streatfeilds, Arthur
Ransomes, Richard Jefferies, Richmal Cromp-

tons. We'd zipped through the Dimsie books, the Angela Brazils, the books about girls who rode horses or learned ballet at Sadlers Wells, or boys in improbable jungle adventures, *Treasure Island*, Rider Haggard, Rudyard Kipling. They showed us another world, a place where angels and demons lurked, and there wasn't always a happy ending. We read all the different colour-ed Andrew Lang *Fairy Books,* except for *The Olive Fairy Book* because we had that at home. We read collections of Norse myths, classical legends, short stories from Russia, Lamb's *Tales from Shakespeare*, Grimm's *Fairy Tales*, *The Ingoldsby Legends*, until finally we were let loose in the adult section.

The town library now is brand new, purpose-built, three times the size of the one where Orlando and I spent so many hours. There are large windows overlooking the sea, landscaping outside the entrance, an exhibition room, and much-expanded children's and reference sec-tions. Sitting at a desk with a plastic marker saying *Chief Librarian*, a man who is unques-tionably Gordon Parker is pointing to a map of the area, his finger indicating Dover Castle.

'You mustn't miss it,' he is saying to an elderly American couple. 'It's an extremely interesting example of a traditional Norman castle, com-plete with keep and drawbridge. The first sign of trouble from the French and everyone in the town below could be accommodated within its walls. The Romans built a *pharos* up there, too.'

'Pharos?'

'A lighthouse, honey,' says the wife. They both

nod in that politely attentive way that Americans have when they're being given information.

'It's quite easy to get there on the bus,' Gordon says. 'Takes about half-an-hour, and the driver will drop you right at the entrance to the keep. I presume you've already been or are planning to go to Canterbury Cathedral.'

'We did Cannerberry two days ago.'

'I think we might just go see Dover.' The husband takes his wife's arm. 'Thank you for your help.' The two of them totter out of the library in the direction of the bus station.

As Gordon turns away, I call his name. 'Mr Parker!' He is still slim, but has lost the pinched look of the post-war years. His hair is still dark but no longer greased back, he wears contact lens instead of National Health specs.

His gaze falls on me without recognition.

'I'm sure you don't remember me,' I say. 'I'm Alice Beecham.'

'Beecham?' His high forehead wrinkles.

'From Glenfield House?'

For a moment he stiffens, and I wonder what insults the name conjures up for him. Then he smiles. 'Alice Beecham ... Goodness! Well, well, well, it *has* been a long time, hasn't it?'

'Would you have time for a coffee with me, Mr Parker?'

'Gordon, please.'

'Or let me buy you lunch.'

He looks at his watch, a wafer-slim affair on a crocodile skin strap. 'We-ell ... it's almost my lunch break, so I could take it early. And since I'm in charge of the place now, they can hardly kick me out for taking too long, can they?'

We laugh together, jolly but wary. I follow him along the front and into the only café in town, he tells me, where you can get a decent cup of espresso. The place is next door to the Top Deck, the little dance hall where Nicola was supposed to be going after my birthday party. In twenty years, it doesn't seem to have changed in any way, including its function.

'It's really lovely to see you, Alice.' Gordon folds his hands together in front of him. He wears a heavy gold signet ring on the fourth finger of his right hand and I wonder what that's meant to signify, if anything. 'So tell me, why are you here?'

'I've moved down here, if you can believe it.'

He looks searchingly at me. 'As a matter of fact, I find that difficult to understand, in the light of ... well, of what happened.'

I shrug. 'I have to live somewhere, and I like the air down here. Besides, it's all so long ago.' I'm lying, of course. 'Do you remember Mrs Sheffield?'

'Vi? Yes, of course. She sings in the same choral group as I do. A nice alto voice. We'll miss her when she goes.'

'She's converted her house on The Beach into flats and I've bought one of them.'

'Which one?'

'The big one on the first floor, with the bay window.'

'Very nice indeed. I've been there.' He reaches into the breast pocket of the Harris tweed jacket he's wearing, despite the heat, brown-and-white herringbone, plaited mock-leather buttons down the front, and pulls out a pack of cigarettes. I do hope he isn't going to light up. I can't abide second-hand smoke. He plays with the packet, but thankfully makes no move to get out his matches. 'Tell me about your mother,' he says. 'Is she well?'

'Very.'

'She was always so kind to me.' He looks out at the beach where seagulls are constantly raucous. 'I would love to see her again.'

'I know she'd feel the same. Perhaps next time she comes down to visit...'

'I really used to envy her ability to write stories. Actually, I've often wished I could write about those Glenfield House days.' He taps his cigarette pack on the table. 'On the other hand, there was quite a spate of books about families exactly like yours. *I Capture the Castle*, for instance.'

'*Our Spoons came from Woolworths,*' I say.

'*The Constant Nymph.*' He smiles. 'You and Orlando were always great readers, weren't you?'

'That's why I used to love books like that,' I say. 'They reminded me of home.'

'They always seemed to feature eccentric harried mothers just like yours.'

'And awkward girls in ill-cut grey flannel skirts.'

'Constant worries about money, an inefficient house to keep up, middle-class values to maintain,' he says enthusiastically, as though recommending the books to a dithering reader.

'Just like Glenfield.'

'Exactly. Yet, you know something?' He sips judiciously at his coffee. 'For all its eccentricities and discomforts, that house was a real refuge for me. And your mother ... she was very good to me, really took me under her wing.'

The image of Fiona as mother hen is unfamiliar to me.

'My own parents were killed in an air raid,' Gordon continues, 'and since I was an only child, without any other family, I was very much on my own.'

Although it had been my brothers who teased him, I am overwhelmed with retrospective guilt. Before I can say anything, he is reminiscing again.

'God, do you remember that evil-tempered geyser in the bathroom? I can tell you, Alice, taking a bath in your house was a definite act of courage!'

We exchange gossip for a while. He has a confiding way of putting a hand on my arm as he speaks, as though afraid I might otherwise get up and leave. I tell him about my marriage, my reasons for coming back to England, bring him up to speed on Ava's death, Dougal's life, and Callum's.

'And how is Orlando?' he asks. 'Such a brilliant boy, we used to discuss everything from Henry James to Mahler's symphonies.' He throws back his head in a shout of laughter. 'And so eccentric! Do you remember how one year he insisted on wearing a black armband throughout the holidays to mark the death of George

215

Orwell?'

'Did he?' I don't remember any such thing. Am I the one with the defective memory, or is Gordon? 'He's a musicologist now – a historical musicologist.'

'I've seen his programmes on the telly, actually. Extremely good.'

'He's attached to Cambridge University and he also has a professorship at Yale.'

'It was obvious even back then that he'd do well, whatever field he went into.' The cigarette pack taps against the table top. 'I hope you won't mind me saying that I thought you children were absolute menaces,' he continues. 'But your nuisance value was quite offset by the fact that you were all so ... so *interesting*. It's a funny thing to say about kids, really.'

'Were you happy back then?' I ask.

He frowns, considering the question. 'Not exactly *un*happy,' he says eventually, 'But certainly not happy the way I am today. For one thing, I fit into my own skin now, and back then, I didn't. And then we were all so desperately poor, with the war so recently ended. Not just individuals, but the nation, trying to put our former enemies back on their feet before getting back on our own. But things are so much better now, aren't they? Especially now that we've passed through the Sixties, been set free, as it were.'

I wonder if there is a message encoded in his words. 'What I wanted to ask you, Gordon, is whether you have any idea what happened to Sasha Elias.'

'Who was that?'

'That sad German refugee who lodged with Mrs Sheffield.'

'Oh, him. Yes, of course, silly me, I knew him very well. As a matter of fact, the Music Society had several musical soirées in his flat – your mother came to one of them and played the viola. And I remember Orlando coming along one evening, singing a couple of folk songs with Vi Sheffield. She has such a fine alto voice, and he improvised a descant so beautifully that it literally brought tears to the eyes. You could see how he got a scholarship to the choir school.'

I try not to look disbelieving. I didn't know Orlando had done that. Nor Fiona. What else had I missed? Had I only seen the woods, and never any of the individual trees?

'Yes,' Gordon chatters on. 'Elias was an eccentric kind of person, I thought. One evening he played the Goldberg Variations, wearing a red brocade jacket instead of the usual tails.'

'Sounds rather fun.'

'Not only that ... after a bit, he took off the jacket to give us the benefit of his braces! Rainbow-coloured, if you can believe it, and about three inches wide. Well! ... it wasn't quite what we were used to in Shale, I can tell you. But he did play very beautifully...'

'So he stayed on down here, did he?'

'Not for all that long, as I remember. Maybe a couple of years. Actually...' He leaned forward. '...there were quite a lot of people here who thought he might have had something to do with that murder. You know, that Nicola girl.

Malicious little thing, I thought she was. Always making unpleasant remarks. Personally, I would not have blamed him if he *had* killed her.'

'So they were obviously able to prove that he had nothing to do with it.'

'There was never any actual *proof*, if that's what you mean.'

'Gordon, that's just spiteful gossip. There was absolutely nothing to tie Sasha in with her.'

'He taught her piano, didn't he? And, rumour hath it, a little more besides.'

'That's rubbish. Just something Nicola said to cause trouble. In any case, he was at my house that night. You might just as well say *you* were under suspicion.'

'*Moi*? *Highly* unlikely, my dear.'

'Anyway, I don't believe he had anything to do with it.' My voice is brisk and positive, though I have no evidence to back up my conviction. My head is full of heat; I feel vaguely nauseous.

'I don't mind saying I always had my suspicions about Ava Carlton's husband. You were probably too young to remember him, but he hung around for quite a long time, that summer, and after. A rough sort of bloke, if ever I saw one. And I saw him talking to Nicola on more than one occasion. In fact, I told the police as much, when they interviewed me. There was another guy, too, always sitting on a bench along the front. I mentioned him to Fiona, as a matter of fact, and I think she Had a Word with him.' He laughs affectionately. 'Your mother's Words were usually pretty effective.'

It seemed fairly clear that whatever Gordon's

reasons for staying here so long, they had nothing to do with Nicola's death, since he seemed completely unaffected by it. But why should he be? If Nicola had been acting true to form, she probably made his life hell. In any case, there was no reason for him to move on, apart from the fact that he originally came from somewhere else. 'So, you don't know what happened to Mr Elias?'

'I'm afraid not.'

Is he telling me the truth? 'You sound as though you were friends, through your choral group and musical evenings. Wouldn't he have said something to you about where he was going, or what he was going to do?'

'Well, it would probably have had something to do with music. I seem to remember vaguely that he took another job in a school somewhere in London, but once he'd left, I never heard a dicky-bird. Now, Prunella Vane – *such* an unfortunate name – always so edgy and brittle, wasn't she? Always so determined that nobody was going to put anything over on her – I know *precisely* what happened to her, because believe it or not, we still keep in touch.'

'So where did she go?'

'She threw up teaching, and took jobs all over the place, as what they used to call a cook-general, until she'd saved up enough money, then she went out to France, bought somewhere near Avignon or somewhere, and set up a cooking school. Very successful I believe, though you'd imagine there was a touch of the coals-to-Newcastle about it, wouldn't you, an Englishwoman teaching cookery in France?'

'I suppose so. Who else is still here from the old days?'

'A lot more than you'd think.' He made a face. 'Including that bastard of an art teacher ... Bertram Yelland.'

'What?' Here was another piece of information linking me to those long-ago days, that summer of continuous heat. 'He lives down here?'

'Not permanently, thank God, or I might just have to slit my wrists! What a bully he was, swaggering about the place, talking in that well-bred over-loud voice of his. I remember him chasing after young Orlando once with a mop! Picked it straight out of the bucket where Ava had left it, dripped a trail of cold grey bubbles all over the house.' Gordon shudders. 'Ghastly man. I told him off once when you, poor little thing that you were, burst into tears when he rushed at you with a knotted wet towel.'

'What happened?' Do I remember this occasion? I'm not sure.

'My *dear*! He actually turned on me, flicking that wet towel at me, and, I may say, raising several nasty welts on my arm before I could reach the safety of my own room and slam the door in his ugly mug.'

I'm touched by this portrait of Gordon as knight errant. 'Thank you, that's sweet of you.'

'It wasn't the first time, either. Remember that lapsed nun, nice looking woman?'

'Attila the Nun?'

'Personally, I called her Angela, that being her name,' he says drily. 'Yelland was always pestering the poor girl. I had a few words with him about it, which he didn't like at all, but in the end she had to leave, couldn't take him hanging about trying to get her into bed.'

'I didn't know anything about that.' I wonder if Orlando did.

'Frankly, I don't know why your mother didn't have one of her famous Words with *him*.'

'Orlando tells me Mr Yelland's become quite a well-known painter.'

'More's the pity. When he announced that he was going to fulfil his dreams and become an artist, I did *so* hope he'd prove to be a total failure. But no such luck. He paints portraits, mostly. Always seems to have something in the Royal Academy summer show. He had an exhibition last year in one of the Bond Street galleries and I read the reviews, the usual claptrap that art critics like to indulge in. I'm extremely glad to say that they all seemed to be of the opinion that this show wasn't a patch on his last one, and that basically Yelland was past his prime.'

He grimaces and I see long-ago insults burn and hum across his face. 'Serve the son-of-a-bitch bloody well right, I say. You wouldn't believe how many times I wanted to smash my fist into that smug jeering face of his, push those large teeth down his foul-mouthed throat. I'll tell you what, Alice, I'd do it now, all right. Wouldn't hesitate for a second. But back then ... well, I was hardly a prepossessing specimen, was I? If it had come to fisticuffs, I was well aware who'd have come off worst.'

'He was a pretty nasty bit of work, wasn't he?'

221

I wonder at the suppressed rage still seething beneath Gordon's bland surface. I'd seen him as mild-mannered and inoffensive, but perhaps he had always been this angry.

'The interesting thing – or the unfortunate thing, depending on your point of view – is that he recently bought one of the cottages down at the North End. Since you left, they've all been gentrified like mad. Very picturesque. It's a regular artists' colony down there now.'

'But he always seemed so keen to get away from here. I wonder why he chose to come back.'

'He only comes for the occasional weekend, but in summer you often see him swanning down the High Street, looking like Oscar Wilde on a bad day, condescending left, right and centre. Thank God it doesn't occur to him to visit the public library or God knows what trouble he'd get up to.'

With difficulty, I try to imagine Bertram Yelland as the Prince of Chaos, barging into the quiet purlieus of the library and causing mayhem, flinging books about, perhaps, or overturning the stacks, sabotaging the filing system, hectoring the librarians.

Gordon rubs warily at his eyes. 'Do you remember those hideous spectacles we had to wear just after the war? National Health they called them; national hindrance would be more like it.'

'They *were* pretty ugly.'

'If I'd had the money back then, I'd gladly have spent it on a decent pair of glasses, even if it meant wearing the same collar two days running or not having my shoes repaired. "Trouble with you, my boy," my mother used to say – before she died, this is – "you've got ideas above your station.'"

'Was she right?'

He smiles at me. 'I didn't have much choice, really, my station at the time being so low that any idea at all would have been above it. Anyway, all that's changed. Thank God for contact lenses, I say, even though they sometimes make my eyes look a bit red.' He glances at his watch.

I can take a hint. 'Gordon, it's been wonderful to catch up with you again. I hope we can meet up soon. You must come round for a drink, once I'm settled.'

'I'd love that.' His voice glows. 'Give me your phone number, and if I find anything more about your friend Elias, I'll let you know.' Getting to his feet, he adds kindly, 'This is a nice place to live, Alice, even if it's not a vast metropolis. There's quite a bit going on, in an amateur sort of way: book groups, the Drama Society, Ramblers Association, plenty of musical events of one kind and another. Talking of which...' He delves into the breast-pocket of his jacket. '...there's a nice concert coming up soon: piano, solo soprano – Helena Wilburton, if you've heard of her – and the Choral Group is singing some madrigals.'

'Thanks, Gordon.' I'm really touched by his thoughtfulness. 'I'll definitely be there.'

'Good. Meanwhile, I'm sure you'll be very happy here, and I sincerely hope you find whatever it is you're looking for.'

'So do I.' Our eyes meet. I wonder how he can be so sure that I am needy. Perhaps he is aware that what I want most is to achieve the same peace of mind that he clearly has. Apart from his feelings about Bertram Yelland.

Twenty years ago, there was obviously far more friction swirling around our house than I had been aware of. In fact, given what I had learned from Vi Sheffield, there was obviously far more of almost everything going on than I had realized.

SIX

'Where are you, Orlando?'

'In Boston.'

'When are you coming back here?'

'Why? Is something wrong?'

'Not really.' I am rolling the pearl recovered from the marble crevices of my mantel between my thumb and first finger. 'Orlando, you didn't tell me you used to go to Gordon Parker's evenings.'

'Didn't I?'

'And you didn't tell me you did stuff with Mrs Sheffield, either.'

'Stuff?'

'Don't be obtuse, Orlando. You know perfectly well I'm talking singing duets with her, helping her clear out her house, all sorts of...' I'm not quite sure why I feel so indignant.

'I'm sure I did tell you.'

'You didn't. Whereas I told you *everything*.'

'Everything? Alice, are you sure?'

'Yes.' I think about it. 'Everything I *did*, even if not everything I thought. I never went anywhere without you, you always knew what I was doing.' Yet, sliding back to that last summer, I can see that I am not entirely truthful. My loyalties lay for a while with Nicola rather than with him; I took her side, not his. And she has come between us again. I have kept things from him, just as he obviously keeps them from me. Which does not prevent me from feeling betrayed.

There is a pause and I can hear the thin line of a flute playing behind him, laughter, someone running arpeggios up and down a keyboard. I feel excluded. Lost. Pressing my nose to the window of someone else's life, without the slightest hope of ever being invited in.

'When you bought me that painting, after I moved in here, did you know that Bertram Yelland has a house in the North End?'

'As a matter of fact, I did.'

'Orlando, you seem to have kept an awful lot of things to yourself. What else should you be telling me now instead of letting me finding it out by accident?'

'Why *should* you be told anything?'

Suddenly, I feel exhausted. 'Stop quibbling, and tell me when you're coming home.'

'When would you like me to come home?'

'Right now, since you ask,' I say, aware of how

childish I sound.

'Complicated to organize,' he says.

'When then?'

'As soon as it's feasible. I'll let you know. But I'll definitely be back in England in time for your birthday – even if the President himself asks the Musick Consort to perform at the White House – about which, I may say, there have been rumours.'

'Wow!'

'I know. Depending on your political views, it could either mean a huge boost for chamber music in the US, or the kiss of death!'

Listening to the cadences of his voice, picturing his familiar face, the way he holds the phone to his ear, the silvery silkiness of his hair, I am suddenly overwhelmed. 'Orlando...' Tears fill my eyes and I start to sob.

'What's the matter?'

'I feel so lonely.'

'Oh, Alice, sweet Alice. It breaks my heart to hear you cry.'

'I keep seeing her,' I say.

'No doubt we both will until the end of our days. But you must think of other things. Go for a walk. See friends. Take on more work. It'll pass. It always does.'

'I miss you,' I say. 'I wish you were here.'

'Believe me, so do I.'

I replace the receiver. I'm beginning to wish I hadn't so hastily cut myself off from the metropolis. In London, I had friends and interests; despite my brave words to Erin, down here there is very little of either. At least I have my work.

And I can always go for a walk. Which I do very shortly, three miles along the seafront to the grassy headland. And as I walk, I wonder just how many other things Orlando knows and hasn't told me.

On my way back, I climb the steep little path between overarching trees and step out on to rough grass. It's all exactly as I remember it, even the Secret Glade, though when I get nearer, I can see that it is overgrown now, the patch of grass in the middle vanished beneath further long curls of brambles to make a single large clump. Unreachable now unless the picker is prepared for considerable damage to tender flesh, the berries tantalize, plumply ripe, lustrously black. The police must have searched the place for clues at the time, but I can't help wondering what lies buried under that thicket of thorns: did they ever find whatever was used to smash her head in, for instance? If not, do they have any idea what instrument had been used to inflict such damage? If I'm determined to find out, my best line of information is probably Gordon Parker.

Another night of shimmering heat. Restless, I stand at the open window staring out to sea. There are lights in the town and I know I can always go and have a drink in a pub or eat at the Chinese restaurant that has braved the frontiers of provincial England and set up in the High Street. Or visit the town's only cinema. Or simply idle along the front while the sea gnaws and nibbles at the shingle.

227

I do none of these things. Instead I sit down and pull another of Sasha Elias's sheets of paper into the light of the lamp. I wonder what I am looking for. If I could find him, unasked questions might be answered, including the one that still bothers me: why he did not get in touch with me again in Paris?

My telephone rings with an urgent commission from Brussels: a hefty number of pages on some complication to do with the coal and steel industries, three days to complete, they will send a courier, they will pay a great deal of money if I think I can get the job done in time, they particularly asked for me since I have the reputation not only of doing a good job but also of getting work in on time. I tell them I can do it, and stay up most of the night to get a head start.

For once, sleep comes easily. I am up again by ten, and seated at my desk. I wear cut-offs and a sleeveless white blouse that ties at the waist. Orlando is right. Work chases away the demons, puts the world into perspective. Under my bare feet, the pile of the rug is smooth, almost sensuous.

At two o'clock, I take a break, eat a salad of cos lettuce and tiny brown local shrimps from the fishmonger, with a slice of wholemeal brown bread and a knob of Caerphilly. I missed cheese in the States. With a cup of coffee to hand, I settle down again to my work. By seven o'clock, from the all-seeing eye of my window I watch the shadows beginning to slant across the green, adding a certain gravitas to the day, a reminder of men coming home from work, sailors returning from the sea, of suppers to be prepared, children to round up. The sea is clustered with white sails as the members of the sailing club come in to shore.

Louise Stone walks along the front with her little dachshund trotting beside her. Despite my deadline, I put down my pen, slip sandals on to my bare feet and hurry after her. She wears a dress that floats behind her like a sail. From behind, she could be a girl. I wonder how it feels to have lost a child, especially a child as wilful, as wicked, as Nicola. There must have been so many occasions when she wished her daughter were elsewhere. How often I've reconstructed that afternoon when she heard that Nicola was dead, and wondered whether I'd correctly remembered how the expression of shock and horror and pain which crossed her face had been prefaced by a fleeting, shamefaced look of relief.

She is a brisk walker and it takes me a while to catch up with her. We are away from the houses now. On our left is the shelving beach and the sea; to our right are the shallow cliffs still tangled with bramble bushes, and above them, the short smooth run of grass leading to the Secret Glade. 'Mrs Stone!' I call.

She stops, turns to face me, eyebrows raised in enquiry at the summons from a stranger, then her face softens. 'My goodness, it's Alice, isn't it?'

'That's right.'

'You haven't changed a bit, even after all this time.'

'Nor you.' I fall into step beside her as the little

229

dog frisks along in front of us.

She smiles. 'I knew you'd turn into a beauty.'

'Well...' It's difficult to know how to answer this without simpering. 'Thank you.'

'Not that it's any of my business,' she says, 'but what are you doing here? I thought you were long gone.'

I explain my circumstances. The divorce, the move to England, my work, the compulsion that led me down here. 'And you've not moved away, after all these years,' I say. It's a question, though it sounds like a statement.

'That's right.' She seems on the verge of saying more, then leaves the syllables in the air without further expanding on them.

I want to ask her so many things but my thoughts feel stuck in quick-setting glue. There is almost no subject I can bring up which won't refer back in some way to Nicola. Why had I ever thought I could talk to Louise about her dead daughter? It's the very last thing I can mention. Even asking after her son, or mentioning Sasha Elias, or any of the people from those days who she might still remember would have the same effect. 'Do you still work in fashion?' I ask finally.

'Yes. It's good to have a profession which doesn't entail going into an office every morning,' she says. 'You must feel the same.'

'Yes.' We discuss our different jobs for a while. The dog sniffs among the stems of pink and scarlet valerian which push through the shingle on our left, interspersed with tall stands of withered tawny grass and fading yellow

230

flowers whose name I don't know. The path veers slightly, away from the sea, magnifying the sound of waves crunching the pebbles at the edge of the shelved beach.

'And how is the lovely Orlando?' Louise asks. 'Such a charming boy. So mature for his age, so gifted.' She sighs. 'How I envied your mother.'

Again, I expatiate on Orlando and his career. 'And ... Simon?' I ask tentatively.

'He's fine. Doing really well. He has his own little business now.'

'Doing what?'

'Well...' She laughs a little hesitantly. '...to tell you the truth, I'm not really sure. I mean, he makes widgets of some kind, but I don't know what they are. Something really essential for boatbuilders, I know that. He turned into something of an inventor, in the end.'

'Is he married?'

'Yes indeed, to a lovely girl, Vicky. They have two adorable little boys, Vincent and Martin. They're living in Norfolk, now, and we see them quite often, much more than when they were living in Singapore.'

I wonder who this 'we' is. Inevitably, the shadow of Nicola, the children she will never have, the dreams she never fulfilled, walks between us. I look at my watch. 'I'd better be getting back,' I say, falsely reluctant. 'I have an urgent deadline.'

We say our farewells. She does not suggest that we meet again; given the particular flat I have chosen to live in, I do not invite her to come round sometime, not wanting to revive unhappy memories. As I turn, I catch a whiff of her perfume and suddenly I am transported back twenty years, Nicola and I are in Louise's bedroom, dabbing that same perfume behind our ears. I see Nicola's tiny frame, her mother's jewelled bracelets dancing up her arm, diamond earrings swinging, a heavy gold locket round her neck, over the thin gold chain she always wore. I see her snapping open her mother's enamelled compact and dabbing powder over her freckles, her greenish eyes narrowed as she looks around for some further mischief to make. I see, too, the photograph beside the bed of a man in a double-breasted suit and a stylish black fedora that shadows his face as though he were a black-and-white movie star, and the way Nicola's expression tightens suddenly as she briefly glances at it. 'I know, let's try on Mum's evening dresses,' she says, her voice suddenly shrill.

'Won't she be cross?' I wonder, but she ignores me and opens a wardrobe, brings out a couple of silk gowns and hastily pulls one on over her clothes. It sticks, refuses to slide down her body, caught on a button or a zip. She swears, her head swathed in material, pulling at the dress. I hear the silk rip, see Nicola's hands tug fiercely at the delicate material, her fingers finding the slash and widening it, the pretty pea-green dress ruined.

'Nicola!' I gasp, and she stares at me, her eyes cold.

'She won't say anything, even if she finds it.' Pulling herself out of the dress, she bundles it up and throws it into a dark corner of the wardrobe.

As I open the door to my flat, the phone rings and I snatch it up as though I had been waiting for it for days. 'Yes?'

'I just wanted to check up on you, see if you're all right.'

It's Orlando. His voice soothes me, sets things back to rights. 'Fine,' I say. 'I'm fine. Guess what? I've just been for a walk with Louise Stone.'

'So she's still living down there.'

'Slightly odd, isn't it, given the circumstances?'

'You'd think she'd want to get away, start afresh.'

'Can you imagine Fiona going on living in the same place, if it had been one of us?'

'Oddly enough,' says Orlando slowly. 'I think I can. If it was the place where the last memories she had of us ... if it was all of us there was left.'

'I suppose.'

Nicola sways between us in her torn white blouse, her rumpled denim skirt, constantly being destroyed by someone's rage, or hate, or frustration.

'Was she wearing a gold chain?' I say suddenly.

'What, when we first saw the ... the body? I don't remember.'

'She always used to.'

'Yes,' he says. 'She did.'

'Thing is, I'm fairly sure it wasn't round her neck when we found her.'

'Do you think the murderer took it?'

'It can't have been very valuable, surely.'

233

'Nor can I believe she was murdered for gain.'

'I suppose it could have been torn off during the ... the attack, and fell into the grass. But then the police would have found it.'

'We wouldn't know whether they did or not.'

'I could ask someone.'

He sighs. 'Alice, you need to put all this behind you. It's long gone now.'

'And it's still right there with us, Orlando. It's the same for you as for me. You said then that you would never ever forget it – and you never ever will.'

'This is true.'

'What bugs me so much is that, if you exclude passing tramps, the murderer is almost bound to be someone we knew. Maybe even someone we liked.'

'I know.'

'Funny,' I say, 'that she wasn't ... she wasn't sexually molested.'

'And what conclusion do we draw from that?'

'That the motive wasn't sexual, I suppose. But she wasn't wearing underpants when we discovered her, was she?'

'No.'

'I wonder if they ever found them.'

'I doubt it. She wasn't wearing any that evening,' Orlando says.

'How would you know that?'

'She hardly ever did. Surely you must have realized. We all knew, all us boys.'

Not wearing underpants? I couldn't have imagined that anyone would dare to go out of the house without them. Or even walk around *inside* the house. I glimpse again, through the curtain of the past, Julian hunched over himself, Charlie's shamefaced smirk, David's hot eyes, while Nicola sat in a corner of the chesterfield in our drawing room. It never occurred to me. Why would it?

Time folds in on itself. At one and the same time I'm standing here, an adult watching the moon slant across the sea, looking at the way my white curtains wave in the cool salt air coming through the window and the ivory glimmer of the magnolias in the next-door garden, and I am also a child again, staring at a dead girl's body, blackberry juice staining my fingers, the scent of crushed grass giving a deceptive air of normality to something which is so abnormal as to be incomprehensible.

'Knickerless Nicola, Charlie used to call her,' Orlando says.

'You never liked her.'

'I loathed her. She was a vicious little creature. But even so, nobody could have wished such a death on her.'

'I know. Oh God. Orlando. It's all so terrible. And it goes *on* being terrible, even after all this time. It's like a curse.'

'It *is* a curse. It's *our* curse, and there's nothing we can ever do about it.'

'Would it make any difference if we knew who was responsible?'

'Knowing's not going to expunge what we saw.'

'It's the same time of year here. The black-berries are ripening, and it's another boiling hot

235

summer, just like then.' Through the window I see the garden gate open and Mrs Sheffield appear. Walking up the path, she glances at my windows, but doesn't see me. 'Orlando,' I tell him. 'I have to go. Mrs Sheffield's come to call. Vi, I suppose I should call her.'

'Say hello from me,' he says, and there is laughter in his voice. 'Give her my very fondest love. And keep some for yourself, Alice, sweet Alice.'

'My dear, how pleasant you've made it.' Vi sits in my big armchair. I've shown her round, poured her a drink, pushed some olives in her direction. 'Modernizing the bathroom and kitchen makes such a difference. And you're so wise to have the window-seat built in. I never got round to it before the war and afterwards, well, there just wasn't any money. You've done a really nice job in here.'

'Well, it's a lovely room to start with.'

'It was our drawing-room, of course, when Freddie was alive. We used to love looking out at the sea.'

'Me too.'

'Endlessly fascinating, isn't it? You wait until you see it in the winter storms.' She laughs. 'But of course you've been here in winter, haven't you? I keep forgetting.' She glances at the piano stool. 'Did you ever sort out about the music?'

'Not yet.'

'Orlando – I'm sure it's something to do with him.'

'I can't quite see why. By the way, he sent –

and I quote – his very fondest love.'

'Did he indeed?' She raises an eyebrow. 'He always was a charmer.'

'Still is, I guess.'

'He was such a funny little boy. So amazingly bright, so solemn. I do hope he's happy.'

Orlando's happiness is something it has never occurred to me to question. Is he? I am ashamed that I never thought to ask. 'He seems to be.'

Her gaze takes in my work table and the open books and papers. 'Look, my dear, I know you're tremendously busy, and I don't want to take up your time. But the reason I've come – apart from inquisitiveness, because I wanted to see what you've done to the place – the reason is I thought I'd have a farewell party before I shake the dust of the place off my feet, and I'd really love you to come.'

'That would be great.'

She gives me the date, a Saturday four weeks from now, in mid-September. The year is already turning. In the gardens along The Beach, dry brown leaves drop lightly to the dry soil beneath and gather at the edge of flower beds. Not autumn, not yet, but preparing.

'The movers will be coming in on the following Monday, so it's the last opportunity I'll have to say goodbye to everyone,' she says. 'And if by any chance your lovely Orlando is around, you absolutely must bring him. I'll hope very much to see him.'

'As a matter of fact, he will be. My birthday's around that time and he's coming down.'

'Yes.' She frowns. 'Of course, I should have

237

remembered. It was at your birthday party that poor Louise Stone's daughter was killed, wasn't it?'

'Not *at*, so much as *after*. And somewhere else.' I make a sudden decision. 'As a matter of fact, I was thinking of having a few people here, a sort of combination house warming and birthday. Do come.'

'I'd love to.' Standing up, she smiles at me, puts her hand on my shoulder. 'I hope it all works out for you, Alice.'

Once, I'd thought she was as old as the hills. Watching her walk away from me into the hazy glow of the town, she seems to carry her years far more lightly than I do. I hope it works out for me, too. I stare at the telephone. Shall I lift it, dial Orlando's number, ask him if he's happy?

I don't. Perhaps I'm afraid of the answer.

SEVEN

By six o'clock, the courier has roared away down the road with my manuscript translation stowed in his saddlebag. The evening stretches ahead of me, flat and uneventful. I am not only restless but also uneasy, besieged by insistent ghosts.

Seated at the piano, I play for a little, but am unimpressed by my lack of expertise. Once, although I was never gifted in the way Orlando is, I was considered an adequate player. Not any more. *Muss i' denn*, I sing softly. *Must I then, must I then, to the city away, and leave my heart here?*

Where is Sasha Elias now? He hovers between the folds of my gauzy white drapes. Because of him, I dreamed away my adolescence; his memory still hangs over me, weighting me down. I know how foolish I am. Apart from a brief meeting, I haven't set eyes on the man for twenty years. He could be anything now, anywhere. He probably barely remembers me. I know all the counsels of wisdom that I must move on, that what I remember is an adolescent fantasy. Yet I cannot help recalling the green star in his eye, the aniseed smell, the touch of the exotic that he brought to my dreary post-war life.

If only I could find him again, surely, surely I would be able to let slip the dogs of the past? But so far, my enquiries have led me nowhere. I am not sure exactly what I search for. A final end to Nicola, a new beginning with Sasha? Is either possible?

My morning's mail waits for me on the marble mantel. I slit open envelopes containing bills for this and that, brochures, a request from a publishing house wanting to discuss a translation of one of their prestigious foreign authors. There are personal letters, too. One from Fiona, one from Bella, Orlando's weekly news bulletin. I glance through the first two then more slowly read the third, typed on a piece of A4 paper. He

239

tells me more about his work in Boston, critiques a concert he has attended, writes an account of a trip to Atlanta. Ends by saying that he'll see me soon.

His voice echoes in my ear. Eventually I put his letter back on my work table and get up, find my keys, go out into the night. Warm air sits on my shoulders like a feather boa. Behind curtained windows, lamps glow. In the yacht club, steel cables tap faintly against aluminium masts.

I walk a couple of hundred yards down the road to Glenfield House and stand looking over the garden wall. The front garden is shadowed, the hedge separating it from the gravelled drive is neatly trimmed, giving off the faintly sour scent of privet in summer. I can smell something dry and peppery – early chrysanthemums, perhaps – and a faint drift of dying phlox.

None of the windows in the house are illuminated, and with a quick look up and down the pavement I slip inside the gate and tiptoe alongside the hedge until I reach the gap which leads into the front garden. The eight cast-iron steps from what had once been our drawing room are freshly painted and gleam in the street light's glare. I stand on the top step. There is the occasional sound of cars in the distance, the rustle of leaves from the shrubbery, a radio playing, seagulls shutting down for the night. Inside the bamboo clump, the lily-pond frogs chatter gently.

I close my eyes. Force myself to concentrate, blocking out the lights, the sounds of the here

240

and now, thrusting myself back into the past. What really happened that night? Twenty years ago I'd stood exactly where I am now, and seen Nicola turn, heard the squeak of the gate opening, behind the hedge. In the drawing room behind me, people had been moving *en masse* towards the dining room, and after a moment, I'd trailed after them. Was there something I'd seen which if only I could prise it from the locked box of the past, might provide some clue?

Concentrate, Alice. If you saw anything, it must still be lodged inside your skull.

She'd been standing by the hedge. Inside the drawing-room, Leslie Hutchinson crooning *Smoke Gets In Your Eyes* was playing on the turntable. I could hear Callum's voice calling to someone, the laughter of girls, someone singing along to Hutch. Anything else? *Think*, Alice.

I try to squeeze the memories from the vault at the back of my head where I've contained them for so long, but I can dredge up nothing that seems remotely significant. I'd watched Nicola for a moment or two, that's all, then turned away and followed the crowd into the passage leading to the dining room, hurrying so I could accidentally find myself standing beside Sasha Elias.

The hall: as I mentally pass through, I recreate it in my mind. It's the same as it always was. The oak chest against one wall, with a bowl of flowers I'd picked from the garden. The threadbare carpet-runner across the coloured tiles. A print of the Lady of Shallott in a dark oak frame. The carved stand holding walking sticks, golf putters, silver-topped canes, a spear.

I move on to the dining room. Like an artist using charcoal to block out a painting, I try to sketch in the scene. The background first: the silky blue wallpaper, a marble fire surround, the uncurtained window at the far end. Makeshift tables set up down the middle of the room, spread with bedsheets worn so thin that in places you can see the grain of the wood beneath. Platters of sandwiches, sausage rolls, savoury tarts, fairy cakes, buns, bowls of trifle and jelly, and in pride of place, my birthday cake, with my name picked out in shiny silver pellets. There is damp on one of the walls, which has stained the paper black. Waxed paper cups stand at the end of one table, with big jugs of orange squash and lime juice cordial, a barrel of cider rests on a cradle suspended above a galvanized iron bath tub recovered from the stables. I try to paint in the faces, though some of the people there I'd never seen before, friends of my brothers, for the most part, or lame ducks swept in under Fiona's wing.

Inside my head, they are gathered together, each in his or her allotted space, as though our dining room has become one of those paper puppet theatres Fiona used to build for us. Just as we used to cut the splendidly Jacobean characters out of a book and stick them to slices of cork, then push them around the stage using knitting needles, so now I push them around my head.

Ava stands by one of the tables, looking carefree but in reality keeping an eye on the family to make sure they don't help themselves too lavishly before the guests are fed. As she talks to Louise Stone, she takes dainty bites from a crustless sandwich. Not far from her is Bertram Yelland, in a canary-coloured waistcoat over an open-necked white shirt into which he's tucked a paisley cravat. He looks rather handsome and from my current vantage point, I can see how young he must have been back then, however old he'd seemed at the time.

There is Prunella Vane, talking to Fiona, while Gordon Parker listens. Each time he nods, a flake of sausage-roll pastry stuck to his lower lip bobs in time. My elder brothers are huddled together near the cider barrel, along with their friends – who seem to include Simon Stone, Nicola's brother. They're laughing a lot. Sasha is there, in the middle of the room, among a group of his pupils and their mothers. A pair of small round spectacles, different from the ones he habitually wears, sits at the top of his nose, giving him a more serious air, as though he is hoping to establish a certain gravitas. He's in his early twenties, I see now, little more than a boy. There are lines under his eyes and a sad twist to his mouth, and I remember how I wanted to cross the room and stand beside him. There are other mothers too. I see Mrs Sheffield, Mrs Tavistock, Mrs Gardner, Mrs Arbuthnot. They are talking, and I remember now how they looked over at him, Mrs Arbuthnot saying she had taken Mary away from him, there were *rumours*, you can't take the chance, can you, not with young girls, she'd heard that a couple of other mothers were removing their daughters, too.

Aunt had been down earlier before retreating upstairs to her room, but there are still two or three old ladies sitting on chairs in their flowered Liberty prints, drinking white wine and cackling slightly, obviously enjoying themselves. In the light from the candles, which Ava and Fiona have set all round the place, their ancient faces melt and blur, and they appear young again, transported for a moment from the end of their lives back to the beginning. There is the man from next door, a retired Rear Admiral, who is wearing baggy yellow corduruoys; there are some of the teachers from Fiona's school; there are a few other neighbours. And Bella, of course, talking to the young Tavistock sisters, and Jeremy's orphaned girl-cousin who lives with them and goes to Bella's school.

But Nicola?

I can't see her, but she must have been there. Someone would have noticed otherwise. Now the puppets in my head move, mingle, form new groups. Dougal has his arm around some girl's waist. Orlando sits down with the old ladies, says something that makes them chortle, refills their glasses. My father talks to Callum by the door. Louise Stone glances round the room and then at her son, who is leaning with one hand against the wall while he talks to Mary or Rosie. Miss Vane is here, Ava there, Bertram by the sideboard. Gordon Parker droops beside the cider barrel, Sasha stands with an elbow on the mantelpiece, surveying the room, Julian and Charlie, David and Jeremy stand in a group with their mothers, then with each other. Orlando moves over to the window and looks out, his back to the room.

And then Nicola appears. She pauses at the door of the room and a small silence falls. I'd forgotten that moment, but now it comes back to me very clearly, how all of us stopped what we were doing to take her in, a girl in a denim skirt and home-made white blouse. The candles shimmer on the thin gold chain round her neck and the little golden studs in her ears. She remains on the threshold and surveys us without smiling, without speaking. And everyone stares back at her. Everyone except Orlando.

She was powerful. I recognize that now. She had no regard for convention. She did what she liked, and what she liked most was the danger of not caring. Young and old, whether we knew her or not, we recognized something alarming about her. From my adult perspective, I can see now how damaged her soul was, how disabled her heart.

Julian breaks away from his friends and pushes through the crowd but she turns a shoulder to him and he steps back, crestfallen. She smiles faintly. The Admiral stares at her and smoothes down his tobacco-stained moustache; his tongue emerges like a swollen red slug and rasps across his lower lip. Miss Vane is holding a paper plate containing a bit of everything; she flushes as Nicola moves past her, puts the plate down on the table, takes one of the little savoury tarts she has made and nibbles at it. Yelland was laughing when she appeared. Now he stands very still as though waiting for Armageddon. Again, now I am an adult, I can see how vulnerable he must have felt, for Nicola was under-age and he could have gone to prison if she chose to broadcast what the two of them had been doing. Sasha Elias, too, watches as she moves into the room, and so does Dougal, a slight frown on his face. Her brother Simon looks wary and resigned; perhaps he recognizes the sign of imminent or recent mischief-making and wonders who is about to become her next victim.

The moment stretches yet can only have lasted for a couple of seconds before everyone returns to what they were doing. Orlando is still at the window with his back to her, peering out into the darkness. Has he seen someone out there? Nicola moves across the room towards him, taking a sausage roll from the table and cramming it into her mouth, picking up a sandwich. What does she want from him? He can see her reflection in the dark glass, he knows she is there behind him. Even when she is standing beside him, he doesn't turn. She says something to him, one small hand gesticulating, the other lifting the sandwich to her mouth. He jerks round and looks at her, his eyes full of loathing.

He says nothing, merely walks away from her as though she weren't there and she swings round to watch him as he stops beside Sasha Elias. Fiona joins them, and Mrs Sheffield. They look down at him, their expressions soft as he speaks, this lovely boy stroking the patch of silver hair above his ear, tightening the knot of his silk tie. Pink silk. I shake my head. It's taken me all this time to realize that he must have chosen the tie from my father's wardrobe to go with my dress of old rose brocade.

Fiona is staring at Nicola and I sense a huge anger inside her. Gordon Parker tries to look nonchalant, as he raises his chin a little and lightly scratches the underside of his jaw. Louise Stone approaches her daughter and puts a hand on her arm. Nicola's expression is cold. Louise asks her something and she listens for a moment, then shrugs indifferently before turning away. I can tell from the angry defeated look on Louise's face as she gazes after her daughter, that whatever she has told Nicola to do, she's not going to take the slightest bit of notice.

And here is my father. He beckons me to stand beside him and puts his arm round my shoulders. He smells of tobacco and Old Spice and gin. 'Ladies and gentlemen,' he calls. 'Today is a very special day. Alice is twelve, and I'd like you to raise your glasses and wish her well in all her future enterprises.' He smiles down at me. 'Happy Birthday, darling child.'

I grip the cool metal of the rail down into the garden. What happened next? At some point, we must have spilled back into the drawing room. The networks of connection between the guests blur and shift again. Vignettes slap into place like cards on a Rolodex. People dance. People chat. They step outside onto the grass in twos or groups. Light spills from the windows; the moon is huge, almost rust-coloured. I dance with Orlando, my father, Sasha, my brothers. Orlando and I chat with the mothers, except for Louise Stone who still lingers in the dining room along with Ava and Bertram Yelland. Gordon Parker tells us that a book on World War Two, which Orlando had requested, came in to the library the day before.

Did Nicola come back to the drawing room with us, or did she slip out through the front door? Am I being wise after the event when I vaguely recall seeing, later, two people walking along the seafront together, one of them Nicola?

It's no good. All I can recall are bits and pieces, not a coherent whole.

I'm shivering. Beneath my thighs, the iron steps are wet with dew. I get up and cross the lawn, go round the hedge, crunch down the gravel drive as quietly as I can. When I get back to my flat, the light is winking on my answering machine. Two messages.

The first speaker is Erin. 'Love to come down for the weekend, sweetie,' she says. 'Tell me what I can bring. Wine? Champagne? Something delicious from Harrod's Food Hall? Tell me what you want and I'll get it. Talk later.'

The second message is from Gordon Parker. 'If you're around tomorrow morning, come and have coffee with me around eleven. Such a coincidence – I can't wait to tell you! No need to reply, if you can't, you can't.'

I pour half an inch of single malt into a glass. Have I learned anything from my attempts at memory recovery?

There are people I can talk to in the hope of obtaining more information. I make a list of them. What worries me most is the strong possibility that the person who murdered Nicola was at my party. That it was someone whom I knew, or even loved.

On the window-seat sit Ava's scrapbooks. I've been putting off looking at them for weeks but the time now seems right. They're both bound in some kind of garish material, with leatherette spines and thick grey pages. The earlier one is almost completely full with cuttings to do with the trial of Nicola's father. The pages of the second one are mostly blank; since there was never a trial, Ava was forced to content herself with no more than the local paper's meagre coverage of the inquest on Nicola, and a four-line mention in *The Daily Mail*.

Orlando and I were back at our respective schools by then, but our evidence was read out to the coroner. Fiona attended, as did Ava, and gave their accounts of the party the night before, Louise Stone's reaction to our discovery, the trauma that Orlando and I had undergone. Most of the partygoers had been interviewed extensively by the police. Despite intensive questioning, no fingers were pointed at anyone. Nor was any evidence uncovered at the scene of the crime. There was a forensic report, which established that Nicola had died of blows to the cranium, and also that she was not killed where she was found. The fact that she was not wearing underpants was explained by her embarrassed brother. A fingertip search of the area turned up no clues. There was absolutely nothing to go on. In the end, the coroner returned a verdict of Murder by Person or Persons Unknown. And that was it.

Holding the closed book on my knee, I fancy I can detect the faint odour of *Nuits de Paris*. Much-missed Ava flitters in my memory like a moth. Reading the dry prose of the inquest conclusions, I wonder whether Nicola had any inkling of what was about to happen to her. I remember the brazen way she had removed her clothes in front of Yelland, completely heedless of whether she might be seen. I remember the man emerging from among the trees higher up, only a minute or two after she was dressed again. But although she deliberately flirted with danger, I don't think she would willingly have gone with her murderer unless it was someone she knew. Somebody local. Somebody who knew about the Secret Glade.

A cold possibility clenches my heart. I shake it clear, watch it disintegrate. *Somebody I know, somebody I love...*

I open the second scrapbook. I see Ava seated at the kitchen table with scissors and newspapers around her, a rounded triangular jar of grey paste in front of her; I recall so clearly its red top incorporating a brush, its delicious smell of almonds. Orlando and I and Bella spent many wet afternoons helping her to paste scraps into books like these. But I believe Ava had a more serious purpose: her collection of newspaper cuttings is as comprehensive as it is possible to be without access to police records.

The cuttings are yellowed now, faded where the paste affixed them to the thick card pages. Reading about it, I realize how sensational the Farnham case must have been in its day. It had all the ingredients that keep a story running for weeks. A war-hero, an only child, a glamorous wife, the victim's angelic friend. The story, as I learned it from the scrapbook, was as follows: Geoffrey Farnham, Nicola's father, had married Louise Dretter in 1935. Simon, their first child was born in 1936, Nicola Jane had been born in 1938. Until war broke out, Farnham had been the deputy headmaster of a south London school. He joined up in 1939, and had a distinguished career, being decorated several times and mentioned in dispatches. Louise, meanwhile, had taken the children to the country, to live closer to Geoffrey's parents, near Llandovery, in Wales. Louise had worked as a buyer in John Lewis's department store until she married. In Wales, with little to do, she began drawing clothes, sending the results to a friend who managed Ladies Fashions in Selfridges. After the war, this had translated into a career and then into fashion work, as she designed the paper-patterns for labels such as Simplicity and Butterick, from which women made their own clothes. Geoffrey Farnham was given his job back when he returned from the front, rising eventually to the post of headmaster, and the family lived comfortably in Battersea, on the fringes of Chelsea.

One Saturday morning in September 1951, according to the accounts of the trial, the Farnham family was going about its normal affairs. Louise was working in the room she used as an office. Geoffrey Farnham was at his school, coaching the under-thirteen football team. Simon

251

had gone camping in the New Forest with his Scout troop. Nicola's friend, Valerie Johnson, had come round and the two girls were in Nicola's bedroom, doing their homework and listening to records. At around twelve o'clock, Louise heard the girls clattering down the stairs and Nicola calling goodbye to Valerie. She then poked her head round the door of her mother's office to remind her that she had promised to take her shopping and to lunch in the West End.

According to Louise's testimony, shortly afterwards, she and Nicola had left the house, returning home at four fifteen or so. Louise had gone to the kitchen where Geoffrey, home by now, was sitting reading the paper. Louise began to put away the groceries she had bought, while Nicola went upstairs to her bedroom to deposit the clothes they'd purchased together, to wit, a new school sweater, a pretty blouse, a pair of jeans and a necklace. Nicola began screaming hysterically. When her parents ran upstairs, they found Nicola crouched in a corner of the room and Valerie Johnson lying dead on the floor, strangled by the blue silk scarf she had been given by her parents earlier that day.

A police officer gave evidence that Geoffrey Farnham had said he had come home at about three thirty, had made a pot of coffee and sat in the kitchen to read the *Guardian*. He said that his wife and daughter had forgotten to lock the back door, and it was possible some outsider had got in. While the body was examined by the medical officer on duty, the family, minus Simon, sat huddled in their sitting room, horrified and grief-stricken. By the time the police officers had the information they wanted and the body had been removed, Geoffrey Farnham had confessed to the murder.

There seemed to be no motive for the crime. Valerie had not been sexually assaulted, her clothing was intact. A colleague of Geoffrey Farnham's testified that at five minutes to four he had telephoned and chatted to Farnham for about ten minutes; Farnham, he reported, seemed agitated and distracted.

A scared teenage girl pupil from Farnham's school, Barbara-Jane Finch, testified that although he had not touched her in any way, he had made remarks which both she and her parents considered inappropriate, given the relationship which ought to exist between headmaster and student.

Although she did not appear on the stand, Nicola had testified to the police that Valerie had gone home without her scarf and must have returned for it, only to find the house empty. Because she was intimate with the place, she must have gone round the back and let herself in through the unlocked back door, at more or less the same time as Geoffrey Farnham returned. 'Something came over me,' Farnham said. 'I couldn't help myself. I made a ... a suggestion to her and when she turned me down, I grabbed the scarf she was holding and pulled it round her neck, trying to stop her screaming. I never intended to take a life. Although it was an accident, I shall never forgive myself for what I've done.'

Louise Farnham was photographed each day of the short trial, dressed in a different fashionable outfit and carrying two red roses in her hand, one of which she handed to her husband's solicitors to give to him.

I read the evidence from Valerie Johnson's father. Her mother wasn't called since she was still heavily sedated. The Johnsons were fairly elderly parents. They had tried for years to have a child and had given up hope, resigned themselves to childlessness, and then – 'a miracle, an absolute miracle!', Mr Johnson kept saying, as tears poured down his face – Mrs Johnson found herself pregnant at the age of forty. Valerie was their pride and joy, their miracle baby, the apple of their eye. She lacked for nothing, she was bright, she was popular at school, and turned out to have a gift for drawing and painting which she'd hoped to turn into a career.

'When she died, it was the end of our lives,' Mr Johnson whispered. According to the crime reporter, half the jury was in tears.

Farnham's defence team did their best, calling upon his war-record, his exemplary teaching career, the dangers he had faced during the war, citing an incident where he was pulled out of a burning tank with thirty per cent burns to his body, an incident which his wife testified still gave him nightmares, but in the face of Farnham's confession, there was little they could do except plead mitigating circumstances.

Counsel for the Prosecution summed up in a moving speech, which ended as follows:

You have heard how this little girl, trembling on the brink of womanhood, went back to the house where she felt entirely at home, in order to recover the scarf she had left behind. Once inside, she encountered the defendant, the father of her best friend, a man she had known virtually all her life.

Imagine her shock as he lunged at her. Imagine how helpless she must have felt as he tore at her clothing. Imagine her terror as he slowly squeezed the life out of her. Imagine how she must have scrabbled in vain at the iron band of the scarf around her neck – her own scarf, Ladies and Gentlemen. We have heard that she loved her friend, the defendant's daughter, that she loved and was loved by her parents, that she was a gifted young artist who hoped one day to turn her talent into a career. I wonder what her last thoughts were as consciousness faded. Did she think of her parents, or her friend, or of the life she would never now live, the dreams she would never fulfil? I ask you to bear in mind that only a timely phone-call from his deputy head-master saved this child from further degradation.

Imagine the grief and shame Geoffrey Farnham has brought upon his family. The only mitigating factor in what is otherwise a senseless and appalling crime, is that the defendant has pleaded guilty in order to spare his loved ones from a long, drawn-out ordeal.

Ladies and gentlemen of the jury, if you feel that beyond any reasonable doubt Geoffrey Farnham bears full responsibility for the unlaw-

ful killing of Valerie Anne Johnson, it is your duty to find him guilty.'

Which, in record time, they duly did.

After the verdict, after Geoffrey Farnham was led down to the cells, and then transferred to prison to serve his sentence, the papers let rip with think-pieces by the columnists.

Valerie Johnson died at the hands of a sexual predator. This must not happen again...

Is it time that Parliament introduced legislation in order to vet our teachers?...

... this appalling double betrayal of innocent trust, for not only was Farnham an adult entrusted with the well-being of our youngsters, he was also the father of the victim's best friend...

Who Can They Trust?...

I turn the last page and read a further paragraph, cut from the *Maidstone & Rochester Times*:

MURDER VICTIM BURIED

Valerie Anne Johnson, 11, was interred today in the graveyard of St Peter & St Philip, Madden, in Kent. The ceremony was quiet, and attended only by family and close friends. Mrs Louise Farnham, wife of the man now serving a twenty year jail sentence for Valerie's murder was also briefly present.

A final paragraph mentions the fact that Valerie's maternal grandparents, Mr and Mrs Herbert

Treadwell, farmed nearby, that he was a Justice of the Peace and that his wife was highly regarded for the active part she took in the community. Valerie was also well known in the village, since she had spent many holidays on her grandfather's farm. There are photographs of the churchyard, the grandparents' farm, the sorrowing parents, holding hands each day as they attend the court hearings. And Valerie herself, a snapshot of her sitting in a deckchair somewhere sandy and rocky, with the usual anonymous features of pre-adolescence: round face, slightly protruding teeth being straightened by a brace, hair kept back in a velvet band. She wears a thin gold chain round her neck as Nicola did, a similar white blouse with puffed sleeves, she grins at the camera. I wonder if the two girls saved up, went together to buy the chains, vowed eternal friendship. It seems dreadful that both of them were dead within two years of each other.

There is a lump in my throat as I reach the end of this sad and shocking story. Perhaps it was no wonder that Nicola had been so disturbed a personality. Not only to have found her best friend dead in her bedroom, but to discover further that her own father was responsible for the crime ... Anyone might be slightly unbalanced after having suffered two such devastating traumas.

I think of my childhood. Of *Mrs Miniver*. Geoffrey Farnham was only one of thousands who returned from the front struggling with an inner disturbance. I think of Gordon Parker, the fatherless boys and their genteelly desperate mothers, of Bertram Yelland, Miss Vane, Ava, Fiona. For them and countless others, the years of deprivation and ever-present danger were probably still having some kind of effect.

I never think of myself as particularly subtle or sensitive to other people, but as I close Ava's album, I wonder just how effective the police investigation had been. Although they had extensively interviewed everyone who had been at the party, they had no way of assessing the ebb and flow, the rivalries and subterfuges which existed between us all, or even being aware of them. Did they know that Julian was infatuated with Nicola? That Orlando hated her? That I was frightened by her or that Yelland was sexually abusing her?

Back then, so many people who appeared to be coping with life in post-war Britain were in reality made quietly desperate by the years of hardship that they had endured. When we were growing up, how sane were any of the adults in our lives?

How sane am I, holding a torch for a man I have only seen once in twenty years?

How sane have I been, attempting to flee my memories?

EIGHT

Gordon is waiting for me when I walk into the library the next morning. 'I was so afraid you didn't get my message,' he twitters, bustling me into his office. He seems hyper-excited, eyes wide with anticipation of my reaction at whatever it is he wants to tell me. For a while he fusses about with kettles and tea bags, mugs and milk, until finally he sits down opposite me in a chair so low its seat is practically on the floor.

He sips his tea, grimaces, puts his mug down on the bleached wood coffee table between us. 'My dear, you'll hardly credit this ... talk about coincidences!'

'Gordon, would you please get on with it before I expire from curiosity.'

'Well ... you know when we had lunch the other day, I gave you a ticket for the concert in the Town Hall?'

'Tomorrow night,' I say, nodding.

'Well, we had a phone call yesterday afternoon, to say that Helena Warburton's accompanist has gone down with the dreaded lurgie, and they'd have to find a replacement. And guess who they came up with!'

I look blank, but my heart begins to thud painfully.

'None other than ... ta dah! ... Alexander Elias! Isn't that the most amazing thing you ever heard, especially after you were asking about him such a short time ago!'

I don't want to disappoint Gordon. 'You're absolutely right. It's totally amazing.' It is more than that. It is fate, I am sure. I find that my hands are trembling.

'So you'll be there tomorrow?'

'I wouldn't miss it for worlds.' At the same time, I feel suddenly nauseous, apprehensive. 'Are there any spare tickets? I have someone coming down for the weekend. You might even remember her– Erin O'Grady. She used to come and stay at Glenfield House in the holidays.'

'The American girl? From California, wasn't it? Yes, indeed I do remember her. She always wore such elegant clothes, a nice touch of glamour for us shabby survivors of clothes rationing! Do please bring her along. There's a little reception beforehand, where they usually serve a pretty good hock and some delicious nibbles. Made by Diedre, our musical director's wife – she's Cordon Bleu trained so they're not to be sneezed at.'

'That's good to know,' I say.

'And after the concert, we usually take the visiting *artistes* out for dinner – or back to Diedre and Malcolm's place. I asked about inviting you as my guest and they're delighted to have you along. So we'll get a chance to have a good old natter with Elias.'

I don't want a natter, I want an explanation. I want ... what do I want? A renewal, a con-

260

clusion? I'm not sure.

'Ghastly old Bertram's also going to be there,' Gordon continues. 'I ran into him – or, rather, his belly – in the High Street yesterday, and he assured me that I could count on his presence.'

'So basically it's going to be Old Home Week at the Town Hall tomorrow.'

'Old Glenfield House Week. Maybe we should start a club.'

The sea lies flat as paper, barely moving. Where the tide chews at the pebbles, gulls wheel and dive, descending in crowds on the intestines of a fish at the edge of the water, tearing at sea-distressed milk cartons, empty crab shells, with their rapacious beaks.

I walk across the sand dunes with a gathering breeze in my hair. Clouds are assembling low on the horizon, the first I've seen for weeks. In the middle distance, golfers move here and there, backs bent as they drag golf carts across baize-smooth grass, or stand cursing in the rough, beating at overgrown summer weeds in the hope of finding lost balls.

Tomorrow I shall see Sasha again. My palms perspire at the thought. Yet he and I have both moved on, we can now have nothing at all in common except a fugitive memory of long-passed summer weeks. Or has he been waiting for me, just as I have waited for him? The sensations I experienced in Paris inflate my heart. After all this time, shall I finally find what I have been looking for?

I feel optimistic for the first time in months, if

not years. Yet, to my surprise, when I examine this sentiment, it has nothing to do with the prospect of seeing Sasha again. Rather, it is a sense of achieving something, as though I were building a house from playing cards and for once, they are not falling down as I attempt to place the next layer. Perhaps playing cards is too flimsy a metaphor. Perhaps I mean that I feel that I have built something on sand, only to find that the sand is in fact solid rock. But no single element stands out to validate this unaccustomed buoyancy. Maybe it's the fact that at last, instead of running, I am turning to look my demons squarely in the face.

Back in my flat, I telephone Orlando in London. 'Come down,' I urge him.

'Any particular reason?'

'Sasha Elias is playing here at the Town Hall tomorrow.'

'Ah.'

I ignore his sardonic tone. 'Erin's coming too, so you can liaise with her. We'll have supper here first.'

'Sasha Elias on his own isn't nearly enough to drag me down there,' he says. 'But you and Erin are more than sufficient temptation. I'll catch the four o'clock from Charing Cross.'

Orlando and Erin arrive at six, carrying wine, port, a ripe Stilton, a tender tart. Erin is wearing a tiny flared micro-skirt in pink and green checks, with green platform soles which make her long legs look even longer. She and Orlando make a handsome couple, both tall and striking, both people who stand out from the herd. It's been a long time since the three of us were together, our various occupations sometimes sending us in opposite directions for months, if not years at a time, and an even longer one since we ate a meal together.

'Alice, Alice,' Orlando says, taking me into his arms. 'You don't know how I've missed you.'

I hug him. Safe at last. *Mon semblable, mon frère.* I know a measure of peace for the first time for ages. 'I've missed you too, more than I can say.'

He opens the stripped pine cupboard set into the corner between two walls near the kitchen and takes out three glasses. He wrests the cork from one of the bottles and pours wine for us all. We toast each other, sit on the window-seat and watch the light fading down towards dusk, not saying much. Just above the horizon, the sky is the purest of crystalline duck-egg blues.

While I organize bread rolls, salad, bowls, Orlando prowls. He picks up the top sheet of a pile of papers on my work table, a copy of the report I've just completed for Brussels. 'Jesus wept,' he says, 'this sounds boring.'

'It is.'

'Why don't you do something more creative, for God's sake?'

'That's what I keep saying,' says Erin. 'She should be translating art books or fiction or poetry, something closer to her real interests.'

I remove the sheet of paper from Orlando's grasp. 'I do this because coal and steel pays well.'

263

'Nobody needs money that bad.'

'Also, I have a reputation to maintain.'

'If you do much more of this, honey, you'll lose the will to live.' Erin flicks a bronze-varnished fingernail at my work. 'Face it, we only have one life so why waste it on teeth-itchingly boring crap like this?'

Orlando takes hold of my shoulders so I'm directly in front of him. 'Alice, you're in a rut. Do something else. If you've got a reputation, ask for something more stimulating. Biography, history, novels ... there's a world of fascinating work out there if you want it.'

'Other translators have more of a literary standing than I have.'

'Then find something that no one's thought about translating yet. Or better still, why work for someone else at all? Why not set up your own business? You're more than qualified to do so.'

I know he's right. They're both right. If I weren't so mired in inertia, this is of course what I would do. 'Actually, I've already had a feeler from a publishing house in Spain...'

'Get in there, babes,' Erin says.

'Maybe I will. But meanwhile, let's eat.' I set a steaming tureen between us at the table, place bowls of *rouille*, croutons and grated cheese within easy reach. 'You can pig out since, apart from cheese and a salad, this is all we're having.'

Erin picks up her soup spoon. 'It smells likes heaven.'

'A fish-flavoured paradise?' Orlando wrinkles

his elegant nose. 'Wonder how God would feel about that.'

As we empty the second bottle, I remember Vi Sheffield's question. Slightly tipsy, I say, 'Orlando, are you happy?'

'How do we know if we're happy?' counters Orlando. 'Are you?'

'I asked first.'

'Well, then...' He looks down at the table, making it hard to read his expression. 'Most of the time I am, I suppose, content. Sometimes, like right now, I might even be termed happy. And you?'

'If I'm honest, I'm content a lot of the time, but not wildly happy.'

'That's me in a nutshell,' says Erin.

'I guess I'm getting a little tired of ... of running away.'

'So young and so jaded,' Erin says.

'Thirty-two isn't young.'

'Unless you're thirty-three.'

'On the other hand,' says Orlando, 'why ask the question? It pre-supposes that one ought to be happy and is somehow failing if one is not.'

'Which just makes everyone even more hassled, because as well as not being totally happy, they're also a failure,' Erin adds.

'You, of course, come from a country whose entire ethos is dedicated to the proposition that not only ought we to be happy, we *deserve* to be,' says Orlando. 'This is a concept I find difficult to hold on to for more than a minute. Why *should* we be happy?'

'Why shouldn't we?' counters Erin.

Orlando looks at me. 'What do you think, Alice-of-my-heart?'

I consider my position, slowly clearing away the bowls, bringing the salad and the cheese board to the table. 'I ... I think I might be happy – I mean I believe I have the capacity for happiness, whatever that means – if I didn't feel the past standing over me all the time, with its foot on my chest, pinning me to the floor.'

'Nicola's murder, you mean,' Erin says.

'I suppose that's it.'

'"*So we beat on, boats against the current, borne back ceaselessly into the past,*"' Orlando says. 'You've *got* to move on, Alice. I told you that the other day on the phone.'

'I thought I had. But recently I've been having nightmares more and more often, ghastly dreams of blood and pain, waking up terrified of something, I don't know what, with tears in my eyes.'

'Maybe you need therapy, hon.'

'Part of it has to do with the fact that they never got anyone for it. The murder, I mean. It's still hanging there, unresolved.' I look at Orlando almost pleadingly. 'Don't you feel that?'

'Very rarely.'

'Do you ever wonder who was responsible?'

'Not really.' He cuts into a softly oozing Camembert. 'And even if I did, I'd find it hard to condemn. It's a terrible thing to say, but I think Nicola got more or less what she was asking for.'

'That sounds heartless,' says Erin.

'Of course it is. But that doesn't make it any

266

the less true. And although I'll never get completely over seeing her lying there that morning, for me, the worst thing has always been the fact that if you analyse the probabilities, it's almost got to be one of us, hasn't it?'

'Do you mean the family?'

'Someone who was there that night, at the party.'

'I wonder.' I tell them about the squeak of the gate, Nicola's surprised expression. 'Someone she knew, but wasn't expecting.'

'Not a passing tramp, for heaven's sake,' says Erin.

'Of course not.'

'Just because you heard the gate doesn't mean it wasn't someone we knew.' Orlando refills our glasses. 'It was a gorgeous evening, as I remember, just like this one. Moon shining, balmy air, all that sort of thing. Several people walked down to the beach at different times. For instance, I saw Julian out there at some point, though I don't know if he was with Nicola. I saw Gordon Parker, and Yelland, later in the evening. And Callum was on the beach with some girl, and I know Dougal organized a swimming party. I walked down there myself, as a matter of fact. The sea was like warm milk. So the fact that you heard the gate scraping open doesn't eliminate any of the people in the house.'

'I suppose not.' I start to clear away the plates.

After a glass of port, more cheese, a tiny slice of tart, the three of us stroll arm-in-arm along the moonlit front. 'Orlando,' I say, 'I know you don't want to talk about it, but remember that night?'

'How could I forget? Especially since you won't let it rest.'

'A couple of things I was wondering about...'

'Such as?'

'When we were all in the dining room, and you were standing at the window, looking out, could you see anyone out there?'

He shakes his head. 'It's so long ago, Alice. How on earth do you expect me to remember something like that?'

'But did you?'

'I'm honestly not sure. There was a full moon, throwing shadows all over the place, and remember how the shrubbery hung across the drive? There might have been someone, but it was impossible to be sure.'

'Second question: what did Nicola say when she came over to you? You didn't seem surprised that she appeared.'

'That's because although my back was turned to the room, I could follow every step the little bitch took. That uncurtained window was like a mirror. I saw her giving poor Miss Vane the evil eye, and Mr Elias, and the way she snubbed poor Julian, and agitated Bertram Yelland – not that I'm an apologist for the old pervert. I saw it all.'

'I only met her once, but boy, that was enough,' says Erin. 'You don't often meet someone who's so effortlessly – evil's too strong a word – so effortlessly unpleasant.'

'Unpleasant's too *weak* a word,' says Orlando.

'What I mean is, she seemed completely oblivious to other people's feelings.' She paused.

'Say, do you remember that book called *The Bad Seed*? She kind of reminded me of the kid in that.'

'You're right,' I say. 'That was Nicola exactly.'

'So, Orlando,' asks Erin. 'When the little monster came and stood next to you, what did she say?'

'I was the one who spoke first. I told her she was a piece of shit, a sadistic little slut. I told her several things.' I can feel his arm shaking.

'And what did she say?'

'She gave me that nasty little smile of hers and then she said, she said...' Orlando pauses. 'Jesus, all these years later, she still has the power to make me flaming mad.'

'*What* did she say?'

'It seems such a silly thing when you look back on it, but at the time, it meant such a lot.'

'What was it, Orlando?' Tensely I wait for some hideous revelation that will alter forever all that lies between us.

'She said...' He laughs, a little shamefacedly. '...that she knew all about the Secret Glade – not that she called it that – and that she and Julian were going to go up and strip it bare before you and I could.'

He's right. The distance of time has changed my perspective. Now the whole affair seems infantile, trivial. But at the time, given how seriously he took his role as hunter and gatherer, he must have perceived her words as a breathtaking threat.

'What did you do?'

'What could I do? Precisely nothing – except

get up there with Alice as early as possible, keep an eye out for the two of them.'

'Hmmm...' Erin said.

'What does that mean?'

'She was probably just winding you up and had no intention whatsoever of doing anything of the sort.'

'Exactly – too much like hard work for our Nicola. And Julian was incapable of getting out of bed before lunchtime, if you remember, Alice.'

'I do.'

Erin squeezes my arm against her side. 'What say we leave Nicola in her final resting-place and talk about something else?'

'Fine.'

But it's not. Because, much as I love Orlando, I am suddenly aware of the fact that not only was he quite capable of killing Nicola, I now know that he also had a motive.

'Since we're talking about something else, who was that woman I saw you with the other day?' Erin asks.

Orlando looks at me. 'Woman?'

'In that fish restaurant at Victoria. Wheeler's, I think it's called.'

'Um...'

'Don't prevaricate, darlin'. London's a small place, and I've seen you with her twice before. You know the one I mean: tall, blonde, rather distinguished-looking.'

Orlando seems disconcerted for once, then annoyed. 'I don't know what you're talking about.'

'Come on, Orlando.'

'It's not illegal to dine with someone of the opposite sex,' he says.

Erin laughs. 'Why so defensive? You're a very desirable catch – rich, distinguished, successful. Any woman would be glad to step out with you.'

'The person I believe you're referring to is a principal flautist with an American orchestra. We've worked together for a number of years. We're just good friends, as they say.'

'Of course you are.'

We stop and look at the houses in the moonlight. 'Isn't it strange how, give or take a coat of paint here, a flower bed there,' Orlando remarks, 'everything's exactly as it was when we were children?'

'Except us,' I say. I feel downhearted, imagining Orlando with a tall blonde flautist. He'd already mentioned her once, but had implied that he hadn't formed a relationship with her because of her penchant for clowns. But if Erin was correct, this obviously wasn't true. I want him to find True Love, of course I do, as much as I want it for myself. But not just yet. And definitely not with a blonde flautist.

When we arrive the following evening, the Town Hall reception room is full of people holding glasses of wine and milling about in the vague way that pre-concert audiences do.

Gordon is waiting for us by the door. He does a double take at the sight of Orlando. 'Goodness,' he says.

Orlando shakes his hand. 'You haven't chang-
271

ed a bit,' he says.

Gordon pouts. 'Then twenty years of unremitting effort have been in vain.' He takes my arm. 'Come along, all of you,' he says. Today he wears an expensive jacket of camel cashmere, with a dusky green tie, and well-cut trousers. 'This is going to be fun.'

Already, in the short weeks that I've been here, I recognize several faces. I wave at Vi Sheffield, at my neighbours from the flat below mine, at one or two others. Although I look for her, I cannot see Louise Stone. Perhaps she doesn't care for classical music. Orlando is seized upon by various middle-aged women who recognize him from his television appearances and want to tell him how much his company had meant twenty years earlier to their lonely mothers, widowed by the attritions of time as much as by the war.

'Look,' Gordon says, indicating the other side of the room. There is Bertram Yelland, gesticulating with a full glass of wine, one of Deirdre's nibbles in his hand. He is surrounded by a group of self-consciously arty people. A peasant skirt here, a beret there, a jacket of pretty patchworked velvets, a leather waistcoat. 'Go and say hello, while I talk to Erin.' He gives me a friendly push.

'Must I?'

'Now that you're a local, dear, you'll have to do it sooner or later.'

I push my way through, and introduce myself into the edge of the circle. At first, nobody takes any notice of me, giving me time to observe Bertram. He is older, fatter, angrier of mien. He is wearing a collarless white linen shirt and baggy black trousers. The ends of his artistically unruly hair are grey.

'And you are?' he says rudely, when he finally deigns to notice me.

I smile, about to utter something enigmatic, but he frowns. 'I've seen you before some-where.'

'You probably don't recognize me face to face.'

I see the possibility of kinky sexual encounters he has forgotten about flit briefly through his mind. 'Er...' His fan club titters.

'A woman of mystery,' someone in a cambric shirt tucked into hipster jeans says, stroking his grey ponytail, grinning as though he's just said something exceptionally witty.

'I own a couple of your paintings,' I say.

'Ah!' Yelland brightens. 'A collector.'

'Not exactly. I have some of your early works.'

He makes an attempt at being ingratiating – at least, that's how I interpret the flabby smile which creases his face and makes it obvious that he has not spent any money on dentistry since I last saw him.

'What paintings are you talking about?' From a passing tray, he grabs another of Deirdre's canapés, something lividly pink and green with a slice of black olive on top, and thrusts it into his mouth.

'Somebody recently gave me one of your can-vasses.' I gesture vaguely towards the windows of the hall. 'A view of the pier before they rebuilt it.'

'I did that from memory.' His dissipated but still handsome face looms towards me as his eyes take me in. I feel that somehow I've penetrated his aureole of self-satisfaction. 'You're very striking, you know. I'd rather like to paint you.'

'I don't want to be painted,' I say.

'Oh...' Yelland rears back, disconcerted. The fan-club murmurs. I gather his suggestion that I act as his model is an honour not lightly bestowed, at least, not down here in the sticks. Some of them move away, as though leaving us to a private moment together.

I smile. I'm wearing a jumpsuit made of peacock-colored silk, with several gilt belts round my waist, and soft rose-pink ankle high boots. 'In any case, you already have.'

Dramatically, he slaps his forehead. 'Am I growing old? It's hard to believe I'd forget a girl like you.'

'It was quite a while back.'

'I used to live here many years ago,' he says. 'Are you local?'

'In a manner of speaking. I've just moved back here.'

A look of faint apprehension travels across his face. 'Wait a minute. You aren't ... you can't be one of those blasted kids, can you, the ones further along the front, with that mad mother, what was it, Flora or Fanny or something?'

'Fiona.'

'Mad,' he says quickly, 'but very kind. She was good to me. Not the finest gourmet cook in the business, though...' He guffaws loudly. 'Yes,

274

you must be...' He snaps his fingers. '...Alice, that's it. Alice, and her brother Orlando.'

'Orlando's over there.' I point him out.

He gazes at Orlando. 'Hmm,' he says in a tone I cannot interpret. His glance shifts. I see that final summer push its way into his mind, the cranking up of mental gears as those years are suddenly alive again, a recollection of Nicola, the hesitation with which he wonders whether to mention her to me, 'Yes, indeed, it comes back to me now.'

A thin woman with Mary Quant hair lays a possessive hand on his arm, giving me a raised eyebrow stare of infinite contempt. 'Darling, do come and meet Peter Agnew.'

He shakes her off. 'One moment, and I'll be with you.' He dips into an inside pocket, muttering that he could swear he ... and brings out a dog-eared card. 'I have a cottage here now, in Mariner Street. You must come and have a drink, a bit of a gossip. I'd love to know how things are with you and the rest of the family.'

'I'd enjoy that,' I say, meaning it. Unprepossessing as he still obviously is, there are things he may be able to explain or amplify. 'When are you next here?'

'I'm staying on down here for a few days, while the weather's fine.' He grins, showing me his terrible teeth again. 'No time like the present.'

'I'll call you in a couple of days.'

We're finally shepherded to our seats by a man whom I take to be the musical director. We're five rows back, in the middle; I'm seated between Orlando and Gordon. The choral group starts to file on stage while he explains the change in the programme and tells us how delighted we all are to welcome back to Shale our old friend Alexander Elias. We are doubly privileged, he adds, since in addition, Mr Elias has agreed to play some Mozart for us.

The chorus sings some *a cappella* madrigals rather well, and follow this with a couple of Negro spirituals. Nobody seems to find any incongruity between the English accents and the plantation vocabulary. Finally the singers file off to much clapping. Helena Wilburton appears and bows to the audience, acknowledging applause. She is generously built, with piled-up auburn hair and a low-cut green gown. She stretches one arm towards the wings and he comes on, Sasha Elias, in a black velvet jacket and black tie. He nods at the singer, bows his head to us, seats himself at the grand piano. He plays a rippling introduction to a Schubert *liede*, and the soprano launches herself into song.

I sit with my hands folded in my lap. I breathe deeply, slowly, deliberately relaxing myself. Outwardly, I appear calm – or so I hope – but I am in turmoil. I can feel Orlando glancing at me from under his eyebrows. As Sasha plays, glancing up at the singer from time to time, I realize how familiar to me he is. I am not conscious of having observed him in such detail, yet the twist of hair at the nape of his neck, the swollen knuckle of his right ring-finger, the star-shaped imperfection in his eye are as known as my own face in the mirror.

His face is rounder, the worry lines smoothed out by the flesh beneath. If there is more grey in his hair, I can't see it. He bends over the keys, he straightens up to smile at the singer as she swoops and soars and emotes.

Erin nudges me. 'I like the look of that,' she murmurs. At first I think she is talking about the rather fine wooden ceiling above our heads, carved and vaulted like a mediaeval hall, but she is in fact indicating Sasha.

'Nice,' I agree. Afraid his gaze will eventually roam the audience, I sink lower into my seat.

The small local orchestra files onto the stage after an interval, and Sasha appears again. Again, they are unexpectedly good, given their amateur status, and he conducts them with a brio which I can see brings them to the peak of their performance.

'Well, this is an extraordinary surprise!' He is smiling, his eyes crinkling so they are almost hidden in the folds of his face. He holds my hand in his. 'Alice! I would have recognized you any-where!'

Behind him, Orlando is watching us as he talks to Deirdre, one eyebrow raised.

'You too, Mr Elias. Sasha,' I say. But is it true? He has filled out. His accent has all but disap-peared. He is taller than I remember him, and more handsome. Though the lines of his face have changed, it is still an interesting face, with high cheekbones with hollows beneath them. He wears his curly hair fashionably long; he waves

277

delicate thin fingers as he talks. He is not tranquil. He moves constantly. Beneath the impeccably cut dinner jacket he wears, it is easy to see that passions seethe.

What I find inexplicable is the fact that after so much wishing, I am at last here, my hands clasped in his, his eyes smiling into mine – and I feel nothing. Not a thing. I've wasted so much of my life on Sasha Elias, worn him round my shoulders like a cloak, and now he has fallen away from me, like wisps of fog in sunshine.

I can think of nothing to say to him. I no longer care that he didn't try to find me in Paris. Embarrassed, all I want to do is get away. Erin arrives at my side and hastily I introduce the two of them. It seems they have an acquaintance in common, a composer from San Francisco, and I am happy to escape and move over to Orlando, who turns in mid-sentence, takes my hand, and holds it tightly at his side.

'Is that Julian Tavistock?' he says. I look over and find Julian staring at us both. His expression is, for some reason, apprehensive. In the harsh overhead light, he seems pale. Sweat shines greasily on his broad forehead.

'Yes.'

'He doesn't seem to be wearing well, does he?'

'Not at all. He's only a couple of years older than you are, and he looks old enough to be your father.'

'Something's obviously bothering him.'

'Could be anything,' I say. 'Perhaps he's embezzling the bank's funds. Perhaps his wife's having an affair. Perhaps he's afraid he might

278

have cancer, or he can't get it up, or something.'

Julian is pushing his way towards us, his wife trailing behind him. 'Hel*lo*, you two!' He shakes Orlando's hand. 'Long time no see, old boy!'

I can tell Orlando debating what answer to give to this absurd remark. Finally he settles for, 'Absolutely.'

'Catch you on the telly from time to time, of course. You're looking good,' Julian says. 'Life's obviously treating you well.'

'What about you?'

'Can't complain, can't complain!' Julian's joviality seems forced. As before, I find it hard to detect the good-looking adolescent of twenty years ago beneath Julian's flabby jowls. Between us lie so many things that, for our different reasons, we cannot give voice to. 'Bit of a turn-up for the book, having old Elias back here, isn't it?'

'It is indeed.'

'Remember the fun we had that summer, when we decided he was a spy?'

'Not really.' Orlando turns to me and raises an eyebrow. 'Do you remember that, Alice?'

'I wonder if he does,' I say.

'I remember your sainted ma came round to our place and gave us the rounds of the kitchen,' says Julian. 'I suppose we deserved it, little devils that we were.' He looks suddenly stricken. 'That was the summer when ... you know...'

'Yes,' Orlando says smoothly. 'I do know.'

Walking back afterwards in the warm dark, Erin is full of Sasha Elias. 'I just can't believe how

279

many mutual friends we have in London,' she says. 'And you know what's a real coincidence?'

'What?' I roll my eyes at Orlando.

'He comes down to Shale sometimes, just stays at a hotel, walks for miles across the dunes, and now he's thinking of buying a place down here for weekends, just like me!'

'Perhaps the two of you could buy one together,' suggests Orlando.

'Share it,' I say.

'Hold your horses,' Erin protests. 'I only met the guy this evening, and you want us to shack up together?'

'*Carpe diem*,' I say. 'No time like the present.'

'Changing the hugely fascinating conversation for a moment,' Orlando says, 'Julian's remembrance of things past is rather different from mine.'

'What's even funnier,' I say, 'is his total inability to mention either Nicola's name or the fact that she was murdered.'

'Julian,' says Erin. 'Is that the bank manager guy?'

'That's right.'

'He was kinda good-looking back when we were kids, apart from the zits.'

'But not any more.'

'I always mistrust a man who loses his hair too early,' says Erin.

'Why?'

'They're usually hiding something.'

'Displaying it, I'd have said,'

'Of all the prejudiced remarks...' I add.

'Whereas your friend Sasha,' says Erin, while

280

Orlando groans, 'he's got a really full head of hair, despite being almost twelve years older than I am.'

'You got that far, did you?'

Erin snorts. 'Come on, guys. Asking someone's age is hardly any distance at all.'

'When are you seeing him again?' asks Orlando innocently.

'Tuesday, we're going to— Just a minute, what makes you think we're meeting up again?'

'I don't know. Do you, Alice? Could it be the pretty flush in her cheeks?'

'Or the fact that she can't stop talking about him?'

'Or the extra spring in her step?'

'Or the song in her heart?'

'What song?'

'Some day my prince will come,' croons Orlando, in his beautiful voice.

'What about your princess?' she retorts.

He ignores her, and the three of us harmonize happily as we walk home beside the sea.

As soon as we're inside the flat, Orlando sits down at the piano and begins to play Chopin nocturnes. Erin drags me into the kitchen.

'Listen,' she says.

'I am.'

'Darling, honeybun Alice baby cakes, please, pretty please—'

'What do you want?' I say suspiciously.

'I suggested that Sasha might like to come to lunch tomorrow. He doesn't have to get back to London until the evening.'

'Suggested?'

'Okay, invited. I knew you wouldn't mind.'

'I see.'

'I'll do the cooking, I swear.'

'No thanks. I'd rather do it myself.' I smile at her. 'Good thing I've some stuff in the freezer.'

'And there's the tart I brought, and some cheese left over ... we'll have a feast.'

Sasha arrives at twelve-thirty. His face lights up when he walks into the sitting room. 'This is amazing!' he says. 'Fantastic!' He looks at me. 'I cannot believe that I am here again. And there is the same piano. May I?'

'Oh *please*,' begs Erin.

I serve dry sherry before we sit down. There is something very pleasant about the four of us sharing this meal, especially now that my heart is no longer abraded by Sasha Elias. I try not to think of the time I have wasted on yearning for him. Or of the new abrasions which might be forthcoming.

'How did you come to England?' Erin asks him. The sun shines through her thick hair and throws a dusky light on her beautiful American complexion. 'If you don't mind talking about it, that is.'

'It's a long time ago. And I have learned to live with what happened.' He looks round at us. 'I wish also that I could forget, but I cannot. I imagine these ugly images will remain with me for the rest of my life, however long I shall live.'

Orlando and I exchange glances.

'My cousin Dieter was sent to England in the late Thirties, by his mother, my Aunt Lena. She

282

was a historian in the university and knew what the consequences of Hitler's rise would be. My father disagreed with her, but she told him he had his head in the sand, like an ostrich. She told him that an old Jew had been beaten to death right outside her house two days before and the local women had watched, had laughed, had held up their babies to see. "What kind of people are these?" she asked of my father, and he said, "They are our people, we are all Germans."'

Erin gazes at him, her mouth partly open. 'We knew so little of this, in California, where I grew up. What did your aunt say to that?'

'She said, "I am a Jew before I am a German, and I know the hatred they have for us. So I am sending my Dieter away before it is too late." My mother refused to send my sisters, but in the end she allowed me to join Dieter.'

'How did you two cope? Two young refugees alone in a foreign country?'

'There were organizations to help such as we were. As for the rest, I will tell you some day.' Sasha glowed at Erin, and the mark in his eye shone like an emerald.

'What happened to your aunt?' Orlando asked.

'She ended up in Dachau, and survived. But she will not talk of those days.' Sasha picks up Erin's left hand and turned it so we could see the thin tendons, the veins running up towards her elbow. 'She has a tattoo right here,' he says. 'Her number, put there by the Germans.'

'How perfectly horrible!'

'Every time I think of that, and the other things: the camps, the cattle wagons, the in-

283

humanity, I am filled with a ... a murderous rage.'

'I don't blame you.'

'But let us talk of other, better things.' He smiles at Orlando. 'Last time we met you were going to America with your Musick Consort. Did that go well?'

'Very well. We've just finished our time out there.'

'And they were even invited to perform at the White House,' I say proudly.

'This is excellent.'

Erin begins an animated conversation with Sasha about some musical function they had both attended, not knowing the other was there.

'Last time we met...?' I frown at Orlando. 'I thought you said you'd never come across him in London.'

'I lied.'

'Why? You knew I wanted to find him.'

'Exactly.'

'But—' I look at him narrowly.

'Alice,' Erin interrupts. 'We must talk about your new translation business.'

'Which one would that be?'

'The one you're going to start like next Monday. I've got all sorts of contacts through the Embassy.'

'And I could find several, also,' adds Sasha. 'So *go* for it, girl.'

It is not until towards the middle of the afternoon that the talk turns inevitably to Nicola.

'Such a troubled girl,' Sasha says. 'In the end,

I told her mother I would not teach her any more.'

'What did Louise say to that?'

'I was surprised. She shrugged, shook her head, said she was sorry but she could understand.'

'Nicola spread some pretty nasty rumours about you,' I said.

'And that is exactly why I terminated the lessons with her.' His sombre expression lightened. 'How is your mother, Alice?'

'Fine. She and my father are still living at the Mill House, but talking about moving, because it's too big.'

'She was a magnificent woman,' Sasha says. 'When I lived here, in this house, Mrs Sheffield was always very considerate to me. But your mother ... she made me feel as though I belonged. For a refugee, this is so important. She lent me German books, helped me with my English ... so very kind.'

'Unorthodox, but wonderful,' I say.

'And how is Mrs Carlton?'

'She died,' Orlando says.

'We were all absolutely heartbroken.' I shift my cutlery about. The loss of Ava is still painful.

'I remember that your mother invited me to your house, and Mrs Carlton was wearing the most beautiful pair of shoes, peep-toe, Italian leather, pre-war shoes, I imagine.'

'I remember those.'

'And her toenails were painted the same red as the geraniums my mother used to grow.' Sasha fiddles with his knife. 'I was so lonely then. I used to walk past your garden wall in the evenings, watch the two of you playing the piano and singing together. So sweet. It reminded me of my two little sisters.' He smiles round at us. 'Let us change the subject. Maybe Orlando, you or I could play the piano and the rest can sing.'

'Play *Muss i' denn*,' I say.

The years drop away. This room, this piano, this man, this song ... *in my end is my beginning.*

I am emboldened to put my hand on Sasha's shoulder. When he leaves I shall give him the diaries, and he will take them away, he will free me. Instead of resenting the years I wasted in longing for him, I shall regard them as strengthening, as instructional. Beside me, Orlando harmonizes with me, as he has always done, and I take his hand, feel his strong fingers curl round mine, remember our childhood, and the happy memories.

Before Nicola came.

NINE

Two days have passed and I'm on my own again. I'd planned to go for a long hike this morning, all the way to the cliff head at the end of my view, then up onto the top and along to where I could catch a bus back to Shale if I feel too exhausted to do the return walk. But clouds lower just above the horizon, turning the sea a thick grey. Bristles of fine rain slant fitfully across my windows. The weather seems to have broken.

I make an alternative plan. I drive into the heart of east Kent, heading for the little village of Madden, thirty-two miles away, where Valerie Johnson's parents still live, as I have discovered from the phone book. I know I am obsessed, but increasingly I wonder if the full-stop I have reached in my life might not be transformed into a mere comma, a semicolon, if only I could rid myself of Nicola for once, if not for all.

I'm not quite sure what I'm doing here, or what I plan to do. I can hardly knock at the door and say I used to be a friend of Nicola's, just as their daughter was. Had she lived, she would have been more or less the same age as I am. Play it by ear, I tell myself. If nothing else, maybe a ghost or two will be laid to rest.

The village of Madden is quiet. And small. It consists mainly of a high street lined with handsome red brick Queen Anne houses or Georgian cottages. There are two or three larger houses set further back, but not many. I spot a chemist, a newsagent, two pubs and a small corner shop. A mobile library van is parked across from a small recreation ground. A broad flat stream flows from the surrounding fields, runs beneath the main road and emerges into more fields. Its surface is littered with reeds and mallards; a third pub sits on its banks, with a terrace overhanging the water.

There are two churches, one brick and Catholic, the Church of St Michael and All His Angels, the other grey stone with a square Norman tower. The churchyard is extensive and well cared for. I park in a nearby side street and walk in through the wrought iron gates. It is ancient and peaceful; holly bushes, yew and a couple of cypress trees add a suitable melancholy. I walk up and down the sandy paths until I finally find the plot I'm looking for. On a rectangular piece of polished black granite, words are carved in square-cut gold letters.

Valerie Anne Johnson. 1939-1951
beloved daughter of Michael and Maureen,
At peace with God.

There are fresh flowers – small pink rosebuds – in a metal vase. The grass around the headstone is neatly mown.

A wooden bench faces the grave. Is it possible for inanimate objects to exude misery? This monument to a much-loved daughter seems to cry out with pain; I imagine that the Johnson parents, Michael and Maureen, have spent hours and hours of their lives here, suffering, weeping. I cannot bear it for very long.

As I am about to leave, someone comes walking towards me. A man in a navy-blue raincoat, his head bare. He wears a blue-and-white-striped shirt with a black tie, and cotton slacks, and carries flowers wrapped in white paper. As he comes nearer, I can see that his hair is thin and white, his eyes a watery blue. Once he must have

288

been a big man, but age has diminished him.

'That's my daughter's grave,' he remarks matter-of-factly, which explains the fact that he seems vaguely familiar. I must have seen his photograph in Ava's scrapbooks.

'She was very young,' I say.

'Eleven, going on twelve,' he says.

'How tragic.'

'She was murdered.' A shadow crosses his over-rosy cheeks.

Unless I tell him why I'm here, I will have no option but to pretend I know nothing about what happened, then turn and walk away.

I draw in a deep breath. 'Mr Johnson, you don't know me at all.'

He nods.

'But Nicola – your daughter's best friend – was my best friend too. Until she was murdered, too.'

'I heard about that. Funny how things work out.' He bends, a little stiffly, and picks up the metal vase. 'I'll take these home to Mother,' he says. He hands the roses in the vase to me, their stems dripping water, then walks towards a tap which rises from the grass about ten yards away. He refills it, puts the fresh rosebuds in and re-places it on the grave, then wraps the original bunch in the white paper. 'She loved pink, did our Valerie,' he says.

'I did, too. I was wearing a pink dress the night before we found ... before Nicola's body was found.'

'I come here every single day,' he says. 'Some-times twice. Mother doesn't get out like she used to, so if it's a nice day, I get her into her wheel-chair and bring her along.' He gazes sadly at the grave. 'It doesn't do either of us much good, to keep on hashing it all over. I suppose we ought to let it go, after all this time, but it's all we have left of her.' He starts to shake. 'Our little angel,' he murmurs. 'Our little girl.'

I put my hand on his arm. 'Mr Johnson, I'm so terribly sorry for you. I can't imagine the pain you've endured.'

'Nobody can. Not unless they've lost a child too.' He looks at me, and a tear runs down his cheek. He doesn't brush it away. 'We often sit here, Mother and I, talking to her. She had so many plans ... we still like to discuss them, even though none of them will ever...' His voice fades.

I think of the two dead girls, all the promises unfulfilled, all the hopes snuffed out with two senseless acts of brutality.

Mr Johnson suddenly turns on me. 'Valerie can't mean anything to you. You're not a journalist, are you?'

'Absolutely not.'

'Then what are you doing here?'

'To be honest, I'm not sure.' I twist on the bench so that I'm facing him. 'I was one of the two children who discovered Nicola Stone's – Farnham's – body.'

He looks astonished. 'It was children who found her?'

'Yes. We were both a bit younger than she was, and—'

'That's terrible,' he says, shaking his head.

'That shouldn't have happened.'

'We can't possibly pretend to be grieving for her,' I explain, 'but I think it's true to say that neither of us have ever really got over it. Especially me. Since the two deaths seem to be interconnected in some way, I thought that maybe if I came here, it would help me to come to terms with it, help me get on with my life – because, quite frankly, I'm kind of bogged down in the past. Does that sound crazy?'

'Not in the least. Maureen – my wife – and I are too.'

'But with much more reason.'

He nods. 'Look, would you like to come back, have a cup of tea, see Maureen? She'd enjoy the company, I dare say. Like I said, she doesn't get out a lot any more.'

'That would be very kind of you, Mr Johnson. I'd like that very much.'

The house is in a side street just off the High Street, a comfortable brick cottage with a narrow front garden separated from the pavement by a low picket fence. There's a little iron-trellised porch with wisteria climbing over it, and diamond-paned windows. A thatched roof is kept in place by chicken-wire netting. The front door opens straight into a dark sitting room which contains a sofa, a big television screen and a high-backed chair. There are low bookcases on two walls, containing twelve matching volumes of the *Encyclopedia Britannica*, the works of Jane Austen bound in limp blue leather, a lot of magazines, a piano tucked under some steep stairs leading to the upper part of the house.

'I'll just go and put the kettle on,' Mr Johnson says. 'Like a biscuit with your tea?'

'That would be really lovely,' I say, over-enthusiastically.

He disappears and I look round some more, though there's not a lot to see. On the piano is a framed photograph of Valerie, a plain child with chipmunk cheeks and a shy smile, an enlarged version of what must have been her last school photo. Draped over the frame is a thin gold chain. The original hearth is still in place, but a modern wood-burning stove has been fitted into the inglenook. There are some watercolours on the walls, simple but promising, which I guess were done by Valerie. There's a portrait of Valerie painted in dreamy sort of pastels, wearing a soft white dress and the gold chain round her neck; she looks ethereal and unreal. I suspect that it was commissioned after she'd died.

'Here we go.' Mr Johnson reappears with a tray holding a teapot and three cups and saucers. There are biscuits on a matching plate.

'That looks great,' I say. 'My favourite biscuits.'

'Chocolate digestives. We always have them – they were Valerie's favourite too.'

Suddenly we hear a voice from some back part of the house. 'Valerie? Is that you, Valerie? Where've you been, you naughty girl? We've been so worried.'

'It's all right, Mother.' Mr Johnson raises his voice. 'We've got a visitor.'

There's a pause. Then the voice says tiredly, 'I

292

don't want a visitor, I want Valerie.'

'Mother's never been the same since it happened,' Mr Johnson tells me. 'And she ... well, she's ... she's not got long, Miss Beecham, so don't mind what she says, will you?'

'Of course not.'

'I'll just go and get her.'

He leaves the room again.

There are photograph albums on the table beside one end of the sofa and I pick one up, turn the thick black pages. Oh my God! I press a hand to my chest. After all these years, here is Nicola again, a black-and-white Nicola, grinning at the camera, her arm through that of a girl I now know to be Valerie. And here she is once more, and again, and still again. The sight of her brings back such vivid memories that I find it hard to breathe. She looks far too innocent to have seduced Bertram Yelland, or shoplifted in Woolworths, far too sweet to have deliberately ruined her mother's evening dress or treated Miss Vane so spitefully.

Many of the photos show Valerie with various relatives at various family gatherings. One woman is obviously her grandmother, the Justice of the Peace, there's an aunt and some cousins, an uncle with Valerie sitting on his shoulders. But there are enough pictures of Valerie and Nicola to make it clear that they were very close. And there are several of Mr Johnson, dark-haired, tall and hunky, muscled arms akimbo, or striking a bodybuilder's pose, or carrying two little girls on his shoulders – Valerie and Nicola, I assume.

Guiltily I put the album down as I hear his voice soothing his wife along the passage. She appears on his arm, tiny and shrunken, looking a good fifteen years older than he is. She is painfully thin; her skin has the waxy yellow look that betokens some mortal disease, cancer, I would imagine. Her tiny claw-like hands are manicured and she wears a wedding band and a diamond engagement ring; both of which must have been resized to fit her emaciated fingers. Behind them patters an aged liver-and-white spaniel, wheezing like a furnace.

'Who are you?' Mrs Johnson shuffles into the upright chair and her husband fusses with pillows, making sure that she's comfortable. I imagine she's had at least one stroke, because her mouth droops on one side and it's obvious that one arm is useless. 'I thought you were Valerie come home at last.'

'This is a friend of ... of Valerie's,' Mr Johnson says.

'What's her name?'

'Hello, Mrs Johnson,' I say. 'I'm Alice Beecham.' I speak clearly, not sure if she's deaf.

'Beecham? I don't remember any Beecham,' she says.

'Yes, you do, Mother. You've forgotten, that's all.'

'Have I?'

'I was just passing through the village, and I remembered somebody telling me you lived here now.'

'So I invited her in for a cup of tea.'

'That's good of you, Mike.' She turns in my

direction. 'He's always been a kind man, ever since I first met him. We were always so happy, weren't we, Mikey? Not like we are now.'

'I'm always happy when I'm with you, Maureen, you know that,' says her husband, his voice not quite steady. He takes her hand in his and pats it.

I imagine that neither of these two have been happy since the day Nicola's father killed their daughter.

The ancient dog totters across the carpet and drools over my sandals.

'That's Minnie,' says Johnson. 'Minnie the Third, actually. We gave Valerie a puppy when she was ten, just like this. Since then, well, we always have the same kind of dog, don't we, Mother?'

'Always call them Minnie,' says his wife.

We sit for a while, making desultory chat. The subjects we wish to talk about – Nicola and Valerie – are too big for this little room, too much present. I am filled with a sudden fear that I will end up like these two, unable to shake off my traumas, unable to move on. I've tried. I fled to Paris, and then to Michigan. But flight doesn't work, I know that now, any more than simply standing still does.

'It's her birthday, end of next week,' Mr Johnson says suddenly.

'She'd have turned thirty-four.' Mrs Johnson raises a hand to her face and starts to claw at her cheeks.

Her husband takes her hand in his. 'Now, Mother...'

'He's free!' She tries to shout but her voice is too feeble. 'That devil, that evil devil ... He's served his sentence, but we're still serving ours. It's not fair, it's not fair...' And she collapses into weak sobs.

I rise to my feet. 'I think I should leave you. Thank you for the tea, both of you.'

'I'll walk you to the gate.' Mr Johnson opens the front door and we both step out onto the carefully tended path. He pulls the door half-closed behind him. 'Sorry about that.'

'Don't be.'

'I know we should move on, but there's little enough for Mother to do, these days.' He sighs. 'When I think of her before all this happened ... in the WI, leader of the Girl Guide pack, volunteer at the church. She used to take part in the local drama society, too ... matter of fact, that's where she met Nicola's mother, only amateurs, of course, but some of their shows were ... she doesn't do any of that now. At least I have my garden, and I'm a churchwarden. There's Minnie to walk. It helps a little.' He straightens himself, adjusts his tie. 'Have you come far?'

'Actually...' I hesitate a little. 'I live in Shale.'

'Nice little place,' he says. 'Unspoiled. I get over there from time to time – Mother loves the sea. I take her down the end of the pier, have a nice cuppa before we come home. Makes a change.'

'Oh,' I say, before I can stop myself. 'You must look me up next time you come.' I scrabble in my wallet for one of my new business cards, cursing myself, for I know that I do not wish to

296

meet the Johnsons again, or be further ensnared in their grief.

He glances at the card, then puts it into the pocket of his shirt. 'Thanks,' he says. 'We might just do that, one of these days.'

As I pull open the gate, I say, 'I hope you don't mind me asking, but were you surprised by Mr Farnham's confession?'

He shakes his head, stretches his mouth. 'To be honest, not really. I was in the Army during the war, and what I learned about human nature ... and none of us are what we seem, are we? We all wear disguises.'

I nod; he is right.

'So when I heard that a reputable bloke like Geoff Farnham had killed my little girl, I ... let's say I was less surprised than I might have been. Over the years, Nicola had let one or two things drop, not just about him but about her mother as well ... it wasn't quite the respectable sort of house it appeared to be on the surface. Sometimes we wondered whether we should try to stop the girls seeing each other, but if I mentioned it, Valerie would get so upset that we didn't have the heart to insist.'

Just like me. 'And your wife said that Mr Farnham's been let out now?'

'That's right. It's been quite a while now, as a matter of fact ... eight years or so? Maybe longer. Whichever it is, it was much too soon for Maureen.'

'I presume you've never seen any of them again.'

He looks at me as though I'm insane. 'Why on

earth would I want to do that? We moved away from the area as soon as we could sell our house, came down here to be near my wife's parents. If you told me that Louise Farnham was going to be staying next door, I'd leave at once. I don't want to see any of them again, ever.' His face has flushed and there is sweat along his jaw. He straightens the collar points of his shirt. 'It's bad enough to be so obsessed with our own memories – we don't need to be part of theirs as well.'

'I'm sorry, I shouldn't have...'

'You probably think we've wasted our lives,' he says. 'And on the surface, that's probably what it looks like. But Valerie was everything to us, she was our ... what's the word? ... *raison d'être* when she was alive, and she still is, even though she's dead.' His smile is grim. 'I'm not saying it's the best way, but it's the way we've chosen to handle it.'

Driving back to Shale, I consider the fact that Geoffrey Farnham is out of gaol, and has been for some time. Why? How? According to Ava's scrapbooks, he was sentenced to twenty years. Even with time off, that would mean fourteen years to serve, so why had he been released even earlier than that? I could find out, I suppose, if I knew where to start looking.

I think too, of Nicola. Is she still loved and mourned, as Valerie Johnson is? Does someone tend her grave and leave fresh flowers?

By the time I get home, the shadows are lengthening as the sun moves lower in the sky behind the town. This is the time of day when the cliffs of Cap Griz Nez are particularly clear, the long green headlands of France seemingly as close as the ones only a few miles further round the coast from Shale. Gulls float on the water like scraps of torn newsprint; streaks of crimson indicate that we shall have yet another fine day tomorrow.

I sit at the table in my bay window and force myself to face facts. I make a list. I am not going to think about what I would do if I were able conclusively to point to a culprit responsible for Nicola's murder, but I am sure that the answer to the puzzle is in front of me, if I can only figure it out.

Julian Tavistock, I write.
Bertram Yelland
Miss Vane
Gordon Parker
Louise Stone
Simon Stone
Edwardes

I arbitrarily dismiss my parents and Ava, my older brothers and their friends. Perhaps wrongly, I also omit Charlie Tavistock, Jeremy Pearce and David Gardner as being too young or too weak to have been responsible for such violence as was perpetrated on the body.

Finally, reluctantly, I add two more names to the list of possible suspects: *Sasha Elias*, and, lastly, *Orlando*.

Each of them had the means, and, to a greater or lesser degree, a motive, though it would be hard to imagine Miss Vane, for instance, wishing to kill Nicola just because of a malicious trick played on her, or, for that matter, Gordon Parker. The same could be true of Ava's former husband, Mr Edwardes. Whatever poison Nicola breathed into his ear, it was hard to see what motive he might have in killing her. In the end, I put brackets round all three names, sidelining them from my list of suspects.

Simon Stone, too. What possible reason could he have to kill his own sister? Unless, as with at least two of the other suspects, there might have been a sexual motive. But according to the inquest, she had not been sexually assaulted. Simon's name, too, I bracket.

I pour myself a finger of Islay single malt. It is easy to see the scenario in Julian's case, Nicola promising, tantalizing, teasing, stringing him along until, at the last moment, she refuses him, and he snaps. My guess is that whatever liberties she might have allowed him in the form of kisses and fondles, Julian was still a reluctant virgin that night. To come so close to his heart's desire, only to be thwarted at the final post ... I remember how he carried everywhere with him that golf club, that weapon. There is the added, if intangible, fact that he has come back here to Shale, when he might have been expected to move on. Is this from some spiritual inertia or a pervasive guilt that pins him here at the scene of the crime?

Bertram Yelland: Orlando and I were in a position to observe him closely, and we had concluded that it could not have been him. But what did we know, back then? We were innocents, we had no inkling of the trouble Yelland might be in if word of his unorthodox sexual arrangements were to leak out. It is easy to imagine Nicola offering another liaison that night, and he falling for it, only to come suddenly to his senses, realize how close to the wind he was sailing, that he would be facing a prison sentence if he were discovered. I can well imagine Nicola at his trial, her big-eyed pretence of ignorance and fear, putting the blame entirely onto him. Maybe she taunted him, pointed out the sword of destruction she dangled above his head. He was certainly big enough, choleric enough, to have killed her.

I face the option of the murderer being Louise Stone. It seems so unlikely, so impossibly wide of the mark, for a mother to kill her own daughter. Yet I recall the look on her face as Nicola gave that indifferent shrug, in the dining room of Glenfield House, the clear intention to take absolutely no notice of whatever her mother had asked. A small enough detail, but add it to years and years of similar actions, to a lifetime of wilful damage, careless disregard, cruelty, even. Like Erin, I remember the *Bad Seed*. Might not Louise have taken a reluctant decision, realizing the impossibility of loosing Nicola upon an unsuspecting world? I recall her agitated behaviour the following afternoon. Looking back, isn't two o'clock somewhat late to start calling on your missing daughter's friends in the hope of finding out where she'd gone? And I remember, too, Mr Johnson, earlier, saying Louise was a member of the amateur dramatic society. If she could act, wouldn't it be relatively easy to pretend to be distraught?

I consider Sasha Elias. His motive was strong enough to make him an obvious suspect. Gordon Parker had hinted that the townspeople thought he might have been responsible, but that could have been no more than anti-German feeling so close to the end of a war which had plunged Britain into poverty. I doubted that anti-Semitism had much to do with it; there'd have been sympathy rather than hostility.

But Nicola's malicious stories were losing him clients. Or were they malicious? I wonder how naive I have been, all this time. I recall his arms round me, his hands over mine on the keyboard, the brush of his arm against my breasts. Then I recall the pages he has written about his little lost sisters, and am once again certain that there was nothing perverted in his behaviour. But if Nicola was deliberately sabotaging his carefully built-up stable of private pupils, it could have meant serious financial repercussions for him. And I know, from the gathering at the lifeboat station, that he had reserves of anger to draw on. But Gordon Parker had implied that Sasha had been cleared at the time of any involvement in the murder.

Finally, fearfully, I look at Orlando's name. I don't want to, but I must. I draw a heart round it, cross-hatch it, add thorny tendrils, berries, each of which I meticulously fill in.

Although he had not yet reached his full height, he was certainly strong enough to kill a slender little creature like Nicola, though he might have had some trouble getting her into the grassy clearing without leaving any trace. There was the fact that he hated Nicola. And she'd threatened to desecrate his blackberry patch...

I seriously contemplate the possibility that the man who is, among much else, my oldest and dearest friend, could be a murderer. Then I scrumple up my list, and go to bed.

TEN

Nothing has changed by the next morning.

Nor had I imagined that it would.

I pick my crumpled list from the waste-paper basket and smooth it out on the table. On a fresh piece of paper, I write down Julian's name, and Louise's. I omit Orlando's. I will face the possibility of his guilt later, if I have to, though it squats at the back of my head like a malevolent toad.

Meanwhile, there are Julian and Louise to consider. Should I tackle them, lay my case in front of each of them, see how they respond? And if so, whom should I approach first? Is it really my place to take such a responsibility on to myself, to behave as though I were an amateur detective? In any case, how can I determine if either of them is guilty? There's always the possibility that one or other might break down and confess, but I can see no reason why they might suddenly end their silence after so long, just because I come round asking questions. And if they did, what would I do, go to the police? And how dangerous would it be to confront someone who has got away with such a crime for so long, and therefore might reasonably either resent or fear my impertinent intrusion?

And then there is the question of their personal trauma. Louise has obviously made a success of moving on from the death of her daughter, Julian is a pillar of the community. If they are innocent, what right do I have to bring it all up again? And again, how exactly would I introduce the subject into the conversation?

My head spins.

I came down here on a whim of the fate I did not believe in. Maybe I should let fate, chance, destiny, intervene again.

Which it does, five days later. It's five fifteen and I've been working for eight hours at a stretch, another boring report from Brussels, this time concerning the use of fossil fuels in East European countries. I sit for a moment, twiddling a pencil between my fingers. My friend and colleague, Anna Krampedach, would never be offered such work, or, if she was, would refuse it. She translates only the things that, as she puts it, 'sink' to her. Plays for the most part, sometimes poetry. In the bureaucratic corridors of Brussels, am I labelled 'the fossil fuel person', the one who can be relied on to accept the boring jobs nobody else will touch? I probably earn twice as much as Anna, but, as Erin has colour-fully pointed out, who needs money that badly?

The pencil snaps, and I get up and walk into the kitchen. My fridge is empty. If I am to eat that night, I need groceries. Walking along the road towards the only shop that stays open late, I glance through the windows of the Wooden Lugger, and spot Julian Tavistock sitting alone with a drink in front of him. He has both fists on the tabletop and is staring morosely into a glass of what looks like gin and tonic. It's not a cosy sort of place: no twinkling horse-brasses or hunting prints, no snug corners or padded banquettes, just glaring overhead lighting, rough wooden tables, and an absence of anything that could detract from the main purpose of the place, which is clearly to consume alcohol.

I can always buy fish and chips, I tell myself, and I push open the door of the pub. The place stinks of stale tobacco smoke; over the years, the walls and ceiling have been stained the colour of fudge by countless cigarettes. I order a drink and stand in front of Julian.

'Mind if I join you?'

He looks up apprehensively and then recognizes me. His face brightens. 'Alice!' He rises to his feet. 'Of course not. Please sit down. Nice to have someone to talk to.'

Knowing that he is as haunted by Nicola's death as I am, I don't beat around the bush. 'Were you sleeping with her?' I ask abruptly.

He has no need to ask whom I'm talking about. Nor does he appear to take offence at my question, though he blushes awkwardly. 'Not exactly,' he says. 'She let me go ... well, at the time it seemed pretty far to me. But what did I know about sex, except that I wanted it? We were so young, so ignorant, really. Innocent. No idea what it was all about.'

'Was it her you were attracted to, or sex in general?'

'Sex in general, I suppose, but only with her. Not that there was anyone else to have it with. Let's face it, back then, nice girls *didn't*.'

'Except for her.'

He looks at me quizzically. 'But then she *wasn't* a nice girl, was she?'

I let the question pass. 'What happened the night of my party?'

Suddenly he looks panic-stricken. 'I ... I don't know. Nothing.' Waving his hands about, he fixes his attention on a local boatman in navy-blue sweater and short rubber boots who has just come through the door.

'Don't be naive, Julian. Something did.'

'Nothing to do with ... with what happened.'

'Nicola's murder, you mean.'

He winces. 'Yes.'

'I saw you kissing her out in the garden.'

'But that was earlier.'

'Earlier than what?'

'Than ... well, than her leaving your house and, presumably, going off with ... meeting up with whoever it was who...'

'Whoever it was who killed her.' I am brutal. I can see that for years he has avoided saying or thinking about the specifics of what happened to Nicola.

'Yes, that.' He raises his glass and drains it.

'Can I get you another of those?' It seems fairly obvious that the drink he has just finished was not his first.

He looks at his watch. 'I shouldn't really. But what the hell.' He has not yet met my eyes.

While I'm up at the bar, ordering for us both, I watch him resume the position he was in, staring at the scarred wooden tabletop. How many times has he sat there brooding, I wonder. I sense that the reason he has answered my questions is that he is desperate to talk about Nicola and until now has not allowed himself to do so.

The boatman has settled on a barstool and is talking about a huge shoal of herring off the Dogger Bank. He glances at me and turns back to the bartender. 'You could lean over the side of your boat and pick them out of the water with your bare hands,' he says.

Back at my table, I push Julian's drink across to him. 'Did you see her leave my party?' I ask.

He shakes his head, still avoiding my gaze.

'Did you go off with her, Julian?'

The blush returns to his face. He stares over my shoulder, and his eyes begin to water.

I lean forward. 'Was it you, Julian? Did *you* kill her?'

There is a silence. He picks up his fresh drink but doesn't raise it to his lip. Ice tinkles faintly against the side of the glass. Have I got him, I wonder? Surely, if he was innocent, he would rush to deny it, be vehement, be indignant. But he says nothing.

'Julian...' I gentle my voice. 'I'm not going to

tell anyone, I promise.'

'Oh Jesus...'

'I'm as hung up on it all as you are. I'm only trying to reach a resolution for myself. I'm not really interested in who did it, or even why.' I'm lying, but he is not to know that.

'Oh God...' He puts his glass down again and knuckles his eyes. 'Oh, dear God...'

'What is it?'

'I wish I knew what to do.'

'What about?'

He shakes his head. Puts his elbows on the table and hides his face in his hands. I wait. When he finally speaks, his voice is muffled and I have to lean forward to hear him. 'I've been living with this for twenty years,' he says.

'So have I.'

'And it only gets worse.'

I feel as though I'm standing on the edge of a high cliff, trying to persuade someone to leap off onto the rocks far below. 'What happened that night, Julian? What did you do?'

From the breast pocket of his bank-manager's suit, he removes a folded white handkerchief and presses it carefully to each of his eyes, then returns it to its place. He takes hold of his glass with both hands. 'I don't really know.'

I try to keep my expression neutral. 'How can you not know?'

'Look...' Julian's shoulders sag, '...if it was happening today, I'd have said she was on something that evening, but of course we didn't know about drugs, stuff like that, not back then...not even her.'

'How do you mean?'

'She was all hyped up. Excited.' His gaze flutters around until it finds the bar behind me. 'Dangerous. You remember how she was.'

'Vividly.' She has brought so much trouble to us all. I wonder what kind of a woman she'd have become.

'She was ... leading me on,' continues Julian. 'Touching the ... the front of my trousers. Slipping her hand inside so her fingers were on my ... on my skin. I felt as though I was going to burst. I thought ... I don't really know what I thought. She said that later, if I wanted to, she would ... she would let me, you know ... let me go all the way.'

He seems so miserable and ashamed that I can hardly bear to look at him. 'And did she?'

He looks at his watch again. 'Look, I really am going to have to get home. Nicola will be—' He stops abruptly, his face appalled. 'I mean *Monica* will be waiting for me.' He pushes himself upright. 'Alice, I really can't talk about this any more.'

'You have to,' I say firmly. 'Sit down, Julian. Just tell me what happened.'

He sighs, as though he knows he has no choice. 'I've never told anybody any of this – in fact, I've tried never to think about it.'

'I'm the same, Julian. I understand.'

He fidgets for a bit with his glass. Then the words come out in a rush. 'What happened is, that at some point, I don't exactly know what time, but quite late, after people started going home, she told me she was going to walk along

309

the seafront and if I really wanted to ... you know ... I was to follow her five minutes later, because she didn't want anyone to see us leaving together. So I did that, waited four or five minutes and then ran along the promenade after her. There were some people walking their dogs, some man wheeling a bicycle, two girls walking along, giggling. I could see Nicola clearly in the distance, the moon was tremendously bright, and it only took me a couple of minutes to catch up with her, so she grabbed my hand, and we walked along and she told me in ... in extremely graphic detail what we were going to do as soon as she reached a place she knew where we could be private.' He stops.

'And then?'

'She ... she made me put my hand up her skirt and...' He swallows. '...she wasn't wearing any underpants.' He shakes his head. 'I can't explain how exciting it was. I was fifteen, nearly sixteen, it was the first time I'd ever felt a woman's ... I couldn't believe I was only a few minutes away from ... well, from losing my virginity. God! I've never experienced anything as frantically exciting. Not before, not since.'

'So what happened?'

'We got up to that area just beyond the castle, and we walked up a lane and out between some trees onto a grassy bit, near a huge roundish area of brambles and bushes. You could see the moon shining on the water, and lights on the horizon, the lightship blinking. Even though it was night time, there were birds singing, and some seagulls, I remember. And she said, she said, This is okay, right here. And she walked up close to me, and started undoing my belt...' Julian looks over at the boatman who is now talking impassionedly about a monstrous catch of cod he'd seen once off the Scilly Isles. '...I have to tell you, Alice, I felt as though I had a flagpole in my trousers. I'd got my putter with me, God knows why – I think I was trying to pretend I was just going to practise putts, if anyone asked – and I dropped it on the ground, put my arms round her. And then, then...' His voice fades to silence.

'Then *what*?'

'She turned away from me and said in that cool little voice of hers, she said, "Actually, Julian, *actually*, I think I've changed my mind."'

His mouth twists and I can see how that long-ago rejection torments him still. 'What did you do?' I am surprised at how accurate my reconstruction of the scene has proved to be.

'I couldn't believe I'd heard right. I said, What do you mean? And she said, I don't feel like it, after all, or something like that. Obviously I was devastated. Mortified. When I finally realized she was serious, I grabbed her by the neck and shook her as hard as I could, I shouted that she was a rotten bitch, words to that effect, I shoved her, so hard that she fell over. Then I ... I kicked her a couple of times. I was ... I was sobbing, not just with the ... the sexual let-down, but with the humiliation of it. I looked down at her lying on the grass and her eyes were shining with triumph, and I realized that she must have planned the whole thing.'

'And then what?'

311

'Oh God, I was so ... so angry, so utterly frustrated. I think I kicked her again, and then I turned away and walked off, walked home. I heard her laughing, so I know she was alive when I left. But for years I've wondered whether maybe she collapsed and died after I'd gone, from my kicking her, or half-strangling her or something.'

'But you must have known that wasn't so.'

'Why should I have?'

'Because she was found *in*side that clump of brambles, not *out*side.'

'As a matter of fact, I've never been entirely sure where she was found. Once I heard that she was dead, I tried never to think about her again.' He smiles ruefully. 'And utterly failed.'

'The point is that after you'd gone, someone else must have moved her.'

'Yes, but Alice, don't you see? What terrifies me is the possibility that it was me who actually killed her.' A spasm contorts his face and for a moment I see again the boy I once knew.

'I don't think you could have, Julian. Did you look back, did you see her get up?'

'I didn't look back at all. You can't imagine how embarrassed and foolish I felt.'

'Which is what she wanted.'

'I suppose so. But on top of that, there's the fact that it was probably my golf club which was used to kill her.'

'You don't know that. They never found the weapon.'

'The wounds on her...' He shudders slightly. 'According to the local paper, they were consistent with a weapon like a golf club.'

312

'Even so, it's not your fault.' Behind me, the boatman chortles at some witticism of the barman's. 'Did you see anyone else on your way back?'

'Someone walking a dog, a couple of teenagers snogging under a tree, a man and woman climbing up the path to the top of the hill. And when I got nearer to your house, I met Orlando on his bike. Otherwise, nobody was around. The place was deserted.'

'What about the police? They must have interviewed you.'

'Of course they did. More than once.'

'Didn't they ask for an alibi?'

'Yes. But it seemed fairly obvious that they couldn't be sure when she left your house. I said I'd been on the beach for a bit, that I'd danced with various girls, I'd been in the dining room and out in the garden. There were so many people milling around that night that nobody could be sure who was where at any particular time.'

'So you lied.'

'Through my teeth. And please don't think I'm proud of it. But I was so terrified that I'd be accused of murdering her. Until now, I've gone on being terrified, if you really want to know, though I realize that, firstly, I didn't kill her, and secondly, nobody could pin anything on me if I had. But I can't have been away from the party more than twenty or thirty minutes, And then I walked home with my brother Charlie, shortly after my mother left.'

'Which Charlie corroborated?' I hated the way

313

I sounded like something out of a crime novel.

'Of course – because it was true. The police believed everything I said because there were plenty of people to say they were pretty sure they'd seen me around more or less the whole time.'

He stands up and stretches, then comes round the table and puts a hand on my shoulder. 'I really have to go, Alice. But thank you for doing something which should have been done years ago.'

'And that is?'

'You've forced me to tell you what happened, to face up to the past. It's immensely liberating. I suppose I ought to feel ashamed of myself, but I don't.'

'Ashamed of what?'

He lifts his shoulders. 'Lying to the police, kicking a girl – and she was such a little thing, wasn't she? I've lived for years in terror that one day I'll feel a hand on my shoulder and find myself accused of murder, and carted off to jail, unable to do a damn thing about it.'

'Even though over the years you must have realized you had nothing to do with her death.'

'That hasn't stopped me feeling that in some way I was *morally* responsible, even if not actually so.' And then he looks at me directly for the first time since he'd started talking, and smiles at me. 'It sounds silly, really, but by telling you about it, someone who was there, someone who knew Nicola, I feel almost ... reborn.'

This rough-and-ready pub makes a strange confessional, I think, as the door opens to let in

314

a waft of sea-flavoured air, and then closes again behind him. The question I have to ask myself is whether I believe him. I suspect that I do.

I long for my own rebirthing.

Crumpling my fish and chip newspaper and stowing it in the rubbish can under my kitchen sink, I make a mug of tea and go over to sit on my window-seat, looking out at the sea.

Orlando. My beloved Orlando. Can he possibly be implicated? If I accept the version of events which Julian has just given me, then I also have to accept that he did indeed see Orlando cycling in the direction of the Secret Glade. What did he find when he got there, if he did get there? Can I really believe it possible that Orlando, of all people, could have killed Nicola?

His story about her threat to lay waste to his special blackberry patch sounded such a Nicola kind of thing to say, and if he'd believed it, if he'd seen her go off with Julian in that direction, he might well have followed, if only to protect what, over the summer ripening, he must have come to consider, in some way, his own property. Had he found her there, in pain, perhaps, from Julian's kicks, found her at his mercy, wanted to inflict some damage? Had he, too, seized her by her vulnerable neck, shaken her – 'such a little thing' – and found, to his horror, that he'd killed her? It sounds all too horrifyingly plausible.

ELEVEN

Do I wait for fate to intervene once again, or do I grab hold of the future? Be reactive, or proactive? In other words, do I bide my time, in the hope that sooner or later, I'll encounter Louise Stone in some casual way, or should I boldly go and knock at her door?

Outside my windows, the green has turned into a dusty plain reminiscent of the African veldt. The sun hangs like a golden clock face in a white-blue sky. Major de Grey's garden is full of shrubs so parched that their dried-up leaves are falling fitfully to the baking soil in which they are planted. It is too hot to work, or even to think. I change into my swimsuit and sit on the shingle, plunging every now and then into a sea which has turned the unreal green of a travel-brochure photograph.

After two days of dithering, while fate does nothing to help, I wait until dusk and then make my way to the North End. Although it is cooler after dark, there is no need for me to delay this visit until the light is fading, yet by doing so, I feel more secure, as though I am a creature of the night, whose natural habitat is the dank and gloom of a subterranean cave, a burrow in the ground.

Eventually I find myself at Number Twelve, Fisher Street, in front of Louise's racing-green front door. The curtains are not yet drawn, and when I glance through the window into the as yet unlit sitting room, I can see it is empty. Perhaps she's out. I hope so because I can then further postpone this meeting. I tap the knocker, just to be sure.

Footsteps approach along the narrow hall. They're heavier than the quick brisk ones I associate with Louise and I surmise that the person now lifting the old-fashioned latch will prove to be the man I glimpsed when I last came down this street, some weeks earlier.

I am right. My smile is ready when the door opens. He raises enquiring eyebrows. 'Yes?'

'My name's Alice Beecham,' I say.

He frowns, as though wondering whether the name should register with him, and then decides it shouldn't. 'How can I help you?'

'I wondered if I could have a word with Mrs Stone – Louise.'

'What about?'

'Er...' I'm not prepared for this question. 'She'll know who I am.'

'Just a moment.'

He retreats down the passage. I hear voices, an angry exclamation, something being banged down on a table. A few minutes later he returns. 'I suspect you're going to try and rake over matters which we much prefer not to think about.'

'Well, yes, maybe, but...'

'In that case, you'll have to forgive us if we appear uncooperative. However, since my wife

317

seems to think you should come in, you'd better do so.'

As I follow him, I try to digest the fact that this pleasant-looking man is Louise's husband. Is this Geoffrey Farnham himself – Valerie's father has told me that he has been released from prison – or has she remarried in the years since I left Shale? He reminds me very much of Mr Johnson, with the same open face, the same haunted eyes. He moves ahead of me into the sitting room, still familiar to me from the past. The wooden beam, now wreathed in pot-plant ivy, still holds up the ceiling at one end of the room, the walls are a simple cream, there are long curtains of ivory and oyster linen.

Louise is sitting on a sofa covered in beige and piped in chocolate-brown. 'Hello, Alice,' she says, without smiling. 'After we met the other day, I knew you would eventually show up here.' She indicates the man now standing protectively beside her. 'This is Nicola's father.' She looks up at him. 'Darling, Alice is one of the two children who found her body.'

He looks me over. 'I'm sorry that had to happen,' he says.

'In fact, it was from Alice's twelfth birthday party that Nicola disappeared.'

'I remember you telling me about it,' Farnham says. His expression is marginally less hostile. 'You were by way of being Nicola's closest friend down here, weren't you?'

'That's right.'

'What do you want from us?' Louise asks. There is a smudge of pinkish lipstick on the rim

318

of her glass, like half a kiss.

'I'm not entirely sure. Any help you can give me. Any ... clarification. Illumination. Something like that.'

She regards me steadily, without speaking. Then she nods. Sighs. 'I suppose it's about time.'

'You don't have to go into all this,' Farnham tells her. 'It's done. It's finished with.'

'Is it? I don't think so. Not for any of us.'

I regret having come here. 'I'll go,' I say. 'I shouldn't have come in the first place.'

'No, Alice, wait. If anyone has the right to hear what really happened, to hear what we have to say, you do. But it won't be easy; we may need a drink to help us through.' She lays a hand affectionately on her husband's arm. 'Would you mind, darling?'

Farnham retreats to a side-table at the end of the room where bottles and glasses wait. Without asking what I'd like, he pours gin-and-tonics for all three of us, slides a lemon slice into each glass, and hands them to us. 'Right,' he says, 'Let's get it over with, shall we?' He's clearly a man used to making decisions, to being in command.

'Alice?' Louise looks at me.

I take a deep breath. Embarrassed by the sympathetic manner with which she waits for me to speak, I stumble through my now-familiar recitation about my inability to move onward, my urgent need for some kind of resolution.

'I apologize for bringing this up,' I finish lamely. 'It must be terribly painful for you both.'

319

Louise nods. 'It is.'

I try not to stare too hard at Farnham, who has seated himself close to his wife on the sofa. This man killed a girl by pulling a scarf around her neck so tightly that she strangled to death. I wonder whether he heard the small bones in Valerie Johnson's neck snap. I wonder if he felt pity as her dying fingers clutched at the suffocating ligature. He seems so ordinary, yet he must surely have nightmares about those brief minutes in which he lost control and an innocent child was murdered. Given his war record, perhaps killing came more easily to him than to others. But that is not my present concern. 'It's painful for me, too, believe me.'

Husband and wife glance at each other as I lurch to a halt. Neither says anything for a moment, as though they are collecting their ammunition, armouring themselves against me. Louise says finally, faintly, 'The shock of finding her must have been...' Staring down at her drink, she says, 'I always remember your faces, that afternoon. Yours and Orlando's. So white and pinched. I think I knew then what had happened.' She grimaces. 'You were far too young to have been through such an appalling experience.'

'I feel that the more I can find out,' I say, 'the clearer it will all become. And that once I can look at it without flinching, the nightmares will go.' And with them, I hope, though I do not say, the inanition which plagues my inner self, holds me mired in the past.

Farnham leans towards me, hands clasped

320

between his knees. 'Maybe we should start with the background which led to me being sent to prison for murder, and why my family moved down here in the first place,' he says.

'All right.'

'I enjoyed my job,' he begins. 'I was a good headmaster. The kids liked me, I liked them. If you're at all conversant with the circumstances surrounding the death of Valerie Johnson...' He waits for a moment, and I nod my awareness of the case. '...you will be aware that a girl pupil, Barbara-Jane Finch came forward to say that I had spoken to her suggestively, or inappropriately, which added to the prosecution's case. And, of course, I confessed to the crime. Open and shut case, send him down, next case, please.'

'I know all that.'

'What you may *not* know is that a few years ago, Barbara-Jane Finch got married and eventually had a baby, a girl. She and her husband then went to the police and withdrew every word of her testimony at my trial.'

'She said that even though her evidence hadn't been crucial,' put in Louise, 'nonetheless she'd been wrestling with her conscience for years, that she'd been terrified she'd be sent to prison herself, for perjury, and it was only when she had a daughter of her own that she realized she couldn't keep silent any longer, she had to put the record straight.'

'Of course it was far too late for me by then, and besides, my wife and I weren't anxious to have the facts made public.'

'What facts were those?'

'It turned out...' Head bent, he clears his throat while Louise puts her hand on his knee, murmurs some sympathetic endearment. 'According to Barbara-Jane Finch, our daughter had bullied her into making a false statement, threatened her with whatever kind of reprisal girls *do* threaten each other with, in order to strengthen the case against me.'

'*Nicola* did that?' I stare at him, disbelieving. 'To her own father?'

'Hard to take in, isn't it? So devious.'

'So downright *wicked*,' says Louise.

'But ... but *why*?'

'Self-preservation, I should imagine.' Farnham's voice is dry. 'Though it was hardly necessary since I'd already confessed to a murder I didn't commit. My wife and I had decided, right from the start, that it was better me than the real culprit.'

'And who was that?'

Geoffrey looks at me in surprise. 'I would have thought it was obvious.'

'Is it?'

Before I can process the nebulous possibilities in my head, Louise says, 'Nicola, of course.'

'Nicola?' I return to that distant summer and try to rearrange it. '*Nicola*?' Nicola had killed Valerie? It was because of Nicola that her father was given a twenty-year prison sentence, because of Nicola that Louise had to move away from her home, set up a new life under a different name and without a much-loved husband, because of Nicola that Simon was forced to start

322

his life over again? I think back to those years, Simon's sullen silence, Louise's brave attempts at normality. I can see that over both of them must have hung the constant fear that somehow, some time, their true identities would be discovered. 'She actually murdered her best *friend*?'

'Even after all these years, it's hard to accept, but yes, she did.'

'I can't believe it.'

'Neither could we. At least...' Louise glances at her husband, '...not at first.'

'Do Valerie's parents know?'

'I doubt it,' said Farnham. 'As far as I'm aware, nobody does. Except us. And the police. And now you.'

'Certainly we've never told the Johnsons,' explains Louise. 'We talked it over and decided it was better if they went on believing Geoffrey had done it, than if they were told that Nicola, the little girl they'd known since nursery school days, was a killer.' She shrugs. 'I don't know ... maybe we were wrong. But having discussed it for hours, that's the conclusion we came to.'

'But the ... murder.' I cannot process this information. 'How on earth could such a thing have happened?'

'It was just the latest – and infinitely the worst, of course – in a never-ending line of problems with Nicola.' Louise sounds weary. 'We long ago realized that just as some babies are born with a cleft palate or a hearing deficiency, so our child was born with a defective sense of morals.'

'She was a premature baby, wasn't she?'

'That's right.' Louise seems surprised that I

323

know this. 'Perhaps she didn't have time to develop a conscience. Today I imagine she'd be diagnosed as a sociopath.'

'She was an almost textbook example,' says Farnham. 'Believe me, I had plenty of time to bone up on the subject. Like most of them, even from earliest childhood, she displayed all the classic features. The charm, the cunning, the manipulative behaviour, the domineering hostility, the constant lying.'

'The worst thing, as far as I was concerned,' says her mother, 'was the complete lack of shame or remorse, if she was caught out. Even when confronted with conclusive evidence about something she'd done, she twisted her way out of every accusation, blamed everyone but herself. And as for any kind of empathy with the people she took advantage of, like poor Valerie, she simply despised them for being weak enough to suffer.'

Painfully I remember the look on Miss Vane's face as she opened the packet containing the corsets. We had all been embarrassed by Nicola's cruelty to someone whom, even then, we recognized in some indefinable way as weaker than ourselves, but none of us had made any objection, about that or about her other unkindnesses. None of us, except Orlando.

'And once she started her periods,' Louise says matter-of-factly, 'there was the constant worry that she'd get herself pregnant.' She presses her lips together, as though trying to hold back tears. 'As well as everything else, she was ... horribly promiscuous.'

'Especially with older men,' Farnham says grimly.

Louise's mouth quivers. 'We tried,' she whispers. 'We tried so hard to love her. To accept her. To see her as disadvantaged, rather than as ... evil.'

Farnham takes her hand in his and holds it tightly. Both of them seem utterly spent, as though the strain of recalling those years of raising Nicola, added to her subsequent violent death, is proving to be too much for them to handle.

'How did she ... what happened with Valerie Johnson?'

'Apparently the poor child had a new scarf, a very pretty silk one which her doting parents had just given her. Nicola wanted it, but for once Valerie dug her feet in and refused to hand it over.' Louise covers her mouth with her hand. 'I hate talking about this. I hate remembering that awful *awful* time.'

'If you'd rather I went...' My head feels as though it might explode with shock. I try very hard not to imagine what happened in Nicola's bedroom, but nonetheless, scraps of horrified speculation wing through my brain.

'I hate the fact that our daughter was responsible for someone's *death*.' Louise has not heard me. Her voice has risen.

'Calm down, darling.' Farnham gives her arm a little shake.

'That she actually *killed* someone.' Louise is breathing hard. 'Someone who was supposed to be her best *friend*. Over a *scarf*.'

325

'As far as we were able to make out from Nicola's hysterical account of what happened,' says Farnham, 'when none of her usual techniques of persuasion worked on Valerie, she more or less said, all right, keep your stupid scarf, grabbed at the ends and pulled it as tightly as she could round Valerie's neck.'

'I don't think ... I don't *want* to think that she *meant* to kill Valerie,' Louise says. 'If I really thought *that*, I'd...'

'But having done so,' continues her husband, 'she came down the stairs from her bedroom, pretending to talk to Valerie, then pretended to see her to the front door, shutting it hard so her mother would hear her and simply assume that Valerie had gone home.'

'Then she came into my office, lounged about a bit, as she so often did, announced that she was bored and reminded me that I'd promised to take her shopping. Which indeed I had. So the two of us went on the Tube to South Kensington.' Louisa looks at her husband.

'Yes,' he says. 'Yes.'

The two of them fall silent. Louise puts her drink down and closes her eyes. Farnham breathes deeply through his nose, relaxes his shoulders.

Seconds tick by. I say nothing. What is there to say? I wish I were somewhere else. Their grief and pain sit beside us in this room where once their daughter existed.

Finally, Farnham starts again. 'When they got back, Nicola went up to her room where she "discovered" the body of her friend, and started screaming her head off.' He presses a hand to his forehead. 'I saw some terrible sights during the war, unspeakable sights, but I have never been so shocked and appalled as when we ran up the stairs and found poor little Valerie lying dead on the floor. I went through some brutal campaigns, but the sight of that child's body...' He falters, '...so cold, already stiffening ... even after all this time, it's still almost beyond belief.'

'And Nicola went shopping...' I can hardly hear Louise's words.

'Of course she tried to pretend that Valerie must have come back to the house and been killed by an intruder, or even that the poor child had strangled herself, but in the end, it all came out.'

'And then we had to work out what to do for the best.'

'The best,' repeats Farnham. He slowly shakes his head. 'If that's what you want to call it.'

Louise sits up straighter, presses herself against the back of the sofa. 'You probably think we sound heartless,' she says. 'But I have to be honest...'

'We've had a long time to face up to our feelings.'

'And the fact is, that when Nicola died, atrocious and heart-rending as that was, it was, quite simply, a relief.'

Her husband nods. His hand grips the stem of his glass, knuckles straining against the skin that covers them.

'I'm ashamed even to have thought it, let alone to be saying it aloud, but it *was*.' Louise looks at me directly. 'If you really want to know, Alice, by the time she died, she'd done so much damage to us all that I ... I almost hated her.'

'Darling, you didn't.'

'I did. I really did. What she did to you ... to Simon ... to me...' She chokes slightly on the words, and falls silent.

They seem so distressed that I feel I ought to leave, but before I can get to my feet, Farnham has risen and is refilling our glasses.

I try to digest what I've heard. Farnham is, of course, exonerated from any part in the murder of his daughter because at the time he was safely incarcerated in one of Her Majesty's prisons. But it stills seems feasible that Louise could have been driven to murder, especially after what I've just been told. But she would surely not be talking so freely to me if she were guilty.

We take our fresh drinks and eye each other. Despite their apparent candour, I am still wary. After all, they've had twenty years to refine their story, to get it straight. I'd already noted that he was a man used to command. He was also a man used to winning, and he had been spectacularly defeated by Nicola. Even if he had chosen, for all the right reasons, to take the rap for her, he must have resented being a loser. Is it too far-fetched to wonder if, through connections made in prison, he could have organized Nicola's murder, taken revenge on his daughter? I see again the moonlit garden at Glenfield, Nicola's surprise as she half-turned towards the voice that had spoken to her from behind the hedge. Reck-less, amoral, daring, it wouldn't have taken

328

much persuasion for her to go off with a stranger, especially if he had mentioned her father. Perhaps money was offered, or sex asked for in exchange for a sum far larger than Bertram Yelland could afford.

My brain spools through the last half hour or so. When I arrived, Farnham had warned me that they might seem uncooperative. But they have been quite the opposite. Almost too much so. Almost too eager to tell me their story, a story which, looking back at the events of that distant summer, I find completely convincing. Perhaps that's what they want. Perhaps by appearing to be totally open with me, and also by showing themselves in a less-than-positive light, they hope to deflect me from further enquiry, persuade me that what they are telling me is the truth, the whole truth and nothing but the truth. But sad though it was, Valerie Johnson's murder is not why I am here.

'You were let out early,' I say.

'Yes, but on parole.'

'How come?'

'What with Barbara-Jane Finch's statement to the police, and those letters which kept—'

Although he is not a man you would normally interrupt, I do so now. 'Letters?'

'Some nutter,' Farnham says. 'After Nicola's death, these letters started arriving. Written to the police, the barrister who'd taken on my case, even me. All saying the same thing: that I wasn't guilty of Valerie's murder, that the letter writer knew who'd done it, that at the earliest possible moment the truth would be divulged. Etcetera,

etcetera, etcetera. Letters like that are always the same, full of assertions but without any solid proof to back them up.'

'Who was sending them?'

'Nobody knew. The police never took them seriously, just buried them in some file or other. After all, why should they bother, when they already had a clear confession of guilt?'

'When Barbara-Jane came forward, Geoffrey's barrister wanted to push for a retrial, on the grounds of reasonable doubt, a confession made for compassionate reasons, and so on,' says Louise. 'But Geoffrey wouldn't let him.'

'Why not? Nicola was dead by then, she could not have been harmed.'

'But Simon could. He was newly married. Can you imagine the fuss there'd have been, a father who'd served years in jail to protect a daughter who was subsequently murdered herself? Can you imagine the press on his doorstep, the notoriety? It wasn't fair on him and his wife.'

'So you just sat there in prison?'

'No. Although I insisted that I didn't want any kind of retrial, my barrister made representations, there was a judicial review, I gave a new statement about what had really happened. Barbara-Jane, bless her, was insistent on her own new version of the truth. They even managed to find those letters mouldering away in the police archives, not that they could be counted as evidence. In the end, they quietly let me out.'

I rise to my feet. 'Thank you for telling me all this,' I say. It is only as I'm about to walk out of the room into the passage leading to the front door that I realize that none of this has any bearing on what I want to know.

I turn to face the two of them. 'But who killed Nicola?' I ask.

'Good question. Excellent question,' says Geoffrey. 'I really wish I knew.'

Again Louise looks at her husband, as though seeking his approval for what she is about to say. 'We thought...' She presses her thumb and first two fingers against her forehead. 'God, how could we have considered such a thing? We *wondered* whether it could possibly have been Simon.'

'Why?'

'He resented the move down here, he hated the change in our circumstances. It was just the wrong time for him, and he never really made friends at school here, or fitted into the local teenage scene. And he never believed for a single moment that his father had killed Valerie.'

'He's told us since then that he knew immediately – not that we ever discussed it – that his sister was responsible,' Farnham says.

'For a while, I did wonder if she could have said or done something, the night of your birthday party, that just pushed him over the top.'

'But in the end, it wasn't him, couldn't have been.' Farnham gives a grim chuckle. 'He turned out to have a watertight alibi – if a whiskey hangover can be called watertight!'

'Apparently he walked Rosemary Mitchell home,' Louise explains. 'Her parents were out at some RAF reunion, in London, and she and Simon got stuck into Squadron-Leader

Mitchell's whiskey. The two of them eventually passed out on the floor of the Mitchells' sitting room and were found there around two o'clock in the morning, dead drunk.'

I remember the hangdog expression on Simon's face the next day, as Louise talked to the police in our drawing room. The smell of him, which I now realize was whisky fumes. But if it wasn't him, it could still have been his mother. Especially after the feelings she has just confessed to.

She comes over to me as I stand hesitant, one hand on the door frame. As though she can read my mind, she says, 'And if you're wondering whether *I* had anything to do with Nicola's death, I will tell you frankly, Alice, there were many many times – God forgive me! – that I seriously considered it. Not in anger, but in fear. What harm would she go on to do when she was an adult? What kind of a life could she expect to live in a world where she wouldn't get away with things as easily as she had so far? Wouldn't it be kinder simply to press a pillow to her face, or hold her under water when she was in the bath? But in spite of everything, she was my daughter, the darling little cherub whom we nearly lost at the very beginning of her life, the red-haired baby we all doted on. When it came down to it, I knew I couldn't possibly have committed such a grossly unnatural act.'

Sitting on the window-seat of my flat, I realize that the baggage Nicola's family drags around is far heavier than my own. They are shackled by it until the grave receives them, with no possibility of ever shedding the burden. Whereas I...

I am luckier than they are. Dimly I perceive a possibility of emancipation, which they can never achieve. An unaccustomed calm fills me. The events of long ago now seem less of a burden; they no longer drag me down quite so deeply. On the horizon, the very last of the daylight streaks the blazing sky with scarlet and flushes the sea crimson. In a band of blue-gold sky, a single star gleams like a promise.

From here I can see the new-built pier. So much of the post-war years has been swept away, subsumed in the bright freedoms of the Sixties and Seventies, and I can't help wondering how much effect the war had on the children who were raised in its shadow. Despite the dullness and the routine, there was so little in our lives of what could be called ordinary; the times themselves were extraordinary. Perhaps Nicola was simply more affected than most by the casual brutalities of war. We grew up inured to death and destruction, even though it was more as a concept than as something particular. We read books, saw films, looked at comics, all dealing with the ruthless elimination of the enemy. We took blood, atrocity, in our stride. The broken pier, the landmine collecting-box, Jewish refugees; we were never clear of it. By then the horrors of the concentration camps had been revealed to a revolted world. Nicola was older than I was, and far more aware, and perhaps that, rather than moral dysfunction, had helped to shape her into what she became.

TWELVE

Orlando sits opposite me, his face glowing in the dusky light. The room is lit only with candles, and in the flickering glow, he seems leaner, browner, more taut than I'm used to seeing him.

He has come by his own invitation, telephoning two days ago to ask if he might stay for a day or two, until after Vi Sheffield's party. 'And your birthday, too,' he said. 'Is there anything you'd particularly like?'

'Just yourself.'

'Ah.'

As always, I wondered at the telepathic link between us. He knew I needed to speak to him, and was probably aware of what – yet again – I wanted to discuss. Was he also aware that I am terrified in case I discover, by confession or intuition, that he is the one who killed Nicola?

She links us together but at the same time keeps us apart. If I could prise her from her entrenched position in our lives, I know that at last we could set right whatever it is that seems to have gone awry between us.

'Are you coming alone?' There'd been a crack in my voice.

'Why should you think otherwise?'

'I wondered if you and the blonde flautist...'

'I'm not quite at the stage of introducing her to the family,' he said.

He has brought wine, which we continue to sip after dinner. A melancholy has settled upon us both, although we have resolutely discussed only the present. Before his arrival, however, with much trepidation I had gone through what I perceived as happening on the night of my twelfth birthday party, placing him at the centre. I did this over and over again, and each time, the pieces of the puzzle seemed welded closer and closer together, until the whole scenario appeared completely seamless. My heart quails. If I discover that he was in some way connected to or even responsible for Nicola's death, how will I feel?

What would I do?

If I say nothing, we can continue as we have for so many years, closer than twins yet constantly divided, though it is hard to say by what. If I say nothing about Nicola tonight, then he will never bring it up. Only a few weeks ago he'd told me that he never thinks of it any more, it's long gone, though I wonder how true that is. I remember his agonized face – *'I shall never, ever forget this, as long as I live.'* and I know he was right then. But over these summer weeks, if nothing else, I have come to a greater acceptance. I see that you cannot disregard the past. Nor can you reconstruct it. In many ways it has a stronger hold than the present.

Leave it lay, I tell myself. It was a favourite phrase of Allen's and I have always admired its lazy tolerance of that which cannot be put right, or is not worth bothering about. Leave it lay...

'Orlando,' I say, and watch his face stiffen, his eyes grow wary. 'Orlando...'

'What?'

'Just tell me, and I'll never ask again, I swear it. I'll never mention any of it, not ever.'

'For God's sake, Alice...'

'Was it you, Orlando? Did you kill her?'

'What would you do if I said yes? What difference would it make?'

'I don't know.' Yet there is no question that a difference of some kind would be made.

'She's dead, Alice.' His voice drops in a comic old-crone tremble: 'Dead and gone these twenty years, m'dear.'

'Did you?'

He looks defeated. 'Oh, Alice...'

'Did you?'

For a long moment, he gazes out of the window. He pulls back his shoulders. Sets down his wine glass. Finally he speaks. 'For a long, long time,' he says quietly, 'I almost thought that maybe I had. I wanted to so badly. Particularly that night, when she tried to sabotage your party – oh, darling Alice, when I saw your face crumple, all your confidence just ooze away, I could so easily have throttled her.' He reaches out to me. 'You were such an insecure little thing. So nervous.'

'Me?'

'Remember how difficult you found it to get to sleep? When we still shared a bedroom, I used to try everything I could to stay awake until you'd finally gone to sleep, so that you wouldn't be left alone in the dark. You had black shadows under your eyes for years. And the nightmares...'

'That's now,' I say.

'And then. Don't you remember? About soldiers rushing into the house through the windows, guns firing?'

'Vaguely,' I lie.

'Anyway, on top of everything else...' He stops.

After a pause, I say, 'Anyway what?'

He twists his neck about, tossing his head like a horse. It's a gesture I recognize, signifying unease. 'The night of your party...' he says. '...you weren't around, but I was standing in the drive – I forget why now – and suddenly Nasty Nicola jumped out at me, yelling something. She was so close that she actually knocked me over. I could feel the gravel on my cheek, and I was terrified in case my school trousers were torn. They were brand new and very expensive. Fiona would have been furious. The worst thing was that she was wearing this horrible clown mask, white, with black crosses on the eyes, and a huge red mouth.' He shudders. 'She was a vile girl.'

'What on earth did she do that for?'

'Who knows? Maybe she was hoping to scare me to death. Maybe it was revenge for something unforgivably rude I'd said to her earlier in the evening. Or maybe it was just her usual generalized malice.'

'What did you do?'

'What could I do? I struggled to my feet, wiped away a surreptitious tear of sheer terror, and pretended I couldn't have cared less. I would have strangled her, I think, if Julian hadn't been standing nearby, sniggering, his zits aglow with sexual repression. Or at least hit her. Knocked her down. I went back into the house, washed the dirt off my face and carried on with my evening.'

'And later?'

'What do you mean?'

'Did you leave the house?'

'Yes. I went down to the beach with some of the others. Sat in the garden swigging some of Callum's beer and hoping Fiona wouldn't see me.'

'Did you see Nicola leave?'

'From my position cowering behind a leaf, hoping she wouldn't attack me again, do you mean? Yes. Her and Julian. They went off towards the cliffs.'

'To the Secret Glade?'

'So I presumed.'

'Did you go after them?'

He twists his head again.

'I know you did, Orlando. Julian met you, when he was coming back along the front.'

'All right. Yes, I did. I went up to the Secret Glade. Julian, obviously, wasn't helping her, since he was back at Glenfield, but she could still have been stripping my blackberry bushes – *our* bushes. It was very bright, a full moon, if you remember.'

'Did you see her?'

He presses his lips firmly together, as though he does not want the incriminating words to emerge. My heart sinks, drops, falls in pieces.

'Oh God, Orlando, what did you do?'

He shakes his head. He gets up and fetches another bottle of wine from the rack, opens it and refills our glasses, while I watch him with growing dismay. My darling Orlando, a killer?

'What I did...' His voice shakes slightly. 'What I *did* ... was nothing.'

'You mean you didn't kill Nicola? I never really thought—'

'What I did was...' His expression is one of distaste, self-dislike. '...I stood by and – I think, I believe, I have always been afraid that – I watched her being murdered.'

'*What*?' I see the black shadow of a boy advance across the moonlit grass towards the blackberry bushes. I see an arm lift, hear a stifled terrified scream, a thud, blows raining down on defenseless flesh. See the boy pausing, frowning, wondering what to do, what he is listening to, realizing, at last, with terror and with impotence.

'Alice, why do you think I've never wanted to talk about this? Do you think I'm proud of myself?'

'Are ... are you sure?'

'Not one hundred per cent. But ninety per cent.' He begins to breathe heavily. His nostrils are pinched and white.

'What happened?' My own breathing matches his. We are joined at the hip, at the head, at the heart. What happens to him happens to me as well. I remember *Wuthering Heights*, Cathy's passionate, despairing cry: *he is more myself than I am. Whatever our souls are made of, his and mine are the same.*

'Jesus, Alice. You should have been there. Or, let me rephrase that, thank God you weren't.' He rests his elbow on the table, drops his head into his hand.

'Tell me, Orlando,' I say, when he says nothing further.

'I went up along the green lane,' he says heavily. 'I could see her, the glimmer of her white blouse, between the trees. She was so small. I think she called someone's name, softly. And then the outline of a person stepped out from the cover of the brambles.'

'A person?'

'I couldn't tell. I'm pretty certain it was a man, or male, certainly, but it could have been a woman, a biggish woman.'

'Like,' I ask tentatively, 'Miss Vane?'

'That sort of size, I suppose. Whoever it was grabbed Nicola's arm, pulled her back behind the bushes. I knew there was something wrong. It was like that ... *incident* we were unlucky enough to witness with Bertram Yelland, though at first I thought it was just Nicola turning tricks again for money. But I gradually realized this was something much more secretive and sinister than that. In fact, I'd started to cross the grass towards them, to see if there was something I could do, when I heard her give a little scream, almost a yelp, which was immediately cut off. As though he'd clapped a hand over her mouth or something.'

'Orlando, this is horrible.'

'It gets worse, darling. I thought, I'm only a

boy, what can I do? And I thought of all the terrible things she'd done and I hesitated, and that's when I saw this ... this hand come up and then down again. Up and down. And each time there was this terrible awful sort of thwack. Awful, Alice, awful. He must have been using a golf club – I could see the moonlight glinting on the shank of it.'

'A golf club?' Julian's putter, fortuitously dropped as he rushed away.

'Unless he was going equipped, as the police say. But Alice, I knew what was happening, I was perfectly well aware that he was ... he was killing her, or at the least very severely assaulting her and I did absolutely nothing to try and save her.'

'What could you have done?'

'That poor little girl.'

'Nicola, a poor little girl?'

'No one deserves to die like that. And I just let it happen. I was too frightened to do anything. Maybe if I'd called out, he would have let her go. But maybe he'd have come after me next, attacked me. And do you know what in a way was the most bizarre thing of all?'

'What?'

'There was a dog barking somewhere, almost in time to the blows. Thwack, bark, thwack, bark ... something so ordinary, combined with something so horribly abnormal.' He sighs heavily. 'So I took off. I just turned and ran down the lane, back to the sea. I didn't do anything to help her. I've had to live with that appalling act of cowardice all these years, and I grow more and

341

more ashamed.'

I shake my head, cover his hand with mine. There is nothing I can say to comfort him. Not meeting his eyes, I ask, 'Did you see anyone else around when you were walking towards the Secret Glade?'

'Apart from Julian, no.'

'He said something about a couple going up the hill.'

'They weren't around when I got there.'

'And someone walking a dog, some lovers kissing under a tree.'

'I didn't see any of them.'

'And there was only the one person involved?'

'As far as I'm aware.' He sighs. 'And the next day, when we went up there to pick blackberries, I almost couldn't face it, except I knew you'd start asking questions I wasn't prepared to answer. I looked for the body when we got to the big bramble patch, and there wasn't anything, not a sign of anything. I was so damned relieved. I thought maybe I'd dreamed it, or misinterpreted the situation – and then we went into the clearing and ... oh God, it was so awful.'

'Why didn't you tell the police all this?'

'I don't know. I didn't know then and I still don't.'

But I do. I remember his terror, his plea for us not to say anything about what we had discovered. He was a boy who had always read too much, and too widely, who knew about miscarriages of justice, about police intimidation, about borstals, bullies, death and sin and retribution, adults who wouldn't listen. As a chorister, he would have regularly listened to the dire warnings of the Old Testament God. He would know that the wages of sin is death. He was too clever not to be aware that sins of omission can be as evil as sins of commission.

We stare sombrely at each other across the dinner table, our gaze shadowed.

Do I believe him? Trust him?

All my life I have done so. In spite of what he's told me, I can see no reason to change now.

'It doesn't solve the question of who *did* kill her,' I say, some hours later. We have cleared the table, tidied up, strolled beside the sea for a while, dropped into a pub for a final whisky. Now we are both showered and in our dressing gowns, as we so often used to be when we were children.

'Does it matter?' says Orlando. 'As long as it wasn't me?'

I contemplate him for a long moment. Consider what he has just said. Is this the secret fear that I have been carrying inside my head for so long, that it was? Until the last few days I would have sworn that I never for a single moment thought that it could possibly have been him, despite the hostility he had for Nicola.

But he is right. What does it matter, as long as the two of us are innocent?

'It wasn't me, either,' I say, laughing.

'No, I don't believe it was.'

I am outraged. *'What*? You can't possibly have thought that *I...*' But I can see that he has at least considered it.

343

'You had the motive – given how slight the motives for any of your suspects seem to have been – you had the means, you had the opportunity. What more do you want?'

'The mindset? Can you honestly see me as a murderer?'

'As easily, my darling, as you seem to have seen me.'

'I did *not*.'

'If you say so.'

I am embarrassed. 'I really don't know what to say.'

'Then say nothing.' He gets up and opens the piano lid. 'This is a nice instrument.' He pats the stool. 'Come over here and we'll sing together like we used to.' The opening bars of *Drink To Me Only* spill across the room like sprayed water.

We sing the *Ash Grove*, and *Greensleeves, Early One Morning*. Songs of childhood and innocence.

There are tears in my eyes for this beautiful night, my lost past, my beloved unattainable companion. 'Oh, Orlando,' I whisper, 'I love you so.'

He puts his arm round my shoulders. 'And I you.'

'I wish ... oh, how I wish...'

'Hush.'

He doesn't know that what I wish is that I could be truly free of my suspicions about him. Despite all his explanations, I am still haunted by possibilities.

* * *

344

He leaves the following morning to stay with a college friend in Canterbury, an organist at the cathedral, and won't be back until the day after tomorrow, the day of Vi Sheffield's party, my birthday.

Is it due to Orlando's calming influence that although I am no further forward to laying my ghosts, I nonetheless feel that I am at last turned towards the future? Too restless to work, I lug out from the cupboards in the back room the three boxes of Aunt's books which Fiona has passed on to me. Many of them are religious tomes of one kind or another and I put them to one side, to be passed on to one of the schools or libraries. At the bottom of each box is a layer of Aunt's green-bound log books and I toss them into a carton to be put out for the rubbish men at the end of the week. And suddenly I hear again her elderly, but still brisk and incisive voice, 'You never know when they'll come in handy.'

I search through the volumes for the one I'm interested in. They're meticulously annotated in old-fashioned copperplate script so minuscule that they are almost unreadable without a magnifying glass, like the tiny books that the Brontë sisters produced. Each volume begins on January the first and ends on December the thirty-first.

I scuttle through the books, looking for the year I want, the month and day. The entries vary in length, some just a line, others, such as the Coronation, taking up several pages. Most entries were shorter in the earlier journals, gradually increasing as – I suppose – Aunt found herself with more time on her hands.

Feb 24th 1948: I read. *Communist party takes control in Czechoslovakia. Vile sausages for supper.*
Sept 4th 1949: *09:28 Queen Wilhelmina of Netherlands abdicates for health reasons – how very sensible of her.*

It's not quite got-up-brushed-my-teeth territory, but pretty close. I choose another volume, and another.

April 27th 1950: 07:03 *news on the wireless that South Africa has passed the Group Areas Act. Apartheid, in other words. A sorry day for Africa.* **18:53** *Ava Carlton leaves the house, a car is waiting for her further down the road. Is romance blooming for our Good Woman?* **19:32** *Callum & Dougal out for the evening with their bikes. Too much Brylcreem, they look like spivs.*
April 1st 1951 April Fool's Day. 09:46 *tell Fiona that Winston Churchill will be arriving for lunch. She is not amused!* **22:16** *Prunella V returns from an evening out. Needs to lose weight. Wonder where she's been, who with. Yelland back at* **23:47** *drunk again. An unpleasant man. Does Fiona know what he gets up to? Is it my duty to tell her?*
July 3rd 1952: *Bobby slamming doors all morning. What a disagreeable child he is. At* **12:32** *he runs down the drive, screaming, kicks the gate until one of the panels splinters. Fiona should*

346

control him better. Buffy Markham arriving 13:30 tomorrow for lunch.

I eventually find the volume for 1953 and turn to the summer months.

June 19th Ethel & Julius Rosenberg hanged for espionage in Sing Sing, on the flimsiest of evidence, most of it false. A thoroughly <u>disgraceful</u> episode.

But June is much too early. On to July, the pages flipping under my impatient fingers.

July 15th 1953: John Reginald Halliday Christie hanged, a good thing too, a monster for all he looks so meek and mild. Feel sorry for the lodger, Timothy Evans, a miscarriage of justice there, I'm convinced. 16:42 Orlando and Alice home from school for the holidays. They are very civilized children. Ava Carlton's girl is nicely behaved, too, which is more than can be said for Bobby. Callum off to France for a month to work in a vineyard, Dougal to Scotland, working as an orderly in an Edinburgh hospital, staying with his grandparents, poor boy. The Yelland man is up to his old tricks. The Canon would have been outraged, were he here today. I suppose I should be grateful that at least life is not boring.
July 16th 1953: 09:26 Fiona's friend Catherine Vinson arrives from Oxford for a short visit. The man with the dog sat on a bench for <u>four hours</u> today, doing absolutely nothing. The children played on the beach all day. Is he watching

347

them? Is he a pervert? Should I report him? There is a great crowd of them, but they are not rowdy. The tallest one, Dickie Tavistock's boy, has a golf club: presumably he is taking up the game. I wonder if he'll be as good as his father used to be, before the war. Am feeling a little under the weather.

***July 18th 1953**: **10:04** Fiona comes in for coffee, brings me a magazine containing her latest story. I often wonder how a woman such as she, with a good degree from Oxford, can write such sentimental claptrap. Still, as she says, it pays some of the bills. **16:07** Children to tea and a game of bezique. Orlando is going to play chess tomorrow with Colonel Strafford-Jones. Alice has started music lessons. 1,700 people have died in floods in Japan.*

***July 19th 1953**: **09:10**, made green tomato chutney. **12:49** Walked to the newsagent. **12:51** Met man with the dog <u>again</u>. Fell into conversation: he is not a local. Nice dog.*

***July 27th 1953**: end of Korean War, thank God for that. How many more wars must there be? **18:30** Orlando brings up supper, Shepherds Pie which is perfectly awful. Poor Fiona is not a good cook, nor, I fear, a hygienic one. Tomorrow I leave for a week in London with the Allinghams. Alice has had her pretty hair cut off.*

***August 2nd 1953**: children on the beach all day. With the good weather, they're so sunburned you'd think we were back in the Congo. Alice's little friend with the red hair seems to be a trifle wayward, heard her arguing with Orlando this morning, using astonishing language. I'm glad*

348

to say that O. is too nicely brought up to respond in kind.

August 5th 1953: 07:00 *up and out for a short walk before breakfast. Weather superb. Wish the Canon were still alive. On second thoughts perhaps not, he would be shocked by much of the world today.* **14:40** *The red-haired girl threw a stone at Bobby and hit his shoulder, making him cry. Nobody noticed except me, and Orlando, who went over and told her off pretty thoroughly, judging by his gestures.*

August 7th 1953: 11:30 *The spaniel man is here again. He has such a pretty dog, reminds me of the hunting dogs my father kept when I was a girl, so good at flushing out game from brambles etc. I had a very similar puppy once, which Father gave me for my 8th birthday, I wanted to call her Claret, because of the markings but he said that was too whimsical so she became Clarrie instead. I think a lot about the past these days, how lucky I have been through the years. The woman with the three poodles has returned: perhaps she has been away on holiday. Also the golden retriever man, the Scottie woman and a new one, a stranger, with a black-and-white sheepdog. All of them leave little piles of poo on the green. The Canon used to say that the Council ought to make it compulsory to clean up after dogs, offer free plastic bags. Sometimes Dougal and Callum play football out there: I should hate them to slip and land in that nasty mess.*

I continue to read. The same cast of characters

appears over and over again, dog-walkers, fisherman, my family, friends from her youth, or her professional life. We move into late August, then on to early September.

August 20th 1953: Mossadegh overthrown in Persia. A good thing, I think, to bring back the Shah, a reforming monarch, who seems especially sound on suffrage for women etc. 15:41 Ava Carlton brings me the skirt she has mended for me. Such a kind woman, where would we all be without her? 16:20 Confused shouting outside my door, that dreadful man Yelland creating a fuss about something or other. And to think I knew his grandmother so well during the War. I wonder what she would make of him now.
August 25th 1953: Now that we are to move back to Oxford, Fiona plans to have a party. 13:06 she came to discuss details. If there are friends you'd like to invite, she says ... I'm not one for late nights, but an hour or two downstairs can't hurt. There is to be dancing, I hope she doesn't expect me to do the samba! 16:01 Alice and Orlando here for tea. The blackberries are almost ready for picking, they tell me, it'll be any day now, can they use one of the walking sticks from the hall?
August 29th 1953: 10:52 Cartland's men bring a barrel of beer and a lot of cider for this party. I shall take a cup of 'tea' before I go downstairs on The Night! 14:22 look at my good Liberty paisley and discover it has moth! Ava Carlton will get me some mothballs, I'm sure, but I really don't want to go round smelling of naphthalene,

it's so ageing. Dickie Tavistock's boy appears to be infatuated with the red-haired girl, who behaves in a most unbecoming way, in my opinion.
***17:40** Ava Carlton brings me some boxes so I can start packing away my books, ready for our move. Somehow I must summon up some energy. I've never felt so listless in my life. I shall miss the splendid sea-view from this window, and the light.*

It's September now, and Aunt is getting ready for the big move.

***September 4th 1953**: Tomorrow is little Alice's birthday. Not that she is so little any more. I gather from Ava Carlton's circumlocutions that the child has in fact started her periods this summer. It's the end of an era in many ways for all of us. Leaving this house will be a wrench, all that is left of the Canon and my two boys is here. But we also lived in Oxford and I shall perhaps find them again there. And of course there are many friends still there, though I fear they're not wearing too well. Saw Professor Mungo Starr at a dinner in London recently and he looked like an ancient tortoise. I remember him as a very well set-up young man indeed. The red-haired child was on the green today, talking to the wild-looking man who tried to take Ava Carlton away. Hard to believe AC could have been married to such a brutish specimen.*
***September 5th 1953**: Spent the morning packing up things. Feeling very tired. I shall throw a lot of my clothes away before we leave here: more*

351

*moths, into everything. I hope we can get rid of them. The mothballs Ava Carlton brought don't seem to have done the trick. The house is buzzing, people coming and going all day, too many to record. Went downstairs at **18:30**, to find everyone looking very nice. Even Yelland seemed to have made an effort, not something he does very often, unless it is to cause fuss and bother. The children were charming, Alice in a pink dress and Orlando wearing a tie to match. I gave Alice a diamond brooch from my jewellery-box, and although it is not his birthday, passed the Canon's gold repeater on to Orlando, since he is the one most likely to appreciate it. Return to my room at **21:09.** Being sociable is very tiring at my age and my hearing is not as good as it used to be. In addition, I am beginning to feel distinctly unwell. Does this have anything to do with Fiona's dubious cooking?! Sit and watch the gleam of starlight on the sea. **21:32** Am astonished to see the spaniel man peering over the garden wall, like a spy. The Tavistock boy is in the garden, kissing the girl with red hair while she strokes the front of his trousers! A real trollop, I don't know what young things are coming to. And she's wearing too much jewellery, in my opinion: a gold chain, pierced ears, so vulgar in one so young, Alice's pearls are just right for her age. **21:47** Orlando appears on the drive and the two break apart. The girl fishes in a bag she's carrying over her shoulders and produces a hideous white mask which she slips over her face and illumines it from below with a torch. Orlando is staring across the garden at* *the man, who ducks down, and the girl jumps on him, yelling. He falls over and she laughs, as does the Tavistock boy. I shall try and have a word with him at some point. I can see Orlando is terrified, and angry, though he pretends not to be. He goes back into the house and the Tavistock boy follows. I tap on the window, wag my finger at the girl who sticks her tongue out at me. Can you imagine?* **22:14** *I pour myself a medicinal tot, since I am feeling rather ill, and it seems to do the trick.* **22:30** *people are beginning to leave. Callum and Dougal go down to the sea with a big group of younger people, presumably to swim, since it is a mild night. At* **22:48** *the red-haired girl sets off towards the cliffs, followed a few minutes later by the spaniel man, his dog trotting along beside him. The Tavistock boy walks in the same direction, carrying that golf club of his, for some reason. An assignation, I suppose, though why you'd take a golf club along on 'a date' I don't know. I hope the boy is careful, I'd hate Dickie's son to find himself in trouble with a girl like that.* **23:08** *Orlando appears, wheeling his bike down the drive, and cycles off after them. Oh dear, I shall have to call Fiona, I think, I'm really not feeli*

The writing trails off, and there are no further entries.

Aunt died of a heart attack three days after she was admitted to hospital that night.

THIRTEEN

I have just taken a couple of roast chickens from the oven when the doorbell rings. Wiping my hands on a tea towel, I run down the stairs to the communal front door to find Mr Johnson standing on the doorstep. He looks like a corpse. There are dark shadows under his eyes, and his skin is grey and waxy. In the days since I last saw him, he must have lost at least ten pounds. I invite him in, close the door and lean against it for a moment, watching him climb the stairs. His steps are heavy, his shoulders bent.

I know why he has come.

I sit him down at the small café table in the kitchen, make coffee, and take a chair opposite him. He fists his hands together on the table, and sits with lowered head.

'Are you all right, Mr Johnson?'

He shakes his head. 'No.'

Behind him, in the big sitting-room, is a table covered in one of Aunt's linen sheets and set with a pile of plates, Aunt's solid silver cutlery, pink linen table napkins. Two crystal vases full of pink rosebuds sit in the middle, and glasses are grouped together at either end. Sixteen people are coming this evening to celebrate my birthday and I am very busy. But the significance

354

of his presence overrides everything else.

'Is there anything I can do?' I ask.

'No. Except listen to what I've got to say.' He sighs tiredly. 'First of all, I want to apologize. Earlier this morning I went to see Louise Farnham, as was – Stone, she's calling herself now – and she told me you've never got over the shock. Over finding Nicola Farnham's body, I mean.'

'That's true. But I—'

'Like I told you when you came to the house the other day, I never ... it never occurred to me that it would be children would find her. Not *children.*'

I say gently, 'Why don't you tell me about it?'

'It was all because of the chain. The gold chain. It wasn't on Valerie's body, you see. I went down to the police station and asked specially and they said there hadn't been any chain round her neck when she was found in Nicola's bedroom. And I knew someone must have taken it, because she wore it all the time, she loved it. And then after they'd put Geoffrey Farnham away, Nicola and her mother came round to see us, to say goodbye, they were going to leave and settle somewhere else. I could hear Mother screaming and crying when she realized who it was at the door.'

'I can imagine.'

'When you think about it, it was so hurtful. So ... cruel, really. I have to say Louise seemed pretty ashamed to be there. She said that Nicola had insisted on saying goodbye and how sorry she was about Valerie, but she didn't *look* sorry. I wouldn't let them in, of course, didn't want to talk to them, and then, when they turned to walk away, I could see the girl was wearing a gold chain round her neck, kept running her fingers round it. I didn't think anything of it at first – I mean, why would you? – but later I remembered how Valerie used to tell us that Nicola was really jealous, wanted one just like it but her parents wouldn't get her one. It took me a long while before I started wondering, putting two and two together and coming up with five. And by then, they'd left town, so I couldn't check.'

'Of course not.'

'It took me the best part of two years to find out where they'd gone – Louise changed her name, you see, can't say I blamed her, who would want people knowing her husband was a murderer? I finally tracked her down that summer, twenty years ago, saw a photograph in the local paper, some arty prize or other that she'd won, and after that, I couldn't keep away. I spent hours watching for Nicola. Of course, Mother was still managing to cope at that point, hadn't given way to depression and illness, so I was freer than I am now. And one day, I'm sitting on that bench out there...' He gestures at the window. '...and Nicola comes up, cool as a cucumber, says, "Hello, Mr Johnson, what are you doing here, nice to see you again," something like that.'

'What did you say?'

'Came straight out with it, asked her about the chain. And she laughed, said it was nice, wasn't it? I said our Valerie had one exactly like that, and she said did she really? She had this nasty sort of a look on her face, almost ... triumphant.'

I'm thinking back. I'm remembering noticing Nicola talking to some man, not Edwardes now, but someone else. The past is refashioning itself in my mind. It must have been Johnson, twenty years younger, his hair still dark back then. 'Did you ask her where she got it?'

'She said she'd got it from a good friend. It was the way she said it, that's when I knew for certain that it must have been her all along, that evil little she-devil. It wasn't her father who strangled Valerie, it was *her*. And what's more, she knew I'd cottoned on to her and she didn't give a damn ... sorry, sorry, shouldn't use language.' Emotion chokes him and he presses thumb and forefinger to his forehead.

'What did you do?'

'I wanted to grab Valerie's chain – I just *knew* it was Val's – off her throat, but I didn't. Too many people about, for one thing. So I just nodded, said it was nice, said I had to get back, even said, God help me, that Mother sent her love. And in the car on the way home, I decided that one way or another, I'd get it off her.' He coughs. 'For Valerie's sake, you see. It seemed only fair.'

'So what happened?'

He sips at his coffee. 'I overheard the young people – that's you and your friends, and Nicola – talking about a party you were having a few nights later and since Mother was out playing cards that evening, I drove over with Minnie – my dog, that is. I'm not quite sure what I expected to do, really, but I was that upset and

357

angry...' His voice breaks.

I get up and refill his cup with coffee. There is so little I can do to help him. The events of twenty years ago blister him now as much as they did back then.

'I kept peering over the wall round your front garden,' he says. 'And then there was a point when that Nicola was alone, out on the lawn, and I decided that was the chance I needed. I called her name – softly, mind – and she looked up and saw me, grinned that triumphant way again. So I pushed at the gate, started to open it and come up the drive, when I saw an old lady up at the window, watching me. Didn't want her calling the police or anything, so I walked round the corner. Still kept an eye on the house, though, and then later, I saw the girl set off towards the cliffs, so I followed.'

'Did you know where she was going?'

'I had a sort of idea, because I'd been up there before, seen her doing ... well, disgusting things with some man or other. I wasn't bothered about that, though. I just wanted to get Val's chain back, she had no right to it, I couldn't bear seeing it round her wicked neck. And then this young lad passed me, started walking along with her, she was teasing him, leading him on ... you know ... and then when they got up to the cliffs, she pushed him away. Told him to get lost.'

I nod.

'He lashed out at her, and she fell down. Swearing, he was, really upset, and who can blame him? I was standing behind some brambles, and when he'd run off, I stepped out and

358

said "I'll have that chain, thank you," and reached out for it.'

'Was she surprised to see you?'

'If she was, she didn't show it. And I said, "It was you, wasn't it, it was you as killed her?" She laughed at me, said, just you try and prove it, and something – I know they all say this, but it's true – something snapped and I ... I hit her, smashed my fist into her face, and it wasn't enough, it wasn't nearly enough, and I looked around for a stick or something and there was a golf club lying on the grass – don't know why – and I picked it up, started hitting her with it.' He buries his head in his hands and again I touch his arm.

'I just intended to hurt her,' he says, his voice muffled, 'but then all the rage and the sorrow, Mother's broken heart, and mine, I don't know, I just couldn't stop. She always looked so innocent and all the time she had such a black heart. And there was our Valerie, so sweet, so good, our only one, gone forever.' He begins to sob. 'Oh God, I didn't mean to, I really didn't mean to kill her.'

There's nothing I can say. I stroke his hand, the lumpy veins, the liver spots, the arthritic knuckles. Compassion for his wasted life brings tears to my own eyes.

He looks up at me. 'I'd have gone to the police then and there, but I looked around and I realized that no one had seen what I did, and in any case, Maureen – Mother – needed me. So I ... I picked her up and ... I ... uh ... I threw her in among the brambles, then I got the golf club and drove back

359

to Madden. Mother was still out, so I'd got time to change out of my ... there was ... blood, you see. I burned them on the bonfire, bit by bit. Mother never knew.'

It occurs to me that when the news of Nicola's murder filtered through, she might have had her suspicions, but I don't say anything. 'That's good,' I murmur.

He pushes himself upright. 'I'm going now, to give myself up. I just wanted to let the Farnhams know, first. I thought they were the only people who needed to hear this but I decided I'd best come and see you too, when they told me that you'd been having ... difficulties.' His voice skates over the word, embarrassed by the possibility of mental instability or psychological problems, both of them likely, in his vocabulary, to be euphemisms for madness.

'What purpose will be served by you going to the police now?' I ask.

'It's only right.'

'Haven't you suffered enough already?'

He smiles faintly. 'Justice has to be seen to be done, isn't that what they say? I've got to take my punishment.'

'I'd have thought that you've been punished enough.' I can see that with this confession, his purpose has come to an end.

'There's the other thing.' His hands twist together. 'I should have said earlier ... Mother died last week.'

'Oh dear, I *am* sorry.'

'It was for the best, really. She's been ill a long time. But you can see there's nothing to stop me from giving myself up now she's gone.'

'Think about it first.'

'I've thought of little else for twenty years,' he says. 'And anyway, without Mother to care for, I haven't got much else to live for.'

We shake hands formally. At the door of my sitting room he stops and looks at the decorated table, and I imagine he's remembering that pink rosebuds were Valerie's favourites. From my window, I watch him climb into an old Hillman Minx, its chrome gleaming, its bodywork shining. The badges of various motoring organizations are fixed to its polished grille. I wonder how many times over the years he has cleaned the car, washed it down, chamois-leathered it, an ordinary man taking pleasure in doing the best job he can, as I imagine he has done with everything in his life. A good man, the salt of the earth, and as he drives away, I am weeping for his sad life, and all his empty years.

He can have no idea of the burden he has lifted from my shoulders.

And then, across the green, I see Orlando. He is looking up at my window, and I wave at him as he comes towards me. The sun glints on his silvered hair. Behind him lies the peacock-blue of the sea, above is the richness of the summer sky. The boats in the yacht club gleam as though freshly varnished; the chrysanthemums in the garden below my window are copper, apricot, flame, crimson, the magnolia leaves a brilliant jade green. Next door, in the Major's flower-beds, marguerites, like miniature suns, nod against the garden wall, egg-yolk yellow hearts, petals white as milk. As Orlando smiles up at me, my heart thrills and soars.

'So terribly sad,' I say, telling him about Mr Johnson. 'What a heartbreaking life. I wouldn't be in the least surprised to hear that he'd killed himself.'

'For nothing now can ever come to any good,' Orlando quotes sombrely.

'That's absolutely right.'

He puts an arm around my shoulders. 'What time's everyone coming?'

'Any time after four. But we're not eating until six.'

'Anything I can do to help?'

'Not really. Just be.'

And so he does, playing Chopin and Mozart on the piano, while I continue my preparations. Finally, I pour us both a glass of chilled white wine and we toast each other, smiling.

He takes my hand. 'Alice...' he says earnestly. 'Listen...'

I take a shower, make up my face, slip over my head the dress I bought specially for today, last time I was in London. Around my neck are pearls; there are more of them in my ears.

As I come out of my bedroom in a sheath of linen – not pink, but old rose – Orlando at the piano launches into *Happy Birthday To You*, decorating the tune with flourishes and variations that turn its banality into something magical. He is wearing a white shirt and a silk tie that exactly matches my dress. 'How did I know

362

you'd be wearing that colour?' he asks.

'Because we're joined at the heart.' I rest a hand on his shoulder as the doorbell rings and the guests begin to arrive.

It is much later. We are flushed with wine and good food. I stand up and tap a glass. 'Quiet, please. I'd like to say a few words.' I look round at them all: my parents, my brother Dougal and his wife, dear Bella and her husband, Erin, Sasha Elias, Gordon Parker, Vi Sheffield, Julian and Monica. Even BertramYelland. 'Most of you were at the last birthday party I had in Shale, just down the road from here, a long time ago. Some of those who were present then are no longer with us – Aunt, for instance, and our beloved Ava – some are unfortunately not able to come. But I want to thank those of you who made it and who remember what it was like back then.'

'I'd rather not, if you don't mind,' trills Gordon Parker.

I raise my glass to my parents. 'Thank you both for everything. Particularly you, Fiona. Gifted, unorthodox, indomitable – you've always been an example to us all. As well as being completely ... how shall I put this? ... different from other mothers...'

'God, how I envied you, having a mum like that,' says Julian.

'Like what?' Fiona bridles a bit.

'Never ... um ... *fussing* about things,' Julian says.

'Is that a compliment?' says Fiona. She takes my father's hand.

'Most definitely,' he says.

'And I want to say thank you to my friends, both old and new.' Again I look round the table, tipping my glass at them one by one. 'Coming back to Shale has been ... everything I wanted it to be – and much more. And finally, since it's my birthday, I ask you to make a special toast to the man who all my life has been my dearest friend, who is everything to me and always has been – Orlando Grahame.'

As I sit down, Orlando rises to his feet. 'First, we should wish our charming hostess a happy birthday,' he says, at which everyone breaks into uncoordinated song. I've forgotten that Julian is tone-deaf, and Yelland can't sing a note.

'Don't call us,' Orlando says wrily. 'Secondly, may I echo Alice's sentiments about the assembled company. And thirdly, and most importantly, I'd like to say that this afternoon, I finally asked Alice to marry me ... and she said yes.'

There are whoops and cheers.

'About bloody time,' shouts Dougal.

'What took you so long, slowcoach?' calls Erin.

'Don't blame me ... I've been waiting forever for her to stop mooning over some unattainable ... uh ... dream,' Orlando avoids looking at Sasha Elias, who sits next to Erin, 'and accept her fate, her destiny.' He reaches into his pocket and brings out a small leather box. 'No prizes for guessing what this is.' He comes round the table and kisses me. 'Darling Alice, I'm so happy today that it was almost worth the wait.'

Fiona, never normally one for sentiment,

364

nonetheless wipes away an unaccustomed tear. 'Oh, if only Morag were here today,' she exclaims. 'She'd be absolutely delirious.'

On my left, Sasha is looking bewildered. 'But, I don't understand ... isn't Orlando your brother?'

'No relation at all.'

'So Grahame isn't just the name he uses for professional purposes on the television and so on?'

'It's his real name. He's the son of my mother's oldest friend, Morag, from her school days,' I explain. 'They'd always promised each other that if anything happened to either of them, they'd look after any children they had. So when Doctor and Mrs Grahame were killed during an air-raid in London, Fiona brought Orlando to live with us, even before I was born.'

'We always used to plan that our children would get married.' Fiona takes a swallow from her glass of wine. 'I can't believe it's finally coming true.' She pats at her hair, greyer now, but otherwise styled pretty much as it was the afternoon she walked me down to the cinema to see *Mrs Miniver*.

'The mystery,' says Vi Sheffield, 'is why it's taken them all this time to get it together. Even when they were children, you only had to look at them...'

Bertram Yelland lumbers to his feet. 'If I may be permitted,' he says, 'I'd like to record that those days living down the road at Glenfield House were among the happiest of my life. Post-war England was hardly the most comfortable place in the world, and Glenfield considerably less so...'

'How very gracious,' murmurs Orlando.

'Nonetheless, I think we would all agree that life then was ... was ... well, I don't know what it was really, but if it hadn't been for Mrs Beecham's encouragement, and Professor Beecham's many kindnesses, I for one wouldn't be where I am today.' He raises his glass. 'So thank you, and cheers!'

'Was I kind?' Beside me, my father seems bemused. 'I can't remember being kind to him. In fact, on the whole I thought the fellow was a bit of a pompous prick.'

'Still is,' says Orlando. 'But a good painter.'

When everyone has left, Orlando and I stroll arm-in-arm along the sea front as we have done so many times before. The sun is well below the horizon now, but the sky is still faintly light. The air smells of salt and wind, a faint scent of cut grass is carried on the breeze. Peace, at last, I think. *Shanti, shanti, shanti.* 'Tomorrow, we'll go and pick some blackberries, shall we?' says Orlando.

'Oh, yes!' Ahead, I see the wraith of Nicola walking away towards the distant cliffs. She is powerless now; we're free of her, or as free as we'll ever be. She looks over her shoulder at us and I watch her begin to dissolve, her red hair, her white blouse, melting, evaporating, fading into the blue air, the rolling water, slipping away until finally she's gone.